taming TROUBLE

Tucker should be spelled T-R-O-U-B-L-E.

JIFFY KATE

Editor
Nichole Strauss
Insight Editing Services

Cover Designer, Interior Design and Formatting
Juliana Cabrera
www.jerseygirl-design.com

MORE BOOKS BY JIFFY KATE

Finding Focus Series
Finding Focus
Chasing Castles
Fighting Fire
Taming Trouble

French Quarter Collection
Turn of Fate
Blue Bayou
Come Again
Neutral Grounds
Good Times

Table 10 Novella Series
Table 10 part 1
Table 10 part 2
Table 10 part 3

New Orleans Revelers
The Rookie and The Rockstar
TVATV (coming fall 2020)

Smartypants Romance
Stud Muffin (Donner Bakery, book 2)
Beef Cake (Donner Bakery, book 4)

Standalones
Watch and See
No Strings Attached

PLAYLIST

T-R-O-U-B-L-E by Travis Tritt
Slow Hands by Niall Horan
Keep Your Hands To Yourself by Georgia Satellites
Lets Get It On by Marvin Gaye
Hands To Myself by Selena Gomez
Mixed Drinks About Feelings by Eric Church
Foolish Pride by Travis Tritt
Tennessee Whiskey by Chris Stapleton
Drink You Away by Justin Timberlake
Fooled Around And Fell In Love by Elvin Bishop
Love On The Brain by Rhianna
Jealous by Labrinth
Ask Me How I Know by Garth Brooks
Blue Ain't Your Color by Keith Urban
Say You Won't Let Go by James Arthur
We Danced by Keith Urban

CHAPTER ONE

FREE-RANGE TITTIES.

I'm not a picky man when it comes to breasts. I pretty much like them all—small, medium, large, larger. A handful can be enough, but I can also handle my cup running over.

But if I had to pick my favorite of all the titties, I'd have to go with free range—any size. They're unobstructed, uninhibited—not being caged in by those pesky bras—and beautiful. Those plump mounds with the sweet orbs in the middle, just begging to be sucked.

Currently, two very nice ones are staring me right in the face. However, in my hungover, possibly still-intoxicated state, I can't remember who they belong to or how they got here. But that doesn't matter. They're here and I intend on enjoying them.

"You're even a perv in your sleep," a groggy voice moans as I tweak a nipple. And I'd know that voice anywhere. It belongs to the person who is often the bane of my existence, but also the source of my greatest pleasure.

"Piper?" I ask, peeling my face away from her bare chest and trying my damnedest to focus in on her face. Her beautifully pissed off face. She's always wearing a scowl, at least when she's with me, even when I'm fucking her against a wall or laying between her legs, giving her an orgasm that rocks her world. Her brows are always scrunched up, turning her petite features into a harsh glower. And, somehow, she's *still* the prettiest girl I've ever seen.

But I'd never tell her that.

I like her pissed off. It works for us.

"Why are you in my bed?" she demands, pulling the sheet up and effectively covering my favorite titties.

I almost whimper at the loss, but don't want to give her the satisfaction.

"Fuck if I know. I'm guessin' I gave it to you so good last night you decided to keep me for a second round this mornin'." I go in for her neck, knowing exactly where to start nibbling to get her to drop her frigid front.

"No," she groans, but her body is saying yes. The way she tilts her head to the side, giving me access to the smooth skin right behind her ear, tells me she wants me. She just hates to admit it. Actually, she never admits it.

We hate-fuck.

And sometimes, we fuck the hate right out of ourselves until we're somewhere between tolerance and indifference, verging on liking each other, but that never lasts long.

"You sure about that?" I ask as I slide on top of her, rolling her onto her back, causing her dark hair to fan out beneath her. Her sleepy face is staring up at me and it nearly steals my breath. I never get the chance to see her like this. Usually, we have sex half-clothed, and we never sleep in the same bed. It's one and done, until the next time. Now, the next time has been later that same day, but we make zero commitment to each other. We set no dates. We have no contract or agreement. When we're finished, we leave things like you would a one-night stand.

Thanks to our mutual friends, we're often forced into being in the same room together. That usually results in stares and glares and sometimes an exchange of words, but as far as everyone knows, that's the extent of it—we hate each other.

And, we do, but we also get each other and we know how to please each other. There's a strange mutual desire to be together and when neither of us can stand it any longer, we give in.

But that's it. That's as far as it ever goes.

Pulling Piper's hands above her head, so I can have control of her body, I'm stopped by an unfamiliar accessory that catches my eye.

"Piper?"

"Yes," she breathes, her way of telling me to get on with it without coming right out and saying it.

"What the fuck is on your hand?" I ask, not able to tear my eyes away.

"What?" she asks, annoyance building the longer I wait to give her what she wants. Piper hates games. I think that's why she's so opposed to relationships. She's slipped a few times and told me bits and pieces of her childhood and about her parents. They're filthy rich and masters of manipulation, especially with each other.

I bring her hand down and thrust it in her face.

"This."

On Piper's ring finger of her left hand, sits a large, shiny diamond.

Much to my disappointment, faster than I can blink, Piper slips out from under me like a ninja.

Much to my enjoyment, she's now standing in front of me, naked and fucking perfect.

Her eyes flicker from the ring to me and then back to the ring, her gorgeous mouth dropping open.

"What the fuck is this?" she screeches, pulling hard until it slips off her finger.

"Uh," I say, because that's all I've got. I mean, give me a fucking break. I just woke up, next to Piper Fucking Grey and she's standing naked in front of me. It's hard to form coherent sentences under any of those circumstances, let alone all three.

"Tucker," she yells. "My eyes are up here. And I'm talking to you!" She snaps her fingers at me and just like that, the bitch face is back. "What the fuck is this? And why am I in your hotel room? And what the hell is this?" With each question, her voice gets louder and her tone more frazzled. I watch as her eyes scan the room, looking for something.

When she spots her black dress from the night before laying over by the chair, she marches over to it and grabs it up and holds it to her chest. Then she's on a scavenger hunt around the room, collecting her belongings.

Lacy panties by the night stand.

Fuck-me stilettos by the door.

"What did you do?" she mindlessly asks, her voice panicked. "What did *we* do?" I don't know if she's talking to me or herself, but I just sit back and watch the show. I've never seen this side of her and it's oddly entertaining, but also disturbing.

Her expression is out of place. Piper Grey is a lot of things— beautiful, annoying as hell, gorgeous, smart, put together, in charge, control freak—but unsure and panicked is not in her normal repertoire.

"Well, babe," I begin with a drawl, but she throws something at me and it hits me in the head. Reaching down, I find the diamond that was on her finger.

"Don't. Call. Me. Babe." She quickly slips her panties up her delicious legs and pulls her dress over her head. Her hair goes up in a quick bun as she inspects herself in the mirror, swiping at the leftover mascara under her eyes.

Reaching for the handle of the hotel room door, she turns back around. "If we got married, or some crazy shit like that, I'm gonna cut your balls off and feed them to you."

I laugh from my spot on the bed, twirling the ring around on my pinky finger.

It's a really nice ring and from the way it reflects the light coming through the opened curtains, I'm assuming it's real.

Like, a real fucking diamond.

"Piper," I call out, causing her to stop just before the door shuts behind her.

"What?"

Another memory starts coming back to me and I jolt up from the bed, walking toward the door.

"Don't come near me with that," she says, pointing down below my waist.

"What?" I ask, looking down at my cock standing half-mast.

"That. It's evil. It makes me do bad things."

"My dick?"

"*Demon* dick," she corrects.

I can't help the laugh that erupts from me. This entire morning is ridiculous.

Did I marry Piper Grey?

Wouldn't I remember that?

"How much did we drink last night? *What* did we drink last night?" I ask, trying to stitch together the holes in my memory.

She drops the tyrant bit for a second, slipping on her shoes and standing taller than her normal five-foot-nothing. "I don't know. I...I can't remember."

I scratch my head, moving my unruly curls out of my face, and reach for my discarded boxers on the floor by my feet. Pulling them on, I rack my brain for my last memory from the night before. "We were with Micah and Dani at that bar...the one with the hidden door."

"Right," she says, placing her hands on her hips. "You morons started taking shots for everyone at the bar."

"One for the guy with the suspenders..." I say with a smile, happy that I can remember something.

"And the girl who looked like a dude," she says, shaking her head.

"And the dude that looked like a girl," I counter.

She tries to hide the smile, but I see it.

"Morons," she reiterates.

"And then Micah and Dani ditched us to celebrate on their own, and I can't remember much after that."

We both stand there, with the door half open, trying to piece it all together. I grab my phone, figuring if I really did drop change on a wedding, it'd be on my bank app by now. Just as I swipe across the screen, a text message pops up on my phone.

Dave: Congrats, dude!!!

Dave is one of my old band members, but for the life of me, I can't imagine what he'd be congratulating me for. I scratch my head again in confusion. What the hell? Come to think of it, I do remember seeing him last night. Sort of.

"Did we go to The Cat's Meow?" I ask aloud, as I type out a similar question to Dave. A fragmented memory of test tube shots and singing along to *Sweet Child of Mine* filters through my brain.

"Who are you texting?" Piper asks, her eyes wide again, the panic setting back in.

"Dave," I tell her, like she knows who I'm talking about. "I think we partied with him last night."

Piper reaches into her slim black purse and pulls out her own phone.

About that time, a video comes in from Dave and I hit play. At first, the picture is out of focus and the background is loud. There's lots of talking and hooting and hollering, and then everything goes silent.

"Piper Grey, you're the best lay of my life," I say, or video-me says, while down on one knee on a stage I know very well. "And you've got great tits. I want them in my bed every day from now til' eternity. Listenin' to Micah pour his heart out tonight got me thinkin'...since I found the person I want to screw for the rest of my life, I shouldn't let you go. So, marry me."

The video spans across the room to a smiling, obviously drunk-off-her-ass Piper. She's not crying, like some girls do, like Dani was when Micah proposed last night. She's just smiling, ear-to-ear, and then she cups her hands around her mouth and yells her response, "I'll marry you."

Everyone in the crowd goes wild, applauding and whistling.

Then, above the noise, Piper gets everyone's attention with a loud whistle, that, if I'm being honest, is sexy as hell, even on a grainy video. "On one condition," she says with a slight slur as she holds a finger up in the air.

Whoever is taking the video, sweeps across the room from Piper, back to me, standing on stage.

"Anything for you, Darlin'," I tell her, jumping off the stage and walking through the mass of people, like Moses parting the Red Sea.

"You buy a drink for all of our friends." She waves her arm through the air at the hundred people packed tightly around us. "And promise me one of those mind-blowing orgasms you give so well...every day, for the rest of my life."

By that time, she's gripping the front of my shirt and we're nose to nose. I'm still holding the microphone from the stage and the place is starting to erupt, everyone telling me to say yes.

"I already said, anything...and I mean, anything."

We kiss and the crowd goes fucking wild.

And the video ends.

Another text comes through immediately after.

Dave: This shit has gone viral!!!

The hotel room is dead silent. Piper is still standing by the door, listening to the sounds of our drunken night coming back to haunt us, while I stare at my phone like it grew two heads.

"Huh," I grunt out, unsure of what else to say. I mean, it's not that bad. So, what? I proposed to her in front of a bunch of drunk bastards at The Cat's Meow? That's not the worst thing that could've happened.

At least we didn't get married.

But I feel the tension filling the room, and I swallow once, my body wanting to take a step back from her in preservation, just in case. For some reason, I'm pretty sure Piper isn't going to think it's quite as humorous as I do.

Taking a chance, I glance up just in time to watch as the blood returns to Piper's face, turning it a shade of pink, as the anger boils. I see it in her eyes and the hard set of her jaw as she grits her teeth together and breathes in deeply through her nose.

And this time, I do take a step back, raising my hands in surrender, phone in one hand, diamond ring in the other.

She takes a counter step toward me, her finger rising as she seethes. "Fix this."

"Hey, babe," I tell her in a soothing tone, trying to talk her down a little before she says or does something we'll both regret. "It takes two to tango." Or maybe I'm trying to piss her off even more, but fuck me, if I'm going to let her put all the blame on me.

"Don't call me babe," she yells, her finger poking into my chest. "I swear to God. If this gets out—goes any further than this hotel room—I'll kill you. And I'll enjoy it. And when they come to take me away, it'll be the happiest fucking day of my life, because you'll be dead and I'll get three-square meals a day, and a roof over my head and I won't ever have to look at your face again...or ward off your demon dick."

Her rant is crazy, almost as crazy as she is, and it's making zero sense, but I let her go. Partly, because I'm afraid of her. And partly, because I really love it when she's all worked up.

"Make that shit go away," she finally says, gathering her wits and smoothing her hair back. "Tell George or Darrell or whoever the fuck to delete that video."

"What about this?" I ask, holding up the ring.

"I don't care what you do with the damn ring, Tucker! Sell it. Pawn it. Stick it up your ass!"

"So, you don't want it?" I know I'm egging her on, but I can't help myself. Maybe I'll get lucky and get a morning fuck session for my efforts.

"No, I don't want it." Her tone oozes disgust. "What I *want* is for this to all be a nightmare and I want to wake up in my bed. Alone!" She screams in frustration and slams the door behind her, effectively ending our banter and leaving me with a semi.

I smile to myself, falling back into the bed, rolling over and hugging Piper's pillow to me.

She might frustrate me to the ends of the earth. And I wouldn't say I like her. I don't even tolerate her on most days. But I love the way she smells. And I love the way she fights. And I kind of like the part where she said she'd marry me...even if she was drunk.

If for no other reason than knowing she's not going to let this go or forget it, and I'll still be pissing her off, even when I'm not with her.

That's enough for me.

A random, hazy thought fills my mind, playing out like a movie—me and Piper, walking down a dark sidewalk, her leaning into my side, laughing.

When I see the flickering gold sign ahead, I stop dead in my tracks.

"I'm gonna buy you a ring." I pull Piper back and look down at her half-shuttered eyes, loving how beautiful she looks peering up at me, without the hard persona she usually wears. She's just Piper and she's gorgeous.

"Yes!" Piper squeals. "I wanna big one." She waggles her eyebrows at me with a sly grin on her face.

"Oh, Darlin', I'm gonna get you the biggest one they got."

The pawn shop light flickers again, almost beckoning us inside...or maybe it's more of a warning, but in my drunken state, this seems like the best idea I've had all night.

CHAPTER TWO

I wake up from a deep sleep, after tossing and turning for hours. From the way the sun is barely creeping in my window, I know it's afternoon and I overslept. Since I'm only working for myself and my dad these days, it's not a huge deal, but I don't like feeling like I've wasted the day away.

This used to be the norm for me. When I was playing gigs all the time, living life on the road, our days didn't even start until afternoon.

Rolling over in bed, I rub vigorously at my face, trying to get rid of the grogginess and also the dream I was having before I woke up. It felt so real—creamy tits and dark hair, belonging to none other than Piper Grey, *my wife*. Or at least in my dream she was. She was wearing the big-ass rock on the third finger of her left hand. She was also smiling as I kissed it and then her.

A lot different than the non-dream experience from the hotel room.

Piper and I have been like oil and water since we met. We rubbed each other the wrong way for so long, until one night, after a party at the Landry's, we couldn't ignore the desire lingering under all that hate and pent up aggression. Since then, we've hooked up any time we're given the opportunity and occasionally, we create the opportunity—bathrooms, hotel rooms, behind a barn. We've been a lot of things to each other over the past six months—enemies, fuck buddies, pseudo-lovers—but the idea of her being my wife makes me pause.

I chuckle. A weird sensation filling my chest.

I've never thought much about marriage. It's not that I'm scared of it or have bad examples. I'm not a child of divorce and I haven't seen a bunch of bad shit. My parents had a great marriage before my mama died. And now my dad is happily remarried to Kay. Then, there's Sam and Annie, who've been married since the dinosaurs roamed. Deacon has made Cami happier than I've ever seen her, and Micah and Dani are now getting ready to tie the knot, sooner rather than later. So, I'm surrounded by amazing examples.

Out of all those people, Dani is the one who deserves the biggest props. She's tamed the beast, something no woman has ever been able to even come close to accomplishing. It's like she's the fucking Playboy Whisperer or some shit.

I've always thought something like that might happen to me one of these days. I'd meet a girl and she'd rock my world, change everything about me, and make me want to settle down.

But that hasn't happened yet.

Maybe it's because I haven't slowed down long enough.

Up until a few months ago, I'd spent the last ten years living out of a suitcase, with my longest committed relationship being my band. I've practically been married to those fuckers since high school.

But this past year was rough. I felt myself spiraling for a while, unable to stop it and not sure I wanted to. When I woke up from a week-long bender, next to some unknown chick, not knowing where I found her...or where I was—it was Biloxi, by the way—I knew I needed a change of scenery. I couldn't breathe, couldn't think, and wanted to peel away the thick layer of mask that'd taken over my reflection.

I looked like shit and felt like shit. The only thing I could think of to make it better was to come home.

I needed some peace and quiet—time to think.

When I stayed sober long enough, I realized I hadn't written any new music in months and that always messed with my head.

Where there weren't words, there wasn't life. There wasn't me.

Without some sort of creative outlet, I was going crazy, and it wasn't the good kind.

As a younger kid, my guitar became a source of therapy. After my mom died, I found solace in the strings, teaching myself simple songs and then gradually moving into writing them. Cami had her canvases and I had my lyrics. When dark, depressing thoughts tried to have their way with me, writing songs was a way for me to express myself. I'd take the sadness and anger and put them into lyrics, until I felt like they weren't going to suck me under.

They're the reason I played my first gig. I realized from the get-go, if I didn't sing my songs, no one was going to hear them. And I thought if the right person *did* hear them, they'd buy them and I'd be rich. I mean, that's what happened to people on television and in movies. Why couldn't it happen to me?

Oh, to be young and naive again.

As crazy as it sounds, I've been chasing that dream for the last ten years. I got a little off-track. I fell in love with the rush of the stage and started playing every bar and small venue this side of the Mississippi.

Until a few months ago, I was still chasing the dream, but something happened that morning in Biloxi. Something clicked or broke, I don't know which.

A week or so later, I woke up one morning and walked away from it all, told my band to go home.

Since then, my life has been in reboot mode. I've moved into my old room at my dad's and started helping him in the sugarcane fields, doing odd jobs. Every day, I try to exert myself so much that all I can think about is a hot shower, a plate of food, and a nice cool bed.

There have been a few hookups with Piper, but for the most part, I've secluded myself in hopes that I'll get out of this hole and find myself again.

One thing that's helped me clear my head has been working with all of this old wood in my dad's barn. He said I could have it and do whatever I want with it. So, I made a shelf and then another. Cami had mentioned wanting an old-fashioned cradle for the new baby, so

I started working on that. I like it. It's rewarding to see a finished product, something I made from scratch. I don't really draw up plans or anything. I just jot down measurements and notes. Most of what I make is trial and error, but it feels good to create.

I can't say that it'll suppress the demons like writing a song, but it's working for now. If I do continue to write songs, I want someone else to sing them, but I don't even know if that's what I want anymore. For now, I'm happy putting in some manual labor on my dad's farm, working with my hands, and feeling completely exhausted at the end of the day.

It's a slow pace. It's three-square meals a day, thanks to Annie and Kay. It's waking up in the same bed every morning. It's boring and routine and exactly what I needed.

Just as I'm thinking about getting out of bed, my phone dings with a message. For a split second, my traitorous dick nearly leaps out of my pants in hopes that it's a sexy brunette texting for a booty call, but it should've known better.

Dave. Good ol' Davie Boy. The same punk who sent me the video a few days ago and ruined my chances of morning sex with Piper.

She hasn't called or texted since she stormed out of the hotel room, not that she does on a daily basis, but she will usually at least answer when I do, but no. Nothing. Nada. Dead air. Radio Silence.

I get it. She's pissed about the drunken proposal and the video... and the ring. But, like I told her, it takes two, and if I had to guess, I'd guess she's just as pissed at herself for letting it all happen. Piper isn't used to being out of control of situations. Shit, I've probably only seen her tipsy a few times since I've known her and never as drunk as she was the other night.

> Dave: Dude, have you seen how many times your video has been re-Tweeted? That shit really did go viral!

What the fuck?

> Me: I told you to take that fucking video down!!! Are your trying to get me castrated?

Dave: Do you even know what that means?

Me: Yes, dipshit! I may talk slow, but I'm not stupid. And I value my dick more than your life. If I go to Twitter and see that video is still up, I'm hunting you down and killing you with my bare hands. I'll give Rambo a run for his money. It'll be Texas Chainsaw Massacre up in your joint. Comprende?

Dave needs visuals. He's a see and learn kind of guy. Point in case, he taught himself to play the drums by watching videos of Dave Grohl. He also stakes claim to being named after him, but that's a load of shit. I know for a fact his parents weren't fans of Nirvana or the Foo Fighters, and I sure as hell know they've never heard of Scream.

Dave: Why so sensitive? Did you grow a pussy since you abandoned us?

Me: Dave.

It's all I have to type before the little text bubbles pop back up on the screen. The cool thing about Dave and me is that he can hear my tone through text because we've done it so much over the years.

Dave: You do know what it means when something goes viral, right?

Sure. It's viral, meaning...

Dave: It's out of my hands. That video has now been posted on Buzzfeed's Best Drunk Proposals AND the Cat's Meow's Facebook page. It's taking off like a wildfire. There ain't no stopping it.

Fuck.

Me: Fuck.

Dave: Sorry, man, but you're famous. And so is that hot as sin chick you proposed to. What was her name? Poppy.

Me: Don't worry about her name. And don't mention it. Ever.

Falling over my twisted sheets while I'm trying to get out of bed, I lay in the middle of my floor, forcing my brain to figure out a fast plan to make this all go away. I believe Piper. I believe everything she says, because she might be a grade-A bitch and spawn of Satan, but she's never lied to me.

Dave: What are you gonna do?

Me: Fuck if I know, dude. Any ideas?

Dave: No, but if she beats your ass, can you be sure to get it on video? It'd make a great follow-up.

Me: Dave.

Dave: Fine. Gotta go, anyway. Later.

Groaning, I roll over and pick myself up off the floor. A sick feeling is in the pit of my stomach and I can't tell if it's from lack of food or impending doom, but I decide some of Kay's leftover fried chicken from last night will help me decide. So, I trudge downstairs to see what I can find.

After eating and getting cleaned up, I jump in my car and head to Baton Rouge. I figure dad is probably half done with his work for the day by now, so I'll just have to make up for being a loser tomorrow.

Right now, I need to get to Grinders. I need to talk this out with someone, and Micah and Deacon are my go-tos. The problem is, since they know nothing about me and Piper, I have to be discreet and I'm never fucking discreet. I could talk to Cami, but she'd see right through my bullshit quicker than a one-legged man at an ass-kicking contest.

No, the boys are the way to go. I just have to play it off like I'm talking about someone else and see how they react.

That's my plan, anyway.

"Tucker the Fucker, you here for a late lunch or an early dinner?" Deacon greets me with his usual wide smile from his perch at the bar. Micah turns to face me after replacing a bottle of booze on the shelf and nods his head my way. I admit, the past few months I was worried these two yahoos wouldn't ever get their panties untwisted. I haven't seen them so at odds with each other since we were kids, but even then, it wasn't as bad as the feud that erupted after Micah went into business with Alex Collins. But they finally kissed and made up, and it warms my rotten, black heart to see them working together again.

"Nah, man, I just came in to see how things were goin'. I took the day off, so I'm here to bother you bitches."

"We haven't seen you in a while. Been holed up with a gaggle of groupies?"

"Gaggle, huh? Is that what they're called now? Oh, and by the way, I forgot to give you this." I show Micah my middle finger and then sit down at the bar. "If you must know, I've been helpin' my dad in the fields, puttin' in an honest day's work."

"Damn," Deacon grunted. "Is he punishin' you or somethin'? Makin' a pretty boy like you do manual labor...you must've pissed him off big time."

"No, asshole. He needs the help, and I don't mind it. I'm actually enjoyin' it. I've even been workin' on a few new pieces of furniture. It feels good to work hard and get my hands dirty."

Micah tosses a bar towel over his shoulder and snorts. "There's our boy. Braggin' about using his dirty hands to work his wood, that's the Tucker we've missed. But, seriously, I'm glad to see you findin' your happy place again. That sunshine is definitely doin' some good, too. You don't look like that shaggy-haired vampire from Twilight anymore."

"Very funny, dickweed." I pick up a napkin and wad it up, throwing it at the back of his head. "The grand opening of Lagniappe is next week, right? You ready?" I ask, changing the subject. I'm not ready to talk about me any more than I have to.

"Hell, yeah, I'm ready. It's gonna be an amazing night, but there's just *one* thing I need to make it perfect." He smiles at me, a bit too sweetly for my taste, and I know that looks. He wants something.

I glance over at Deacon and, when he sees my questioning expression, he shrugs at me. "Don't look at me."

Micah ignores us and continues. "Well, I was gonna ask if you knew of any guitarists I could hire for the night...you know, a little acoustic set would be nice but..." He drags his words out, letting me read between them.

"Are you askin' me to play at your restaurant opening?" I croon, pretending to be flattered, which I kind of am, but I don't want him knowing that.

"Well, I mean, I know you're busy playin' in the sunshine and workin' your wood, but I was thinkin' about it," Micah teases. He's never going to run out of woodworking jokes.

"Of course, I'll play. I did it for Grinders and Pockets and I'd be pissed if you wouldn't have asked me for the new one."

"Consider yourself hired, Tucker Benoit. You can even bring one of your lady friends to be your personal assistant, and all your food and beverages will be on the house."

My blood runs cold for a second at the words "lady friend". The only one I'd want with me that night is Piper, but she hates my guts even more than usual right now. I have a feeling she'll be there anyway and there's no way I'd bring anyone else and make things worse between us. I don't mind Piper being a little rough on my balls, but that doesn't mean I'll willingly let her rip them off my body, which is exactly what she'd do if I brought another girl to the opening. Ours is a fucked-up relationship, for sure, but we know our boundaries.

"Now that that's settled, Tucker, I'm gonna need you to fill us in about your recent conquests," Deacon declares. "With Cami getting farther along in the pregnancy, things are kinda...cooling off in the bedroom, if you know what I mean. Unfortunately, that means I have to live vicariously through you."

I stand up so quickly, my bar stool nearly topples over. "That's my sister you're fuckin' talkin' about, Deke," I snap. "Don't make me kick your ass because you know I'll do it."

Deacon raises his hands, palms facing me, in supplication. "It's not a diss toward Cami, I swear. She's the most beautiful woman in the world, especially when she's pregnant. It's all me." He really does look remorseful, but he's going to have to do some fast talking to get me to understand what the hell he means. I don't want any explicit details about their bedroom antics, but if he says one disrespectful word against Cami, his ass is mine.

"What the fuck, man?" I'm staring Deacon down, showing him I mean business, when Micah busts out laughing. He's about to be number two on my shit list today.

Micah is bent over with his hands on his knees, laughing his ass off. Eventually, he stands back up and wipes his eyes, still chuckling. He looks at me but points at his brother. "Deacon thinks he's gonna poke the baby with his dick if they have sex!"

I slowly sit back down on my stool and look at Deacon. Not only does he seem apologetic, he's also completely embarrassed based on how red his cheeks are right now.

"Is this true?" I ask. I have to ask. This is a gold mine of retaliation. I can't let this opportunity pass me by.

"Well, yeah. I mean, the doctor has already said this baby is gonna be a big one and we all know how much I'm packing." He grabs his crotch and Micah pretends to gag while I roll my eyes. "It only makes sense that, if I go *in*, some things that should not be touching, will be touching! It's biology!"

"You're a fucking idiot, you know that? I can't believe my sister actually married you," I scoff.

"Maybe that's what happened to you, Deke," Micah goads. "I just assumed Mama dropped you on your head, but maybe it was from her and Dad doin' the wild thing when she was pregnant with you!"

"That's enough! Our parents did not ever do *the wild thing*, so shut your face," Deacon says with a horrified look on his face. "All I wanted to know was who Tucker hooked up with the night you proposed to Dani and we got completely off topic, fuck."

Micah just shakes his head, laughing, and goes back to drying the bar glasses.

"Come on, man," Deacon says, giving me a pointed look. "You never hold out on me."

It's true. I don't. Actually, I make it a point to tell Micah and Deacon about all of my sexual conquests. It's well-known that my goal in life is to plant my flag, and by flag, I mean my dick, in every country. Now, I don't necessarily need it to happen in that country. The pussy just needs to have originated there.

I let out a breath and roll my eyes. He's not going to give this up and I guess I should take pity on him for the mess of a conversation we just had.

"Yeah, I hooked up that night. She was...hot," I tell him, trying to quickly come up with a lie or partial truth to suffice.

"Was it that blonde bartender?" he asks. "Tits McGee," Deacon says, like I should know exactly who he's talking about.

"Who?"

"Come on, man! There's no way you could've missed those...I mean, her."

I glare at him, because he better not have been looking at some other chick's tits. My sister will beat the shit out of him. Also, because how could I have missed that? I never miss a set of good titties. It's just not my style.

"Right," I lie. "Tits McGee." I give him a look like *you got me.*

"I knew it, you fucker," he says gleefully, like he just guessed the answer to a million dollar question. "So, was she good?" Deacon asks, waggling his eyebrows.

Such a fucking horn dog. Deacon and Micah like to say *I'm* bad, but that's because they use me as their cover.

"Where did you take off to after the bar that night?" This time it's Micah who's giving me the Spanish Inquisition. "Did you dump Piper and take Tits to a hotel?"

Fuck, he knows.

He knows Piper and I were together at the bar when he and Dani called it a night.

Think, man. Think.

"Uh yeah, I left with her," I tell him, giving him a wicked smile. "You know I can't resist big tits and long legs."

"You left Piper alone?" he asks, his eyes narrowing in on me accusatorily.

"Ooh, Dani is gonna be pissed," Deacon adds.

"No, man." *Shit*. This is why you don't lie. One lie turns into two and then you're lying about your lies. "I didn't leave her alone. She started talking to some guy, but then she said she was tired. So, I, uh, called her a cab."

Rule number one: never leave the girls alone.

Micah, Deke, and I might be partiers, and we know how to have a good time, but we always make sure the girls are taken care of. If I made them think I let Piper leave alone or with some stranger, they'd either know I was lying or string me up.

Shit, I don't know if I'm playing this off well enough. I feel like I'm losing my bullshitting ability.

They both look me up and down, like they're trying to decide if they believe me. A few seconds pass, feeling more like days, but Micah and Deacon eventually let it go and relax on the interrogation.

Crisis averted. For now.

"Hey, Micah, I, uh, heard there's this video circulating the web of some drunken couple gettin' engaged the same night you proposed to Dani. At first, I thought it might be you two, but it's not. Have you, um, heard anything about that?" I'm suddenly very nervous and starting to sweat. I really don't like lying to my best friends, but I know Piper would kill me for sure if I told them.

"You know I don't pay attention to that kind of shit. Plus, Dani would've ripped my balls off if I had proposed to her while we were drunk. And then posted a video of it? Fuck that. I feel sorry for that dude."

I feel sick. Bile is churning in my stomach, trying to make its way up my throat, and I've got a full sweat going on. How in the hell am I going to fix this?

"Yeah, totally. Poor bastard," I grumble. "Uh, it's been great hangin' out, but I just remembered something I have to do, so I'll see y'all later."

I don't give them a chance to respond, I just haul ass out of the restaurant and practically jump into my truck.

CHAPTER THREE

When i was growing up, all Micah and Deacon ever talked about was opening their own restaurant. Well, that and girls, of course.

They'd go on and on about what food they'd cook, what the place would look like...Frankly, it bored me to tears sometimes but I never said anything. No way would I try to discourage their dreams; they just weren't as exciting as my dreams. Traveling, performing on stage, selling a shit ton of records, and all the women I could ever want—that's what I wanted, and for a very brief time, I had a taste of it.

You know when you want something so badly and you have it built up so much in your mind, there's no way reality can live up to your expectations? That's what life on the road was like for me. I had fun, don't get me wrong, but instead of feeling fulfilled at the end of the day, I was left empty and dried up.

As I sit here in the parking lot of Lagniappe, I feel nothing but pride that my boys achieved their dreams. Micah and Deacon have both worked their asses off and the last few months have been tough for damn sure, but they're stronger for it. Micah has always been in Deacon's shadow, but that officially ends tonight. I can't wait.

Micah is slowly walking around the dining room when I walk inside the restaurant with my guitar strapped to my back. He seems to be mentally cataloging something, so I try not to bother him but that can only last for so long.

"Man, those wheels are turnin' so hard, I swear I can smell something burnin'. Everything ok?"

He looks at me and gives a relaxed smile. "Everything's perfect. I'm just soakin' it all in."

"It looks great, Micah. It really does. This place is gonna be huge," I tell him. I'm not just blowing smoke either; Lagniappe has success written all over it.

"Thanks, man," he says, slapping me on the back. "I have an area for you right over there, if you want to get set up." He points to a small space in the back corner of the dining area. It's just me and my acoustic guitar, so I don't need much, but I appreciate him placing me where everyone will be able to see and hear me.

"I was kinda worried about you the other day when you left Grinders like a bat out of hell. Everything alright with you?"

I was hoping he wouldn't bring that up. After getting his and Deacon's take on the proposal video, I had to leave and clear my head. Piper still isn't talking to me, so I'm really at a loss on how to fix this.

"Yeah, I'm all good. Don't worry about me." I give him my typical shit-eating grin, like I always do, and I hope he buys it.

"You didn't bring anybody tonight?" he asks.

"Nah, I can't be worried about hookin' up tonight. I got a job to do." I wink at him then lean my guitar against the wall in the corner.

"Whatever you say, T. I'm sure you won't be hurtin' for company after your set tonight. The ladies always love a rock star."

"Damn straight and hallelujah!" I exclaim, relaxing when I see Micah buying my act. Six months ago, I'd have my wallet fully stocked with rubbers in preparation for tonight. Somehow, things have changed and I can't make heads or tails out of it.

As I set up my amp and test my mic, Randy, Micah's right-hand-man and the guy in charge of the amazing food, walks over and hands me a drink.

"Thanks, man." I nod my head in appreciation and take a healthy sip of the amber liquid.

Southern Comfort. He knows me well.

"That's Micah's go-to, figured you'd like it as well."

"You're a smart man, Randy. I'm glad Micah has you around."

He laughs, shaking his head. "Boss man is the brains of the organization, I'm more the brawn."

"Don't let Micah hear you say that. His pussy ass'll get offended. Always thinkin' he's gotta be the brains *and* the brawn." I shake my head, but it's the God's honest truth.

About that time, people start filtering into the restaurant.

The entire Landry Clan, including my sister, are the first to arrive. Shortly after, my dad and Kay walk in. Between all of them, they take up a fourth of the seating, but from the beaming smile on Micah's face, he couldn't care less. He's happy. This is exactly what he wanted.

I'm also happy to see the genuine look of admiration on Deacon's face. This recent blow-up between the two of them was a long time coming. Micah's had that brewing in him since we were kids, and Deacon knew it. I think it's why he fought it so hard.

Deke knew Alex wasn't in it for good or for all the right reasons. He was trying to protect Micah from getting burned, but what he didn't realize was that he was also making himself sound like an asshole dictator. His way or the highway. I think they both learned some good lessons these past few months.

The night gets off without a hitch. The wait staff are busy seating people and charming the pants off of them, while the kitchen staff whips up the best tasting food you've ever put in your mouth.

"What do you want to eat?" Micah asks, walking up as he looks out over the place.

"I'll eat later, man. Don't worry about me."

"Nah, eat. I want you to enjoy the night too."

"Fine, give me the house special."

At that, Micah's eye light up. "Comin' right up."

Just as I'm getting ready to walk over and take the empty seat between Dani and my sister, in walks Piper Grey. She doesn't look my way, just swoops in and kisses cheeks and takes my seat.

Fuckin' A.

She didn't tell me she was going to be here, but I guess that shouldn't surprise me since she won't return a text or a call. Inside, I'm suddenly worked up, but I put on my game face and grab my guitar. The food will have to wait, because I'm going to make damn sure Piper sees me. She'll have no excuse to not listen to what I have to say.

An hour into my set, and I feel as though my mission is accomplished. There's not an empty chair, plate, or glass and everyone seems to be having a great time, including Micah, Dani, and *Piper*.

My song choices have been directed at her, but no one else would know. I mean, maybe if they knew about us, they might piece it together or make some guesses, but that secret is still safe with us, for now.

"Ladies and gentlemen, I'm taking a little break. Hope you enjoyed the music and the food." I give the crowd a wink before taking a chance to look for Piper. As soon as she registers that I'm watching her, she grabs her glass and slams back the clear liquid inside before storming to the hall that leads to the restrooms.

Game on.

Calmly, I stand and place my guitar on its stand, bowing to patrons who are still clapping, before discreetly making my way down the hall, following Piper. I try the knob and it turns. Pushing the door open, I walk in to find my beautiful target leaning over the sink. Her hands are gripping the edges of the white porcelain, and her head is hanging down below her shoulders. My fingers itch to touch her, to try and soothe her, but that's not how we work.

"What's a girl like you doin' in a place like this?" I ask, breaking the silence in the room as I reach behind me and turn the lock on the door, insuring our privacy.

Piper's body straightens as her hand flies to her chest, her breathing accelerated. "What the fuck are you doing in here? This is the *ladies'* room, Tucker."

I make a show of looking around the room as I walk—no, stalk—toward her. "I don't think anyone's in here, darlin."

She steps back until her body is flush against the wall.

"I haven't heard from you in a while. You're not still pissed about the video, are you?" I move to tuck a piece of her hair behind her ear and she smacks my hand away.

"Don't touch me, asshole. Of course, I'm still pissed. I told you to fix it and you didn't. Now, the whole world knows we're engaged!"

"Oh, so we're engaged, huh?" I snicker when she rolls her eyes. "I don't know why you're so worried. None of our friends or family know anything about that video, so who cares what anyone else thinks?"

"*I care.* I have a professional reputation to uphold and *your* family may not know, but what if mine sees that video? They'll disown me!"

My jaw clenches as I try to escape the burn of her words. I'm not sure what would anger her parents more: Piper getting engaged in a bar in New Orleans or Piper getting engaged to *me*. Either way, I know it wouldn't be good for her. I'm not good for her, not good enough anyway. It doesn't make me want her any less, though.

She reaches out and touches the crucifix that's hanging on the chain around my neck and I bite down on my bottom lip to hide my smile. I don't know if she realizes it, but she does this every time we're together, sometimes more than once. She never asks about it, but there's something about it that always seems to get her attention.

I can't be this close to her and not touch her, so I place my hands on her hips. When she doesn't fight me on it, I take a step closer. "Look, babe, it's out of our hands now. We can't stop it, so we just have to deal with it."

"You know I hate it when you call me that. You're just trying to get a rise out of me so I'll fuck you."

"What's wrong with that?" I slide my hands around her petite frame and grab her ass.

"Maybe I don't want to anymore. Did you ever think of that?" she spits out.

"Nope," is my answer even though it's a lie. I think about the possibility of Piper being done with me way more than I'd care to admit. "You can't quit me, you just don't want to admit it."

I kiss her just below her ear and work my way down the column of her neck. Piper's responses to my actions are there—obvious to me because I know her body so well—but it's not enough. I want her to push back. *Feel something. Do something.*

When my teeth graze her collarbone, she gasps and grabs onto my shoulders.

"Oh, sure, that's it," she says sarcastically in between quick breaths, "It has nothing to do with me just needing to get laid. What do you care anyway? I'm just another notch, another groupie to you. You could have almost any woman in this restaurant but, instead, you're in the bathroom with me. Who can't quit whom, huh?"

She palms my dick through my jeans, smiling wickedly when she feels how hard I am.

"You're my groupie now? I kinda like that." I trace the skin across her chest with my tongue. "Although, none of my groupies have ever irritated me as much as you do."

"Pompous ass," she mutters.

"I think it would be much more productive if we took our anger out on each other, don't you?"

Sliding my hands up her skirt gets her attention. "Tucker, we're not fucking in the bathroom of Micah's new restaurant."

She says that like it's the dirtiest place we've fooled around. It's not, believe me.

"You're right, we're not. But I'm still gonna make you wish that we were."

"Don't start what you can't finish," she warns.

I pull her lacy panties to the side and find her completely wet for me. I know we don't have much time before my next set starts, so I go right for her clit. I switch off between rubbing circles and stroking it with my fingers, just like I know she likes.

Piper makes the best noises when we're screwing and being in a public place is no exception. Her moans are low and breathy, completely guttural and natural. None of that fake porno-sounding bullshit. Piper is better than porn, any day.

I briefly toy with the idea of teasing her to the point of orgasm then pulling away before she can finish but that's too cruel, even for us. Besides, Piper coming is a thing of beauty, an amazing sight to behold. I wouldn't be doing myself any favors by denying us both the experience.

When I start rubbing faster, her hips begin moving on their own accord, causing her to grunt in frustration. She's too close too soon for her taste, but that only makes me move faster, harder. She can try to fight it all she wants, but I will make her come on my hand right fucking now. I need it as much as she does.

Her thighs are shaking and her pussy is even wetter now, so I push two fingers inside while keeping pressure on her clit with my thumb. As her orgasm hits her, her cries echo throughout the bathroom just before I place my free hand over her mouth. Giving her a smirk and a shake of my head, I keep pumping my fingers as she rides out her climax, holding onto me for dear life. Her eyelids flutter and her legs start to give out as the waves of pleasure slow down, so I remove my hand from her mouth and wrap my arm around her waist, holding her to me. When I know she's clear-headed and able to stand on her own, I slowly pull my fingers out of her and put them directly inside my mouth, moaning at how she tastes.

Piper watches with great interest but catches herself. She clears her throat while straightening her skirt before she speaks. "I hope that was good for you because that's all you're getting tonight."

I laugh because I know she's lying. "I do believe you're mistaken, darlin'. This was just the appetizer. After my next set, I'm gettin' the whole entree, plus dessert."

She tries to hide her smile, but I see it. I see her.

I adjust my dick so my erection isn't too noticeable, but there's only so much I can do. I catch her watching me and give her a quick wink before unlocking the door and walking out.

There's a lady approaching the bathroom and I give her a huge smile and tip my head. "Ma'am."

I'm sure she recognizes me from my performance and her eyes go wide as she notices where I just came from.

Never looking back, I make my way back out to the bar and request a refill on my drink. The bartender obliges and I take it with me to my barstool, ready for my next set.

Ready to make Piper squirm as she thinks about what's coming.

In my head, I pick songs I know get to her and I'm ready to give the performance of my life, but before I can even pick up my guitar, Piper walks over to the table, whispers something in Dani's ear, and walks to the door. She stops before leaving, taking a second to glance back over her shoulder. The look on her face is a challenge. She's taking the ball back and placing it firmly in her court.

This is the Piper I love fucking with—the one who gives it back to me, just as good as I give it.

Sure, she's leaving me with a case of blue balls, but it'll make the next time we're together that much sweeter.

And she knows exactly what she's doing. She knows all I'll be able to think about from now until then is her—her scent, her tits, the way she moves. Everything about her was custom made for me, which makes this game of ours that much more enticing, and completely frustrating.

After my second set, I make my way over to the table where my sister is sitting with Dad, Kay, Sam, and Annie. Dani is up taking pictures and Deacon found his way to the kitchen.

I give him six months. He's smitten with this place. I can tell. He'll find some way to weasel his way into this business.

"Great job tonight," Kay says, reaching over to pat my hand.

"Thank you," I tell her with a wink.

"Yeah, it was good to see you play. It's been a while." My dad nods his approval as he slips an arm behind Kay, resting it on her chair.

"This whole night was wonderful," Annie adds. "I'm gettin' spoiled. You're gonna have to drive me to the city once a week, Sam."

Gettin' spoiled. I'd say Annie already is, but I'd *never* say that to her or out loud, for that matter, in fear she'd catch wind of it. Annie is definitely the queen of the Landry castle. Everyone knows it and no one more than her husband.

Sam leans over and kisses her cheek, chuckling his agreement.

"Tucker, looked like you were a big hit with the ladies tonight," Sam says with a quirk of his eyebrow. When I say the apples don't fall far from the tree, I mean, Micah and Deacon get their horn dog ways honestly. I can imagine Sam was a rounder in his days. He just happened across the perfect woman to make an honest man out of him early in life.

"Stop," Cami says from beside me. "His head is big enough as it is. Don't go fillin' it with more hot air than what's already in there." She rests a hand on her small protruding stomach and I give her a smile. I couldn't be annoyed with her if I tried. Something changed as we grew up. She went from being my irritating little sister who ratted me out and was always in my business, to someone I admire and couldn't imagine my life without.

I don't really tell her that, at least not very often.

Everyone thinks I don't have mushy feelings, but I do. I just keep them under wraps. I have an image to uphold, after all. Instead, I pull the end of her hair that's up in a high ponytail, like we're still in grade school. She swats at me and my dad clears his throat.

This is a ten-second replay of my life. Cami says something sassy. I retaliate. My dad keeps us both in line. Just because we're now twenty-six and twenty-eight, instead of six and eight, doesn't mean anything has changed.

"I usually get my pick of the litter," I say, for Sam's benefit, because like Deacon, he likes to live vicariously through yours truly, and I can't let him down. Also, even though I admire the shit out of Cami, it doesn't mean I still don't like to annoy her from time to time. Old habits die hard.

Perusing the room, I see a woman with long brown hair, someone I might've hit on six months ago, and I smile at her.

It's all for show, of course. Unless Piper is waiting for me at my truck when I leave, I'll be going home alone.

"I'm glad you're all here," Micah says from behind me, clapping his hands loudly and practically scaring the shit out of me.

Turning around in my chair, I see Dani standing beside him, holding his hand. Deacon has walked up behind Cami, rubbing her shoulders gently. The entire family is present and accounted for, except for Carter. And Piper. She's been adopted in, even if she's not aware or wants to be. When Annie Landry decides your family, there's nothing you can do about it.

"Dani and I are getting married," Micah announces with a big ass grin. "A week from tomorrow. You're all invited."

"A week?" Annie practically yells, before remembering that there are still other people in the restaurant. "A week?" This time her question is quieter and directed at Micah with a pointed stare. "How in the world do you expect us to plan a wedding in a week?"

"You're not." Micah takes a deep breath and smiles down at Dani, before looking back over at his mama. "We're getting married at the chapel down the street, and the reception will be here. It's just gonna be all of us and a few of our friends and employees. Y'all can invite some close family friends, but we'd like to keep it under fifty." He pauses, kissing Dani.

"I've never really wanted a big wedding," Dani adds, reaching up and touching Micah's cheek. "Besides, there's no use in waiting. I know what I want." Her eyes never leave Micah's.

"Well, I guess that's settled." Annie has a pleased grin on her face as she looks over at Sam.

Her kids are happy, that's all she's ever wanted. She's said it a million times. So, even though Micah and Dani are robbing her of what she does best, entertaining the entire state of Louisiana, she's happy, because they're happy.

CHAPTER FOUR

Piper has gone radio silent again.

I broke down and texted her late Sunday night, trying to feel her out and see when she'd be making the trip back to New Orleans for the wedding, but she's yet to reply.

That's okay. She won't be able to ignore me come Sunday. Micah is making me and Deacon his best men, and Dani is having Piper be her maid of honor and Cami her matron of honor. So, Piper will be stuck with me, whether she likes it or not.

And, I have to say, that pleases the shit out of me. It's kind of put a little pep in my step.

I was up at the crack of dawn this morning, but by the time I made it downstairs, my dad was already on the tractor in the back forty acres. It's like he never sleeps, or if he does, it's only a few hours.

Clay Benoit is one of the hardest working men I've ever met, if not *the* hardest working man. My entire life, I watched him work all day, come in and cook for me and Cami, go to bed, and do it all over again the next day. When my mama died, he became the mom and the dad. He wasn't the best at either, but he tried. One thing is for sure, Cami and I never went hungry and we always knew we were loved. He set a good example for us. We learned you never give up, even when times are tough, you stick it out and keep going. It's something I've always carried with me.

"You forgot this," I hear a voice behind me call out from the front porch.

Kay is standing there with a jug of water, make that *two* jugs of water, and a smile. I love her. She's not my mama, but she's perfect for my daddy. She came along at just the right time and pulled him out of the dark hole he'd been living in since my mama died. Sure, he made appearances for me and Cami, but his heart was still shattered. Kay helped him glue back the broken pieces.

"One's for your daddy. I'm not sure how long he'll stay out there, so I thought he might need an extra."

"Thank you," I tell her, leaning in and kissing her cheek. "And thanks for the breakfast and coffee."

"You're welcome." She smiles and pats my face. "Don't work too hard today."

"I'm gonna try to." I laugh and she swats at me. "It does me good."

"Alright then, work hard."

I wave and turn toward the barn. Since my dad is already out in the fields—doing God knows what, because even though I help out, I'm not a sugarcane farmer—I decide I'm going to do something I know.

Setting the jugs of water down on my makeshift workbench, I walk to the corner and plug in my saw, grabbing the two large pieces of wood I started on last week.

Cami mentioned something about wanting an old-fashioned bassinet for the baby, so I'm giving it a whirl. I've never made one before, but the first time I made a shelf, I hadn't done that before either, and it's now hanging on the wall in the living room. So, surely, I can make a bed for a baby.

Jotting down my rough plans on a scrap piece of wood, I get lost in my work—placing the first piece of wood on the sawhorses and flipping the switch on the circular saw. I feel the slight twinge of adrenaline as the blade whirs. Carefully, I begin to cut along the lines I traced and before too long, one piece becomes two, and then two become four.

Laying them out side-by-side, I inhale deeply, loving the smell of sawdust mixed with a little dirt and sweat. It's done more for my mental stability than any five-star spa or rehab facility.

As I walk over to grab some water, movement from outside the barn catches my attention. An unfamiliar car is parked by the large oak tree out front and a petite frame is walking this way. I can't make out who it is, but I can tell it's a girl.

I wipe the sweat from my forehead on the sleeve of my t-shirt and walk toward the large opening of the barn.

She gives an awkward, unsure wave when she sees me, but continues walking my way.

"Hi," she says timidly, pulling her long sleeves down over her hands.

Something about her is familiar, but I can't quite place her.

"Hey," I reply, taking another step closer. "You lost?"

She laughs lightly, shaking her head. "No. I thought I was, back up the road a little, but just like the guy at the gas station told me: just past the big white house, you can't miss it."

"Guy at the gas station?" I ask, confused.

"Yeah, I just asked around until someone knew you. Didn't take long, actually."

"Well, that's a little creepy."

Funny that this girl is standing in my barn, because not too long ago, Dave was teasing me about my groupies missing me and that it wouldn't be long until they came looking. If Dave put this girl up to stalking me, I'm going to kick his ass. He has it coming, anyway.

"Yeah, I know it sounds creepy, but, uh..." She drifts off and her eyes dart around the barn. "Well, I'd have never guessed you live on a farm. This is nice."

"Mind me asking your name? Your face looks real familiar, but..."

"Sophie," she says abruptly. "My name is Sophie. I met you a little over five years ago at a concert in Houma. You were playin' a dive bar in town. My friend and I met up with you and your band after the show. Tracy...she was actually datin'—"

"Dave," I finish for her, because it's all coming back to me now, and I make a mental note to drive to Dave's house and kick him in the balls. Between the video and now this, he has it coming.

"Dave," she concurs, nodding her head and taking a deep breath.

"So, Tracy found out from my douchebag of a friend where I live and you thought you'd just show up?"

"It's more complicated than that. I promise, I wouldn't be here if I thought there was another way."

"Another way for what?" She's really got me confused now. If she was here to pick up where we left off—and if I'm remembering right, that'd be with her naked and screaming my name—I'm guessing she'd be going about this a little differently. From the look on her face, she looks like she either wants to cry or run.

And now that I really take a good look, she doesn't look like she's feeling so good. That's when my manners kick in and I start trying not to think the worst of her.

"Sorry, I'm just confused about why you're here, Sophie."

"I think that's the first time I've heard you say my name." She quirks a smile and shakes her head. "The night we were together, you said it was easier to call me babe." The way her eyebrows arch up and she presses her lips together, I'm guessing I didn't score any brownie points with that one.

"Sounds about right," I laugh. "I'm sorry. I know I can be a grade-A dick sometimes."

Maybe that's what she's here for—some closure for some lingering fantasy that there'd be more for us than a one-night stand. I know that sounds crazy, but I have no other explanation for why she'd go through all that trouble to track me down.

"You're different than I remember." Her tone is thoughtful and she pauses a second before continuing. "Maybe it's the change of scenery—no stage or smoke machine, no bright lights or band members. But you're...normal, I don't know. I'm just...I guess, I'm glad. I'm glad to see you live in a house and not a tour bus." She laughs again, but this time her smile doesn't reach her eyes and I see a layer of sadness I didn't notice at first. She seems to have a lot on her mind—something she needs to get off her chest—so I let her talk.

"This isn't easy for me and I have no idea how you're gonna respond, but please just hear me out," she says, her eyes as pleading as her words and tone.

"Okay." I lean up against the open door of the barn. Maybe I need it for support or maybe to come across as being unaffected. I'm not sure, but something deep inside my gut twists a little.

The way she keeps looking at me makes me feel like I'm under inspection or a test.

Sophie turns around, looking back where she came from, and for a second, I think she's going to leave. But when she turns back around, her face is determined.

"I'm sick," she says, nodding her head, like she's trying to convince herself as she's telling me. Her eyes are on the dirt floor of the barn, but before she continues, they meet mine and I notice how blue they are. They're a lot like mine, actually. But her skin is darker and her hair, if it was down, and my memory serves me correctly, is longer with tight, spring-like curls.

"I've been sick for a long time. I was originally diagnosed with Leukemia when I was sixteen."

"I'm sorry." It comes out before I can stop it. I know people who are sick don't want pity, but I'm genuinely sorry.

"Me too. It sucks," she admits with a small laugh. "I went into remission when I was eighteen, just a few months before I met you, actually."

"Oh, well, that's great. I'm happy for you." I try to remember the girl from five years ago and I can recall that she seemed younger. I remember Dave giving me a hard time about hitting them young, but her friend vouched for her being over eighteen. I'm glad she was telling the truth.

"It came back two years ago," she says, swallowing the words like bile. "I thought I had it beat again that time too, but I was wrong."

She stands there for a moment and for whatever reason, I know she's gathering her strength for whatever she's about to tell me.

"I'm sorry." I repeat my apology from earlier and I mean it. I fucking hate cancer. For a second, I think maybe she's here to ask if the band can do a benefit concert or something, because we've done that sort of thing in the past, but then she continues.

"I had a baby four years ago—Sammy. She's literally all I have in this world."

I nod, trying to figure out where she's going with this. It's a sad story, probably the saddest thing I've heard in a long time, but I don't know why she's telling it to me.

"My mother is in prison. She'll be there for at least another ten years. And my father has never been in my life. I don't even know his name. The lady I live with...I call her Mamie, but she's not really my grandmother, not by blood, anyway." She stops and squeezes her eyes shut and I feel the need to do the same, because I feel bad for her. My chest literally aches.

I think about giving her a hug or something—anything to take away a little of her pain. But just as I'm getting ready to take a step toward her, she blows out a harsh breath and looks up to the rafters, like she's praying or seeking some kind of answer, so I don't interrupt her.

"What did you come here for?" I ask, eventually, wanting to get to the point of her visit.

"Sammy," she says, simply, quietly. "I came here for Sammy."

"Your daughter?"

"*Our* daughter."

It's a good thing I'm leaning against this giant oak door, because if I wasn't, my ass would be on the dirt floor. My eyes are fixed on my filthy work boots and the ragged hem of my jeans.

I can't look away.

I can't breathe.

I can't make sense of what she just said.

Our daughter.

That can't be right. That can't be what I heard.

I stand there, frozen in space, waiting for her to correct herself.

Seconds pass by, maybe minutes.

When Sophie doesn't speak, I finally look up at her and I'm met with pale blue eyes that are also waiting—waiting for me to say something.

"I don't...I'm not sure I..."

"Our daughter, Tucker. That's what I said and it's what I meant. Sammy is ours...yours and mine." Her voice is thick with unshed tears and I still can't process anything beyond those two words—our daughter.

Nothing in my brain is working right. I can't focus on anything, so I blink over and over, trying to clear my vision. That clarity I had earlier from working on the bassinet for Cami is gone.

A baby.

No, a kid.

She's four.

And she's mine?

"I don't understand," I mumble, pushing myself off the barn door and stumbling over to the wooden stool in the corner. I need to be lower to the ground, just in case.

"It's not hard to understand. We had sex. We made a baby. I had that baby—"

"And you kept her from me?" I blurt out, my voice raising as the raw emotion of her revelation hits me. "All this time...why wouldn't you find me and tell me? If I'm really her dad, I had a right to know."

I can't believe I'm yelling at this girl who just told me she's dying, but I can't help it.

"I didn't think you were the kind of person who'd want to know about some random chick he knocked up after a concert." Her words hold a bit more strength and bite than earlier, and looking up at her, I see the shadow of a fighter in her eyes. "I did what I thought was best for Sammy. I thought I was giving her stability and a home, something I never had." Her slender hand tightens into a fist as she presses it against her chest.

Shaking her head, she continues. "The last I knew about you, you were on some West Coast tour. I didn't want the fight. I've done enough of that in my life. I just wanted my baby and to live."

She leaves it at that. She doesn't say to *live in peace* or to *live in quiet*. She just wanted to live.

"And now?" I ask. "What do you want now?" I feel so helpless and a bit lost. I don't know what she wants or is expecting. "I'm not sure I could tell you what color the sky is right now, so you're gonna to have to spell it out for me."

"I'm dying. The doctors want to try another round of chemo and radiation, but it'll probably kill me, if the cancer doesn't get the job done first. At my last visit, my oncologist told me I have anywhere from six weeks to six months. Sammy was practically a baby the last time I went through chemo, but it was still tough on her. It made her sad...so sad." She pauses and closes her eyes, no doubt searching for that last bit of strength. "And it made her grow up too fast. She was only two and she was getting her own milk out of the fridge."

Sophie stops and she lets the first tears fall down her cheeks, unchecked.

"I can't let her watch me die, Tucker. I want her to remember *me*..." Her words are desperate now, with her hand on her chest, she implores me with those blue eyes to understand what she's trying to say. "Not the me I'll be at the end. I want her to remember playing at the park and baking cookies. Not what I look like when I take my last breath. I hope I've done enough. I hope I've left enough of myself behind, but even if I haven't, I don't want her to remember watching her mother die. And when I'm gone, I want her to have someone who loves her."

"Me?" I ask—out loud, I think. Is she talking about me?

"You'll be all she has left."

"But I don't even know her. She doesn't know me." Fresh panic spikes in my chest and I feel the blood pumping hard from my heart to my head, making my vision swim and my entire body feel numb.

Doubt follows the panic, and I can't keep it inside.

"What if she's not even mine?" I question, standing from the stool, needing to move—maybe run. "Have you considered that?"

"I don't have to consider it. You were the only person I was with..."

She huffs, rolling her eyes. "I'd been with people before you, but it'd been a while, and after you, well...I had Sammy to worry about." She pauses, her eyes boring into me, like she's trying to see under my skin. "She doesn't know you either. I don't know you. Don't you think if I had another solution, I'd take it? I came here today on a gut feeling and out of last resort. This isn't easy, probably the hardest thing I've had to do in a long time...maybe ever."

I stare at her for the longest time, searching for an inkling of dishonesty—anything to make me believe this is an elaborate lie—but I come up empty handed.

She clears her throat and wipes at the dampness under her eyes. "I know you'll want a paternity test. I don't blame you. I want you to have that...whatever you need to help you come to terms with this."

Come to terms?

Like I'm the one who's sick?

"What am I supposed to do?" I ask, not particularly to Sophie, but to anyone who's listening. The universe. God. Anybody.

"I don't know. I'm kinda overloaded on the decision making." She pulls her sleeves back down over her hands. The timid side of Sophie is back and I see the unsureness again on her face. "I'll be back in a week. If you want me to bring a paternity test, I can get one and bring it with me. They have ones that you can do through the mail now."

"Right...okay."

I can't feel anything.

I can't even feel the cool breeze coming through the barn, only see it because of the sawdust it's kicking up in the air.

"I'll bring Sammy with me next time. I think it'd be good for you to see her...and for her to meet you."

I don't reply to that. I just watch Sophie walk back to the car she drove up in and get inside. After she starts the engine, she sits there for a few minutes, staring back at me and then at the house...and I wonder what she's thinking.

Is she thinking this will be a nice place for her daughter to grow up?

If so, she's right. This is a great place to live as a kid. All of my best memories are here.

Is she thinking I'll be a shitty father?

If so, she's right again, because I have no idea what I'm doing with my own life. How can I possibly be responsible for someone else's?

And dying? How does that feel? How does she deal with that? How does she die and leave a little girl behind?

My mama did that. She knew she was leaving me and Cami behind, but she wasn't sick for very long. She didn't have a lot of time to think about it and dwell on it. She was just here and then she wasn't. We all hurt. We hurt for years. We still hurt.

Sammy is going to hurt. Even though she's only four. She's going to feel that loss.

My hand goes to the cross that used to belong to my mama. I squeeze it, feeling the pointed edges dig into my palm. It's the first sensation my brain has registered since Sophie's life-changing words. *Our daughter.* I squeeze again, harder, because I need the twinge of pain to ground me.

Without knowing for sure whether or not Sammy is mine, I already feel for her. I understand what she's about to go through. But it's different. At least I had my dad and Cami...and Micah and Deacon... Annie, Sam. I had people around me who loved me, and I knew it. Without that, I'd have been lost.

Sammy will have no one.

CHAPTER FIVE

After sophie drives off, I forget what I was doing before she stepped into the barn and flipped my world upside down. I don't want to face Kay. If she saw Sophie drive up, I don't want to field questions from her, because I don't know a fucking answer to anything right now.

So, I bail.

Climbing in the cab of my beat up truck, I crank the engine and pump the gas until it roars to life.

When I turn out of the dirt drive onto the gravel road, instead of turning right, the way to the Landry's and the highway, I turn left and head for the old road that dead ends at the river.

I need to be alone. I need room to think.

The short five minute drive is done on auto-pilot. My hands and feet know these roads. They know how to get me home half-sober. They know every pothole and secret spot. And thankfully, they remember how to get to the river, because I can honestly say, I'm not all here. Sure, I'm breathing, but that's about it.

My brain is taking up too much energy, spinning with the information Sophie just dropped on me like a fucking bomb.

When the river is in front of me, I hit the brake a little too hard and the truck sputters and then dies, but it's okay, because I made it.

The water is peacefully flowing in front of me, moving along without a care in the world and I want to scream at it for being so fucking calm. So, I do. I push the truck door open and jump out, slamming it behind me. With everything I have in me, I scream and yell, my voice getting swept away with the wind and the water. I let the river have it, every emotion flooding my body—disbelief, hurt, anger, sadness. So much fucking sadness.

Life isn't fair.

Everyone has their fair share of struggles.

I already knew that, but for fuck's sake, this feels like more than a fair share.

Sophie doesn't deserve cancer. Nobody fucking does.

Sammy doesn't deserve to lose her mom.

As for me, I'm not sure what I deserve.

There was a time when I thought I'd be the one to die young. The way I've lived life up until a few months ago was full-throttle, no-holds-barred. I've always approached life with vigor.

My mama lived a good life, always played by the rules and did everything she was supposed to do. She was a good wife, a great mom, a loyal friend...she went to church every Sunday and prayed every night. I figured if God would take her, he'd take anybody. So, I wanted to live like I was dying, because we're all going to at some point.

None of this makes sense.

After I finish yelling at the river, my throat aching and my lungs screaming from exhaustion, I walk back to my truck and dig under my seat, finding an emergency stash of Crown Royal. Unscrewing the cap, I put the bottle to my lips and toss it back, drinking until the burn is too much to handle.

It's not good, but at least I feel it.

The warm liquid begins to infiltrate my body and the numbness that was taking over begins to fade.

For most people, what I just drank would be enough to make them tipsy, if not drunk, in a matter of minutes, but I've built up a nice tolerance over the years. It's just enough to take the edge off and help clear my head, but it doesn't do shit for all of the questions churning in my brain.

Sitting down in the dirt, facing the river, I lean against the front of my truck and continue to take sips off the bottle, willing answers to fall from the fucking sky.

At some point, I must fall asleep, because the vibration in my back pocket where I keep my phone, has me nearly jumping off the ground. Looking around, it takes me a second to remember where I am.

The river.

And then the fresh memory of Sophie comes flooding back.

I wipe my eyes, rubbing them to try and get the fog to clear.

When I pull my phone out, I have a message from *No Caller ID*, aka Piper.

Part of me wants to open the message and lose myself in the nonsense bullshit we usually talk about, but the other part of me can't. I can't pretend. And Piper doesn't want to hear all of the shit that's running through my head right now. That's not how we do things. Ignoring the text, I put the phone back in my pocket and get up off the ground, dusting my pants off and stretching my sore muscles.

I'm not as young as I used to be, and that hard ass ground is a stark reminder.

There were days gone by that I could've slept there and woke up feeling like a million bucks, but not now. I'm too old for that shit.

Instead, I climb back in my truck and sit there until the sun goes down.

WHEN I FINALLY DRIVE BACK TO THE FARM, I DON'T STOP IN THE living room or go to the kitchen to see what I missed for dinner. I can't talk to my dad or Kay. I need a little more time to figure shit out before I do.

The night is restless. I spend it tossing and turning, and what little bit of intermittent sleep I manage is riddled with dreams of a little girl with pale blue eyes. Each time, she's alone and crying and I try to get to her, but I can't. And each time, I end up jolting awake, with my heart trying to pound its way out of my chest.

Before the sun has a chance to rise, I hear my dad's bedroom door creak open and then his footsteps pass down the hall, briefly pausing at my door.

I lie in bed, waiting until I hear the front door open downstairs before I get out of bed and throw on my jeans and a hoodie. I can feel the chill in the air, even from inside. The coolness seeps right through the old wood of the house. Without carpet on the floors, there's not a lot of insulation, which typically is great in Louisiana. But on the few days of the year, when the temps actually feel like winter, it's freezing, especially for us warm-blooded southerners.

Sneaking my way past the kitchen, not even glancing to see if Kay is in there, I hurry onto the porch and put my boots on as I'm walking to my truck.

I need to talk to someone and the only person I can think of, who won't judge me or my feelings, is my sister. Plus, she's really good at coming up with solutions to difficult situations. She's had plenty of practice. Even though I'm older, I'd say she's definitely wiser.

Hopefully, she'll be able to help me figure my shit out.

On my way into town, I pass the big house and a vision hits me so clearly, kind of like when I'm writing a song and a brilliant lyric comes to my mind. I see a little girl running down the tree-lined lane and I have to stop my truck in the middle of the road.

What the fuck is happening to me?

Leaning over on the steering wheel, I close my eyes and try to get a grip.

Tires crunching pulls me upright in my seat.

When I see Sam's car pull up behind me and then inch up to the side of my truck, I cringe. I don't know if I have it in me to put on a fake smile and bullshit my way out of this, but I'm going to try.

Rolling down my window, I give him my best smile and wave.

"Tucker," he says, with his own, much more genuine smile. "Everything alright?"

"Oh, yeah." I look down at my dashboard and then laugh lightly. "Old trucks, ya know?"

"Havin' trouble?"

God, am I.

"Just a little."

"Need some help?" he asks, because that's Sam Landry. Even in his suit and tie, briefcase in hand, he's willing to get out and help someone on the side of the road. If it hadn't been me, he still would've stopped.

"Nah, I'm good."

"Bring it over to the house later, we'll pop the hood and give it a look," he instructs. "And if you're hungry, Annie's got a fresh batch of muffins she just took out of the oven. Carter's over this mornin'. Cami just dropped him off."

"Actually, she's who I'm headed to see."

"Alright, well, I guess I'll get on down the road."

"Have a good day," I tell him, waving him on.

After he's around me and on his way, I fall in behind him, following him to the main road.

Something inside me eats away and part of me wants to follow Sam to Baton Rouge and apologize for not telling the truth, even though he bought it and probably won't think another thing about it.

As I pass the church, I consider a mid-week confession, but Cami will have to do, for now.

I CAN ACTUALLY SAY THIS IS PROBABLY MY FIRST TIME TO BE downtown French Settlement this early in the morning. Downtown, as in, the main drag, not downtown, as in, hopping little juke joints and fancy restaurants. That's Baton Rouge and New Orleans, not French Settlement.

The only thing this downtown has to offer is a few small shops, like my sister's art studio, the post office...and the bank, which happens to be where the busybodies of French Settlement go to dish on the latest gossip.

I'm sure I've been the topic of their conversation recently, if for no other reason than the fact that I'm back in town. With a place this small, it doesn't take much to get the rumor mill turning. I don't care what they have to say about me. It's never mattered or bothered me. I figure if they're talking about me, someone else is getting a break.

However, I wouldn't trade living here for anywhere else in the world. It's home and it's comfortable. Over the years, I've realized that even the busybodies and old gossips are part of what make a small town what it is.

Parking my truck, I can't help the smile on my face. This early in the morning, the only people out and about are a few old men in overalls sitting on a bench drinking coffee. There are large potted plants full of fall color and a few of the shop doors are open, inviting in the morning breeze.

I love that Cami chose this place for her studio. It fits her.

The little bakery across the street has an open sign in the window, so I decide to run over and get a coffee and whatever else they might have to offer, anything to sweeten my surprise visit. I'm going to need all the help I can get this morning.

"Good mornin'," Mrs. Martin says from behind the counter.

"Mornin', Mrs. Martin." I tip my head to her and offer a smile.

"Been a while since I've seen you around here. Thought you were off becomin' a big rock star?"

"Yeah," I start, scratching my head at the way that sounds so crazy now. Rock stars. Gigs. Bars and venues. All of that seems worlds away. "I decided I needed to slow things down for a bit."

"Good for you," she says with a nod, like she completely understands what I'm talking about. "One of these honey buns would be good for ya too. You're lookin' a little skinny."

I laugh and nod. "Alright, I'll take two honey buns."

"Goin' to visit your sister?"

As I was saying, gotta love small towns.

"Yes, ma'am." I take out my wallet and pull out some money. "I'll have a coffee too, please, and..."

"Cami likes chocolate milk. I make it special for her."

"Okay, then. A coffee and a chocolate milk."

After Mrs. Martin fixes me up, I walk back across the road to the Cami Benoit Studio.

I wonder if she felt as proud of me when she'd come to my shows and see my name on a billboard as I do of her when I pull up and see her name on this sign?

The front door is locked when I try the handle, but Cami must hear the noise from the back and comes to investigate, frowning when she sees me.

"You look like shit," she says, opening the door.

"Well, good mornin' to you too, sweetheart."

"Sorry, I just...it's been a while since I've seen you look so..."

"Shitty?" I ask, showing her the bag and the chocolate milk from Mrs. Martin.

"Did you not sleep last night or somethin'?"

"You could say that."

"Somethin' wrong?"

This is why I came to her, because she always knows. There's no bullshitting with Cami. So, I knew I'd be forced to just come out with it.

"Yeah, you could say that," I reply again.

"Sit, let me have my chocolate milk first and then you can talk."

I laugh at how serious she seems about this milk and I do what she tells me to—I sit on the bright red sofa that stands out against the stark white wall behind it.

"Wow." Taking a sip of my coffee, I notice the painting hanging across from me.

"You like it?" she asks with a scrunch of her nose as she tilts her head to one side.

"Yeah, it's amazing."

"I feel like it needs a little somethin', but I can't decide what. Thought about taking it outside. Sometimes, I get a fresher perspective when I'm immersed in what I'm trying to paint."

The painting is of a cypress swamp and the way she's captured the light reflecting off the water...hitting the bark of the trees perfectly...it looks like a photograph.

"If I didn't know any better, I'd think it's one of Dani's photographs."

"Well, thanks." She tilts her head back the other direction and looks at it a little longer. "Maybe I'll just leave it alone then."

"Yeah, it's great just like it is."

"I might need you to come by more often and tell me how awesome my paintings are. I could move along a lot faster if I didn't get so caught up on the tiny details sometimes. Deacon says I'm the only one that even notices the small changes. I don't know whether to punch him or not. The baby does that to me. Makes my emotions go all haywire..."

I'm just smiling, listening to her, when she notices she's rambling.

"Sorry, the baby makes me do that too."

"Oh, really. What else does the baby make you do? Drink chocolate milk and eat honey buns?"

"Yeah, he really likes chocolate milk." She pats the small bump and gives me a mischievous smile.

"He, huh?"

"Oh, shit!" Her eyes go wide and she covers her mouth. "I mean, shoot. I wasn't supposed to say anything until Sunday dinner."

"Well, cat's outta the bag now."

"Tucker Benoit, you better keep your trap shut," she warns, with the glare I know all too well. It's the same one she used to give me when she knew I was up to no good and was trying to keep my ass out of trouble. *Try* being the key word.

"So, another nephew?" I ask, teasing, but also fucking stoked that I'm going to be an uncle again.

"Yep," she says with a smile, loosening back up and leaning into the couch beside me. "Another boy, which I can't say I'm sad about. Sure, I'd love a little girl," she sighs. "But I'm already used to boys and I can reuse all of Carter's things I have saved."

"That's good," I tell her, my mind leaving the news about the baby and traveling to the news I got yesterday, what brought me here this morning. I feel the familiar spike of fear and adrenaline in my chest.

"What's wrong?" Cami asks, sitting her cup down on the floor. "You look like you've seen a ghost."

"Fuck," I groan, rubbing my hands over my face.

"Just tell me Tucker, because you're startin' to freak me out. Are you in trouble?"

"Not with the law or anything like that..." I start, trying to decide what to tell her first.

"Then with what? You know, I've been worried about you since you came home off the road, but when you told me it was just time to come home and slow down, I believed you. So, if there's more to that story, now would be a good time to come clean." Her voice matches her posture, on alert and ready for action. Maybe it's the mother in her, but she's always ready to take care of business. Although, she was like that before Carter came along. When she got pregnant with him, she never once waivered in her decision. From the moment she knew she was going to have a baby, it was all about Carter—providing for him, taking care of him, loving him.

"This isn't about that. I was tellin' you the truth. I needed a change of pace. Life on the road isn't the life I want anymore."

"Then what is the life you want? What's this about?" she asks, like it's a simple as that.

"I thought I knew. I thought I wanted to help Dad and work on my furniture, try to sell a few songs. Maybe buy a house somewhere close by..."

"What's wrong with that? Sounds like a great life to me."

"Yeah, it does."

"So, what's wrong? What's with the bags under your eyes like you've been on a bender for three days? Are you seein' someone I don't know about? Is this about a girl?"

Oh, Cami.

So much I should say, but where to start?

Tears spring into the corners of my eyes and I press my fingers against them, willing them to stay put. I can't cry. I don't even know why I feel like crying. I don't know the last time I did cry, because fuck that.

Cami's hand lands gently on my back and I swear, if she's starts trying to soothe me, I'm going to turn into a fucking girl right here on this couch. So, I blow out a frustrated breath and stand to my feet.

"You're gonna have to talk. I suck at readin' minds." Her words are soft and reassuring. I know this is my safe place—Cami is my safe place—but it doesn't make what I'm about to say any easier.

"This *is* about a girl," I begin, deciding to start by telling Cami the way Sophie told me. "I had a visitor yesterday, a girl I met out on the road about five years ago."

From the quirk of Cami's eyebrow, I know she's probably jumping to all kinds of conclusions, but to her credit, she stays silent and just listens.

"Her name is Sophie. I met her after a gig in Houma. Dave was dating her friend at the time and we all hung out after a show." Wiping my now sweaty hands down the sides of my jeans, I take a seat back beside Cami. "We hooked up, but I was gone the next day and I never saw her again." I pause, because I'm unsure how to go on from here. What do I say?

"Until yesterday," Cami says, filling in the silence, helping me tell my story.

"Yes, she found me at the barn, after asking her friend Tracy where I lived and then stopping to ask around town if anyone knew me. If I had to guess, Dave had something to do with her figuring out my whereabouts." I still owe him a visit.

"Persistent, I like that." She nods her head in approval.

"She's sick," I finally say. "Dying, actually."

"Oh, my God." Cami's hand flies to her mouth and I can already see tears springing to her eyes.

Shit.

"She was diagnosed with leukemia when she was younger and went into remission a couple of times, but it's back and there's basically nothing the doctors can do." I take a deep breath and try to find the strength inside to go on. Seeing Sophie's face in my head, as she told me yesterday, is what does it. If she was strong enough to find me and tell me, surely I can relay the message to someone else. "They've given her anywhere from six weeks to six months."

"That's awful," Cami says, shaking her head. "I fucking hate cancer. It's so unfair."

"It is." I nod. Resting my head in my hands, I plead with God and the universe, even the floor beneath my feet, to offer up a miracle—anything to make the next part I'm getting ready to say any easier. "It's really unfair for her daughter."

"Oh, God," she breathes out again, her eyes doubling in size. "She has a child?" That's when the waterworks start. Cami sniffles, but then she can't hold it in. Her hand goes to her stomach, and I can only imagine what's going through her mind, probably thoughts of Carter and her unborn baby. Maybe she's even thinking the same thing I thought yesterday, about our own mother.

Then, she gasps, her hand flying back to her mouth. "Tucker."

It's in that moment that I know my smart, witty sister has figured it out. She knows where this is going. I don't even have to say the next words, because she already knows. But I do need to say them. I need to say them so they'll stop haunting me and I can figure out what I'm supposed to do with them.

"*Our* daughter, Sammy. She's four."

"You have a daughter." It's not a question or an answer, it just is. The way Cami says it makes it sound like a miracle or a blessing... something wonderful.

"I guess I do." I exhale sharply and shake my head, like it's going to magically make all the pieces fall in place.

"What do you mean, you guess?"

"I mean, I haven't met her. I didn't even know it was a possibility until yesterday. I haven't seen Sophie in over five years...in all honesty, I hadn't even thought about her. So, I don't know what I mean, but I can tell you that I have no fucking clue what I'm supposed to do." The more I talk, the louder I get, and the next thing I know I'm pacing the studio, and Cami's on her feet with her hands on her hips, staring me down.

"So, get a paternity test and then get your shit together," she says with a bit more edge than I expect. "That little girl didn't ask for any of this, Tucker. You need to think about her...what she needs. She's four, for God's sake!"

"And I'm supposed to know how to raise a little girl!" I throw my hands in the air, feeling myself begin to unravel. "Most men get a little bit of time to figure this shit out. In a matter of hours, I've found out that a girl I hooked up with got knocked up, she had a baby, and now I'm supposed to be an insta-father!"

"She wants you to have her?" Cami asks, a slight bit of confusion clouding her anger.

"She's dying, Cami!"

"Yeah, but..."

"She has nobody...no mom or dad. No aunts or uncles. She's not like us. She doesn't have a big family of people who care about her. From what she said, Sammy is all she has. Sophie is all Sammy has."

"And when Sophie dies..."

"I'll be all Sammy has."

"Sammy," Cami repeats, a hint of a smile on her lips. "I like that." She rubs the small bump again. "If this one was a girl, we'd thought about naming her Samantha, after Sam, and calling her Sammy."

I like it too, now that she mentions it, and for a second, I let my mind wander to the what ifs.

What if I'd known about Sammy from the beginning?

What if I'd been in her life for the last four years?

Would I have been a good father?

Or would I have let the rock star life I was living come between me and her?

I don't know.

I'm not the same guy I was even a few months ago. Things have changed.

"What if she's not mine?" I ask, speaking out my fears, giving them life, knowing Cami won't judge me for them. "What if I go through all of this and it's a big scam or Sophie is mistaken and she's not mine?"

"But what if she is?" Cami counters.

"What do I do?"

"You get that paternity test, and then you step up. You can't let that baby girl be without a parent, Tucker. You and I both know what it's like to lose a mother." She pauses for a second and when I hear her sniffle, I look back up to see fresh tears in her eyes. "Do you ever think that things happen for a reason? Even bad things. Like, maybe God knew that you were gonna need to know what it's like to lose a parent one day."

"I don't know," I tell her honestly, because after all these years, I've never come up with a good enough reason for God to take my mama away. Maybe I've been a little pissed about it, actually. Or a lot pissed. But something about what Cami is saying brings me a tiny bit of peace in a place that's been dark for a long time.

"When do I get to meet her?" Cami asks.

"I don't know that either." The tears that were threatening earlier are back and I have a huge lump in my throat. "Sophie is coming back next week. She's bringing Sammy. But I don't want to do anything or say anything until I know for sure that she's mine."

"You'll know," Cami says with confidence. "When you see her. You'll just know."

CHAPTER SIX

EVERY MORNING THIS WEEK, AND EVERY NIGHT FOR THAT MATTER, I've been counting down the days.

Not to the wedding or to seeing Piper, but to Sophie's return and meeting Sammy.

I've never over-thought something this much in my entire life. Usually, I just do what feels right in the moment, but this has me thinking and re-thinking, and when I feel like I've explored every nook and cranny, I find something else to worry over and think about.

My newest worry is that this thing I've been doing with Piper might have to come to an end.

Our relationship, if you can call it that, has been built around secrecy. Most of our hook-ups happen on the fly and usually by one of us driving or flying somewhere to meet the other.

Lately, we've been forced into the same situations, which have given us opportunities to sneak off and get our kicks. But after Sammy comes to live with me, *if* Sammy comes to live with me, all of that will come to a halt.

There's no way I'll be able to run off on a whim to Birmingham, or leave in the middle of the night to meet Piper in Baton Rouge. And I know her, she won't want to come here. Besides that, I can't do the shit we do with Sammy around. That wouldn't be setting a good example or providing a stable environment, and that'll be my job. That's what kids need.

This kid, *my* kid, that I don't even know.

For someone who is merely a thought—an idea—she's sure found a way to infiltrate my mind.

Speak of the devil.

I pull out my vibrating phone and see the incoming text message from *No Caller ID*. All I can see is the little bit of text that comes up with the notification, because I refuse to open the message.

Today's says: *You're a dick.*

At least that gets a snicker out of me. It's the only thing that gets me out of my head for a second, and I think about opening it up and replying. But I can't. I can't pretend everything is fine when it's not and I can't tell her about Sammy. I've never lied to Piper, so I'm not going to start now.

Besides, I don't have enough room in my brain to think about Piper, Sophie, and Sammy. It's too much.

But tomorrow, I'll have to see her. It's Micah and Dani's wedding and there's no getting out of it. Not that I'd want to, but I'm just not in the mood for a wedding. I can barely lie my way through a day on the farm. I don't know how I'm going to get through an entire day of putting on a show for people who know me far too well.

At least here, my dad doesn't ask a lot of questions and he keeps me busy. When he doesn't have a job for me, my woodworking is there to occupy my time.

Maybe that'll be my game plan for tomorrow, just keep myself as busy as possible. I'll play the dutiful best man and be at Micah's beck and call.

No Caller ID: You can't ignore me all weekend.

Piper's message pops up on my phone as I pull onto the main highway, headed to New Orleans.

Me: I know.

It's the first reply back I've given her and I know it's short, but

I don't know what else to say. Of course, I won't be able to ignore her. I know that she'll be drop-dead gorgeous. And, honestly, I'm not ignoring her. I'm saving her. Because I know what Piper wants. She wants convenience. She wants someone she can call and have them jump when she says jump. She wants no-strings attached and no commitment.

I thought I could give her that, but I was wrong.

When my phone rings a few minutes later, I'm not surprised.

"Hello?" I say, putting my phone on speaker and placing it on the dashboard in front of me—redneck hands-free.

"What's your deal?" Piper's voice is hushed and if I had to guess, she's probably with Dani and my sister and she's trying not to be heard.

"Nothin', darlin'."

"Don't darlin' me. You haven't answered any of my text messages this week. Are you that pissed about last weekend?"

"No."

"Then what's wrong? You aren't going to be weird today, are you?"

"No weirder than usual."

"You know what I mean." It's a half-whisper, half-yell, and I wish I could see her right now. I love when she gets all worked up.

"It's not gonna be weird, Piper. We're gonna play our parts and that's that."

"That's that?" she questions and pauses. "You're pissed, aren't you? This is your way of getting back at me. You need to give me a taste of my own medicine?"

Her tone goes a bit playful and I don't know if I should keep up the charade or tell her right now that it's all over. Everything.

"You got me. Now, tell me what you're wearin'." I decide to go with the charade. Except, it's really not, because hearing her voice has me wondering if there's a way I can keep this thing with Piper and do whatever else I need to do.

"Wouldn't you like to know," she purrs. "Guess you'll just have to wait and find out. Maybe I won't wear any panties. You always like that."

"Now who's bein' mean?" I drawl, appreciating the vision of Piper in a sexy dress with nothing underneath.

"I'll see you at the altar."

I know what she means, but the sentiment isn't lost on me.

After Piper hangs up, my mind is immediately back on the events of the past week and tomorrow. I think about calling her back, making her distract me.

A few weeks ago, my biggest concern was trying to cover up a wedding proposal that went viral and now I'm trying to figure out fatherhood and contemplating mortality.

When I pull up to the chapel, just down the street from Lagniappe, I hesitate to get out of the solace of my truck. This isn't me. I'm Tucker the Fucker. I'm fun-loving, life of the party, and the guy everyone else depends on for a good time.

You can do this.

Put on a fucking smile and play the part.

It's Micah and Dani's wedding day. Don't fuck shit up.

Reaching under the seat, I feel around in my hidey hole for the half-empty bottle of Crown. I need a little liquid courage to get me through the day. Unscrewing the lid, I tip the bottle up and down a few good swallows before getting out of the truck.

Cami is the first person I see when I get inside and she grabs my arm, pulling me into a dark hallway.

"Are you okay?" she asks, straightening my tie.

"Yeah, why?" I ask, raking my hands through my hair. I probably could've used a haircut, but it'll be fine. At least, I shaved.

"Just checking. Any word from..."

"No," I tell her, cutting her off before she mentions names and ruins my mojo I worked up in the truck. "Probably won't until she shows up tomorrow, *if* she shows up tomorrow."

"Okay," she says with a nod. "Piper's in a mood. Just wanted to give you a heads up, seein' as how you'll be walkin' her down the aisle."

"10–4," I tell her with a mock salute.

"Can y'all play nice for one day?"

"Sure." I give her a placating smile, hoping she'll drop the talk and let me get back to pretending like everything is fine, at least for today. "Go take care of your girl stuff. I've got manly things to do," I tell her, holding up the bottle I brought in with me.

"Tucker," she warns with a pointed glare.

"Camille," I reply in a placating tone.

"Be on your best behavior," she demands. "No, actually, be on someone else's best behavior. Like, a good person. Someone who follows the rules and doesn't get drunk before a wedding. That person. Be on their best behavior."

"Stop worryin'. It's bad for the baby."

"Maybe you're bad for the baby," she snaps back.

"Whoa, hold on there. I'm the favorite uncle. You better be tellin' him that every day."

"Keep that to yourself!" Cami's small fist is now gripping the tie she just fixed.

"Whoa, whoa, whoa. It's fine. Everything is fine," I say calmly, like I'm speaking to a caged animal.

"Okay." She loosens her grip and takes a deep breath. "Sorry, I've just been feelin' a little crazy today. I'm tired. Being pregnant is exhausting."

I don't know what to say right now, except *God bless Deacon*.

"I'm sorry." It's the only good thing I can think of at the moment, so I say a silent prayer it was the right choice.

Cami doesn't respond. She just straightens my tie again and pats my chest, giving me a tight smile before she leaves me standing in the hallway.

The fuck?

I've gotta find Micah and Deacon. I have a feeling they might need the rest of this bottle more than I do.

Walking down the hall, I see a sign that says "Bride" and assume that's where Cami went, so I keep walking. I don't need to see a sign for where Micah and Deacon are because I can hear them before I get there.

"You did not!"

"Yes, I did. It was at least three months before you!"

"You're a lyin' sack of shit." Deacon's voice booms from the other side of the door and I have to get in there and see what this argument is about. Also, I need to shut them the fuck up before my sister comes down here.

"Would you two fuckers shut up," I tell them as I slip through the door and shut it behind me. "Do you know the level of bat shit crazy your wife is runnin' on today?" I ask, looking at Deacon.

"Dude."

"Exactly. I just got a healthy dose of it before I barely stepped foot in the door."

"Glad it was you and not me...this time," he says with a wince.

"So, what's the argument about? I bet I can settle it."

"Deke claims he lost his virginity before me."

"Bullshit." I turn to Deke and hold up the bottle of Crown, pointing it at him. "You did unspeakable things to my sister in the back of your truck after graduation. Micah fucked the Johnson twins the night of prom. So, he beat you by at least a month."

"Give me that," Deacon says, grabbing the bottle from me. He takes the lid off and tilts it up, keeping his eyes on me. "Why you gotta take his side? Just because it's his wedding day doesn't mean shit."

"Because he's right...I'm right. You know this is like Fort Knox," I tell him, pointing to my head.

Micah is smirking at the two of us through the mirror, where he's attempting to tie a bow tie.

"Let me help you." I walk over and undo the mess he's got going, evening the two sides and then deftly turning them into a work of art. Pulling the two ends tight, I step back and smile. "Who's your best man now?"

"You both are. Don't get him started," Micah says, motioning over his shoulder.

"You tryin' to squeeze me out of this one, Deke?" I ask, turning on him and snatching the Crown back and handing it to Micah.

"Well, Micah was my best man...and I thought he could be yours. You know, we all get a turn."

"Tucker's never gettin' married," Micah says, taking another swig from the bottle before handing it to me. "Ain't that right?"

"Probably not," I tell him, wanting that conversation to die fast. "But you are." Looking down at my phone, I see a text from *No Caller ID* and swipe right to clear it off my screen. "Less than an hour to go. When's your mom and dad supposed to be here?"

"Any minute. Dad said they're riding with Kay and Clay and bringing Carter with them."

About that time, there's a knock on the door and Sam sticks his head inside. "How's it goin'?"

"Good, get in here and have a drink with us," I tell him, handing him the bottle and shutting the door behind him.

The four of us finish off the last of it, passing it around.

"I can't believe y'all are old enough to get married and shit," Sam says with a wink.

"Well, you should've been here earlier, your two prized ponies were arguing over who lost their virginity first." Micah cuts me a glare while Deacon slaps the side of my head, but Sam makes my day.

"Micah," he says without thinking, like it's a no-brainer.

"Told you," Micah says, flipping Deacon off.

"He wouldn't take mine and Micah's word for it."

"Never has, why would he start now?" Sam asks, smirking as he adjusts his own bow tie, looking like he just stepped out of a men's fashion magazine. He's always been one of the smoothest mother fuckers I know.

"What is this? Gang up on Deacon day?" Deke's arms fly in the air and he looks like he's actually offended that nobody is taking his side, even though he's wrong. "First Cami tells me I can't do anything right, then I get here and everybody is against me. Shit."

"Some days are just like that," Sam says, in all his infinite wisdom. "That's a lesson for both of you, even you, Tucker. Some days, you've just gotta take the beating and say you're sorry. Admit you're wrong, even when you're not. It's easier that way. You'll save yourselves a lot of grief."

"That's just messed up," Deacon mumbles.

There's a knock at the door and Annie is the next person to pop her head inside. She smiles, shaking her head. "All my boys. Look at y'all. You're so handsome."

"Don't cry, Mama," Micah warns. "I already told you. It's a happy day."

"And I told you I can cry if I want to. Besides, they're happy tears."

"Remember what I said, son," Sam whispers through his teeth, smiling over at Annie.

"Sorry, Mama. You're right."

"That's a good boy." She reaches over and swipes at a piece of Micah's hair, putting it in its place. "Now, your bride is ready to meet you at the altar. Don't be late."

"I'll be there with bells on," Micah tells her, kissing her cheek.

"Sam, I need an escort." She holds out her hand and he, of course, obliges, giving the three of us a nod on his way out.

Walking up behind Micah, I give him an encouraging slap on his shoulder. "Ready to do this?"

"I think I've always been ready. I just hadn't met her yet."

"Are you getting mushy on us?" Deacon asks, coming to stand on the other side of Micah.

"Maybe. But it's my wedding day. If you can't be mushy on your wedding day, when can you?"

"Well, I have to say that I've known Dani was it for you since the first time I met her at Pockets," I tell him, because it's the truth. Until that day, I'd never seen Micah that enamored by a girl. He couldn't look away. She challenged him and made him rethink his whoring ways. Ever since then, he's been a changed man—committed, devoted, and completely in love.

"You wanted to hit on her," Micah grumbles.

"Can you blame me?" I ask, looking over at Deacon for a little back-up. "You've seen her, right?"

That second part I tacked on just to get a rise from him.

"Don't," Micah warns.

"Actually, I've always seen Dani as a little sister," Deacon says, smiling back at me.

Fucking ass kisser.

"Wipe your nose off, Deke. You've got a little somethin' brown on it."

"Would you two dickwads knock it off?" Micah walks toward the door and opens it. "Get your asses out there and don't fuck it up."

"We haven't even practiced," Deacon retorts.

"You've been walking for twenty-eight years. I think you can manage."

"Do we have a special song?" he asks, still standing in the middle of the room.

"Are you a fucking girl?" Micah growls. "Get your ass out the door and walk your wife down the aisle. For fuck's sake."

I walk out and Deacon follows. Cami and Piper are standing at the end of the hall when we get there. Cami smiles at Deacon, all signs of her earlier melt down gone without a trace. Piper looks over at me, but then quickly faces forward.

Thankfully, Cami takes the reins.

"You two are walking first. When you hear the music start, walk slowly, but not too slow. Deacon and I will be right behind you."

"Sounds easy enough," I tell her, turning around and offering Piper my arm.

She takes it and I feel the light squeeze she gives it, causing me to glance over at her just in time to see a small smile on her beautiful lips. They're a light pink, not too much, but enough to set off her skin tone. Her dark hair is hanging in loose curls down her back, with the sides pulled up, showcasing her slender neck. I have to look away before I forget where I am and who we are...and just everything.

The music starts and we walk. I smile at the familiar faces we pass, but the entire time I'm thinking about how good it feels to have Piper this close to me. When we get to the end of the aisle in the small chapel, I reluctantly let go of her hand and walk to a spot on the right side, next to Micah.

As Cami and Deacon are making their way down the aisle, I steal one more look at Piper. The soft light coming in the stained glass makes her look like an angel, even though I know she's not. I almost snicker to myself at the thought. She's definitely no angel, but she is a good person. Our arrangement is a unique one and it's based off of hating each other, but even I can admit that Piper isn't the devil. She's genuine and giving. I've seen her be a great friend to Dani, and Micah likes her, so that has to account for something.

Deacon steps into place between me and Micah, blocking my view and it's a good thing. With the space between us, I'm able to focus and it's then I remember what my life is about right now. I also remind myself that Piper doesn't fit into it, just like I don't fit into hers. We were never meant for more than a good time.

Turning my attention down the aisle, I watch as Dani walks through the chapel doors. Her eyes light up when she sees Micah. Glancing over at Micah, I see the same. He's looking at her like she's his favorite thing in the whole world.

The vows exchanged are simple and sweet. Micah and Dani add their own personal touches and then the minister announces them as husband and wife.

It's short and to the point, but it's perfect.

CHAPTER SEVEN

"Bathroom in five," a whispered voice says in my ear.

Everyone else at the table is so caught up in their own conversations that they don't notice, but I do and I can't. Actually, I could, but the longer I've had to clear my head of the Piper haze it was under during the ceremony, the more I know I can't do this anymore.

It's going to be hard enough, so like everything else in my life I decide to quit, I'm going to do it cold turkey. Starting tonight.

Before she can get out of arm's reach, I tug at the hem of her dress. As she snaps her head around, the look on her face could kill.

She's about to lash out, but my dad turning in his seat toward me stops her dead in her tracks.

In the split second before she turns to walk away, I give her a slight shake of my head, letting her know I'm not meeting her in the bathroom in five minutes. She shoots a glare that most would miss, but I catch the slight squint of her gorgeous eyes. I've been the recipient too often to miss it. It tells me she doesn't like my response and if we were still playing our game, which we're not, she'd get some type of retaliation later.

"Surprised you're not playing tonight," my dad says, getting my attention.

"Micah told me I could if I wanted to, but I didn't want to steal the show...you know, it's his wedding, after all." I give him a wink and take a long sip of my drink.

"Right, well, it was good hearing you play the other night. I've missed it."

That's about as much as you'll get out of my dad. He's a simple man who doesn't waste words on small talk. He says what he means and means what he says. I like it that way, because when he speaks, I know I should be listening.

"It's time for the toasts," the DJ Micah hired for the evening announces. "First up is Deacon Landry, brother of the groom...and the bestest man," he says, with a questioning tone.

Deacon's smile is wider than the Mississippi as he steps up to the mic.

"Hey, y'all," he says, tapping the microphone. "Micah told me to keep this short, so I wrote a few things down." Clearing his throat, he pulls out a card from his pocket and begins to read from it. "First, I'd just like it to be known that I met Dani first. So, technically, I introduced them. Micah, I've known Dani was it for you since the first time the two of you met at Pockets."

Fucker is stealing my lines.

"I'm glad you finally found someone to tame the beast." Deacon pauses for the laughter and hoots and hollers, looking mighty pleased of himself. "And Dani, you're the sister I never had. You make this family better and I'm happy to call you a Landry. It'd be great if y'all could make me an uncle sometime soon, because Tucker and Micah get all that fun and I'm tired of missin' out. Oh, and I'd like to take this moment to tell everyone...we're having a boy!"

"Deacon!" Cami yells from her seat across the table from me. "What a jackass," she mumbles, rolling her eyes as everyone claps for Deacon's speech and congratulates him and Cami on the announcement.

"What, babe?" Deacon asks as he comes back over and takes his seat. "You *told* me I could be the one to tell everyone."

Let us be clear, Deacon may act dumb, but he knows exactly what he's doing and he knows how to manipulate situations to get what he wants.

"At *Sunday dinner*, Deacon. Not here," she seethes.

"Babe, I'm sorry. I was just so excited and you know how horrible I am at keepin' secrets." The odd look Deacon shoots me over Cami's head has me confused, but I just give him a smile and shake my head at his equal parts of genius and stupidity.

"Congratulations," Kay says, hugging Cami from behind.

"So happy for y'all," my dad chimes in. "I can't believe I'm gonna be a grandpa again."

"Thanks. We're pretty happy about it," Cami says, giving Deacon a warm smile.

"I'm gonna be a big brother!" Carter yells, running over from where he'd been sitting with Annie and Sam. "Woo!"

"Are you excited, baby?" Cami kisses his cheek and hugs him to her.

"Yeah, I was so scared you were gonna have a girl."

"And what's wrong with a girl?" she asks, laughing as she kisses the top of his head.

"They talk too much and wear pink...and I want someone to play Transformers with."

"You know I'm havin' a baby and not a six-year-old, right?" Cami teases.

"Duh, Mom. Your belly is big, but it's not *that* big." Carter's eyes go wide as saucers, giving Cami a side glance. We all laugh, but only Carter could get by with a statement like that.

"The next speech is from Dani's best friend, Piper Grey," the DJ says, keeping things going.

I watch as Piper stands from her seat beside Dani and walks up to the microphone. She's composed and sure of herself, not over-confident, but someone who comes across as having their shit together.

"Hello, I'm Piper." She smiles and gives a little wave. "I know a lot of you don't know me, but I've known Dani since we were freshmen in college. She's been my best friend, and at times, my only friend. We've been each other's family, kept each other from eating pints of Ben & Jerry's during breaks-ups, and been there for each other through all of life's ups and downs. So, believe me when I tell you, this is the happiest I've ever seen my best friend. Because of that, I'd like to thank you, Micah. I'm going to miss looking out for her, but I feel confident leaving her in your hands. To Dani and Micah," Piper says, raising her glass of champagne.

"To Dani and Micah." Everyone joins in, raising their glasses to the newlyweds.

"That was a lovely speech," Kay says, dabbing under her eyes. "I just love that girl."

"She's a good one," my dad agrees.

Maybe I'm feeling over paranoid tonight because I've had so much on my mind and I feel like I'm walking around living a lie. But I swear they're all baiting me, waiting on me to crack and spill my guts.

Before anyone can say something else or look at me weird, I stand up from the table and mumble something about looking for another drink. Instead, I bypass the bar and head straight for the back door. If it wouldn't be considered rude, I'd get in my truck and get the hell out of here. But I can't do that. It'd draw attention and I sure as hell don't need any of that. So instead, I take a few deep cleansing breaths and try to pull myself together.

"What's going on with you?"

I groan, not wanting to turn around, because Piper is the last person I want to see right now. She's the reason I'm out here in the first place. The reason I feel like I'm about to lose my damn mind, well, one of the reasons.

"Nothing. Nothing is goin' on with me."

"Bullshit. You've been weird for over a week. I thought you not answering my text was part of your retaliation for me walking out on you last weekend. But today, you've still been avoiding me." Piper takes a step closer, pointing her finger into my chest. "I know you, Tucker. I know what you want and I know how you want it. It's not like you to turn me down. So, something is going on and you're going to tell me what it is."

"You don't want to know," I tell her, honestly. She stops and cocks her head in surprise.

"You want me to tell you nothing is wrong and then we go fuck and everything is back to normal." I swallow, wondering where I'm going with this. Nothing coming out of my mouth is planned and I'm afraid if I keep talking, I'll say too much. "So, don't ask what's wrong when you don't really want to know."

"Maybe I do," she challenges.

"No, you don't. You want convenience, no strings attached, booty calls in the middle of the night, and secret rendezvous...you don't want to hear about me or my life. That's not how it goes between us. So, stop pretendin' you care."

Her face morphs from shock to resolve. I watch as she tilts her chin down in preparation for whatever she's getting ready to fire back at me with.

"You don't know me. You don't know what I want." Her tone is cool and even. "You use me as much as I use you, so don't start playing the victim."

Turning around, her dark hair flows behind her like a cape as she stomps back into the restaurant.

Fuck.

I run my hands through my already unruly hair and growl out my frustration, wishing I was back at the river so I could scream again and let it all out.

Making my way back inside, I walk down the hall. Part of me wants to check the handle on the women's bathroom and see if Piper's in there, because any other time, that's how one of our little tiffs would end—me fucking her into oblivion until we're unsure where the hate ends and the lust begins—but I force myself to keep walking. When I get back to the main part of the restaurant, I'm just in time to see Dani and Micah feed each other a piece of cake.

Sitting back down at my place by my dad, I'm eternally grateful for his lack of need to fill silence with frivolous conversation. He's good at letting me deal with my own shit, so even if he thinks something is wrong, he won't ask. He knows if I need to talk, I'll talk.

The rest of the evening goes smoothly, or as smoothly as it can. I try my damnedest not to track Piper's every move, but fail miserably.

I see her.

I see her laughing with Cami and Dani.

I see her going after the bouquet and letting some waitress from Grinders catch it instead.

I see her talking to Sam and Annie.

I see her helping Kay with a button on her dress.

I wish I didn't see her, because it would make this so much easier. After tonight, it'll be better. I won't be forced to see her for a while. Some distance will do me good.

I tell myself that, like a mantra, until the last dance of the night.

Piper leaves ahead of Micah and Dani. I overhear someone say something about her going to get something out of their hotel suite that Dani forgot. Again, I try not to listen, but it's like my ears are trained to hear anything about her.

Cami, Deacon, and Carter leave right after, followed by my dad, Kay, Annie, and Sam.

In the end, it's just me and a few of Micah's employees from Lagniappe. We all make quick work of clearing the dishes and glasses, piling them in the kitchen.

"Don't worry about the rest of this mess," Randy says from the kitchen door. "I'll be back in here tomorrow sometime to make sure it's all back in order by Tuesday."

"Y'all go," I tell him. "I'm just gonna pack up these gifts and make sure they get to the big house. Micah and Dani can pick them up there."

"You sure? I can help if you want."

"Nah, I'm sure. Y'all go. I'll be right behind you and I'll lock up and set the alarm. Micah gave me a key and the code."

"Alright," he says, waving as he walks back through the kitchen, turning off lights as he goes.

I gather a few more straggling cake plates and take them to the sink. When I walk back out into the dining room, scanning the place for anything else I can clear away, I notice a purse or something laying at the table where Micah and Dani were sitting.

Walking closer, I realize I've seen it before.

As I pick it up, a flash from a night in Baton Rouge hits me out of nowhere.

I pull up to the hotel Piper gave me the name of and let the valet park my truck, because I can't wait another second to get up to the room and see what she has for me.

Is she going to fight me?

Will she let me in or make me wait in the hallway?

Or will this be one of those nights where she's done with the games and wants me just as much as I want her?

The anticipation is killing me.

When I knock on the door of her room, she opens immediately, with this black clutch in her hand. It's satin and sleek. She opens it and takes out a tube of lipstick and applies it, like she's going out for the night.

I don't fucking think so. *Those are my words, because she's not spending half an hour telling me about every detail of the black thong she's wearing and how she wants to tie me up with it and then not deliver.*

What? *Her reply is rehearsed and part of the act. I can see it by the way her pale brown eyes go wide and her lips form into a pout. It's not real Piper. It's the Piper who wants me to suffer. It's the Piper who loves making my life miserable for the sake of our twisted game. It's the Piper who'd rather bust my balls than give in to what we both know she wants.*

I take the purse from her hand and toss it across the room. A sly smile forms on her perfect lips and she quirks an eyebrow.

Game on.

A light tap on the window causes me to jump and turn. I expect to see some drunk who can't find his way back to Bourbon Street or a homeless person looking for a handout, but instead, it's Piper.

She holds her hand up in a semi-wave and then motions to the door.

I hold up her purse and question silently, asking if that's what she's here for.

Her hands immediately go to her hips as frustration over me not complying sets in.

Walking slowly to the door, I turn the lock and open it.

"Lookin' for this?"

"I do need that," she says, reaching for the purse, but I yank it back before she can grab it.

I don't know why I do it, maybe out of instinct or maybe out of habit. Maybe because I know for me and Piper, this is the end.

"Don't make me be mean to you," she warns, pursing her lips in a way that always turns me on.

I love it when she looks at me like that. Her eyes are hungry and her smart-ass mouth is begging to be kissed, even though we don't do that. But maybe I will tonight. Maybe I'll take what I want, just this one last time.

"I thought maybe you were comin' back to see me," I tease, but it's not really. "I thought maybe you might wanna kiss and make up."

"Are you going to tell me what's been going on with you?" she asks, crossing her arms over her perfect chest.

"No."

She stands there, like we're on opposite sides of a battle line, glaring at me because I won't do what she wants me to...say what she wants me to.

"Did someone go and grow some feelings?" she asks in a mocking tone. "Is that what this is all about?" Her words are harsh and meant to sting, and if I'm being honest, they do.

But I'll never let her have the satisfaction of seeing that hurt.

"No, no feelings here," I tell her, putting on the cockiest front I can manage. "Just tired of givin' and never gettin' anything in return."

"Fuck you, Tucker. I give just as good as I get, and you know it."

"When it suits you, darlin'. It's all about Piper, twenty-four-seven. You don't give two shits about me or anyone else, for that matter. You're just always lookin' for who can get you what you want, make you look good to your stuck-up parents, and be at your beck and call."

Most of what I'm blowing is smoke, but I know it's going to get a rise out of Piper. She's hitting below the belt, so I decide to join her.

"You don't know anything about me," she sneers, repeating her words from earlier. "You're a washed-up rock star who's run home to lick his wounds after not making it in the big leagues. So, don't fucking judge me. Worry about your own life!"

Before she can say another word she'll regret, I grab her by her waist and pull her into the restaurant, slamming the door behind her and pushing her up against it.

My mouth is on hers in an instant, taking what I want. Normally, I wouldn't kiss her, but if this is the end, I'm doing it my way.

She pulls away, gasping for air. "What the fuck are you doing?" The edge in her tone is already fading and I can tell she's forgetting about everything she just said, and as I grind my erection against her sweet pussy, she might even be forgetting her name.

"Wrap your legs around me, baby. I'm gettin' ready to show you."

Carrying her away from the windows and into the dark hall, I press her against the wall with my body, using one hand to unbuckle my pants and free my cock. Taking it in my hand, I stroke it once and then brush it against her wetness. As promised, there's no panties—nothing standing between me being inside her.

"You're nice and ready for me, just like I like it," I whisper, going in for her neck and breathing in her sweet scent. "Fuck, I love the way you smell, but you wanna know what I love even more than that?"

"What?" she asks, breathless and completely under my control.

"This," I tell her, thrusting forward and sliding into her wet heat. "I fucking love the way it feels when I'm inside you."

It takes an intense amount of control to not come on contact. Even though she's on the pill, I still always wrap it up. I thought it was mind-blowing before, but this...this is like heaven, so fucking perfect.

If this is my last time with her, I want it to be like this.

She moans loudly and I couldn't be happier about the fact that she doesn't have to keep quiet, or that she's not objecting to the fact that I didn't put on a condom, but I'd be a dick if I didn't ask her first.

"Tell me now if you want me to put on a condom," I growl, using every ounce of restraint to keep from moving inside her.

"Just do it," she groans.

"Do what? You've gotta be specific, Piper." My resolve is slipping. "Fucking tell me what you want."

"This. You. I just want to feel you...Just fuck me."

"That's my girl," I moan, allowing my body to give into its carnal urges. My hips thrust forward again as I bury myself inside her, our hips flush, eliciting a glorious cry from Piper.

"Let me hear you," I demand. "Tell me, Piper. Tell me how good this feels...tell me how you think about it at night when you're alone."

"I do. I think about it all the time," she says, holding my face in her hands as I pound inside her while she's pinned against the wall.

"Do you touch yourself while you're thinkin' about me?" I don't know why I'm asking this. It's going to be torture later, but damn it, I want to know. I'll gladly live with the regret.

"Every time."

"No one else?"

"No one."

"Hold on," I tell her, grabbing her ass tightly. "I'm gonna fuck you so hard that you'll feel it for the next week. Every time you walk, you'll think of me."

"Oh, my fucking go—" Her words are cut off with a scream of pleasure. She throws her head back, knocking it into the wall, but is completely unfazed as she grips my shoulders. "Fuck, Tucker. Holy shit."

I continue to push into her, rubbing against her clit at the perfect angle to send her into oblivion.

While she's in the upper stratosphere, I watch her, burning the vision of Piper having an orgasm into my mind. I'll always remember the way she looks when she forgets about hating me and is just... being—completely vulnerable and transparent. This is the Piper I want to remember.

When she begins to relax, I pick up my pace again, holding her to me and bringing her one last orgasm before I come—harder than I've ever come in my life. My cock pulses over and over, and I'm afraid that I won't be able to stand, let alone hold Piper, so I drop her legs and we both lean against the wall.

She's caged between my arms and for a moment, I drink her in. Her eyes. Her high cheekbones. Her lush lips. Her angled jaw.

Before I let her go, I kiss her again, devouring her mouth with mine, and to my surprise, she doesn't fight me. She gives in, gives me access, and kisses me back.

Coming up for air, I stay close, breathing her in, but it only lasts a moment.

"I gotta go," she mutters as staggers away a few steps, obviously still feeling the aftereffects of the mind-blowing orgasm she just experienced. Before I can say anything, she reaches down and fixes her dress, righting herself. With one last look, she turns and walks away.

Standing in the dark hallway, I tuck my cock back in my pants as I watch her, unsure of what to say.

With her hand on the door handle, I decide I can't let her leave without saying something. I deserve the last word and she deserves some indication that this is it.

"Goodbye, Piper."

We never say that. We might say *see ya later* or *until next time...fuck you*, but we never say goodbye.

She pauses for a second, but she doesn't turn around. And then she's gone.

CHAPTER EIGHT
Piper

GOODBYE.

I had a feeling that was coming.

There's been a weird vibe this whole week. I felt like something was wrong and that Tucker was pulling away. But when I saw him today, I knew it. Maybe it was the way he looked at me like he was memorizing my face. I don't know how I knew, I just knew.

And, what just happened was not normal for us. The fucking, yes. But the intensity and emotion behind it, no. We've never had sex without a condom, for one. Why I didn't stop him, I don't know. I just wanted it. I wanted to know what it felt like, and now I regret it, not because of possible repercussions but because it was earth-shattering. It was one of those sexual experiences you read about, the ones that bring people to tears. But there was no way in hell I was crying in front of Tucker.

And then he kissed me.

And I kissed him back.

What the hell was I thinking?

He's wrong about a lot of things, but one thing he's right about is that we don't do feelings. We don't kiss. We don't discuss our personal lives. We're not even nice to each other. It's how we keep things from getting personal. At least, that's it for me. When I'm hating him, I forget about how sweet he is and how funny...and sexy as hell. If I focus on all of his annoying traits, like always being right and never taking anything serious, I don't have time to think about anything else.

When I asked him earlier today what was wrong, I knew he wouldn't tell me. I actually wanted to kick myself for even asking, but I wanted to know. I don't know why, I just did.

Actually, that's a lie. I do know why. Somehow, through all the hating, I've grown attached to him. He's become my stress-relief, my distraction, the person I turn to when life gets too complicated.

I thought we had a good thing going. It's not perfect or conventional, but it serves its purpose.

However, the feelings that have been coming to the surface are not part of the arrangement. I didn't expect them. I can't control them. And they're freaking me out and pissing me the hell off. I want to scream...or fight with Tucker, but since I can't do that, I have to get the fuck out of here.

Slipping off my heels, I run the rest of the way to the hotel.

Maybe there's an earlier flight back to Birmingham. It's worth a shot. And it's better than sitting in the hotel room by myself for the rest of the night, thinking about Tucker and trying to make sense of what's happening.

When I get to my room, I pull off my dress and throw it into my weekender. In my hang-up bag in the closet, I have an outfit I brought in case I took a later flight and went straight to the office, so I go ahead and take that out.

Part of me wants to just change and leave, but I need to wash the sex off. The last thing I want is a reminder of Tucker and this night.

Jumping in the shower, I begin to wash and I realize he was right. I feel him. If I close my eyes and allow myself to relax, I see him...hear him, smell him.

Fuck him.

Fuck him for making me feel.

Fuck him for changing the game.

The tears are a surprise. It's been years since I've cried over a guy and the last time I did, I swore I'd never do it again. But I can't stop them, so I let them flow and mingle with the water, flowing into the drain at my feet.

I stand there until I feel like I can breathe again. It takes a while. The water runs cold, but eventually, I regain my composure.

When I get out, I waste no time drying off and tossing my hair up into a twist at the nape of my neck. By the time I slip on my linen pants and cropped sweater, I feel more like myself.

More in control.

More put together.

Grabbing my bags, I give my room a once-over and try not to think about what I had fantasized about happening here this weekend.

By the time I call for a cab and ride out to the airport, which is a good thirty minute drive from the French Quarter, it's almost two o'clock in the morning.

My original flight is supposed to board at five, so I decide to just wait it out at the terminal.

Horrible idea.

The worst ever.

Every guy who walks by reminds me of Tucker in one way or the other—cowboy boots, worn out jeans, a crazy hat, long blond hair, blue eyes. Of course, none of them have *all* of those characteristics. If they did, they'd be Tucker. And they certainly aren't him.

He's...well, he's Tucker. He's different from anyone I've ever dated. He's so far from my idea of boyfriend material, and don't even get me started on marriage.

According to my parents, the only acceptable man is a professional and preferably someone who went to school for at least six years, and not because they were a slacker. The person should also come from money. If they're in politics, even better.

My degree and profession aren't quite up to their standards. I've listened to them lament about my wasted education for the last six years. But it was the one thing I've stuck to my guns on. I decided I couldn't and wouldn't choose a profession based on what they wanted me to do. There was no way in hell I was going to be miserable every day of my life because of my job.

Maybe that's why I never officially date anybody.

Because just like I couldn't choose a career they approved of, I also don't think I'll ever be able to choose a guy they approve of. So, it's easier to have an arrangement like I have with Tucker.

"Is this seat taken?" a deep voice asks, pulling me out of my thoughts.

I look up to see a dark-haired man, dressed in business casual, staring down at me. Taking a glance around the terminal, it's obvious that we're one of the few people waiting on the flight, so I shake my head.

"No, no one is sitting here."

Subliminally, I'm saying *no one is sitting here, including you.* There are fifty other seats available. Why must he choose this one?

"These are the best flights," he says, not taking my hint and helping himself to the seat and the plug-in between us. Firing up his laptop, he taps on a few keys, bringing it to life.

"Yeah," I reply, trying not to engage, while also trying not to be rude.

"They're always on time."

"Yep."

"So, were you in New Orleans for business or pleasure?" He pulls a pair of glasses out of his bag and slips them on, smiling at me in the process.

I bet this works for a lot of women. The whole glasses, charming smile, winning personality thing, but I'm not in the mood.

"My best friend got married," I tell him, hoping a direct answer will get him to shut up and mind his own business.

"Ah, maid of honor?" he asks.

"Yes."

"Did she make you wear one of those tacky bridesmaid's dresses with the frills and big bow?"

I laugh, because this is starting to become absurd and because it's kind of funny, and maybe I should just appreciate the distraction and give in to his attempts at conversation.

"No, she's actually one of those awesome brides who let us pick our own."

"Wow. She's like a unicorn or something, right?" He chuckles. "I mean, aren't most girls bridezillas these days?"

"I wouldn't know. That was actually my first wedding to be in."

"No way," he says in disbelief. "Gorgeous girl like you. I'm sure everybody wants you in their wedding. That's the thing, right? Picking pretty girls, so your photos turn out good?"

I laugh, like full on laugh, because he's probably right, but it's still ridiculous. "I have no idea!"

"Yeah, that's how it works. See, I have a theory." He closes his laptop and turns in his chair to face me, fully engaged. "The women are so obsessed with the perfect wedding. They scour magazines and Pinterest themselves to death, until they have these completely unrealistic visions of their perfect day. So, instead of it being about them, it ends up being more like a Broadway production."

"Man, you've really got this all figured out. Are you sure you're not secretly a girl?"

This time, he laughs, and it's not annoying. It's actually a bit infectious and I join in.

"No, but I do have four sisters. Three of them are married and the other is planning her *perfect day* for next June. Not like the one coming up, but the one after that."

"Oh, God," I say, laughing again as I shake my head.

"Yeah," he says with a nod, taking a second to just look at me. "I'm Greg."

He offers me his hand and I take it, shaking it firmly.

"Piper."

"I like that name."

"Thanks."

"You don't have to say you like Greg. I know it's incredibly boring. And I wish I could tell you that it's Gregory...like Gregory Peck, all distinguished, but it's not. It's just Greg."

"Well, *just* Greg, it's nice to meet you."

"You too."

He smiles, before turning his attention back to his laptop and we sit in comfortable silence for a while. After checking my phone for missed texts or phone calls, even though I know there won't be any, I pull out my planner and check my schedule for the week, making a fresh to-do list.

"Would you like a coffee?" he asks, standing up and stretching. "I need a pick me up and the coffee place should be open now."

"Uh," I pause, because I almost immediately agreed to a coffee from this virtual stranger.

"Piper? Coffee or no coffee. It's not a life or death decision."

I laugh nervously, this guy throwing me off of my usual game. I intended on coming here, running from my current situation and throwing myself back into my work. Meeting Greg wasn't in the plan. "Right. Well, um, I don't have any cash. I don't travel..."

"It's my treat."

I shouldn't say yes. Nothing is every truly free, even coffee. Like anything else, it leads to other things and I'm not looking for other things.

"Tell you what, since you're having such a hard time deciding, I'll bring back two coffees. If you want one of them, you can have it."

"Okay," I reply mindless, a bit lost in my over-thinking.

"Watch my bag?" he asks, nonchalantly, like we're old friends.

"Okay," I reply again.

I watch him walk away and I must admit he's handsome. You'd have to be dead to not notice. His pants fit him perfectly and narrow at his ankles, setting off his shoes that match his belt. He's dressed like someone walking an H&M runway show. His hair—intentionally messy on the top, while perfectly groomed on the sides—is the culmination of his persona.

Everything about him is well-maintained, putting off an air of success.

I wonder what he does for a living?

Doctor?

No, too laid back for that.

Lawyer?

Definitely not. Too friendly. But then again, Sam Landry is a lawyer and he's one of the nicest people I've ever met.

Definitely not a rockstar. I almost snort at the thought. Greg and Tucker are polar opposites.

Fucking Tucker.

Get out of my head!

In less than two seconds, I go from blissfully relaxed to completely annoyed. Tucker always has the ability to turn me on and piss me off, but he shouldn't be able to accomplish it when he's not even in the same vicinity.

I wish I could flip a switch in my brain. An anti-Tucker Benoit switch. I don't want to think about him. I don't want to think about what his goodbye meant. I don't want to think about the ache in my chest when the thought of not being with him enters my mind. I don't want any of it. So, why can't I control it? I control everything else in my life, why not this?

Maybe I do need a Greg.

Maybe I need someone to make me forget.

My parents would approve of Greg.

"Coffee, my lady," he says, sitting back down in his seat and not giving me a chance to decline.

"Thank you, kind sir."

He smirks and it's cute, but it's not Tucker.

Stop it.

WHEN THE PLANE ARRIVES AT OUR GATE AND WE FINALLY GET TO board, as fate would have it, Greg's seat is across the aisle from mine.

"Nice coincidence," he says with a boyish smile.

"It is," I agree.

"Here, let me help you with that." He grabs the bag from my

shoulder and puts it in the overhead bin.

After we're both seated and fastened in, he looks across the aisle. "So, what do you do, Piper?"

"I'm an editor for *Southern Style*," I tell him, much more forthcoming than I normally would be. The South has definitely rubbed off on me, making me more trusting of people.

"Ah, the magazine business. Nice."

"And you?" I ask, wondering if any of my guesses from earlier are true.

"I work for Bromberg's."

"Jewelry," I say, a little surprised, but not really. I figured it was something lucrative.

"Yes, business development. We're thinking about opening a new location in the French Quarter."

"My best friend's boy...uh, husband," I say, correcting myself. "Her husband just opened a restaurant down there. You should try it out sometime."

"What's the name?"

"Lagniappe," I tell him, still thinking about how weird it feels to say husband...I can't believe Dani is married. "It's a great place. The ambiance is unique, but posh. The menu is inventive and delicious. I promise, you won't be disappointed."

"Sounds like my kind of place. I'll be sure to check it out sometime. I have a feeling I'll be there quite often."

"You should tell them I sent you."

"I will." He nods his head with a contemplative look. "Maybe I could take you there sometime. I'm sure you go to New Orleans often."

"I visit occasionally." Probably not as often now that things are... whatever they are between me and Tucker.

And there he is again.

I swear, he's like a plague.

"I tell you what, I'll give you my card and the next time you're in town, call me. If I'm there, we'll meet up, and I'll treat you to dinner at Lagniappe."

"Okay," I agree, before I even have time to think about it, obviously. Because if I was thinking, I wouldn't have. The worst thing I could do is have dinner in Micah's restaurant with Greg. I don't know why, but it doesn't sit well with me.

"Here," he says, pulling a card out of a leather holder. "This is my personal cell." He writes a number on the back of the card before handing it to me across the aisle.

WHEN WE GET TO BIRMINGHAM, WE GO OUR SEPARATE WAYS. HE'S nice. There's honestly nothing wrong with him, but I know I'll never call him.

And I don't want to think too much about why I'm so sure about that, because every reason has to do with the one person I'm trying to forget.

Instead of going to my apartment, I head straight for my office. It's early, but not too early. Besides, it'll be nice to get a jump start on the day before my asshole boss shows up for our nine o'clock staff meeting.

Drake Montgomery has been thorn in my side since I took this job. He's pretentious, comes from old money, thinks his shit doesn't stink... basically, he's my parents wrapped up in a tailored suit and slicked back hair. He also thinks every woman wants him and even though he's constantly preaching about workplace behavior, he's made advances on every female at *Southern Style* magazine.

He's a literal walking contradiction and total douchebag.

If I thought I had a chance at getting him fired, that would be my mission in life, but his grandfather was one of the founding partners for the magazine, so he's not going anywhere. Therefore, my goal is to get promoted and take his job. He's our current editor-in-chief, but what he really wants is to be promoted to publisher. I realize as long as I'm at *Southern Style*, he'll always outrank me, but I have hopes of at least getting to run my own department. At least then I wouldn't have to see him on a daily basis.

Or make his coffee.

My dreams of a peaceful morning losing myself in my work are crushed when I pull into the parking garage and see his black Audi already in his spot. I want to cry, but I refuse to allow myself to be that weak twice in a twenty-four-hour period.

The universe hates me.

Some time, in a past life, I must have been a horrible person, and I'm currently reaping what I sowed. It's the only explanation, because, despite my flaws, I try to be a good person. I'm a loyal friend. I donate to charity. I don't litter. I occasionally pay-it-forward at Starbucks by buying the person's drink behind me. I conserve water. I don't listen to disco. I'm nice to animals. Kids love me.

Yet, I always feel like I'm being punished.

When I get to the top floor, I walk out of the elevator and keep my head down as I make my way to my corner office in hopes he'll not notice me and I can escape the torture for a couple of hours.

Taking a deep breath and holding it, I walk past Drake's office.

"Piper." His tone is annoyed and it immediately sends me on edge. "In my office. Now."

Turning around, I squeeze my eyes shut tightly and gather all the strength I can muster, before I walk to his door and brace myself for whatever shit he's getting ready to put on my plate.

I can do this.

"Good morning, Mr. Montgomery." I smile sweetly, even though inside I'm planning his murder.

"Sit."

He continues to type away on his keyboard and I start to get impatient.

"What did you need to see me about?" I ask, struggling to keep my fake positivity going.

Fake it til' you make it, right?

"This," he says, turning his monitor so I can see it.

A grainy video begins to play and the sounds from a ruckus crowd flows through his office. Thankfully, we're the only two people on the floor this early in the morning, because what he's showing me is the video of Tucker's proposal, and my heart drops out of my chest.

I try to think fast, come up with something to say—an excuse or explanation—but end up looking like a gaping fish. So, I press my lips together and keep my mouth shut, wondering if I can plead the fifth, as we listen to Tucker's drunk words come through the speakers.

Piper Grey, you're the best lay of my life.

We watch the entire video, from start to finish. When it ends, he turns his monitor around and clasps his hands in front of him, leaning over his desk. His eyes bore holes in me, as we sit in mind-splitting silence.

I have a brief moment of delusion as I consider the fact that Drake Montgomery, womanizer and all-around manwhore, might find this humorous. Maybe he wants to ask about my engagement...or impending nuptials.

I'd gladly fake that.

"Care to explain yourself?" His words hold no humor, and along with his frigid stare, feel like ice water pouring down my spine. My back straightens and I swallow hard, my mind scrambling for the right response.

"I was—"

"Drunk," he provides, his jaw twitching as he levels me with his gaze.

This is what I was so worried about. My parents were a concern, sure, but in the back of my mind, this was the real fear.

"Yes," I concede, deciding to take the high road. There's no sense in lying. The proof is in the video. Maybe if we hash this out it can all go away.

"How do you expect to be promoted with this kind of trash floating around. What would my grandfather think?" His question makes me feel about two inches tall. The video is highly unprofessional, but is it against company policy to have a private life?

"Drake—" I begin, before he instantly cuts me off.

"Mr. Montgomery," he corrects, cocking his head and straightening his tie. "If I found this, anybody could find it. Do you know what a video like this can do if it gets in the wrong hands? It's a publicity nightmare, Piper. No magazine in their right mind would take a risk hiring someone like you, after seeing this. This isn't *Rolling Stone*. We don't pay you to party and make yourself famous for debauchery. *Southern Style* makes its money from wholesome people, looking for wholesome content."

My heart stops at his words, because he's speaking to my fears, feeding them. I want to have a smart comeback for him, but I have nothing. I feel like a child being reprimanded by a parent and he's rendered me speechless.

Hearing his take on the whole ordeal makes me feel like I've committed a federal offense. Before now, I was worried about embarrassment, but Drake Montgomery has me feeling like I should be worried for my job, my professional reputation. I swallow hard, wondering how I'm going to get myself out of this.

"What do I need to do?" I ask, hating the way the words taste in my mouth, because being at his mercy is the last thing I want, right above being out of a job.

CHAPTER NINE

My hands feel sweaty as I pace the length of the barn.

I think about putting all of this nervous energy to use and make something, but I can't. My nerves are getting to me and I'm afraid I'll chop off a finger or something. Besides, the barn is beginning to look like a furniture store with all of the odds and ends pieces sitting around.

My dad asked me last week what I was planning on doing with it all, but I have no clue. He suggested I sell it, and honestly, that thought hadn't even entered my mind. I've been building things to relieve stress and clear my head. It never dawned on me that someone would want to buy any of it, and I'm still not convinced they would.

The bassinet for the new baby did turn out pretty awesome. I put a hundred pound weight in it to check out the sturdiness, and it held up just fine. I'm kind of impressed with myself.

When I hear a car coming down the dirt road, my heart leaps into my throat and I hurry to the barn door to see if it's the same one from last week. I know it's not my dad or Kay, they left half an hour ago to make their weekly shopping trip to Baton Rouge and should be gone the better part of the afternoon.

Kay always talks my dad into lunch before they come back home.

At least, that's what I'm banking on.

As the car gets closer, I notice it's driving slowly, slower than cars usually drive, but it's finally close enough for me to see that it's Sophie.

I wonder if she's as nervous as I am.

Who am I kidding? She's probably scared out of her mind.

I would be.

Over the past week, I've caught myself getting sucked into a dark hole, where I try to put myself in her place—trying to feel what she feels—and it's horrible.

It feels like I'm suffocating.

It feels like desperation.

However, I'm not Sophie. I don't know what it's like to be a parent. I only just found out about the potential, so I can't truly empathize with her.

I watch as the car pulls in, and without being obvious, I try to catch a glimpse of Sammy, but I don't see her. Maybe Sophie changed her mind.

But then, she parks the car and eventually gets out and goes to the back seat, opening the door and disappearing from my line of sight for what feels like forever, but is probably only minutes. I think about calling out for her, wondering if she needs my help, but not wanting to rush her.

When she emerges, a small head of blonde curly hair follows her out of the car.

The world stops spinning for a brief moment. I forget to breathe. My heart continues to pound in my chest, but other than that, my body freezes.

I'd recognize that mess of hair anywhere.

It's just like mine.

The closer they get, the more her features come into focus. She has light brown skin that reminds me of cafe au lait, and her pale blue eyes, like Sophie's, are stunning. I can imagine people stare at her, maybe even stop her on the street, because she might be the most beautiful little girl I've ever seen.

And it has nothing to do with the fact that she's mine.

Because just like Cami said, I know.

I'd hope that even if we met on the street somewhere, I'd still recognize her. Something inside me pulls me to her. I expect her to hide or shy away, something most kids her age do, but she doesn't. She holds her head up and meets my eyes, giving me a wide smile.

"Hi," she says, crinkling her nose against the sun and I instantly see Cami.

"Hi," I reply, unable to fight the smile on my face.

"I'm Sammy."

"I'm Tucker," I tell her, squatting down to her level. "Nice to meet you."

"I like your barn. Do you have horses?" She looks past me, searching the open space for animals.

"No, no horses," I tell her, feeling the disappointment inside my chest. I wish I had a fucking horse.

"You've got lots of furniture. Is this your house?" Her brows furrow in confusion.

I look up at Sophie who's wearing a faint smile, like this is completely normal behavior. She also looks tired and fragile, thinner even, like she's lost weight since last week.

"Wanna sit on one of my chairs?" I ask Sammy, but I'm hoping Sophie will take me up on the offer as well.

"Sure." She lets go of Sophie's hand and walks confidently into the barn, testing out one chair, before moving to another, until she finds one she's satisfied with. "Do you have a baby?"

"Sorry," Sophie says quietly. "I should've warned you that she asks a lot of questions."

"It's okay. She talks really good for four," I comment, watching Sammy swing her legs and take inventory of the rest of the barn.

"Yeah, product of always being around adults, I guess." Sophie shrugs and takes a deep breath, her eyes closing for longer than necessary.

"Do you wanna sit?" I ask, motioning to an open chair.

"Thanks." She finally sits and smiles over at Sammy.

"So, *do* you have a baby? Or is this for a doll? I have one like this, but it's not big." Sophie gets up from her chair and walks over to the bassinet, swinging it and frowning when she sees the bricks inside. "Why's the rocks in it?"

I laugh, walking over and taking the bricks out and setting them on the ground. "I was testing it out for my nephew."

"What's a nephew?"

"My sister's havin' a baby. So, he'll be my nephew. I already have one. His name is Carter."

She nods thoughtfully. "You have a sister?"

"I do," I nod, still completely mesmerized by this tiny person and how much I see myself in her. I want to reach out and touch her soft skin, feel her curls...see if she's real. Hug her. There's so many foreign feelings rushing through my body, my head is spinning, but I force myself to keep it together. "Her name is Cami."

"Rhymes with my name."

"It does," I agree. "Well, it's actually Camille, but we call her Cami."

"Mama calls me Sammy. I'm *actually* Samanie," she says, repeating my word choice with care.

I look to Sophie for explanation.

"Samanie is Creole. It's an old family name. I just wanted her to have something to remind her of where she came from. The name originates in Houma, where I'm from."

"How do you spell it?" I ask with an odd need to know everything there is to know about Sammy.

"S-A-M-A-N-I-E. Sa-mon.ee." She spells it and sounds it out for me with a smile and a crinkle of her nose. "I know it's different." She shrugs.

"Samanie," I say, trying it out. "No, I like it."

"Samanie," Sammy chimes in with a big smile, like it's a game.

"That's really pretty," I tell her. It fits her. Somehow the name encompasses her—the blue eyes, the tone of her skin, the blonde hair. She couldn't have an average name. It just wouldn't work.

She smiles at the compliment and just like everything else I've witnessed from her, she takes it in stride and says, "Thank you." Her attention goes back to the bassinet for a minute as she swings it lightly. "Are you *actually* somethin' else?"

I start to laugh, but remember how Carter is when someone laughs at something he's serious about, and I can tell this is a serious question. Straightening my face, I reply, "nope, just Tucker."

I'm your dad, I think to myself, but I don't say it, because that'd be weird and I don't want to freak her out. I'm sure there's some sort of process for that kind of revelation. Hopefully, Sophie knows how to do that, because I'm at a loss.

Sammy takes a deep breath in and then lets it out, and I can see the wheels in her little mind turning. "Is that your swing?"

I look out the back door of the barn, where the old tire is tied to the large oak, and I nod my head.

"Would you like to swing on it?"

A smile grows on her face, so wide it forces her eyes into tiny crescent moons, as her blonde curls bounce with a vigorous nod of her head.

"If it's okay with your mom." I look over at Sophie who smiles her approval. As Sammy runs out to the swing, I watch as a world of emotions pass across Sophie's face—adoration, happiness, sadness, worry...maybe even a hint of relief.

"Do you need help?" I call out to Sammy, but I know she can do it. Carter has been swinging on that thing since he was old enough to walk. My dad lowered it to the ground so he could get in it on his own, and also so my dad wouldn't fret over him falling out. I swear, when Cami and I were kids, we swam in the river and climbed trees, but none of that is safe enough for Carter.

"I can do it." Her tenacity and independence shines through in every move she makes and I feel like I could watch her for hours.

"She's amazing," I say without thinking, to myself, to Sophie.

"She is," Sophie agrees and I can see that she's fighting back emotions. "I'm sorry." She shakes her head and presses her lips together before continuing. "I know *I* came to *you*. And I've had a lot of years to come to terms with this, but it's so hard. I feel like I'm forcing myself to put one foot in front of the other. My head knows what I need to do, but my heart fights it every step of the way."

"I'm sorry." It's the only thing I know to say and my throat tightens as my own emotions rush to the surface. "This fucking sucks, Sophie. I...I don't know what to say."

She clears her throat and sits up straighter. "Sorry." She blows out a breath, collecting herself. "Look, I know you didn't ask for this and I'm sure you still have your doubts—"

"I—" I start to cut her off and tell her I don't have doubts, not anymore, but she doesn't let me. She keeps going, like she needs to get it all out.

"Here," she says, handing me an envelope I didn't notice before. "Sammy's swab is already in there. You just have to do yours."

"What's this?"

"A paternity test. You just swab your cheek, put it in the other tube, and mail it in."

"Okay," I tell her, a brief wave of reality hitting me.

Right. A paternity test. Because there's still a chance that the little girl swinging on the tire swing, with her head tilted up to the sky and her little purple sneakers up in the air, isn't mine.

Right.

"I had my doubts and I didn't ask for this," I begin, working through the kaleidoscope of feelings swirling through my chest. That part's true. But how do you ask for something you didn't know you wanted? How do you know that when you're face to face with something you helped create that the world shifts on its axis and you realize you'd move heaven and earth to make them happy and safe. "I can't explain it, but somehow I just know...I know she's mine. I'd like to think, even if you hadn't told me, I'd still know."

"I've been doing some research on the process of adding you as Sammy's father," Sophie says, her tone turning more business than I've heard before, like she's separating herself from the situation. "If the test comes back positive, we'll have to file an Acknowledgement of

Paternity in front of a notary. The paperwork has to be filled out and filed at the vital records office."

"Okay." The numbness from last week begins to seep back in as the truth of what all of this means comes crashing down around me. Paternity tests, vital records...father—all of it seems so surreal, yet right, like this is how it's supposed to be.

"If..." Sophie begins, but hesitates as she watches Sammy swing for a minute. "If you don't want her, I'll understand."

The words literally break my heart. I feel my chest fracture and practically crumble as I too watch the little girl swing like she doesn't have a care in the world.

"I don't have a doubt she's yours," Sophie continues. "But if you can't take her, I'll figure something else out. I know I blindsided you with this. Showing up here last week, out of the blue. It was a pure shot in the dark. I was so desperate. After my last doctor's appointment, I went into panic mode and all I could think about was getting Sammy somewhere safe—somewhere she'll be happy. I didn't even know if you'd be here or if I had the right Tucker Benoit. When I contacted Tracy and she said y'all weren't touring anymore, I took it as a sign from God. And when I drove up and saw you in the barn, working... and this peaceful house...I felt like I was doing the right thing. But after I left, all I could do was think about how much of a shock this must be to you."

I listen to her and try to find the right way to say what I'm feeling. It's off the cuff and more transparent than I've been with anyone in a long time, but somehow, my confession feels safe with Sophie.

"To be honest, I've been home off the road for a few months now and I don't know what I'm doin' with my life. I've been tryin' to figure that out, takin' it a day at a time. Most days, I feel like I'm barely takin' care of myself. I don't know how I'm gonna take care of Sammy. I have a nephew, but all I've about is bein' a good uncle—playing army men and running around the yard...feeding him chocolate." I chuckle, shaking my head. "That's the extent of my experience when it comes to kids."

"Well, you'll be happy to know Sammy is very self-sufficient," she says with a small laugh, both of us trying to make light of the situation. But the heaviness is still sitting around like a thick fog.

"I need time," I confess. "But I'll do this." I hold up the test. "And I'll meet you in Houma for the paperwork."

I can at least give her that much.

"Thank you."

CHAPTER TEN

THE ENVELOPE SOPHIE GAVE ME IS READY TO BE MAILED AND currently burning a hole in my pocket. I was hoping to run into town this morning, but my dad needed me to run the tractor for him. We're tilling up the fields that were harvested in December, getting them ready for planting again.

Most people probably don't realize how long of a process it is to grow some sugarcane. Crops can take over a year to be ready for harvest. As a kid, my favorite thing about harvest time was when they set fire to the crops. It helps get the critters out and cuts down on the time it takes to gather the stalks by getting rid of the undergrowth. I used to sit up on the roof of the house and watch the smoke rise.

This morning, I'm thankful for the cooler temperatures, because I'm stuck in the old tractor and it doesn't have any air conditioning. Sometimes, I think my dad does it on purpose, like he's still teaching me lessons. Maybe he is. I know I'm definitely learning the meaning of hard work. He pays me well, probably more than he would a typical farm hand, but I feel like I earn every red cent.

As I make the pass down the last row, I head straight for the barn.

After I park the tractor, without cleaning up or changing, I jump in my truck and head for town. There's still time to make it to the post office before the cut-off and I should also be able to catch Cami at the studio. Since she's the only person who knows what's going on, I need to talk to her.

Walking into the small post office, I buy enough stamps for the envelope and instead of handing it over to the old man behind the desk, I do it myself. The last thing I need is for wind of me mailing off a paternity test getting circulated. Everyone will know soon enough, and to be honest, I don't care, but I'd rather not have to deal with that on top of everything else.

Dropping it into the box on my way out, I smile at a couple familiar faces I pass as I head back out the doors to my truck.

When I pull up in front of Cami's studio, she's standing out on the sidewalk, looking pensively at a large canvas leaned up against the window.

"Does this yellow look too *buttery*?" she asks, turning her head from one side, then slowly to the other. "I brought it out here to see it in natural light. I think it has too much white."

"You're the expert, so I'm sure my opinion means nothing."

"I need it," she insists, practically whining. "Come on, you've seen a sunflower in person. Don't be a dimwit. Is it too light or not?" At that, she turns on me with her hands on her hips and I see a glimpse of what I got at the chapel last weekend and quickly retreat.

"Maybe a *bit* too much...uh, white? I guess...." I pause, unsure if this is the right thing to say or not. I just never know these days. "Sunflowers are usually a darker shade of yellow, right? So, maybe a bit more—"

"Brown." She cuts me off, finishing my thought and I'm grateful, because I wasn't sure what she added to the yellow to make it darker.

"Yeah," I agree, hoping that's what's expected of me.

"That's what I was thinkin'. I'm really glad you stopped by." She goes to grab the canvas, but I beat her to it, lifting it up and motioning for her to get the door.

"Where do you want it?"

"In the back." Walking ahead of me, she grabs a palette off the table and collects a cup and brush as we go. "Here is good." She points me to a large easel.

Looking around the small room, I give a low whistle. "Damn, you've been busy."

Letting out a deep sigh, she sits on the stool in front of the painting of the sunflower. "The problem is that I can't finish anything," she says with another whine, that is very un-Cami. "I have all of these scenes and images in my head, but when I sit down to put them on canvas, I can't make them come to life! It's this baby, he's taking all of my brain cells."

She frowns down at her belly and I want to laugh, but I'm afraid.

"Well..." I drawl, pausing. "What you've done is really great. I'm sure you'll get them finished at some point."

"That's what Deacon said," she says with another sigh. "What about you? I know you didn't stop by to hear me complain or discuss paintings."

"No, that's exactly why I came. I was walkin' out of the post office and I said to myself: Tucker, Cami needs someone to bitch and moan to. Get your ass over there. Stat."

"Stop," she says, laughing as she picks up her brush and begins to make light strokes across the canvas. I stand there, watching as she paints, and it's oddly soothing.

After a minute or so, Cami breaks the silence. "I know Sophie was supposed to come back. I'm sure that's why you're here, so you might as well spill it."

"I saw her."

"And?"

"And you were right."

Cami's brush stops mid-stroke and she slowly turns on her stool to face me.

"Tell me about her."

"She's..." I start, but I don't know where to begin. "She's perfect." It's the only thing that comes to mind. "And I know she's mine, but that's not what makes her perfect. She talks a lot, asks a lot of questions. And she has this gorgeous curly, blonde hair." I laugh to myself, running my hand through my own hair as I think about hers. "And her eyes... they're this crazy color of blue. I've never seen anything like them." They are like Sophie's, but they're different too. Unlike Sophie's, Sammy's have a darker ring encompassing her pale blue, making them stand out against her skin and blonde hair.

When I stop, looking back up at Cami, she's staring back at me with a soft smile on her face. "I told you."

"I know." I nod, feeling a tightness in my chest as I think about Sammy. I've thought about her since the day Sophie showed up and told me about her, but since I saw her...I find myself missing her. It's so strange.

"It's weird, right?" Cami asks, crossing her arms over her chest and resting them on her belly. "The way your heart expands and encompasses them. You don't even know you can love someone that much...until you do."

"Yeah, I guess." I think she's right. Actually, I know she's right, but admitting it isn't easy. It's scary. I've never felt anything like it.

"You'll feel like your heart is walkin' around outside your body and you'll consider bubble wrap and padded rooms...sometimes the padded room will be for you, but you'll never question love again, because every day, for the rest of your life, you'll look it square in the face."

I take a deep breath, soaking in her words. "What do I do now?" I ask, needing my younger, but much wiser sister to tell me what to do. "I don't know the first thing about being a dad, especially to a little girl."

"Well," she says, switching gears from her dreamy state she's been in for the last few minutes to a more practical, down-to-business attitude. "All kids need the same basic things: love, a safe place to land, and someone to be there for them."

"You make it sound too easy." Ever since I met Sammy, I've been trying to imagine her in my life and what that will look like. So far, all the scenarios have ended in me screwing her up. I have so many what ifs running through my mind, I can hardly sleep at night.

What if she turns out like me?

What if she hates me?

"It's not easy, but you'll be great. I've seen you with Carter. You're a natural."

"I've never been with Carter for longer than a few hours. You've said yourself that you don't trust me to keep him overnight," I tell her, feeling the jolt of all-consuming fear resurface.

"I was being an overprotective mom, Tucker. It's my job, but I trust you. I know you'd do anything and everything in your power to keep him safe, and you'll do the same with Sammy. And that's all you can do. And you'll make mistakes. *I* make mistakes. Deacon makes mistakes. Dad, Kay, Annie, Sam…they all make mistakes. No parent is perfect."

A parent.

I'm still having trouble wrapping my head around that idea.

"So, what next?" Cami asks, pulling me out of my thoughts.

"Uh, well, I just mailed off the paternity test before I came here." I nod my head, taking a deep breath. "As soon as the results are back, I'm supposed to drive to Houma and meet Sophie at the vital records office to file the paperwork."

"And then what?" she asks. "How are you going to support her?"

I take another deep breath and blow it out, taking a seat on the empty stool across from Cami.

"I have some money in savings. It's not much, but it's enough for a while, until I figure some things out. Dad pays me good for helping him…and a month or so ago, I sent one of my songs to a guy in the industry I know who's trying to find someone to buy it." I shrug, because this is where I stall out.

I don't know what's next.

There's no five-year plan.

"Where are you going to live?"

"Not at Dad's," I tell her, because I've already figured out that much. I know he'd let me and would probably be happy about it, but I wouldn't do that to him and Kay. They're used to their peace and quiet. They need their space back. I wasn't even planning on living there forever. This is just speeding up the process.

"How about our house?" Cami suggests. "The cottage is only a week or so away from being finished. Deacon and I decided we're going to use the house for rental property. You can be our first tenant."

"Really? Are you sure?"

"Yeah, we'd much rather have someone we know live there, and it's a great place for kids. There's already a swing out back. I'll help you get Sammy a room ready."

The more she talks, the more my head spins with the reality of how my life is getting ready to change. Most parents get at least a few months to adjust to the idea, but I'm barely going to get a few weeks.

"I need a minute," I tell Cami, grabbing my head and cradling it in my hands as I rest my elbows on my knees. Taking deep breaths I try to calm the rush of panic mixed with fear. It's not a good combo. It makes me feel like running—fight or flight—and I know I can't do that.

"I hate to be the one to tell you this, because I can only imagine how you're feelin'." She stands from her stool and walks over to me, her funky purple sneakers coming into view as she places a hand on my back, reminding me a little of the one's Sammy was wearing. "But you don't have much time. If you drag your feet on this...who knows what'll happen."

"I've thought about that," I admit. "Actually, I had a dream about it last night. I was standing in this long hallway and Sammy was at the other end, screamin' for me. Not Tucker. She was yellin' "Daddy" as these people took her away. I ran and ran, but I could never catch up to her. When I woke up, I was drippin' in sweat and I had the worst feelin' in the pit of my stomach. I couldn't shake it."

"It was just a dream," Cami soothes. "I find the best thing to do in situations where you feel completely out of control is to find something you can control and work on that. Since you can't really do anything until you have the results on the paternity test...while you wait, take me up on this offer, and as Deacon and I are moving out, you can move in. Get a place, check one thing off your list. It'll be good for you too."

"What's Dad gonna say?" I ask, because I don't think I'm ready for that. Not yet.

"He'll be fine with it. Tell him you need your own space. No one is gonna question that." She snickers and shakes her head at me. "Actually, I think you'll put Deacon and Micah's fears to rest a little. The two of them have been gossipin' like old women since you came back, wondern' what's wrong with you. They're really thrown off by the fact that you're not hookin' up with all the locals. So, havin' your own place should make them feel a little better...at least they can pretend you're gettin' some."

"Cami," I say with a mixture of disgust and awe.

"What? You think I don't know you're *Tucker the Fucker?*" She quirks an eyebrow at me, before shaking her head with a chuckle.

"Okay, we are not discussin' this." I stand from my seat and walk to the doorway that leads to the front of the studio.

"Fine," she says with another laugh, raising her hands in surrender. "I have to admit. This change is a bit disconcerting."

I roll my eyes. "Nosy asses, all of y'all. Why don't you worry about your own sex life and I'll worry about mine."

"Oh, don't even get me started on my sex life," she says with an exasperated sigh. "Deacon thinks he's gonna poke the—"

"Lalalalalalala." I plug my ears with my fingers, a total childish move, but I already know where she's going with this and I do not want to hear about the woes of their sex life from my sister. It was bad enough coming from Deacon.

"Such a prude," Cami teases, swatting at me.

"You two are annoyin' as shit." I scowl at her while she smiles at me, perfectly happy with my discomfort.

"Just wait," she says, walking past me. "One of these days, you'll meet someone you want the whole world to know about."

Her words hit me in my chest and my thoughts go directly to Piper. We've had enough heavy talk for one day, so I decide that's my sign to leave. "I gotta go," I tell her, moving to the door like my pants are on fire.

"Hey, Tucker," Cami calls out before I can escape. "You're gonna be a great dad."

"Thanks," I reply, but I don't believe it. I'm not sure if she believes it either, but I appreciate her being in my corner. I'm not sure what I'd do without her.

Walking out to my truck, I think about driving to Baton Rouge and going to Grinder's to see Deacon or driving the other direction and heading to Nola to see Micah, but instead, I drive straight home.

As I pass the big house, I notice Sam's car is home, so I turn down the long drive on impulse.

There are some things that have been plaguing me since my talk with Sophie, and Sam is the only person I know who can answer them.

Pulling up closer to the house, I park in the front and get out.

Normally, I'd walk right in, but seeing as though this isn't Sunday dinner or a planned family occasion, I knock.

As I wait for someone to answer the door, I begin to pace, trying to come up with the right way to word my questions without giving too much away.

"Tucker?" Annie says, pulling me out of my thoughts. "What on earth are you doin' standin' on the porch? Come in."

"Sorry, Mama A. Is Sam home?"

"Yeah, he finished up a case today, so he came home early. Want me to get him for you?"

I start to have second thoughts and think about making up some excuse for my impromptu visit, but the knot in my stomach pushes me forward. "Uh, yeah. Unless he's busy. I can come back."

"Nonsense," she says, walking back into the foyer and leaving the door open for me to follow. "I was just thinkin' about you this mornin'. How's everything goin' since you've been home?"

This is Annie's way of prying, without prying.

"Good, just workin' for Dad, keepin' myself busy."

"That's good." She smiles as she walks closer to the bottom of the stairs that lead up to the bedrooms. "Sam! Tucker's here. He needs to talk to you."

"I'll be right down," Sam calls back.

"So." Annie leans against the banister, giving me a once-over like only a mother can do. I swear, sometimes I think she has x-ray vision or some crazy super powers that lets her see into your soul. "Besides work, what else have you been up to?"

"Uh, well." I swallow, feeling like she's going to see right through me and it makes me nervous as shit. One thing is for sure, I can't lie to Annie, so I go for the one truth I don't mind sharing. "I have made some furniture." Annie has always been a fan of my woodworking skills.

"Oh," she says, her eyes growing wide with interest. "I'd love to see what you've made. I've been lookin' for a few new pieces to redo one of the upstairs bedrooms."

"Well, come over any time. All the pieces are in the barn."

"Hey, Tucker." Sam shows up just in time to save me, walking the rest of the way down the stairs and stopping at the bottom to plant a kiss on Annie's cheek.

They've always been like this—open, affectionate. It used to drive Micah and Deacon nuts, still does, but they realize now that the more they moan and groan about it, the more Annie and Sam play it up. But it's not just for show. It's real. They're the shit fairytales are made of.

"Did you want to take a look at your truck?" he asks, as he unbuttons the sleeves of his dress shirt and rolls them to his elbows.

"Yeah," I reply with a nod, appreciating the excuse to get him to the garage. I kind of forgot about the truck. I should've thought of that.

I follow him to the garage and he lifts one of the doors.

"Pull it around and we'll pop the hood."

Doing as instructed, I walk over to my truck and it purrs to life like it's fresh off the lot.

Of course.

"Soundin' pretty good today," he says, tapping the hood for me to pop the latch.

"Yeah, you know old trucks. They only mess up when you don't want them to." I smile, but I'm not sure he's buying it.

"So, what's been goin' on?" he asks, getting his hands dirty as he goes in to check all the normal culprits—spark plugs, hoses, oil.

I think about giving him a similar response to the one I gave Annie, but Sam's a no-bullshit kind of guy, besides that, I don't have a lot of bullshit left in me.

"I actually have somethin' I was needin' to talk to you about."

Sam stands up slowly, grabbing an old towel on the bench behind him and wiping his hands.

"Shoot," he says, leveling me with one of his famous stares. I bet it makes people sing like a bird when they're on the stand.

"I have a friend," I begin, trying to ask what I need to without telling everything...and without lying. "She's...uh, dyin'. She has cancer and she's not gonna make it."

"That's awful." Sam brings his strong hand down on my shoulder. "I'm really sorry to hear that."

"Yeah," I agree, swallowing as I gain some strength for the next part. "She also has a daughter—a little girl, Sammy, who's four."

"Great name," he beams.

"Well, it's Samanie, but she calls her Sammy." I use the small talk to try and calm my nerves. "She's the cutest little girl...big blue eyes, curly blonde hair."

I watch as Sam's expression shifts and I realize I might've said too much. So, I quickly spill the rest of what I need to say.

"My friend, Sophie, she doesn't have anyone...no family, and I was wonderin'...what will happen to Sammy after she dies?"

This is hypothetical, of course, but I need to know all the possibilities, from someone who knows the law, and Sam knows the law—front, back, and sideways.

"Well, I'm assumin' the father is out of the picture?"

I reply with a shrug and he takes it as a response and continues.

"If there are no immediate family members at the time of death, the child will go to the state."

"And if the father is alive, will they try to find him?" I ask.

"If paternity was never determined, they usually don't have a lot to go off of. However, if paternity was determined, at some point, they'll follow protocol. Eventually, they'll try to locate the father. It's not always an easy process and tends to get messy. More than likely, the child will end up in the system. It might take years before they find the father or another living relative."

Images of Sammy being taken away hit me again, visions from the recurring dream I've been having slamming into my mind. As much as I want to go back to a few weeks ago, when my only concern was figuring out my own shit, I can't, because now I know about Sammy and I can't turn my back on her.

I can't leave her alone.

"My advice to your friend," Sam continues, "is for her to get her affairs in order. I'm not sure how much time she has, but it'd be in the best interest of the child if she tries to work this out before the time comes. I'm sure it's difficult. Actually, I can't even imagine the pain she's going through, but she'll be more at peace, if she knows what's going to happen to Sammy."

Sam using Sammy's name makes everything more real. The idea that she's going to be part of this family has me wanting to tell him everything, but I can't yet. I need to get the paternity test back and then meet with Sophie. I need to know she's truly mine before I bring everyone else into the mix.

CHAPTER ELEVEN

"ALLEGED FATHER: PARTICIPANT #X9724833 IS NOT EXCLUDED AS THE biological father. Probability of relationship: 99.99%"

I read the words over and over until my vision blurs.

That's me, Participant #X9724833, and according to the paternity test results printed on the paper in my hand, I'm Sammy's dad. Not that I thought otherwise, but seeing it here in black and white, all official and shit, makes it sink in just how real this is. I'm a father and soon, I'll be solely responsible for a little girl who knows very little about me or how her world is about to be turned completely upside down.

I allow myself a few more minutes of selfish introspection then text Sophie, letting her know I have the results and am ready to meet her in Houma to file the paperwork. We agree to meet at a local park first so I can spend some more time getting to know Sammy. And for the first time in days, I find myself genuinely smiling, and it's because of her.

That same smile falters when I'm closing out my phone from shooting Sophie a text and notice the missed messages from Piper, but I don't open them. I can't.

LATER, WHEN I'M DRIVING TO HOUMA, MY PHONE RINGS. FOR A SPLIT second, I think it could be Sophie, letting me know something's changed, but as I glance over at it in the seat beside me, I see *No Caller ID* flash on the screen, and I let it go to voicemail.

Again.

I don't know why she keeps trying. She's a persistent woman, but she should know by now I'm not worth the trouble she's putting herself through. Every inch of my body is wanting to hear her voice and speak to her, but I'm a weak man and I know that won't be enough. As soon as I have a small piece of her, I'll want more. I'll have to see her and touch her. Taste her.

There's no time for selfish needs. I have to hold onto what little strength I have and save it for Sammy. She needs me more...more than Piper. She doesn't need me. She might need what I can give her, but that's where it ends.

When I finally make it to Houma and find the park Sophie told me about, I step out of my truck and hear a high-pitched squeal coming from the playground. It's Sammy, I just know it. I've never heard that particular sound from her before, but I feel it deep in my bones that it's her.

How crazy is that?

Sure enough, I quickly spot Sophie and Sammy at the swing set. With every push, Sammy is laughing and throwing her head back, wild curls blowing in the wind like a dandelion being released of its seeds, full of life.

In stark contrast, Sophie seems paler than the last time I saw her, less than two weeks ago, and visibly weak. She looks as if she's using her last bit of energy to push Sammy. The closer I get, I notice her hooded eyes and the way she barely manages a smile when she sees me. Concern rises inside me for this person I barely know, yet share so much with.

"Mind if I have a turn?" I ask Sammy when she turns to see me.

She gives me a surprised smile and then responds. "You want Mama to push you on the swing?"

"No, silly, I want to push *you*. Your mama is havin' all the fun, and I think she should share. What do you think?"

Sophie eases up on her pushing while Sammy ponders my question. When Sammy agrees to let me have a turn, Sophie gives me a grateful smile before walking to a nearby bench.

"Have you touched the clouds yet, Sammy?" I ask, pushing her swing a little bit harder with every turn.

"No. I can't do that. I'm too little." Sammy doesn't speak like most kids her age. Not that I have a lot of experience in the matter, but remember when Carter was four, he still said "wittle", instead of little. Sammy doesn't do that, and it feels like physical proof of how she's had to grow up so quickly. She already seems wise beyond her years.

"You're not too little, you're just right. Wanna try?"

She only thinks for a second before answering with a loud, "Yes", so I increase the force of my pushes. The higher she gets, the louder her laughter is. My heart reacts, as well. It feels...warmer, bigger and I notice I'm breathing easier for the first time in weeks.

"Look at that! You're gettin' closer and closer to those clouds," I tell her. Thankfully, she's in one of those swings that has holes for her legs, wrapping around her back, keeping her secure. When Cami was little, this was her favorite thing to do. She'd beg me to push her on the swing and make her touch the clouds. I see similarities between Sammy and my sister, me too. It's so weird that she'd share familiar characteristics and traits, without ever knowing us.

"I am! I think I can touch them!" She reaches her tiny hand out, grabbing at the air. Sammy does this a few more times before relaxing back into the swing. She looks tired, so I stop pushing, letting the swing slow on its own.

"So, how did you do? Did you grab any of them clouds?" I ask, walking around so I can see her face.

"I tried really hard, but they kept slippin' through my fingers. I had no idea they were so slippery!" she exclaims. Laughter bubbles out of me at her wild imagination and it feels good. So good.

Sammy reaches her arms again, but this time, they're directed at me, and I'm caught off guard until I realize she needs me to help her out of the swing. Grabbing her gently under her arms, I pull her out of the swing, setting her feet on the ground and pausing at the way it feels to hold her, even briefly.

My daughter.

Not paying attention to my weird behavior, she says, "Thanks, Tucker" before running off to the sandbox a few feet away. I'm still standing there, dumbfounded and staring after her, even when she looks back up and waves.

When I finally take a seat by Sophie on the bench, I notice an odd expression on her face.

"You okay?" I ask. "You need some water or somethin'?"

"I have some, thanks. She's somethin' else, huh?"

"She's perfect," I say, honestly. "I don't know many kids, but she seems so smart and mature for her age."

"Sammy's been an old soul since the day she was born," Sophie replies thoughtfully. "She was an easy baby, never colicky or fussy. She started walking at nine months, talking before that. When she was two, she was already potty-trained. I know moms at the group we used to go to for playdates were always amazed, telling me how lucky I was... am." She swallows, her smile fading a bit as she grows silent, her eyes drifting over to Sammy. "It's like God knew exactly what I needed."

"Tell me more about her," I encourage, feeling like Sophie needs this just as much as I do. "What she likes, what she doesn't. I want to know everything."

Sophie blows out a breath and chuckles. "Wow, where do I begin?"

I watch as she takes her time. It must be extremely difficult to try to wrap up everything about your child in a few words, but I try to be patient, because I really want to know.

"Well, she loves music."

My heart literally leaps at those words. I swear, she couldn't have started off with a better attribute.

"I'm sure you're thrilled to hear that," she says, shielding her eyes from the sun as she looks over at me. We smile at each other and it's then that I see Sophie. I mean, really see her. Her skin is dark under her eyes and her cheeks are sunken. I bet she's lost a good ten pounds since the day she showed up at the farm. She's weak, frail, nothing like a young woman her age should be. I feel my blood begin to boil as I fight the anger bubbling up, trying to imagine how hard this has been on her.

I hate cancer.

Sophie's not just taking care of Sammy, she's trying to take care of herself as much as she can, and she's fighting death every step of the way. It's so fucking unfair.

Life is so unfair.

"She loves to dance and sing and will cover everything with glitter, if you let her," she continues, her words flowing faster. "She loves to be outside and pick flowers during the day and watch the stars at night. She'll try just about anything once. People used to tell me all the time how great it must be to have such an adventurous child and it is, as long as you can keep up with the adventure. I don't want her to lose that, Tucker. I don't want her innocent spirit to be crushed. Promise me you'll make sure she doesn't."

As fragile as Sophie seems, she's still tough. I like seeing the fire in her eyes.

"I promise." And I mean it with all of my heart. "What about her favorite foods? Things she doesn't like?"

"That little girl could eat pizza every day for the rest of her life, I'm fairly certain. But, like I said, she'll try anything, so don't be afraid to encourage her. The two things I've never been able to get her to eat are green beans and cabbage but, who can blame her, right?"

I smile, because those were two things I hated growing up, but I love them now. "Well, she definitely knows what she likes, and she has no problem bein' an individual." I sigh, looking over at the sandbox where Sammy has made a couple of friends and is leading them all around the square in a line resembling a parade. It makes me laugh, again. "She's so special, Sophie. You've done a helluva good job raisin' her."

There's a hint of a blush in her skin that makes me remember a bit more of our brief time together—that one night so long ago. Would things have been different if I'd treated her better? Called her? Dated her? I can't bear the thought of her being punished for my womanizing ways, but I also can't regret it because it resulted in Sammy.

There's definitely nothing about Sophie that deserves this sentence.

"Mama! Mama!" Sammy runs over with her hand behind her back. She takes a second to catch her breath before presenting Sophie with a bunch of dandelions.

"Thank you, baby. You're the sweetest girl in the whole world." Sophie leans down and kisses Sammy's cheek, just before a coughing fit hits her.

Before I can offer her anything, Sammy has already grabbed Sophie's bottle of water and handed it to her. I watch as this four-year-old rubs her mama's back, soothing her until the coughing subsides.

My heart breaks witnessing this tiny person taking care of her sick mother, but I'm also proud to see how caring and thoughtful she is. I hope later, when the time arrives and Sophie is no longer with us, that Sammy allows me to console her—take care of her—because it's taking every ounce of strength I have not to pick her up and hold her—protect her from the harshness of her reality.

I understand, now, why Sophie doesn't want Sammy to see her get any worse, but the question is, how much is too much? Hasn't she already seen her mama suffer enough? Does she even know that Sophie is dying and what that means for her? My head swims with possible outcomes from not answering these questions correctly and not many are good.

How am I supposed to know what's right or what's best for Sammy? Her life is going to change forever, Sophie is going to die, and I'm going to be left picking up the pieces. I don't feel like I'm good enough for that or like I've earned the right. But now that I know Sammy and know she's mine, I'll do everything in my power to take care of her the best I can.

It's not much, but it's all I have to offer.

"I want to tell her," Sophie says as Sammy runs back to the sandbox.

"Tell her—" I begin to question, but she answers it for me.

"That you're her dad. She needs to start getting used to the idea. I'm not getting any better, worse, actually. I know it's kind of fast, but I don't feel like I have another choice."

Choices.

I've been frivolous with the choices I've made in my life, using up chances and taking for granted the life I've been given.

This is real talk if I've ever seen it. The fact that Sophie can sit here and speak so matter-of-factly about her mortality and what's to come amazes me. I don't know where she gets her strength from, but I hope that same strength lives in Sammy.

"When?" I ask, feeling my nerves spike, but also feeling something else mixed in with them—anticipation, happiness...Am I allowed to feel happy at a time like this?

"You need it too, Tucker." Sophie turns to face me. "I can see it on your face, in your eyes when you look at her—you want her to know. You both need this."

I nod, watching Sammy as I play it over in my head, trying to predict her reaction.

"Besides, we're getting ready to go file the paperwork and Sammy will know something is up. You can't keep much from her. She's entirely too perceptive for four." Sophie joins me, watching Sammy. "I can't even begin to imagine what she's going to be like when she's older."

That last sentence comes out soft, quiet, like an inner thought Sophie let slip, somewhere between heartache and awe.

She wants Sammy to live. She wants her to grow and become whatever she wants to be.

She just wishes she was going to be here to see it.

I get that.

I wish that too.

My heart aches as I watch Sophie watch Sammy.

After a few minutes, she calls her over.

"What do you need, Mommy?" Sammy asks in her tiny voice. "Are you okay?"

"I'm fine, baby." Sophie tells a white lie, but it's one of those kind that I think God looks right over. He can't fault her for wanting to put off the pain as long as possible. "Wanna sit down?"

"Okay," Sammy says, scooting between me and Sophie.

"Remember how I told you that Tucker is a special friend?" Sophie asks, making eye contact with me over Sammy's head, her eyes glistening in the sun.

"Yeah, you said we're gonna see him a lot and he's a good person."

"That's right, baby." Sophie gives me a small smile, hugging Sammy to her side.

Sammy also turns toward me, giving me a big cheesy grin, showing her adorable baby teeth, like she just let me in on a secret between her and her mom.

"Remember when you asked about having a daddy and I told you when I found him, I'd tell you?"

"Uh huh," Sammy says, turning back toward Sophie.

"How would you feel if I told you Tucker is your daddy?"

Just like that.

No pomp and circumstance.

Sophie just comes right out with the truth, connecting the dots for Sammy as best as she can, and I take note.

"I think I would like that," Sammy says thoughtfully, her head turning to her lap as she plays with her fingers, thinking it over. She's quiet for a second and I don't say a word, because I've momentarily lost my ability to speak. "Yeah, I like that a lot. Do you like that?"

Her stunning blue eyes turn to me and I almost laugh, my emotions all over the place.

"Yeah, Sammy. I like that a lot, too."

"I've always wanted a daddy. Have you always wanted a Sammy?"

She renders me speechless again and I fight for the right words to say—something honest, but also something that lets her know how much I want to be her dad. I didn't before, but it was only because I didn't know her. Now, that she's here and she's mine, I can't think of anything else I want to be.

"I think I did, I just didn't know it."

She smiles and it warms every fracture in my chest, molding pieces that have been broken back together. She finds her own spot and settles there.

"Can I call you daddy?" she asks, scrunching her nose up at me in question.

"Call me whatever you want," I tell her sincerely, but daddy sounds kind of perfect.

CHAPTER TWELVE

Five o'clock in the morning and I'm wide awake.

What the fuck?

During my touring days, I was usually going to bed at this time and now, I'm waking up to do manual labor? It's crazy how much my life has changed in these last few months. And the changes just keep on coming.

After getting dressed and brushing my teeth, I head downstairs where my dad and Kay are up and cooking eggs and bacon. As much fun as life on the road can be, nothing beats a home-cooked country breakfast.

"Mornin'", I mumble, heading straight for the coffee pot. They both greet me with smiles on their faces and are way too chipper for this early in the day.

"Tucker, you feelin' alright?" Kay asks. "You look like you didn't sleep well. Or at all." She places her hand on my cheek and gives my face an inspection. It makes me smile. Kay has always respected the memory of my mom, and I appreciate that, but also I appreciate her care and concern more than I can say.

"I haven't been sleepin' well lately." I shrug and take a sip of my coffee. "I guess I just have a lot on my mind."

"Thinkin' about goin' back out on the road?" my dad asks.

"No, not that." I sit down at the table and think about spilling it right here and now, but a lump rises up in my throat preventing me from saying a word.

"Well, good." He takes his cup of coffee and sits across from me. "You've been a great farm hand. I'd hate to lose you. We've got some plantin' comin' up soon and I'm gonna need you."

"I'll be here," I tell him. I'll definitely be here, as in French Settlement, and here, as in helping on the farm. But the idea of moving into Cami and Deacon's house has been weighing heavy on my mind. I know I need to start making some changes and getting my own affairs in order, but lately, I feel like my feet are made of lead. It's like if I tell everyone about Sammy and make a place for her, I'm leaving the door wide open for Sophie to die. I know that's not the case, but the mind plays dirty tricks.

"Cami's bringin' Carter out this mornin'," Kay says, leaning over to top off mine and my dad's coffee cups. "So, that pretty much sums up my day. She's got some appointments this afternoon and that new art class this evenin'."

"Well, I've gotta get the last twenty acres tilled up today," my dad says, standing up to kiss her. "But with Tucker's help, I should finish up pretty early and I'll take y'all out to dinner."

"Sweet talker." Kay smiles at him and gives him another kiss. It's not too sloppy, just sweet. And totally foreign. With my mom dying when I was little, I remember some affection, but I was young and I probably didn't notice it as much...and it's been a long time. For the better part of two decades, my dad was alone. He used to be sad, even during happy times, I could see the longing for my mom, but he's finally happy again.

I stand and kiss Kay too, except mine is on the cheek, and she follows it up with her usual pat to my face.

"Thank you for breakfast," I tell her.

"You're welcome."

On my way out the door, my phone chimes in my back pocket and I almost ignore it, thinking it's probably another text from Piper. With my lack of sleep, I'm liable to give right in and text her back.

But I can't ignore it completely, so I take it out to read the notification, lately I've been taking solace in the fact that she's still trying. When I notice it's actually a text from Sophie, I nearly drop the phone.

Sophie: call me.

I watch my dad until he's inside the barn, far enough away to not notice my sudden panic. "I left somethin' in the house," I call after him. "I'll be right there."

With a dozen different thoughts swarming through my head, I open my phone and press Sophie's name. The possibilities of why she needs me to call begin racing through my head.

There could be something wrong with the paperwork.

She could've changed her mind.

Maybe it's even something good, like a different diagnosis. That's possible, right?

"Hello?" a weak voice answers, and my heart drops further into my stomach.

"Sophie?" I ask, knowing it's her, but unsure of what to say.

"Hey." She pauses for a second and I can hear her labored breathing. I grip my phone tightly and consider running to my truck—running to Houma—but she coughs and continues. "I was just wondering if you would maybe mind taking Sammy for a couple of days."

"Sure." It's a knee-jerk reaction, no thinking involved. Of course, I'll take Sammy.

What the hell am I saying?

"I can maybe meet you halfway," she suggests hesitantly.

"I can do that, or I can come to you. You don't sound too good. Are you okay?" I know that's the stupidest question that's ever left my mouth the second it's out there, but I'm a bit lost for eloquent words right now.

She laughs a humorless laugh. "I've been better."

"Is there somethin' I can do? Anything I can get for you?"

Anything. I would do anything to make this better for her.

"No, I'll be okay. I just need a day or two to rest, that's all. And I feel bad that Sammy's cooped up in this house with me...and I thought it'd be a good test run for the two of you." She says those last words like they're painful, but also like she's ashamed of herself, but I wouldn't know why. It's smart. Sammy just met me. It's crazy to think that she'd go from not knowing me from Adam to living with me. Maybe an overnight stay is exactly what we need.

"I could probably be there around two. Would that be okay?" I ask, willing to drive there now, if she needs me sooner.

"That's great." She breaths a shallow sigh of relief. It's quiet, but I hear it. "I'll have her ready and I'll text you the address."

"Okay."

"See you then."

When Sophie disconnects, I stand there staring at my phone until my dad calls my name.

I'm going to need to have that talk with him and Kay sooner than I thought.

I spend the rest of the morning helping my dad out in the fields. When the sun is high in the sky and we've finished tilling the portion of field he wanted to get through, we both head to the house for lunch.

Carter is sitting on the living room floor in front of the television with all his toy cars and Army men spread out around him, but he gives me an excited wave when he notices me.

"Hey, Carter-man," I call out.

"Hey, Uncle Tucker-man," he replies with his eyes still fixated on the screen in front of him. I know that's as good as I'm going to get from him for now. Once he's in the "TV zone", that's all he can focus on. It's actually better that he's distracted because I'm about to come clean with Dad and Kay.

My dad and I fix our plates and sit at the kitchen table, ready to dig in. *Hard work makes for a hearty appetite.* That's one of his famous sayings, and he's right. I'm fucking starving.

"You've been quiet today," my dad remarks. He glances at me before taking a bite of his sandwich. He's always been a quiet man, himself, which also makes him very observant.

"I have? I hadn't noticed." *Lie.*

"Well, normally, I have to tell you to shut up and get to work at least a few times before lunch and I didn't have to at all today."

I can't help but laugh because it's true. I've just been too wrapped up in my head to notice.

"So, what's goin' on with you? You know you're gonna have to tell me at some point." He sighs, resting his elbows on the table, like he's been expecting this conversation. "Are you in some kind of trouble?"

When I look at my father's face, I see nothing but concern, causing his tan, weathered skin to wrinkle more than normal. I'm sure I'm the cause of some of those lines. I wasn't the easiest kid to raise. And I know it was hard for him to let me go out on the road with my band, especially at such a young age, but he's always supported me.

I'm hoping that doesn't stop today.

I take a drink of water and think for a bit, trying to get everything straight in my head before speaking. For someone who's so prolific with words, in times like this, I find it hard to piece together what I need to say. Write a song? No problem. Tell my dad that *surprise, I have a kid?*

Shit.

"I'm not in trouble, but I do have somethin' goin' on," I hesitate for a second, willing the words out of my mouth.

My dad pushes his plate away and focuses on me. "What is it, son?"

"I, uh..." I pause, clearing my throat. "I found out recently that I'm a father." I blurt the words out because they still feel funny on my tongue. Wrong, out of place, even though they're true. "But there's more to it than that. The girl's—Sammy's...my daughter's," I correct, "her mom...Sophie is dyin'. This is the third time she's had cancer in the last ten years and the doctors have only given her a few weeks to a few months to live. She doesn't have any family and she wants me to have custody of Sammy, sooner rather than later."

I dump it all out there, barely taking a breath. My dad takes in the information, barely blinking.

Eventually, he sits folds his napkin, laying it beside his plate, before leaning back in his chair.

I mimic his actions and wait. My appetite is gone now, replaced by a bundle of nerves settling deep in my gut. All I can do is stare out the window and wait for his response.

Thankfully, it doesn't take too long.

"A girl, you say? Sammy?" my dad asks.

I feel the smile break across my face before I even think to do it. "Yeah, it's short for Samanie. It's Creole."

He looks off, still deep in thought, before saying, "It'll be nice to have a little girl around here."

His response catches me off guard. It's short and to the point, exactly like something he'd say, but I expected this to be different. I thought he might yell at me or look disappointed, but there's none of that.

"Tell me more," he commands. "Have you met her?"

"I have. A couple of times, actually. She, um, she's four years old and she looks like me. It's crazy, but I can even see parts of Cami in her too, especially her personality. There's no mistakin' she's mine. I knew it before I ever took the paternity test."

My dad looks surprised at this information. "Paternity test? You've already got that far?"

I shrug, filling up my cheeks with air and blowing it out. "Yeah, I didn't want to tell anyone before I knew she was mine. I didn't want to put y'all through that, just in case..."

"You could've told us. The things you go through, the things that are important to you, are not burdens to us. We're your family, Tucker." Now, he looks a bit disappointed.

Feeling somewhat ashamed for not telling him sooner, trusting him with the important things in my life, I look down at my plate and pick at my food, trying to think of what else to say—what else he wants me to say.

"I'm not surprised," he continues, his tone lightening a bit. "I'm more surprised it didn't happen sooner, if I'm bein' completely honest."

I smirk at that admission, but it also kind of pisses me off. Sure, I've made the rounds, but typically, I'm very responsible. I think about telling him that, but it seems like a pointless argument at the moment.

"Tucker," he says, exhaling a deep breath. "Family is family. You know that. We're here for each other. So, you don't have to carry all this on your own. It's no wonder you've been actin' like a crazy person lately—quiet, on edge, not sleepin'. I was beginnin' to worry you were on drugs."

This makes me laugh. The irony isn't lost on me. A few months ago, my recreational drug use and abuse of alcohol were what brought me home. I didn't tell anybody. But those issues seem like a drop in the bucket to what I'm dealing with right now. I think about telling my dad exactly that, but some secrets are better left unsaid. So, I decide to not go there and drop the rest of the bomb regarding Sammy.

"Sophie, Sammy's mom, called me this mornin'. She's not feelin' well and wants me to pick Sammy up this afternoon and keep her for a few days." I pause, feeling the tightness in my chest, partly from what I've agreed to and partly from what I'm getting ready to ask. Dad and Kay are nice enough to let me live here, but they didn't sign on for having a four-year-old running around.

"Can I bring her here? Cami is gonna let me take her and Deacon's place once they move into their cottage, so we'll be out of your hair as soon as we can. But, for now, I don't have anywhere else to take her. I'm sorry to throw this at you all at once, but I swear, it's not on purpose. I'm tryin' my best to figure everything out. It's just a lot."

"I have no doubt you are, but don't feel like you have to move out. I can only imagine how you're feelin'." He pauses, shaking his head. "Actually, I've got a pretty good idea. You have a lot on your plate and a lot of decisions to make, so take the time you need. I'm glad you've at least talked to Cami about this. I bet she's just fit to be tied," he says, snickering.

"She's already wanting to decorate Sammy's room." I smile, scratching the back of my head at the thought of Sammy and Cami finally meeting...and everyone else, for that matter.

Kay walks in and must sense the lingering tension in the room. She looks from Dad to me, and then back to Dad. "What's wrong?"

"Nothin's wrong, darlin'. You're just gonna be a grandma again," my dad tells her, smirking over at me, giving me that look that says *you've made your bed, now lie in it*. He's not above making me pay for not telling him about Sammy sooner. Leaving me hanging, out on my own with Kay is his way of teaching me a lesson. There's a lot left to be said, but those words are enough to set me as ease for the time being.

Kay's hand flies to her mouth as she eyes turn from my dad to me. "Really? Tucker, I didn't even know you were seein' someone."

I feel the twist in my chest and immediately think of Piper, but I do my best to ignore it. If I was *seeing* anyone, it'd be her. I know I said goodbye, and from my lack of communication with her, I'm sure she knows by now that I meant for good. However, the fact that she has no clue what's going on in my life right now bothers me, even though we don't have that kind of relationship, I want to tell her. The past week or so, it's been weighing heavy on my mind, but I keep pushing it back. I'll deal with it later. Right now, I have Sammy to worry about.

"I'm not. *Sophie* is someone I slept with one time five years ago, and I just found out we have a four-year-old daughter together. Her name is Sammy and she'll be movin' in with me soon." I figure the honest truth is the best option.

"Oh, my goodness! This is wonderful news, Tucker. With a baby boy on the way and now a little girl to love on, not to mention a cousin for Carter to play with, my heart feels like it's gonna burst," she says. Her eyes are tearing up and she looks so happy. I don't know why I was so hesitant to tell her and my dad about Sammy. I should've known they'd react this way. The relief I'm feeling right now is indescribable and it eases some of the tightness in my chest.

"When do we get to meet her?" Kay questions. The excitement in her voice is unmistakable.

My dad stands up from the table and grabs his plate, giving her a kiss on the cheek. "Honey, I'll fill you in on the details. Tucker has somewhere to be right now, isn't that right, son?"

"Oh, yeah," I look at my watch. "I've gotta run. I'll, uh, be back. It'll probably be around six or so. She lives in Houma. Takes about an hour and a half to get there."

"Drive safe," my dad says with a pointed stare and nod. "We'll be here when you get back."

"Right," I agree. "Okay."

"It's gonna be fine." Kay's hand comes up to rest on my cheek and it calms me a little. "She's gonna do great and so will you. You'll see. Everything will work out like it's supposed to."

Without even knowing all the details about the situation, she still manages to say the right thing. And I hope she's right.

I smile and give her a kiss on the cheek before I head out the door and climb in my truck.

I'm a nervous wreck as I drive to Houma—nervous-excited, as well as nervous-nervous. I'm happy to see Sammy again and the chance to spend some quality time with her, but I'm also scared shitless.

Then there's the guilt.

When I remember why she's in my life now, all I can think about is how unfair life is. If Sophie wasn't sick, would I even know about Sammy? I'd like to think I would eventually, but truth be told, I might've never met her. It sucks that the main reason I'm getting my daughter is because her mama is dying.

These conflicting emotions are stressing me the fuck out. It's a miracle I haven't turned back to my wicked ways—when booze, drugs were my escape. I won't deny that I'm tempted sometimes, but I know it'd just leave me feeling empty inside. I'd be back to that sorry ass fucker who woke up in the hotel room without a clue where he was or who he was with.

I can't do that anymore.

I don't want to do that anymore.

Besides, I have Sammy to think about now. I refuse to do anything that might jeopardize my relationship with her.

What I really need is a few days with Piper—a chance to lose myself in her. But those days are long gone, even if she does still text me from time to time. It's over between us. Honestly, I don't know why she still bothers, but I dread the day I realize she's stopped trying and has moved on. Those texts, even though I don't return them, are my life line to her—a thread that still links us together. When they stop, I'm not sure what I'll do.

It makes me sick to my stomach to think about her moving on and being with someone else. That's twisted as fuck. I know it is, but I can't help it.

I still want her.

I still think about her every day.

But she wants casual and convenient, and I can't do that anymore. My life is neither of those things and it's getting ready to change drastically. There won't be any time for a secret relationship or booty calls. I'll be taking care of Sammy—being a dad.

Sophie isn't the only one who's dying. The old Tucker is too.

Shit is getting ready to get real.

That's not okay with Piper. It doesn't fit her needs. *I* don't fit her needs.

I'm who she called when she wanted to shake things up—cause some trouble.

I was her guilty pleasure.

I was Piper's middle finger to her parents, even though she never intended for them to know about us. She says she doesn't care what they think, but secretly she craves their approval.

Don't we all? Even when we're older, we still want our parents to be proud of us.

One of these days, I hope she gets it—all of it. I hope they accept her for who she is and can be happy for her, because she deserves it.

As I get closer to Houma, I try to clear my mind of Piper by turning up my radio and singing loudly to one of my favorite songs. Soon, my hair is flying around my head and I'm a sweaty mess as I put every emotion and frustration into my performance on the steering wheel—playing air guitar and even a little drum solo.

It eases my soul for those few minutes.

That's what I miss about the stage—the release and the rush I'd feel when the world faded away and all that was left was me and the lyrics. And maybe my guitar.

Smoothing my hair back, I pull up at the first stop light and grab my phone to open Sophie's text with the address. It's close by and only takes a few more minutes before I'm pulling up in front of a small pink house.

The paint is chipping and the grass is a little high, but other than that, it's a cute place. There's a short white fence enclosing the yard, with an old swing set off to the side that's seen better days.

Hesitantly, I reach out for the latch on the gate when I hear my name from the front door. It makes my heart leap into my throat and I swallow hard as I look up to see Sammy standing there.

She's wearing a yellow dress with a little white sweater and matching white tights. Her blonde curly hair is hanging around her face and she brushes it away as she glances up at me.

But it's the smile that kills me.

"Hi, Tucker," she says with a cockeyed grin as she squints her eyes into those little crescent moons that I've come to love so much.

"Hi, Sammy."

It doesn't escape me that she didn't call me dad. She hasn't yet, but I'm okay with that. I don't want to rush her.

Shit.

I don't want to rush myself.

All of this is so new and sudden. I'm having a hard time with it, and I'm a fucking adult. I can't imagine how hard this is for her.

"Where's your mama?" I ask, looking behind her looking for Sophie.

"She's laying on the couch. She's sick." Her face falls and I see the deep concern etched on her forehead. I'm sure she's also scared. By now, she has to know that the kind of sickness her mama has is serious. I wonder what Sammy has told her. Does she know her mama is dying?

"I'm sorry about that," I tell her sincerely. "That's why I'm here, though. Thought you might like to come stay with me for a couple days, give your mama a chance to rest and get better."

Those words taste like acid on my tongue, because they're a lie. Sophie's not going to get better. But I can't be the one to break that to Sammy. I can't hurt her, ever.

Sammy frowns and looks behind her back toward the house, before turning back to me. "I don't wanna leave her by herself." Her words are sad and they hit me right in the gut.

I didn't even consider that Sammy might not want to come with me. Of course, she doesn't want to leave her mama. What the hell am I doing? Not just in this moment, but with everything. One second, I feel like I've got a plan and in the next breath, I get the rug swept from under me.

"I just need to rest, baby," Sophie says, coming up behind Sammy and kneeling beside her. "Mamie will be back tomorrow. I've gotta be here to make sure she gets back from the hospital okay." She smiles at Sammy and smoothes back her hair. "You go with Tucker and have some fun for me, okay?"

"Mamie is in the hospital?" I ask, because that's news to me.

"Yeah," Sophie says with wide eyes, as if to tell me it's not open for discussion. "She just needed to see her doctor for a check-up. She'll be back tomorrow."

"Okay, well...that's good." I nod, trying to follow along with her.

"You sure you don't want me to keep you company, Mommy?" Sammy asks, reaching out and putting her tiny hand on Sophie's fragile cheek.

She looks worse today—worse than the last time I saw her and ten times worse that the first day she showed up at the barn. There are dark circles under her eyes and her skin has a sallow tint.

Again, I feel the need to do something—anything to make her better.

I also want to yell at the universe—stomp my feet like a child—and tell it to stop this shit. Because it's not fair.

None of this is fair.

I bite down on my lip to keep myself together, because I have to be the adult. It's not a role I've played much through life, always living in the moment, without a care in the world, but I have no choice right now. I'm the one Sophie and Sammy are depending on, and it's the scariest feeling I've ever felt in my life.

"Let me get your bag," Sophie says, standing up and catching herself on the door frame.

"I'll get it." I reach out for her and pause with my hand on her arm.

She looks up at me with the oddest expression. Her pale eyes are a contrast to her darker complexion, and even though she looks like death warmed over, I can see how I would've been attracted to her. She's beautiful.

"I'll be fine. Just stay here with Sammy."

"No, let me help. Go sit or lay down. I've got this."

I stand firm, knowing I have the upper hand in the situation, because the way her eyes flutter from time to time, I can tell she's about to give out.

"Go," I insist and I make my mind up that from now until however long, I'll be here as much as I can. For Sammy. And for Sophie. We might've only had one night together, but from that one night came a lifetime connection.

We created a life.

It might've come as a surprise. And it definitely wasn't the best timing, but that's the way things work. We don't always get to decide how or when things happen.

No matter how brief mine and Sophie's time together was, she's the mother of my child, and I refuse to let her go through this alone. How could I live with myself? How could I look my daughter in the eyes later, down the road, if I let her mother die alone?

I couldn't.

I won't.

Sophie reluctantly goes back inside. I know she's not used to having help, but that changed the day she reached out to me. I wasn't raised to turn my back on family. My dad reminded me of that today. And Sophie is part of my family.

After I'm inside the small house, I look around. Everything is neat and tidy—in its place. Although, there's not much choice in that. The living room and dining room are together, and the small kitchen is off to the side, with a hallway that leads down to what I assume are the bedrooms.

"Uh, where's her bag?" I ask, standing there, unsure of what I'm supposed to do and feeling a bit out of place, like I'm invading Sophie and Sammy's personal space—their little corner of the world.

"Sitting on the table." Sophie's winded after her short walk from the door to the couch and I wonder how I'm going to leave, knowing she's in such bad shape.

I walk over and grab the small pink bag. It's light, like there's nothing in it, but after unzipping it, I see there's plenty. Tiny clothes. Tiny shoes. Tiny everything. So, it doesn't weigh much. The heaviest thing in it is a ragged old monkey that's laying on top.

"That's Bubba," Sammy says, watching me as I take inventory of the bag.

"Nice to meet you, Bubba," I tell the monkey, smiling over at Sammy.

"He doesn't talk." She shakes her head, but gives me an adorable smile anyway. "But he loves tea."

"Oh." I nod. "That's good. We have plenty of tea. Kay always keeps us well stocked on tea."

"Who's Kay?" she asks, cocking her head.

"Uh, she's married to my dad." I don't know how much to tell her.

She's four. Four-year-olds don't understand things like stepmoms and shit like that, do they?

"So, she's your mom?" she asks with scrutinizing look that is far past her four years.

I laugh, shaking my head as I look over at Sophie who's enjoying our conversation.

"No, she's my stepmom, but she's a great one."

"She sounds nice." Sammy leans on the chair and fiddles with a placemat on the table. "Am I gonna meet her?"

"Yeah, she's really excited to meet you."

Sophie smiles softly at me and then closes her eyes.

"Who else am I gonna meet?" she asks and I'm kind of glad she's bringing it up, because I wondered how all of this would go. Now, I realize that there's no need to worry. Sammy will take care of it. She's not afraid to ask the right questions or say what she thinks and feels.

She's just open and smart...so *so* smart.

Once again, I'm amazed with her, by her. I can't believe I helped make her. She's too good to come from me.

I swallow hard before answering. "You'll meet my dad, your grandpa. His name is Clay. You can call him whatever you want."

Sammy's smile is mischievous. "What about..." She thinks for a minute, tapping her chin with her pointer finger. "Gaga?"

"Sammy," Sophie admonishes with a firmer tone than I've heard her use.

"What?" she asks with mock innocence. "That's what Mamie calls me."

"And what did I tell you," Sophie asks, looking at her with a pointed stare from her spot on the couch.

"Don't repeat Mamie."

"Right."

I laugh, because I have no idea what they're talking about, but seeing this side of Sammy is entertaining, to say the least. "What's gaga?" I ask.

"Someone who's nosy," Sophie responds. "Like Sammy. Mamie

thinks she asks too many questions."

I laugh again, but stop abruptly, because the scowl on Sammy's face tells me she doesn't approve, and the last thing I need is to be on her bad side. "Sorry, not funny."

"Well, it's kinda funny," Sammy agrees, but still has a pout on her face. "But I like questions. I can't help it." She shrugs her little shoulders and sighs. It might be the cutest thing I've witnessed all day.

"And what did I tell you?" Sophie asks, leaning her head back on the couch with her eyes closed, conserving her energy for her conversation with Sammy.

"Questions are good."

"Right."

Sophie coughs and Sammy runs over to her, grabbing the cup off the table beside the couch. "Here, Mommy. Drink this."

Sophie takes a small sip and gives Sammy a weak smile. "Thank you, baby."

I stand there, watching, unsure what to do. I guess we should leave, but taking Sammy away from Sophie feels wrong. Leaving Sophie alone feels even more wrong.

"Sammy, go grab your pink blanket," Sophie instructs. "I forgot to pack it."

"Okay." Sammy carefully sets the cup back on the table and then runs down the hallway.

"I can stay," I tell Sophie when Sammy is out of the room. "I can just hang around and—"

"No," Sophie demands. "This is what I don't want."

"Well, *I* don't want to leave you alone."

"Don't make me beg, because I will." Sophie tries to sit up, so I go to her and pull the pillow up for her to lean against. "I'll be fine. I just need some sleep. I had a blood transfusion a couple of days ago, and—" She winces, closing her eyes.

"Are you in pain?" I ask, reaching out for her, but afraid to touch her. I've heard that people who have cancer are often in a lot of pain, but I don't know much, if anything.

"Sorry," she says, finally relaxing back into the pillow. "I have medicine, but I'm afraid to take it when it's just me and Sammy. When I do take it, the pain is manageable."

"Okay." I still have no idea what to do. All of this is so foreign to me. I feel like I'm having an out of body experience, looking down on myself walking through this scene from a movie.

A terrible, tragic movie.

The kind you know doesn't have a good ending.

"Really," Sophie continues. "I'll be fine. A couple days of rest and meds and I should be back to normal...or whatever this is." She gives me a small smile and I try to return it.

"Are you sure?" I ask as Sammy runs back into the room.

"Found it," she says proudly, holding up a tattered blanket that doesn't look much better than the monkey in her bag.

"I'm sure." Sophie reaches out for Sammy and pulls her in for a hug, kissing the top of her head and inhaling deeply.

I don't blame her. If I was Sophie, I would be soaking up as much of Sammy as I could.

Sammy is life.

She's everything good in the world.

"Have fun with Tucker, okay?" Sophie instructs.

"Okay, Mommy."

"Call me. If you feel sad at all, just call me. I'll be here when you get back."

"Okay." Sammy's demeanor shifts again and she leans in for another hug from Sophie, squeezing her little arms around her.

The interaction breaks me deep down in my soul.

"We're just an hour and a half away," I manage. "If you need anything, call." I pin her with my stare, willing her to listen to me—to do as I'm asking. I need that much from her.

"I will." She nods, pulling a blanket up higher on her chest. "Thank you."

"You're welcome."

I'm not sure why, but before we leave, I lean down and place a kiss on her forehead. It's not out of love, not the romantic kind, anyway. It comes from a place of wanting to soothe her, make her better, take away some of her pain—set her at ease—tell her she's not alone.

I'm here.

I'll be here until she isn't.

And then I'll be here for Sammy.

CHAPTER THIRTEEN

After i get sammy's booster seat out of Sophie's car and put it in my truck, I lift Sammy up and buckle her into the seat.

From being around Carter, I know kids are supposed to sit in the back seat, but I don't have one of those. I'm going to need to get something safer to drive her around in as soon as I can, until then, this will have to work. I give an extra tug on the straps, making sure Sammy is as secure as possible.

"That's tight enough," Sammy says with a grunt.

"Sorry," I tell her, giving her an apologetic smile.

"S'okay." She watches me as I watch her, and then I finally break our little stare-off and run around to my side and hop in.

"What kind of music do you like?" I ask, needing something to distract the both of us from leaving Sophie, as I start up my truck and slowly pull away from the curb.

"I like fun music," she tells me with a smile. It's so innocent and sincere. I want to laugh at the simplicity of her answer, but I don't. After the incident earlier, I now know she doesn't like being laughed at, even if she is being incredibly adorable and funny.

"I like fun music, too."

Turning the station to something easy, and *fun*, we drive down the street and out onto the main highway. The knot from leaving Sophie is still in my stomach when we reach the highway, but I put on a brave face for Sammy. When I look over, she's fully engrossed in the song, kicking her little feet to the beat as she watches the outside world go by, seemingly without a care.

I want to talk to her, somehow prepare her for what's to come, but I don't know how. So, I let her be. If I've learned anything about Sammy, it's that she's not afraid to speak her mind. I'm hoping if she has questions or worries, she'll ask me, eventually.

A few miles out of town, when the song ends and the station starts playing commercials, Sammy sighs.

"You okay?" I ask, keeping my eyes on the road.

"Yeah," she replies in a somber tone, pushing her blonde curls away from her face.

"What's wrong? You can tell me, you know. I'm a great listener."

Listening really is something I'm good at. I've always been a sounding board for Micah and Deacon, so I feel comfortable offering that up. I might not have the right response, but I can definitely listen.

When she doesn't reply, I give her a little push. "Are you worried about your mom?"

"Yeah." Her head bows to her chest and I'm afraid I might've said the wrong thing. I don't want her to cry. I'm never good with girls crying. "I don't want her to be sick," she confesses. "But she's bad sick. She told me the doctors tried to fix her, but they can't."

My heart sinks with this revelation. I guess that answers my question about how much Sammy knows about Sophie's illness.

"Do you know what happens when the doctors can't fix you?" At that question, I turn to look at her, afraid of what comes next, wondering if she's asking or telling.

"You go to heaven," she finally replies, solemnly.

I swallow, relieved that she's answering her own questions.

"You're really smart for a four-year-old. Has anybody ever told you that?"

"Well, I'm almost five."

She says it so matter-of-factly that I have to laugh, but I cut it short when it dawns on me I don't even know when her birthday is. I remember seeing a spot for it on the forms Sophie and I filled out at the vital records office, but she did that part. I was so distracted by what was happening, I couldn't think about anything else except the fact I was a father...*am* a father.

"When's your birthday, Sammy?"

The question makes me feel an inch tall. Dads are supposed to know this stuff.

"May twenty-fifth. I'm a Gemini."

Again, her response makes me laugh. Not the birth date though, that makes me swerve a little and grip the steering wheel harder.

"May twenty-fifth?" I ask, making sure I heard her right.

"Yes, and it means I'm a Gemini," she says it slowly, sounding it out for me, as if I'm hearing it for the first time. "Mommy says that explains why I'm so smart."

"Oh, really?"

The air around me feels thicker and I try not to read too much into the date of her birth, but I can't help it.

"My mom's birthday was May twenty-fifth." The words are out of my mouth before I even think about them.

"Where's *your* mom?" she asks, her little mind working as she tilts her head and looks over at me.

"Heaven." I train my eyes back on the road. For the millionth time since I found out about Sammy, I'm lost for words. I don't know which way is up or down or if I'm saying the right thing. So, instead of saying anything else and possibly opening a can of worms I'm not ready to handle yet, I turn the radio up a little and Sammy begins to hum along.

She doesn't ask anything else until we get off the main highway and are headed into French Settlement.

"Do you like grilled cheese sandwiches?"

"I love grilled cheese sandwiches," I tell her, grateful that we're onto lighter subject matter.

"I'm hungry. Can we have grilled cheese sandwiches?"

"Absolutely."

As we turn down the dirt road, I feel my heartbeat spike. I'm not nervous about my dad and Kay meeting Sophie. They're going to love her. And she's going to love them. But tomorrow is Sunday, and like every Sunday, I'm expected to be at dinner at the Landry's. Which means tomorrow, I'll be telling everyone about Sammy, and they're going to meet her.

"There's the castle," Sammy whispers as we drive by the big house.

"Castle, huh?" I ask, trying to ignore the nerves building in my stomach.

"Yeah, it's big and white. That's where princesses live. In big, white houses."

"What if I told you I know the people who live there?" I ask, almost hating that I'm going to ruin her fantasy about a princess living there.

"Really?" Her eyes grow wide and her little mouth drops open. "You know the princess?"

"Well, I know the, uh, king and queen of the castle."

"There's no princess?" Her eyebrows furrow at the disappointment.

"No, just a couple of ornery princes." I smirk at the thought and the idea of Micah and Deacon finding out about this conversation.

"What's the king and queen's name?" she asks, turning around as far as she can to watch the house in the distance.

"Sam and Annie."

"And the princes? What's their names?"

"Micah and Deacon, but they don't live there anymore."

"Oh." She turns back around and frowns. "Well, I'd like to meet the king and queen." The words are a bit more proper sounding than her normal tone and she crosses her legs and places her hands daintily on her lap.

It's the cutest fucking thing ever.

"I can arrange that."

Annie will get such a kick out of her. And just wait until she finds out that Sammy was born on my mama's birthday. I'm not sure if that'll make her happy or sad, but I'm guessing it'll be a little bit of both.

Maybe tomorrow won't be so scary after all.

They're all my family, and Sammy is now a part of that. It's just a matter of taking the leap and telling them. Cami, my dad, and Kay are already in the know. Sam will probably have a pretty good idea once I start to talk. Annie, Micah, Deacon, and Dani are the only ones who will be blind-sided, like me.

But looking over at Sammy as we turn into the drive at the house, I can't imagine anyone not falling in love with her. I remember what Annie told my sister when she was pregnant with Carter: *a baby is never a bad thing*. Sammy isn't a baby, but she's also not a bad thing.

She's perfect.

After parking the truck and staring at the house for longer than necessary, I finally get out and jog around to Sammy's side.

"Ready to meet Kay and Clay?" I ask, unbuckling her seatbelt.

"Yep." She smiles up at me and stretches out her arms for me to pick her up and my heart flips in my chest.

I wish I would've known her before now.

That's the thought that's running through my mind as I lift her up and place her feet on the ground.

I wish I would've known her from the beginning.

Bending down, I take a page from Sophie's book, and get on her level.

"Kay and Clay are super excited to meet you," I tell her, hoping to calm any fears she might have. "And tomorrow, you'll get to meet the rest of my family...*our* family." I give her a smile, hoping she understands that she's not alone. It's not just her and her mom and Mamie anymore. She's got me. And she's got all the rest of my crazy family. We might not be conventional, but there's a lot of love—plenty to go around and plenty to share with Sammy.

"Let's go," I grab her bag from the back of the truck and hold out my hand for her to take.

When she puts her hand in mine, I melt a little more.

It's so little and soft, and a bit tentative at first.

As we reach the bottom step of the porch, the front door opens and my dad is standing there with an expression that matches how I'm feeling inside—nervous, but excited...maybe a little scared, because this is a little girl and what do we know about little girls?

Sammy's grip on my hand tightens when she sees him.

"Dad, this is Sammy," I say, kneeling at her side. "Sammy, this is Clay, my dad...your grandpa. Remember what I said?"

"I can call him whatever I want to?" Her words are quiet, and it's the first time I've seen her act timid. I want to hug her and tell her everything is going to be okay—shield her from the world and every uncomfortable situation.

Give her a soft place to land.

My sister's advice from a few weeks ago comes back to me.

"That's right." Pulling her into me, I squeeze her shoulder in reassurance.

"*Anything* you want." My dad mimics my pose and kneels in front of us.

"I never had a grandpa before," she says, looking over at my dad with an intense gaze, like she's searching his soul. She must like what she sees, because slowly, she eases up and releases her grip on my hand.

"Well, I've never had a granddaughter before," my dad counters.

Sammy smiles and looks around my dad, into the house.

"Where's Kay?" she asks.

We both laugh, but Sammy is serious. She looks over at me with those incredible blue eyes, questioning what's so funny.

"Kay went into town. She's gonna be real sorry she wasn't here when you showed up," my dad answers.

I stand up and my dad moves away from the door, allowing us to step inside.

"Let's put your bag in the room you'll be staying in and then I'll make you a grilled cheese, okay?"

Without hesitation, she reaches out and grabs my hand, following me to the stairs.

I look back at my dad who looks like he's trying not to cry, so I look away.

I can't see that.

I'm still trying to keep it all together myself. If I saw my dad shed a tear, I'd be done for.

When we get to the top of the stairs, I lead Sammy down the hallway, past my bedroom and to the door of Cami's old room. It doesn't look much different than when Cami lived here. The pale-pink curtains are still on the window. Kay put a new white quilt on the bed not too long ago. That's probably the only thing that's changed, except for Cami's personal stuff she took with her when she moved out. The rocking chair our mama rocked us in as babies is over in the corner and Cami's vanity is still against the far wall. It's a nice room.

"This is where you'll sleep," I tell Sammy, sitting her bag on the bed. "Should we set Bubba free from his cage?" I smile, unzipping her bag.

"Yeah, he's probably tired. He needs some tea."

"I bet Kay will hook you and Bubba up with some tea."

Sammy walks over to the bed and puts her blanket up by the pillow. Taking Bubba out, she holds him up, inspecting him and then crushes him to her chest.

For some reason, it makes my own chest ache.

"How about that grilled cheese?" I ask, needing the distraction.

Back downstairs, I sit Sammy up at the table with a glass of sweet tea. I'm not sure if Sophie is okay with her having it, but at this point, I'd give her anything to make her comfortable and happy. I even poured a small glass for Bubba.

She's watching me as I move about the kitchen, pulling out the necessary ingredients for grilled cheese. It's crazy, but it's making me nervous. I've made hundreds of grilled cheeses in my life, but I'm suddenly afraid I'm going to mess this one up. I feel like I'm on one of those cooking shows Annie and Kay are always watching.

"You just like your grilled cheese regular?"

"Um, yeah?" Sammy scrunches up her little nose and gives me a funny smile. "Just like Mommy makes it—bread, butter, cheese." She counts each ingredient off on her fingers. "Then you cut it two times." Holding her little arms up in an "x", she shows me how Sophie cuts it for her.

"Bread, butter, cheese; and cut it into triangles. Got it."

"And cook it. Don't forget that part."

"Right. I'm glad you reminded me," I joke.

"That's the only part Mommy won't let me do. So, sometimes, when Mommy's bad sick, I make cheese sandwiches."

"Cheese sandwiches are good," I tell her, trying to sound like I'm not affected by her confession, but I am. It guts me.

All I can see in my mind is Sammy taking care of herself, and it kills me. I can only imagine what that does to Sophie, because one thing is for sure, she loves Sammy more than life itself.

"I heard we have a special visitor." Kay's voice is soft and melodic.

I turn around in time to see Sammy smile widely at her. "Hi," she says, waving a little hand in Kay's direction.

"You must be Sammy." Kay walks around and sits in the chair beside her.

"You must be Kay," Sammy counters.

Kay gives me a wide-eyed smile, her hand going to her mouth as she tries not to laugh or cry, or both.

"Me and Bubba are having tea. You want some?" Sammy asks, like this is her kitchen and she's the hostess. "It's not fancy tea, but he still likes it."

"Well, I'd love some." The expression on Kay's face tells me she's mesmerized, completely under Sammy's spell with their short exchange of words.

"I smell grilled cheese," my dad says, walking into the kitchen and sitting across from Sammy, like it's something he does every day.

And that's what we have for dinner—grilled cheeses, sweet teas, and cookies Kay baked earlier in the day. I watch Sammy's every move, listen to every word, and watch for any sign that she's unhappy, but I never see it. She talks to Kay and my dad, making them laugh and wowing them with how smart she is.

Occasionally, I catch my dad looking at her with a soft, sad expression, and I wonder what he's thinking.

That she looks like me?

That she reminds him of my mama?

That she acts like Cami?

Because those are the things I think of and it amazes me too, makes me a little sad, but more than anything, it makes my heart expand—wrapping around Sammy.

When I see her yawn, I look at my watch as realize it's already almost nine o'clock.

"What's your bedtime?" I ask, thinking that's probably something I should've asked Sophie.

We should call her.

"I have to go to bed at eight thirty. Not eight thirty-five. Eight thirty," Sammy says seriously and I can hear Sophie in her words.

"Well, I hate to break it to you, kiddo, but it's past your bedtime. And we need to call and check on your mom."

Sammy frowns and looks at my dad, and then at Kay.

They're both smiling these goofy, sappy smiles at her, kind of like the ones they had on their faces the day Carter was born.

I realize they're not going to be any help in the bedtime enforcement. From the look they're giving her, they'd let her eat chocolate and stay up until two in the morning. She could bring a horse into the house or burn it down, and it'd be okay.

And then I realize I know nothing about putting a four-year-old to bed. I was on the road a lot when Carter was a baby, so I wasn't ever around for that kind of thing. I've heard Cami talk about the horrors of bedtime, but never witnessed it myself.

Suddenly, I'm dreading walking upstairs—fear of the unknown and all that jazz.

"Will I see you tomorrow?" Sammy asks Kay, sadness lacing her words.

"Of course, honey." Kay reaches over and squeezes Sammy's hand. "How about I make you some pancakes in the mornin'. Do you like those?"

"Yes," Sammy says with a fervent nod, her frown quickly changing into a smile.

"Let's go call your mom, okay?" I ask, thinking that's a good way to get her up the stairs.

"Okay," she says, still with a bit of reluctance in her voice.

"Good night, Grandpa." Walking over to my dad, she hugs him and I watch as he turns into a pile of goo.

"Good night, Sammy," he replies, hugging her back. His voice is thick with emotion, but he clears his throat to hide it, looking away when she pulls back.

As I'm walking her upstairs, she yawns again and I stop and pick her up, carrying her the rest of the way. When she lays her head on my shoulder, I close my eyes, wondering what I did to deserve this.

What makes me worthy of getting to raise this little girl?

Why me and not Sophie?

The familiar questions that have been plaguing me the past few weeks are on constant repeat in my mind.

Once we're in the room, I sit her down on the bed and open her bag, looking for a nightgown or pajamas of some sort.

"I can do it," she says, reaching over and pulling out a blue and pink polka dot shirt that looks like it's two sizes too big for her. "I'm big. I can do it by myself."

"Okay."

She jumps off the bed and starts pulling off her yellow dress, but gets stuck halfway. With her arms up and her face hidden by the dress, she walks closer to me. "Help."

I laugh to myself, shaking my head at her simultaneous independence and dependence.

Once I get her arms unstuck, she takes over, changing from her dress to her polka dot shirt.

"This was mommy's, but she let me have it." She smiles proudly, looking down at the shirt. "I love it."

"I love it, too. How 'bout we call her and check in...tell her goodnight."

"Yes," she says, climbing back up on the bed and sitting beside me, with Bubba in her lap.

I dial Sophie's number, waiting a good six rings before she finally answers.

"Hello." Her voice is still weak and tired, but she does sound a little better than earlier.

"Hey, it's Tucker," I tell her, unsure of what to say.

"And Sammy," Sammy chimes in, smiling up at me.

"And Sammy." I convey the message to Sophie with a laugh. "Who is up past her bedtime. Sorry, I forgot to ask and then we lost track of time."

"It's okay. It's definitely not the first, won't be the last," Sophie says, her tone sounding a bit relieved and I wonder if she's been waiting on us to call. "How is she?"

"Good." I look down at Sammy, pausing for a second. "Want to talk to her?"

"Sure."

When I hand the phone to Sammy, she stands up and starts pacing around the small room as she talks, like she's sixteen instead of four.

"Yes," Sammy says, but I'm not sure what the question was. "Grilled cheese. Tucker made them. And Kay made cookies. And we had sweet tea. Grandpa said he made that. I didn't make anything."

I listen and watch with rapt attention, soaking in every second of Sammy talking to her mom. I think about recording it, because it's so cute.

I hope she remembers this. I hope when she's my age, she'll be able to recall being four and talking to her mom on the phone like they're old friends.

After a few minutes, Sammy stops pacing. She nods her head as she listens to whatever Sophie is telling her and then says, "Okay, Mommy. I love you."

Sammy hands the phone back to me and I wonder if Sophie's hung up, so I check, just in case.

"Hello?"

"Thank you for taking care of her," Sophie says.

"You're welcome."

There's no thanks necessary, but I don't know how to tell her that taking care of Sammy is now my job. I'm her dad. She doesn't have to thank me.

"How are you feelin'?" I ask.

"Better." I think she's trying to convince herself as much as me, but I can hear the weariness. It seeps through the phone. "I'll be better. Just give me a day or so."

"Alright. Call if you need us." I give Sammy a wink, because she's looking at me with pensive eyes. She's perceptive. I doubt I'll ever be able to hide anything from her for too long.

"I will."

After a second, the phone goes silent and I pull it back to make sure Sophie hung up before putting it in my pocket.

Turning to Sammy, I feel the nerves from earlier back in full force.

How do we do this?

What does she like?

I barely remember my mom putting me to bed as a kid, but what I do remember was every night, she would go into Cami's room and tuck her blanket in tight around her. I would hear her in there asking Cami what she was going to dream about. Cami would giggle and tell her she didn't know, and mama would tell her to think of something good and keep thinking about it until she fell asleep. That's what she'd dream about.

Maybe that's why Cami always had her head in the clouds, chasing dreams.

"You have to tuck me in," Sammy instructs, pulling the blanket back as I stand there in the middle of the room. "Then we have to say three things we're thankful for." She hops up on the bed and grabs her pink blanket and Bubba. "Then you kiss me on my head and tell me to go dodo."

At first, I'm confused by that last part, but then it hits me. Dodo is Cajun for go to sleep. If I had to guess, I'd say that's another Mamie word.

Pulling the blankets up around Sammy's shoulders, I tuck them in around her. "How tight do you like it?"

"Really tight." She laughs when I tuck it into her sides, squirming around and untucking part I've already done. "That tickles."

"Oh, you're ticklish?" I ask, quirking an eyebrow at her. "That's good to know."

"Do it again." She laughs and her wild, blonde hair gets crazier as she flails.

I tuck the blankets in tight, intentionally tickling her sides just so I can hear her laugh again.

After a few seconds, she calms down and pushes her hair back off her face with a contented sigh.

"What are three things you're thankful for?" I ask, knowing that she's on my list.

She starts ticking off own, one-by-one on her small fingers.

"Mommy, you, Grandpa and Kay."

That's four, but I don't correct her. She could go on all night telling me what she's thankful for and I would sit here and listen to every one of them.

She pats down the blanket around her, and then positions Bubba just so at her side. "What's your three?"

I think for a second, trying to figure out exactly what to say.

"You," I tell her, swallowing hard. "And I'm thankful for grilled cheese sandwiches and fun music."

Sammy smiles. "I like those things too."

"Good night, Sammy."

This is the first time I've ever told her that—the first time I've ever put my little girl to bed and it's hitting me hard that this is my life now—*she's* my life.

Sammy stretches her arms out and waits for me to come down to her. When I do, and her little body is close to mine, I'm afraid I won't be able to stop hugging her. Taking a deep breath, I get my first good whiff of Sammy. She smells sweet, with a hint of lavender and outdoors.

Kissing her on her forehead, I sit up and smile down at her. "Good night."

"I'll be right next door, if you need me. And Grandpa and Kay will be in the room across the hall."

I stand up and walk over to the door, unsure of what to do next.

"Do you need a nightlight or somethin'?"

"No." She hugs Bubba to her and rolls over on her side.

After I turn the light off, I walk out the door and slide down the wall in the hallway. I sit there, thinking about the day and the little girl sleeping a few feet from me, and I don't leave until I hear a faint little snore coming from inside the room.

CHAPTER FOURTEEN

I TOSS AND TURN ALL NIGHT. IT'S NO DIFFERENT FROM MOST OTHER nights, except tonight, when I find myself unable to sleep, I can't help getting out of bed and going into the next room to check on Sammy. Every time, she's sound asleep, so I don't know why I'm feeling the need to check on her again, but I am.

Normally on Sundays, I sleep in a little. Mass doesn't start until ten, which gives me at least two extra hours of sleep if I want it, but that's not going to happen this morning.

After checking on Sammy one more time, I head downstairs and am met with Kay whisking batter in a bowl.

"Can't sleep?" she asks, barely turning around to see it's me.

"No," I groan, heading directly for the coffee pot. "Tossed and turned all night."

"I think I checked on Sammy half a dozen times." She laughs, shaking her head.

"I'm surprised we missed each other." I lift the coffee up to my mouth and inhale the aroma before I take my first sip. "We must've been like two ships passin' in the night."

Kay walks over to the stove and pulls out her iron griddle for the pancakes she promised Sammy.

"You're really good with her," she says, turning to me and smiling.

"I knew you would be, but seeing you with her last night was just..." She drifts off, shaking her head. "She's so precious, Tucker. My only regret is that we didn't know her sooner, and...well, I'm just so sorry about her mama."

"Yeah, it's definitely not the best-case scenario."

"She's real sick, huh?" Kay asks and I can see the worry and concern on her face. She's a mama and she knows. Like Annie, Kay loves taking care of people. It's what God put her on this earth to do, so of course, Sophie's story bothers her.

"She is." I nod my head, taking a deep breath. "A lot worse than I even realized at first."

Kay bites down on her lip and draws her brows together. "I really hate it. For her and for that precious baby. It just doesn't seem fair."

"I know. I've thought the same thing a hundred times. I hate it too, for Sammy and for Sophie. She's a good mom, Kay. You'd really like her. She loves that little girl more than anything. I can't say I'm too happy about the fact that she waited until now to search me out, but I can't fault her. It was a crazy situation and she didn't know me. She just wanted to live her life with Sammy and be happy, but it's not going to work out like that."

Kay sighs and turns to the stove. She's quiet for a minute, probably collecting herself.

"I talked to Cami this mornin'." She sniffles once before continuing. "She's a little upset that you didn't call her and tell her Sammy was comin' yesterday."

Shit.

"I forgot. Honestly, the only thing I could think about yesterday was getting Sammy and trying to figure out how all of this is gonna work."

"She knows that, and she's not mad, but she is comin' over first thing this mornin'."

I should've seen that one coming.

"Coffee," my dad groans, walking into the kitchen, looking as tired as I feel.

"I might've left you a cup." I give him a smirk and he messes up my hair on his way by, like he always did when I was a kid.

"Pancakes will be ready shortly," Kay offers, leaning over for a kiss from my dad. "And I'll make another pot of coffee."

"I got the coffee under control." He pours himself a cup and then goes about fixing another pot.

"Were you up checkin' on Sammy, too?" I ask my dad.

"I didn't have to; I had you and Kay doin' it for me." The expression on his face would seem stern to the untrained eye, but I can see the softness around the edges. Still, I feel the need to apologize which, of course, he dismisses with a wave of his hand. "It was the same when Cami had Carter and was stayin' with us. In an odd way, it was comforting." He smiles before sipping his coffee.

"So, um, I remember when Carter was a baby and we weren't allowed to wake him up unless it was absolutely necessary. Sammy isn't an infant, obviously, but does the same rule apply? Do I wake her up for breakfast or do I let her sleep? I mean, I don't want to mess with her sleep routine, but it just doesn't feel right eatin' without her."

"It's probably best to let her sleep in a bit," Kay says, smiling. "Here's some bacon to hold you over." She winks at me as she sets a platter of the delicious meat in front of me.

"I like bacon, too."

My dad, Kay, and I all turn in unison toward the dainty, but clear, voice of Sammy, who's standing at the bottom of the stairs watching us. I can't explain the feeling that comes over me, but it's as if I can breathe again, just from seeing her. In an instant, I'm out of my seat and walking toward the stairs. When I reach her, I bend down and kiss the top of her head.

"Mornin', sunshine."

"How'd you know to call me that?" She looks up at me with such a curious and skeptical expression, I almost laugh.

"I didn't know, it just came to me," I tell her honestly.

"My Mamie calls me that. She says I light up every room I'm in."

"Well, your Mamie is a very smart lady. Would you like some

breakfast? Kay made pancakes, just like she promised."

"Yes, please! And don't forget the bacon." She grabs my hand and pulls until I have no choice but to follow her to the kitchen table. I quickly realize I'll gladly follow Sammy anywhere, this is just the beginning.

We're cleaning up after breakfast when I see Cami's car pull up in the driveway.

"Looks like we have company," I announce.

"Who's here?" Sammy asks. "Is it Mama?" She seems to be a mixture of excitement and uncertainty and my heart breaks for this little girl again. "No, it's my sister and her son, Carter. He's about your age, just a little older."

"Oh, okay."

I watch Sammy take a deep breath and compose herself before facing the front door. How she's learned to do that at such a young age, I'll never understand.

We hear a knock just before Carter opens the door and runs inside.

"Son," Cami calls after him, "you're supposed to wait for someone to open the door for you, not open it yourself!" My sister walks in with a huff and I'm not sure if it's because of Carter's manners or the fact she's so freaking pregnant, but it's probably both. Either way, I'm not saying a word. "Sorry we just barged in," she tells me before kissing my cheek.

"No, you're not." I laugh and close the door behind her.

I'm startled by the gasp that leaves Cami's mouth and when I turn back around to her, I see her staring at Sammy. Her hand covers her mouth and she looks up at me with tears in her eyes.

"Tucker," she whispers.

I nod my head and give her an understanding smile. "I know."

My sister and I stand together and watch as Carter walks up to Sammy. He removes his backpack from his shoulder and holds it out to her. I can see from here that it's opened and full of toys.

"I'm Carter. I like cars and dinosaurs. What do you like?"

"I like everything and my name is Sammy."

"Cool," he responds. "Wanna play?"

"Sure!" Sammy takes the backpack from Carter and follows him, sitting on the living room floor.

"Hey, Sammy, before y'all start playin', there's someone I'd like for you to meet."

She hops back up and walks over to me, grabbing my hand.

"Hi, Sammy, I'm your Aunt Cami," my sister says, waving her hand.

Sammy tilts her head while her eyes scan over Cami's face, examining her closely. It doesn't take long for her to smile, though.

"Our names rhyme," Sammy states matter-of-factly.

"They sure do," Cami agrees.

"And you have the same crazy hair as me and Tucker!"

We all laugh at that observation.

"I think Tucker's hair is the craziest, though," Cami confides with a fake whisper.

Sammy laughs and looks up at me. "Yeah, but I like it."

For some reason, hearing that Sammy likes my hair makes me feel like I've officially received her stamp of approval. It makes my chest warm and I might even be blushing a little bit.

"Can I play with Carter now?" Sammy asks.

"Of course, darlin'. Go ahead." I loosen my hold on her hand but before she runs off, Sammy wraps her arms around my legs and squeezes. I have enough sense to hug her back, but I'm too stunned to do much else. Thankfully, Sammy doesn't seem to notice my awkwardness, so she skips, literally, over to where Carter has every toy from his backpack spread out on the living room floor.

I know my eyes are still wide when I look back at Cami.

"Well, big brother, I'd say that little girl is quite smitten with you." She's smiling at me and she looks so proud, and for the first time I feel like I might be able to do this dad-thing. Even crazier than that is, I *want* to.

Cami, Dad, Kay, and I sit and watch Sammy and Carter play like we're watching a movie or looking at fine art. They're fascinating. The way they're immediately drawn to each other and talk to each other like old friends is mesmerizing. If only adults could do that—let down walls, let go of insecurities, and just be.

We skipped church this morning. I'm sure Annie is wondering where everybody is, well, except me. I haven't been to mass or confession as often as I should since I got back and this morning, with Sammy here, it just didn't happen. However, the rest of them will have some explaining to do, or I guess, I'll be the one doing the explaining. The thought makes my stomach flip, but I'm ready for everyone to know about Sammy.

When it's time to get ready for dinner at the Landry's, I freeze.

"What's wrong?" Cami asks as she hands Carter the backpack for him to load up his toys.

"Uh, I guess Sammy needs a bath or something, right?"

Cami laughs. "Yeah, she might need a bath."

I stare at Sammy and then back at Cami, shaking my head. "I don't think I can do that."

"Sure, you can." Cami smiles at Carter as he tosses another toy into the bag and then at Sammy as she brings a handful over. "It's easy. I'll show you."

After the kids are finished picking up the living room, my dad heads out to work on a tractor until it's time for dinner and Kay goes into the kitchen to clean up from breakfast. We've all been a bit preoccupied and off our normal schedule since Sammy showed up yesterday. I know at some point we'll have to get used to the idea of her being here and go on with life, but for now, she's still a novelty.

And she's mine.

I still have to remind myself of that, often pinching myself to see if this is all real.

I'm a dad.

I have a little girl.

"Ready for a bath?" Cami asks, pulling me out of my thoughts and making my heart leap into my chest.

Sammy stops what she's doing and turns to look at me. "My mommy doesn't give me baths. She gives me showers."

"Well, okay then," Cami says, rolling with the punches. "Shower it is. How about I go up and get the water started for you and then you tell me what you need help with."

"I can do it by myself." Sammy's little chin juts out and she blinks her eyes, like Sophie, letting us know she's capable of completing the task at hand.

"Sounds good." Cami smiles over at me and shakes her head, trying not to laugh at Sammy's stubbornness. Obviously, she comes by that honestly. "The shower upstairs is a little tricky. How about I show you how to work it and then you can do the rest?"

"Okay," Sammy agrees, taking the stairs with confidence.

"Always make it seem like it's their idea. That's the secret." Cami's words are hushed, but I'm taking notes every step of the way.

After Cami shows Sammy where everything is and gets the shower started, double checking the water, she steps out of the bathroom. With the door still partially cracked, she leans against the wall beside me.

"Quite a little firecracker you've got there." She smiles, pointing over her shoulder. "What is she? Like, four going on fourteen?"

"Seems like it, sometimes." Sammy seems wise beyond her years and it makes my heart ache for the little girl who's had no choice but to grow up too quickly. But there are times, like with her stuffed animal and being tucked into bed last night, she's every bit the four-year-old she should be. I want to savor those moments. I've missed out on so much. I don't want her to grow up too quickly.

"She's perfect." Cami sighs, peeking her head into the bathroom. "Everything okay in there?" she calls out.

"Yes," Sammy replies from behind the shower curtain. "I'm a big girl. You don't have to stay in here."

"Oh, I'm not, just checkin' on you."

"Is it okay for her to be in there by herself?" I ask, feeling nerves in the pit of my stomach.

"She's fine." Cami smiles, pinning me down with those blue eyes that are so similar to Sammy's. "She's not gonna drown or anything. And if she wants to do it by herself, you've gotta let her. Keep things as normal as possible. She needs that."

"Right," I agree, letting out a pent-up breath. "I just don't know what I'm doin'. I feel like I'm gonna mess up, do somethin' wrong."

"That's called being a parent."

We hear the water turn off and then silence. I want to give Sammy her space, but I also need to know she's okay. So, I'm the one to crack the door this time.

"Everything okay in there?" I ask.

"Yes," Sammy says with exasperation. The annoyance is thick in her voice and I have to close the door so she can't hear mine and Cami's muffled laughs.

"Get used to that," Cami whispers. "She's gonna be usin' that tone for the next fifteen years."

I smile, shaking my head at the thought. "Is it wrong to be happy about that?" I ask.

"No."

"I mean, the fact that I'm gonna have her for the next fifteen years... and the fifteen after that. I missed out on the first four years of her life, but I get to watch her grow up. That makes me happy. It doesn't make up for it, but it makes me happy...but in the same breath incredibly sad, because Sophie's not gonna get that. The guilt kills me sometimes."

"I'm not gonna lie. It sucks," she says, resting her hands over her belly. "But you've gotta stay positive. She's gonna need that."

We hear something scoot across the tiled floor, and this time, we both poke our heads into the bathroom. When we do, we see this adorable little girl with her hair wrapped up in a huge towel, and she's standing on the step stool, with another towel wrapped around her, looking at herself in the mirror.

It's the cutest thing I've seen all day. I would say ever, but since Sammy came into my life, I feel that way every time she does something new, something I've never seen her do before.

"I need to brush my teeth."

"Okay, well, after you're finished with that, I've got some clothes laid out for you on the bed."

"Thanks for letting me sleep in your old bed," Sammy says, looking at Cami through the mirror. "It was really soft."

"I'm glad you liked it."

By the time Sammy is dressed, her hair is almost dry and I'm left to figure out what to do with it. I know my own curls are pretty much uncontrollable, especially when they air dry, but I just let them do whatever they're gonna do. The longer my hair gets, the crazier it is.

"What do we do with this?" I ask, picking up the end of one of her curls and letting it fall back to her shoulder.

"Ponytail?" she asks, with an adorable scrunched up face.

"Ponytail. Right. I can do that."

I start brushing her hair, but quickly realize that's not going to work. If we were going to brush her hair, it needed to happen before it dried. I'll remember that for next time. So, instead of taming the curls, I start gathering them on top of her head. Once they're all bunched up, she hands me a pink ponytail holder.

Wrapping it around a couple of times, I give it a wiggle to make sure it's not going to fall. "How's that?" I ask, stepping back so she can see herself in the vanity mirror.

"It'll work," she sighs, rocking her head from side to side, watching the messy curls bounce. "You'll get better." She pats me on my cheek and goes to the bed to get Bubba.

I can't ignore the squeeze I feel in my chest at her vote of confidence. I needed that more than I knew.

"Ready?" I ask, offering her my hand.

She looks up at me and lets out another sigh, but this time it's long and the way her eyes search the room, I'm worried. Maybe she misses her mom or is feeling sad.

"What's wrong?" I ask, pausing at the door.

"I'm nervous about going to the castle," she confesses.

I laugh, because it's so fucking cute, I can't help it, and it's a relief because it's so much less than the concerns I had going through my mind.

"Oh, Sammy, don't be nervous. It's really not even a castle. It's just a big white house where Sam and Annie live. And Micah and Deacon will be there. Deacon is married to Cami, so you've already met her. And you'll meet a really nice girl named Dani. And Carter will be there," I say, trying to set her nerves at ease, but I watch as her face falls.

"It's not a castle?" she asks, her forehead scrunching up in disbelief.

"Well, I mean, it's not like a *castle* castle...it's, uh, it's...yeah, it's a castle." I'm lying. *Why am I lying?* That's so wrong. I'm supposed to be setting a good example and I'm already screwing it up.

"But there's no king or queen?" she asks, still trying to fit it all together.

"Right. No king or queen, just Sam and Annie. They're really nice. You're gonna love them. I promise."

"Okay." She gives me a small smile and finally takes my hand.

I'm pretty sure I suck at this dad thing.

"So, you want us to wait out here?" Kay asks as we walk up on the front porch at the Landry's. We talked earlier that it'd be better for me to go in and tell everyone about Sammy and then let her meet everyone, instead of bringing her into the mix without warning.

I know they're going to be awesome about it, but I want to make it as easy as possible for her.

"Yeah, just hang out here on the front porch with Kay," I tell Sammy, kneeling in front of her. "I'll let you know when to come inside. It won't be long, okay?"

"Okay." Sammy nods her head, the lopsided ponytail bouncing, mocking my lack of skills. Regardless, she's still the cutest thing I've ever laid eyes on and I know everyone in there is going to agree with me.

Surprisingly enough, I'm not as nervous as I thought I might be. Maybe it's because I've already been through this a couple of times now and it's getting easier, or maybe it's because I really *want* everyone to know about Sammy. I want them to meet her and see how amazing she is.

When my dad and I walk in, Cami is already giving me an eager, excited look. The other amazing thing is that my sister has managed to keep all of this a secret. Not even Deacon knows. Carter is looking around me, obviously searching for Sammy, so I know I need talk fast before he spills the beans.

"Uh, I have something I need to tell everyone," I announce, gaining Annie's attention as she pulls a roast out of the oven.

"Okay." She smiles at me and walks to the dining table, placing the roast in the center. "Sam, boys," she calls out, getting everyone to the table quickly, like only she can.

I clear my throat as everyone takes their seat, giving me mixed looks of concern and intrigue.

"Where's Kay?" Sam asks, taking his seat by Annie.

"Uh, she'll be here in a minute," my dad replies, answering for me.

I glance over and he gives me an encouraging wink, nudging me along.

"So, yeah, I have something I need to tell all of you."

"I know," Carter says with excitement, raising his hand like he's in school.

Cami quickly pulls him closer to her, whispering in his ear. I watch as his expression changes and then he smiles up at me.

"Are you leavin' again?" Micah asks. "I was wonderin' how long you'd hang around, but I've never known you to make any grand announcements about tour dates."

"This isn't about the band."

"Did you finally sell a song?" Deacon asks, stealing a roll from the table and getting a disapproving look from Annie.

"No." I shake my head, suddenly feeling the tiniest bit of nerves. I decide to just go for it, before anyone else can offer up another guess. "Uh, I recently found out that I'm a dad."

"What?" Dani's jaw practically hits the table.

I hear a gasp come from Annie, but it's Sam's look of solidarity that keeps me going. I'm sure he's putting the pieces together as I speak.

"I, uh, have a daughter. Her name is Samanie, Sammy for short. She's four."

"Holy shit." Micah looks like a deer in headlights.

"Whoa," Deacon adds.

Everyone seems to be letting it soak in, so I continue.

"Uh, her mom is sick. She's had cancer since she was sixteen. She thought it was in remission, but it's back and they're not givin' her long to live."

"Oh, my God." This time it's Annie who speaks.

"Her mom's name is Sophie. She's someone I met after one of my concerts. We didn't know each other past that." I clear my throat, not wanting to go into details, because Carter is sitting at the table. "When she got her last diagnosis, she started seekin' me out, finally trackin' me down about a month ago. I wasn't sure what was gonna happen, so I didn't want to say anything until I did. But Sammy's here this weekend. She's stayin' for a couple of days, and sometime soon, she'll be stayin' for good."

"Is she here? Now?" Annie asks, looking around the space like Sammy's going to pop out from the corner or something.

"She's outside with Kay. I wanted to tell y'all first before I brought her in. She's been through a lot, but she's amazing and one of the smartest kids I've ever met."

I give Carter a wink.

"She's nice," Carter adds. "We played dinosaurs."

"Well, can we meet her?" Annie asks, her impatience growing.

"Yeah, sure. I'll go get her." I start to walk away, but turn around quickly. "Oh, she thinks this is a castle. So, if she asks about it, just play along, okay?"

Annie smiles and nods. "Of course."

CHAPTER FIFTEEN
Piper

Dani: Hey, girl! Is now a good time to chat?

Piper: Hey! It's perfect, actually. I'm working from home.

Dani: Nice! Working hard? I haven't heard from you in a while. What's going on?

Piper: Why don't we Skype instead?

Dani: Sounds good. Let me get my laptop.

A COUPLE MINUTES LATER, MY LAPTOP CHIMES, LETTING ME KNOW Dani is ready to video chat. When I click to accept the call, I start singing.

"Oh, Dani, girl...the Skype, the Skype is call-ing..."

She immediately starts laughing, making me smile, which is something I haven't been doing a lot of lately. It feels weird but good.

"Piper!" Dani gushes. "It's so good to see you. I miss your face."

"I miss you, too, girl. And, B. T. Dubs, you look amazing. Married life must be treating you well."

My best friend blushes, making her beautiful green eyes light up. I love seeing her so happy. She deserves it, and even though I can only admit to myself, I'm a bit envious, but I'm thrilled Dani has found her happily ever after.

"Stop. I don't look any different."

"Whatever. If you were glowing anymore, I'd ask if you were knocked up."

That comment earns me a middle finger salute, which is mostly why I said it. I love riling her up.

"So, what have you been up to, Piper? I haven't seen you since the wedding. Catch me up on your wild and single life."

I roll my eyes and snicker. If Dani only knew how *wild* I've been. There have been times over the past few months when I've wanted to tell her about Tucker. She used to know everything about me, and I know she wouldn't judge my decisions, but if I'm being honest, I enjoyed the secrecy. I loved having something that was just between the two of us. It made our arrangement uncomplicated and convenient. But there's really no need to mention that now; he dropped me like a bad habit. I can't even get him to return my texts or calls. And I can't believe I've chased after him for as long as I have. Usually, I'm the one who ends things. And I never chase. If a guy doesn't want me, I don't want to give him the time of day. The only good excuse for my recent behavior is that I've been in shock. I didn't see the end coming and it's rocked my world, throwing me off kilter.

"Earth to Piper. You okay over there?" Dani waves her hand in front of the screen and finally gets my attention.

"Sorry, I must've zoned out."

"Have you been working more than usual? You seem stressed."

"I'm always stressed, you know that. But, yes, my boss has been a major asshole lately and making ridiculous demands at work."

That's putting it mildly.

"Damn, girl, I'm sorry. Sounds like you could use some time off. Why don't you come here for a few days?"

What I wouldn't give for some time off, especially if I could spend it with Dani and the rest of the Landrys. However, that would also mean seeing Tucker, and I don't know if I can do that. I don't know how to be around him anymore. We've played this game for so long, but now it's changed and I don't know the rules anymore. I don't know if I can just be friends, and I'm tired of pushing myself on him and getting rejected. If I showed up in French Settlement and saw that he's moved on with someone else, I don't know what I'd do. In everyone else's eyes, we hate each other, so they wouldn't think any differently about the two of us, but I'd know.

It'd kill me.

I can admit that I miss him—his body, his mouth, the fucking—but even more than that, I miss talking to him. Sure, Dani's my best friend, but there was something liberating about venting to Tucker that I still crave. He never judged. He didn't throw it back in my face or try to pretend like he knew what was best for me. He just listened. I've never been so attracted to someone in my entire life. I think that's what made me hate him so much in the beginning. I couldn't stand that he made me feel the way he did—vulnerable, exposed.

"I don't know, Dani. It sounds great, don't get me wrong, but I don't know if I can spare a few days with all these projects I've got going."

Dani sticks her bottom lip out, officially giving me her pouty face, and I laugh.

"Come on, Piper. Your boss can't *not* give you time off; it's illegal! Stay with me and Micah, even if it's just for a weekend. It'll be fun! I know Cami would love to see you, and Annie is always asking about you. Oh, and get this, Tucker has a daughter!"

I hear Dani's words just as I'm taking a sip of my diet soda and, I swear, I nearly choke to death. The carbonation is powerful and painful as it burns its way up my throat and nose. Waving at Dani to signal I'm okay, I cough until I can catch my breath, tears streaming down my face.

Surely I heard her wrong. She didn't really say that Tucker has a daughter, *did she?*

I clear my throat one last time and wipe my face before asking Dani for clarification. "Did you say *Tucker has a daughter?*"

"Yes, and she's the cutest little girl you've ever seen—blonde curly hair like Tucker and Cami, with big blue eyes. We all got to meet her last week while she was visiting, and I swear she already has everyone wrapped around her little finger."

Trying to play it off like this isn't huge news to me is extremely difficult, but I must be doing okay because Dani hasn't noticed.

"Wow. That's, uh, very interesting. A secret kid, huh? I bet that has rocked Tucker's world."

Seriously, I should win an Oscar for this performance, because inside I'm freaking the fuck out.

"It has but, honestly, he's doing great. He's completely in love with Sammy. It's pretty adorable."

"Who's Sammy? The mom?" I blurt out, feeling panic rise in my stomach.

"Sammy is his daughter. The mom's not really in the picture." Dani's face is now somber, the complete opposite of what it was just a moment ago. There's obviously a story there, but I don't want to hear it from Dani. I want to hear it from Tucker, and I'm kind of pissed he hasn't told me any of this. It's irrational, I know, but I can't help how I feel.

I have to see this with my own eyes, hear it from Tucker's mouth. If this is the reason he's gone radio silent on me, I have the right to know.

I guess that means I'm going to Louisiana.

"Maybe I can get away for a few days," I say, like I'm reconsidering her offer, but there's really no choice in the matter. I'm going to make Tucker talk to me. "I could really use the time off to clear my head."

I watch as Dani's expression lights up. "Awesome! Maybe we can stay at the cottage. It would do me some good to get out of the city for a few days. Besides, Cami and Deacon have been moving into their place. They finished the add-on and Cami's trying to get the nursery set up. I'm sure she could use your help. You're so good at that stuff."

"Sounds great," I tell her, trying to not think about all the news she's dumped on me and the fact that I'll be just down the road from Tucker. All of this is a bit too much. "I better go. There's a deadline waiting for me and if I don't meet it, there's not a snowball's chance in hell I'll be able to get away."

"Okay," Dani says. "Go. Work. Call me when you know what days you'll be down."

SINCE I'M MEETING DANI AT THE COTTAGE, I DECIDED TO DRIVE TO Louisiana instead of fly.

The time in the car does me some good, giving me a chance to get my head on straight before I'm face-to-face with Tucker.

I've thought of several scenarios.

There's the one where I ignore him, but I know that's futile and not what I came here for.

Then, there's the one where I sneak out of the cottage and go find him in the middle of the night, but that seems juvenile and I really don't like the dark, especially out in the middle of nowhere Louisiana.

So, I've settled on the one where I suck it up and drive to his house like an adult and confront him. I realize this might mean outing our relationship, but that's a risk I'm willing to take.

I think.

Pulling down the small lane that leads to Micah's cottage, I can't help but smile. This place is really something. It's what dreams and fairytales are made of. Sprawling plantation, quaint cottages, tree-lined drives—all adding up to a Southern paradise. I've been enamored with it since we ran the article on the plantation in *Southern Style*. Man, that issue sold like hot cakes. I think it's still the highest selling issue I've worked on to date.

Across the field and past the pond, is where Deacon and Cami are living. They've transformed their two-bedroom cottage into a family-style home, and it's gorgeous. The wrap-around porch is a nod to the big house, keeping with the style and architecture of your typical plantation home.

Dani waves when she sees me and I quickly park my car and hop out. The Louisiana sun immediately starts warming my skin. Most places in the country are just now experiencing their first taste of spring, but not here.

It's hot as hell today.

"I feel like it's been forever," Dani gushes, jogging over to me and wrapping me in a hug.

"Just since the wedding," I laugh, squeezing her back.

"I guess it's just that we haven't talked much. I swear, I'm not going to be one of *those* girls." She gives me a pointed stare and we both laugh. We know those girls. The ones who find a man and forget their friends. That's not us.

"Hoes before bros," I tell her, offering her a fist, which she bumps.

"Come inside, I've got a salad made and wine chilling. Micah's gone until late tonight, so we've got the place to ourselves."

I glance over my shoulder as we walk up onto the porch and catch a glimpse of blonde hair and broad shoulders walking from the barn toward Cami and Deacon's cottage. My heart leaps in my chest and I clear my throat, trying to not react to him, but it's been too long and I've missed him too much, a fact I'm only willing to admit to myself.

"How're things over there? Do you think Cami needs our help?" I ask, trying to sound nonchalant, but wanting to run over there and...I don't know...tackle Tucker, make him talk to me. Maybe piss him off so much he pulls me behind the house and fucks me.

That doesn't sound too bad, actually.

"Oh, Cami's in Baton Rouge today with Annie and Kay. They're picking out bedding. I promised her our services tomorrow. Until then, we're free for debauchery and gossip."

I laugh, glancing one more time over my shoulder before following Dani into the house.

As much as I need to talk to Tucker, I also need this time with my best friend. So, I try to put him and the lingering questions in the back of my mind.

"*PLEASE* TELL ME THERE'S BEEN A MAN IN YOUR LIFE AND YOU'VE JUST been holding out on me," Dani says with desperation. We've both claimed an over-sized chair and are curled up in our pajamas, sharing a bottle of wine. Our second bottle of wine.

I swallow the fruity, fermented goodness and try to school my features.

"Um, no," I say, shaking my head.

"Come. On." Dani slaps the arm of the chair, leaning closer to me. "No one? Not even a one-night-stand?"

The look she's giving me is one I'm familiar with—raised chin, quirked eyebrow. She knows me better than anyone. There's no way I'll be able to lie my way through this one, and the wine makes me want to tell her. It'll be one less thing weighing on my mind.

"Well," I draw out, taking one last sip of truth serum.

Dani's phone rings and she jumps up to grab it. "Hold that thought," she calls out as she runs into the bedroom where she left it charging earlier.

Was I honestly getting ready to tell her about Tucker?

On the other hand, why shouldn't I?

Besides, it's over now, and Dani can keep a secret. She's my best friend, for God's sake. If I can't trust her with my truths, who can I trust?

"Sorry," she says, coming back and resuming her position in the chair beside mine. "Where were we? Oh, yes. You were telling me about your many conquests."

"You need to lay off the wine, sister. There aren't *many* conquests. My life is definitely not a harlequin romance."

"Fine. *Conquest.* I know there's at least been one! Tell me about him."

"Well, I haven't *conquested* him yet," I laugh, hiding the truth and making a last-minute play call to keep my secret a little while longer. "But his name is Greg. I met him on my flight home after your wedding."

Greg is safe. Originally, I thought he might be a good distraction to get Tucker off my mind, but I haven't been able to follow through.

However, Greg is the perfect distraction for this conversation.

"Greg," Dani sighs, taking his name for a spin. "I like it. He sounds nice."

"How do you know? I haven't even told you about him." I can't hold back the full-on laugh. Maybe it's the wine. Maybe it's hanging out in my pajamas with my best friend. Whatever it is, it feels good. I needed this.

We spend the rest of the night talking and drinking wine. I tell her about Greg, enough to suffice her curiosity. She talks about married life and how happy Micah makes her, which makes me happy.

THE NEXT MORNING, I'M UP EARLIER THAN I WANT.

My phone rang at six this morning, waking me from the best sleep I've had in ages. It doesn't help matters that it was my boss, the asshole from hell, needing me to do edits on a layout he gave approval for a week ago. Not to mention, they're edits I'd suggested last week, but he said they weren't necessary. So, of course, since I'm out of town for a few days, he's decided they're now necessary.

This has been my life the last month or so, ever since he discovered the drunken proposal video, he's decided to make me jump through every damn hoop he can find.

Last week, I was given the unglamorous task of getting his coffee every morning. Not coffee from our well-equipped break room, I could live with that, but coffee from three blocks down the street at this hole-in-the-wall coffee shop that every hipster in Birmingham frequents.

Which just so happens to be the same place Greg gets his morning joe. Fitting.

Since then, he's texted me every other day, asking if he can take me out. He's always polite and sweet about it, but I'm not interested.

When I said I needed a break from my life, I meant it. However, I feel like everything would be manageable if Tucker would just talk to me. I hate myself for depending on him so much. I don't even know when that happened. I don't know when it went from a casual fuck to feelings.

But there are definitely feelings. If there weren't, I wouldn't be so hurt over the fact that he's a dad and I had to find out that information from my best friend, instead of him.

"Hey," Dani says, walking into the kitchen with her red locks in a messy bun on top of her head. "Sleep well?"

"Yeah, I slept great. Just didn't last long enough."

"Why are you up so early?" She pours herself a cup of coffee that I made earlier.

"The asshole called and woke me up."

"Your boss?"

"That's the asshole." I sigh, closing my laptop down after I make sure the email and attachments are sent.

"God, does he ever stop?"

"No, he doesn't."

"Maybe it's time to start looking for a new place of employment. I mean, don't get me wrong, I love you working for *Southern Style*, but nobody deserves to work for someone like him, especially my best friend. I don't like it."

"I've thought about it." The thought has crossed my mind and if this wasn't a position I felt could lead to bigger and better things, I might've already left. Then there's also that part about Drake and the video. I'm not sure what he'd do with information like that if I left. I feel stuck between a rock and a hard place.

"But?" she prods, leaning up against the counter as she sips her coffee.

"But where would I go? I've worked so hard to get to where I am. If I leave, I'll be starting over somewhere else. My parents already think I'm a failure. The fact that I'm *this* close to making editor-in-chief and taking Drake's job is what keeps me hanging on. If I could do that," I pause, letting out a sigh. "I don't know, maybe they'd finally consider my career a success."

"Your career *is* a success." Dani sets down her mug and walks toward me, planting her palms on the table in front of me. "You're working for one of the biggest publications in the industry, doing something you love. And you're damn good at it. Don't let their warped thinking get to you. You're better than that."

"I'm glad someone thinks so."

"What is this?" Dani asks, her voice dropping as she squints her eyes at me like she's trying to see beneath my skin. "This isn't my confident, feisty best friend. What's going on with you?"

"I don't know," I groan, cupping my head in my hands. "I just feel so out of whack lately. I can't think straight. Everything is a foggy mess. I think it's the stress. It's getting to me."

"Have you been laid recently?" Dani levels me with a stare and I roll my eyes at her. This is a question I would've asked her before Micah came along. Now, I'm on the receiving end.

Oh, how things change.

"What?" I ask with a laugh, deflecting her question.

"Laid. This is exactly how you act when you haven't had sex."

"Oh, God. I'm not *that* bad. And seriously, I can go without sex. I don't need a man for a good release," I scoff, trying to convince myself as much as I am her.

"Say what you want, but I've seen this before." Dani's tone is thoughtful as she paces the floor beside the table.

"Stop with the Dr. Phil shit!" I crumple up a piece of paper I'd written notes on earlier and throw it at her, because I'm done talking. If I say anymore, it'll get messy and complicated and I don't want to think anymore. I need a distraction. "Maybe I need some physical labor. Let's get dressed and go decorate a nursery."

Half an hour later, we're up to our elbows in baby stuff—freshly washed baby clothes, courtesy of Annie and Kay...baby blankets, baby shoes, baby diapers. Everything is tiny and adorable.

"What's his name?" I ask as I line up the framed pictures and paintings Cami picked out for the nursery. Earlier, I went around the house and collected a few odds and ends to make up a gallery wall, and it's all coming together perfectly.

"It's a secret." Cami stuffs a stack of onesies into a wicker basket and puts them on a shelf in the closet.

"That's translation for they haven't settled on one yet," Dani says, ironing out the wrinkles in the curtains we're getting ready to hang. "Because if they had, Deacon would've already told the world."

Cami laughs. "She's right. I actually know what I want the name to be, but if I keep up the pretense that I haven't decided yet, Deacon won't say anything."

"Come on, you can tell us! We're great at keeping secrets. Right, Dani?" I ask, nudging her with my elbow as I step back to get a look at the wall.

"The best," she agrees, shaking out a mint green piece of fabric, looking it over for lingering wrinkles.

"Deacon would be so pissed." Cami snorts, but from her tone, I can tell she's considering it, probably still wanting to get back at him for blurting out the sex at Micah and Dani's wedding reception.

We're all laughing when Annie and Kay come back in with the mobile they've been working on.

"Done," they say in unison and with pride.

"That looks great," Cami gushes, taking it from them and holding it in the air. "Now, all we need is the rocking chair that Deacon's picking up this evening on his way home and the bassinet."

"Where's the bassinet?" I ask, standing back and making sure the picture I just hung is perfectly level.

"It's in the barn," Kay offers, sitting down in the floor to fold more baby clothes. "I can have your dad bring it over later."

"I'll go get it." I volunteer before I even think about it, maybe a bit too quickly, but no one seems to notice. The barn means it's at Kay and Clay's, and that's where Tucker probably is. If I'm going to get a chance to talk to him, this might be my best bet.

"You can take the truck," Kay offers. "Keys are on the table."

"You sure?" Cami asks. "My dad won't mind bringing it over later. Besides, we've got a while before we'll need it. I don't think I've ever been this prepared." She laughs, looking around the room that now resembles a nursery. This morning when we got here, it was just a room with boxes.

"It's great that you're getting everything ready. Besides, it'll give you a chance to rest the next couple of months." Annie pats Cami on the shoulder as she leaves the room.

"And you just never know if you'll go into labor early," Kay adds.

"All the more reason I should go get that bassinet," I say as nonchalantly as possible.

"Don't rush the baby," Cami demands. "I'm not ready yet."

While everyone goes about their tasks, I casually leave them and grab the keys on my way out.

It's now or never.

Climbing in the cab of Kay's truck, I start it up and tamp down the nerves building in my stomach, reaching deep down and finding my old self. The Piper who takes charge of situations. The Piper who gets what she wants and doesn't take no for an answer.

I've been missing her lately and I need her desperately.

I'm tired of taking a backseat and feeling like my life is out of control. I'm taking it back, starting with Tucker.

Pulling out onto the road that leads to the Benoit's, I take a deep breath.

What am I going to say?

Should I just play dumb?

That's not really my style, but if it gets me what I want, I'm willing to give it a try.

When I get to the gravel drive, I turn the truck off and hop out. Walking past the house, I see that the large doors of the barn are wide open, but I don't see anybody inside. There's a faint noise coming from a tractor off in the distance. I hope Tucker's not working the fields. He's told me that's what he does on most days. I've had daydreams about what he looks like all hot and sweaty after a hard day's work. I wouldn't mind seeing that in person.

"You trespassin'?" a deep, smooth voice asks from behind me, causing me to jump and spin around. "Looks like you stole Kay's truck, too."

I huff out a laugh. "I, uh, came to pick up the bassinet for the nursery. Cami sent me."

"Thought I saw a strange car over at Micah's cottage last night."

"Yep." I bite my lip because I didn't expect this to feel so awkward. It's never like this between us. "Dani invited me down for a few days."

"That's good." He nods his head while his eyes give me the once over. That, I'm used to, and it feels nice. I like that he's still interested enough to look at me like that. It gives me hope that maybe things aren't completely over between us.

"So, the bassinet?" I ask, needing something to break the ice between us and give me a chance to work up my courage.

"It's in here." He nods his head toward the barn and begins walking that way.

I can't help but return the favor of checking him out. His white t-shirt and dirty jeans are finished off with a pair of scuffed-up work boots. And his hair—it's longer than the last time I saw him and pulled back in a ponytail. If I'm not mistaken, it's with a pink ponytail holder. I almost laugh, but am caught off guard when I look around me.

The barn is filled with furniture—beautiful, handmade, wood furniture.

"Wow, who does all this belong to?" I ask, looking around at every wall. There are chairs and tables, interesting accent pieces. It's stuff you'd see in a magazine. Even from a distance, I can tell the time and effort that went into each piece.

"Me." Tucker walks over to the back corner and picks up a piece of furniture covered by a large piece of cloth.

"Why do you need all of this furniture?" I ask. "You don't even have a house."

"I made it."

My eyes go wide at this piece of information. "All of it?"

"Yeah, all of it." He gives me one of his crooked smiles, setting down what I'm guessing is the bassinet and smoothing back his hair. "I guess I got a little carried away. Making furniture is kind of my therapy...guess I needed a lot of therapy." He laughs, but his words are vulnerable and I realize I never knew this about him. I had no idea.

"I didn't realize you were so talented." I'm in awe, really. Every piece is amazing and showcase-worthy. I just can't believe he made it all.

"Gee, thanks, Piper," he says with a quirk of his eyebrow and just like that, the familiar tug between us is back, and I feel myself relax a little.

"Well, you know what I mean...with your hands," I tell him, getting just the reaction I was hoping for. I watch as he takes a step toward me, tilting his head.

"Oh, darlin'." He drops his voice to a low whisper, giving me another smirk. "I think you and I both know how talented I am with my hands."

"You always have to turn everything sexual," I tease.

"And you don't?" he counters.

We stand there in a stare off for what feels like forever. I want this. This is what I came for. I want the push and the pull. I want the back and forth. I want to be called on my bullshit. I want to be challenged.

I want Tucker.

"Why didn't you tell me about your daughter?" The question tumbles out of my mouth before I can even think about what I'm saying, and I watch as Tucker's walls go back up and he takes a step back. "Don't do that. Don't shut down on me now. I came all this way. I think I deserve an answer."

"Oh, don't think for one second I believe that shit." He picks up the piece of furniture he carried over from the corner and starts walking toward the truck. There's no way in hell I'm letting him dismiss me that quickly.

"Believe what shit?" I yell, wanting his attention.

He stops, setting the furniture back down and turning on me. "You didn't come down here just to talk to me. I think we've already agreed that you don't care about my personal life."

"No, you want to believe I don't care about your personal life, but I do. Okay? I care. I don't know why or how that happened, but somewhere between all the fucking and fighting I started to care. Shoot me!" My heart is practically pounding out of my chest and my fists are clenched so tight my nails are digging into my palms. I welcome the sting of pain. It's a release against the fury that's building inside me.

Tucker laughs a sardonic laugh. "Oh, this is rich. The girl who didn't want any complications or inconveniences is now the one who wants it all."

My jaw tightens and I have to work hard to not reach up and slap his beautiful face. I want him to shut up before he says something he'll regret—or something I'll hate him for—something that will break my heart.

"Believe me, Piper." His voice is softer when he says my name. "When I said I was saving you from complications, I meant it. My life is messy. It's complicated. It's more than you would ever want to handle."

"So, that's it? We're just over?" I can't help the pain laced through my words, because it hurts. "Things get real and you bail? Is that why you've never been in a serious relationship?"

"Don't," he warns.

"Don't what? Call you on your bullshit?" I square my shoulders, ready to face off with him. "You sure don't hesitate to call me on mine. Why shouldn't I return the favor?"

He swallows and then lets out a frustrated growl.

"You think I don't want this? That I don't want you?" He huffs out in frustration, shaking his head. "I want you, Piper. You have no idea how hard it's been for me to ignore your texts and phone calls, but I knew I couldn't let myself give in, because if I got the smallest taste of you, I'd be on the next plane to Birmingham. And I don't have that luxury anymore. I can't run off and meet you at any given time or place.

My life doesn't work like that anymore!" He's the one yelling now and I see the confliction on his face. There's a struggle going on and it's visible as he paces the yard between the barn and the house, like part of him wants to give into his instincts—back me up against the wall and show me how much he wants me—and the other part of him wants to run.

When he comes back to stand in front of me, his blue eyes lock with mine and I see him. For the first time in a long time, there're no walls or pretenses. It's just him and me.

"Tell me how your life works," I plead. "Tell me what to do to make this work."

His face falls as his eyes leave mine and go to the ground between us.

"It doesn't."

With those two words, my heart shatters. There was a time when I wondered if my heart even worked like other people's. I wasn't sure if I could fall in love or feel so strongly about someone that I'd want to be with them forever. At least now I know it's possible.

"I'm barely hanging on by a thread," he confesses, dropping any last bit of protective armor. "Most days, I'm playing it by ear, hoping I don't drown. I don't have the slightest clue what I'm doing or how I'm doing it. Sammy, my daughter, she's four and she's getting ready to lose her mother. I don't know how to deal with that. I'm guessing when the time comes, I'll figure it out, because I have to. She's the most important thing in my life now. She needs me and I can't let her down."

"I'm *so* sorry," I tell him, emotion thick in my voice, and I mean it, for everything.

"I'm sorry I didn't tell you," he replies, reaching out and grabbing my hand. The contact surprises me, but I squeeze it so he won't let go. "I wanted to. You're the only person I wanted to talk to about it when I first found out, but I didn't know if that was okay. Everything has been so confusing and complicated, and that's just not us."

"It wasn't us, but things change," I tell him, still holding onto a small thread of hope that maybe we can work this out.

"There's no way I can be in a relationship right now. I'd be horrible at it. You'd hate me," he says, giving me a small smile.

"I couldn't hate you. I tried that. It didn't work."

He laughs, pulling me into his chest and it feels so good. Breathing him in, I relish in the way his arms feel around me, and I can't help the tears that fill my eyes. I didn't give them permission, but they came anyway and it's all I can do to keep them from falling.

"I'm sorry," he whispers into my hair.

"Me too," I whisper back, letting one rogue tear slide down my cheek.

We stand there in silence for a few seconds, Tucker's arms wrapped around me and me holding onto him. Finally, he says "If I was writing a song about us, this isn't how I would end it."

His confession brings a smile to my face, but it also crushes me.

Love.

Hate.

Place.

Time.

All things we have no control over, yet they have the power to change everything.

CHAPTER SIXTEEN

I MISS HER.

There's a feeling deep down in my gut that I can't shake, and there's an ache in my chest I can't relieve. Telling Piper it wouldn't work between us—letting her go—was hard. I wouldn't say it's the hardest thing I've dealt with recently, but it ranks up there in the top three.

Becoming a dad to Sammy.

Coming to terms with Sophie dying.

Letting Piper go.

I'm still not sure I'm doing a very good job at the dad part, and I know for certain I'm not ready for Sophie to die. Who can ever be ready for that? But letting Piper go, that's a done deal. I haven't heard from her since last week. There haven't been any missed calls or late night texts.

She's the one who's gone radio silent now.

I knew she would. I knew after our talk, that it was over. I told her it was. I did that. So, why do I get up every morning and check my phone?

Habit?

Hope?

I don't know what I'm hoping for, though. Maybe for that stubborn streak that runs so deep through Piper to show up, and for her not to take my no for an answer, but I know that won't happen. I know that, because I know Piper fears rejection.

Her parents have done a number on her self-esteem. She may come off as confident, but deep down, she craves acceptance. It kills me to think she took what I said to her last week as rejection. It wasn't that at all.

I could never reject Piper.

I just reject my abilities to be in a relationship with her.

But I refuse to send her mixed signals, so I'll wait until she reaches out to me. She promised she'd call. So, when she's ready, I'm hoping she will.

I can't lose her completely.

But I also don't have time to sit around and dwell on my decision or how badly I miss her, because today's the day I'm moving into Cami and Deacon's old house. Between my personal belongings and things Kay and Cami have given me, I have quite a bit to get unloaded today.

When my phone rings, I jump on it.

"Hello?"

"Hey," Sophie's weak voice comes from the other end of the line.

"Hey. Is everything okay?" I ask, my mind always going to the worst-case scenario.

"Yeah, I just have a favor to ask." She's hesitant as usual, but I'm glad she's asking. I've learned over the last month or so that Sophie hates asking for help. If she has a bad quality, that's it.

"You know you don't even have to ask."

"Well," she says, pausing. "We moved Mamie into an assisted living facility today, and I'm exhausted...and Sammy's sad. I thought maybe a change of scenery would be good for her."

"How are you handlin' all this?" I ask, sensing the sadness and weariness in her voice and I also feel like there's more she's not saying.

"I'm hanging in there. What else can I do?"

"Maybe I should come stay in Houma for a couple of days. I can be there for Sammy and if you need my help with anything, I'll be there."

"I can't ask you to do that." She coughs and it immediately puts me on edge as she begins to wheeze while she's trying to catch her breath.

"Sophie?"

She coughs again and then takes another second to catch her breath.

"I'm fine."

"You don't sound fine."

There are no words spoken for a minute or more as we both sit on opposite ends, trying to put into words the inevitable and hating every moment of it.

"I'm dying, Tucker," she finally says. "I'm dying, and I hate it. I hate my body. I hate that I won't see Sammy turn five or go to school or graduate or get married. I hate it. All of it." Her voice is thick with emotion when she finally stops to take a breath.

I take one of my own, mustering up the courage to say what she needs to hear. "I know," I admit, more to myself than to her. "I hate it too. I want to take it all away. If I knew how, I would."

"I'm also tired," she confesses. "And I hate that too."

I don't know why she's telling me all of this. I don't know what's making her open up to me, but I'm glad. I'm glad she's talking. Sometimes, I feel like her words and actions are all so fucking planned they don't feel real. This is real. Anger is real.

"You've fought this for a long time. You have a right to be tired," I tell her, schooling my voice to not show the emotions that are clawing at my throat.

"I'm selfish. I'm so fucking selfish," she sobs. "Everything I've been doing is for me...for one more day. I've taken chemo, radiation, medicine...anything for one more day. And now, I don't want to do any of it anymore. I'm sick of being poked and prodded. And if one more doctor looks at me with pity and hopelessness, I'm going to scream."

"Don't say that. I mean, scream, if you want to. But don't say you're selfish. You're the least selfish person I know. All those things you mentioned, you did them for Sammy. *Everything* you do is for her."

She goes silent again. Her breathing is ragged. When she finally begins to speak, it's a whisper, like she's afraid to speak the words into the universe. "I think I'm ready for you to take her. For good."

"No," I tell her without a second thought.

She's not ready.

I'm not ready.

"You don't see the way she looks at me, Tucker," she cries. "You don't see the worry on her little face or the way she watches my every move. I can't live my last days like that."

"I won't let you steal these moments from her. She needs you, Sophie. She needs as much time with you as possible." I think these feelings are coming from deep down inside, somewhere that's been hidden since my mama died.

"It's not your choice," she says with a little more strength than she's managed at any other point in our conversation. "You promised you wouldn't let her watch me die. I'm dying!"

I take a deep breath, closing my eyes. "I'll be in Houma later tonight. We'll talk about it then."

She doesn't respond. I wait for her to, but the next thing I know, the line goes dead, and I'm left holding it to my ear in disbelief.

I'm not ready.

"Damn, Tucker, for a career bachelor who still lives with his parents, you sure do have a bunch of shit to move."

"Less whinin', more workin', Deke," Micah commands.

Deacon drops a box onto the living room floor that is now mine. "I'm not whinin', I'm just sayin'. The man has lived out of a suitcase for the last ten years, how on earth did he acquire so much crap?"

"Quit callin' my stuff crap, asshole," I tell him, pointing my finger his way. "And watch the floors. That hardwood is the real deal, you know."

"Dude, I just moved out of this house last week. Don't try to act like you know more about hardwood than I do."

"Oh, I know all about *hard wood*, don't worry." I grab my crotch for emphasis, making both of my friends roll their eyes and groan.

I'm also an expert on blue balls lately, but I'm not telling them that.

"Come on, let's start bringin' in the furniture." Micah slaps Deacon on the shoulder and heads out the front door. "The sooner we finish, the sooner we drink."

Damn, I've missed this. Even though we all still live relatively close to each other, the three of us don't get to hang out as much as we used to. I know we've each got things going on in our lives that keep us busy, and that's great, but sometimes I wish we could go back to when life was simpler.

I need a beer. It's way too early to be this sappy.

"Watch out, man," Micah calls out from the front porch. "We're headed to Sammy's room with this, right?"

"Yeah, just put it on the rug that's already laid out," I instruct.

As Micah and Deacon are setting the bed up, I run outside to grab the remaining pieces. When I'm back in the room, I lay the parts on the floor and help the guys finish up. Once Sammy's bed is complete, I take a step back and take it all in. This is now my house and my daughter has her own bed here. It's overwhelming in the best kind of way.

"A canopy bed, huh?" Deacon asks. "This is really nice. When did you have time to go shopping for it?"

"I made it," I admit. I'm proud of my work and I pray that Sammy loves it as much as I do, but I can't help but smile at the idea that Deacon thought this was made by a professional.

"No shit?" Micah questions.

I nod my head and try to fight the blush that I can feel warming my face.

"This is some amazing work, Tucker. You've really outdone yourself." Micah continues to admire the bed, running his hand along the smooth wood. I decided to leave it bare, with a light coat of finish. "It's heavy as fuck, too," he laughs while pushing on the footboard.

"Micah just ain't used to luggin' around heavy wood like we are, T. Bless his heart." Deacon slaps his knee, laughing at his own joke.

"What the hell ever. You both know I'm packin' just fine. You're just a jealous bitch, Deacon."

Deacon begins to respond, but I cut him off. "Do not mention my sister and the size of your dick in the same sentence in front of me, got it?"

"Fine," he concedes, crossing his arms over his chest with a pout.

"Anyway," Micah continues. "Little girls love this stuff, right? Sammy is gonna flip out."

I let out a deep breath. "I hope so. I just want her to feel comfortable and be happy, you know?"

The three of us walk into the kitchen and decide to take a beer break. Deacon tosses me and Micah a can before adding his two cents.

"I know your situation is fucked up, man, but you're kickin' ass with this whole parenting thing. Two months ago, I might not have thought you were ready to be a dad, but you've proved me wrong. I'm proud of you, bro."

Looking him squarely in the eye, I nod my head in thanks. "I really appreciate it, man. This has been the hardest thing I've ever went through, and we still have a long road ahead of us, but it's gettin' easier to imagine my life with Sammy now. Movin' into this house helps a lot, so thanks for that, Deacon."

He shrugs off my words and finishes his beer instead of speaking. Our conversations aren't usually this serious, but our friendship runs deep. Honestly, I don't know what I'd do without these two.

CHAPTER SEVENTEEN

Hopefully, things aren't as bad as Sophie made them out to be and I'll have a while longer to get myself together before Sammy comes to live with me.

Sammy *is* coming to live with me.

It's still something I'm coming to terms with. It's not that I don't want to have her—to see her every day and take care of her. I want that. But I know what it's like to lose your mother. I would've given anything for one more day with my mama. Cami would've too. So, I'll do whatever I need to do to make that happen for Sammy.

The drive to Houma is becoming so routine that I'm pulling onto Sophie's street before I know it, and just as the sun begins to set behind me. Parking along the curb, I hop out and walk up to the small gate. Before I can get the latch open, the front door swings wide and Sammy's smiling face is looking back at me.

"Hey there, sunshine."

"Hey there, Tucker," she says back to me. When she jumps down the steps and runs toward me, my heart tries to jump out of my chest and meet her halfway.

Every time she hugs me, it becomes a little less startling and chips away at the awkwardness between us. I realized, when she came and stayed for the weekend, I'm the one making it awkward. Kids don't know awkwardness. They don't know boundaries. They don't put their feelings in a box. They just live out loud and love even louder.

We could all learn a thing or two from them.

I hug her back fiercely, picking her up. "I missed you," I admit.

"I missed you too," she says solemnly, her little arms wrapped tightly around my neck.

"How's your mommy?" I ask, expecting Sophie to appear in the doorway at any second, but she doesn't.

"She's sick," she whispers.

"I know," I tell her, hugging her tighter to me. "She's tired."

"That's what mommy said." Her words are so matter-of-fact that it hurts me. She's wise beyond her years and it kills me that she's going through this.

When I sit her back down, kneeling in front of her, she reaches up and pushes my hair out of my face. "Where's your ponytail?"

I pull the pink holder out of my pocket and show her. She gave it to me when I brought her home last week. She told me to keep it and practice on my hair, so I'd be better the next time I do hers.

"I think you need to use it." She scrunches up her face, totally judging my hair.

I laugh, loving her honesty. "Wanna do it for me?"

Her eyes light up. "Yes."

"Have you had dinner?"

"No." She shakes her head, making her blonde curls bounce.

"Okay, let's go inside. You fix my hair and I'll make grilled cheeses for dinner."

"Deal."

She holds her hand out to me, like I often do to her, and I take it, following her inside.

Later, after Sammy has eaten two grilled cheeses, complimenting me on my skills, we're sitting in the living room as Sophie begins to stir on the couch.

"Sammy?" she croaks out and Sammy runs to her side, offering her a drink of water.

She's been asleep most of the time I've been here, waking once calling out for Sammy. When she saw I was here, her entire body deflated in relief and she's been asleep since.

I've checked on her periodically, as has Sammy. Being here with them like this, I see what Sophie's talking about. Sammy doesn't get too far from Sophie and even when she's wrapped up in play or a television show, every so often, she stops what she's doing to check on Sophie.

Earlier when I was in the kitchen, fumbling my way around, I called out for Sammy, but she didn't answer. Walking around the counter, I saw her kneeled beside the couch where Sophie slept. She watched her so intently, almost like she was counting her breaths and I wondered how often she does that. How many days are spent right there beside her mother as she sleeps.

My heart broke.

"Tucker?" Sophie's voice is weak, so I walk over where she can see me without moving.

"Hey," I greet her, looking down at a shell of the person I met only a little while ago. Someone who walked into my barn and changed my life forever. I hate seeing her like this. I can only imagine what it's doing to Sammy.

"Thanks for coming." She gives me a weak smile, but I know she means it.

"Anything I can do?" I ask, wanting to feel useful.

"No." She shakes her head and slowly starts to sit up, adjusting the pillow behind her. "I'm fine," she says, offering Sammy a small smile and a squeeze of her little hand that's still resting on Sophie's arm.

"How 'bout I start Sammy a shower," I suggest.

Sophie looks at the clock on the wall, realizing the hour. "Oh, yeah. That'd be good."

"I don't wanna go to bed yet," Sammy whines, sounding like any other kid her age, for once. "I wanna stay up with you and Tucker."

"How about after your shower, I read you a book?" Sophie suggests.

Sammy's whine turns around on a dime. "Okay."

"That's my girl."

As I'm following Sammy down the hall toward the bathroom, I turn around to see Sophie watching us. Her face is shadowed with sadness and exhaustion, but I also see a hint of happiness there too.

"I left you a grilled cheese on a plate in the microwave," I tell her. "Want me to get it for you?"

"No, I need to get up. Thank you, though."

"No problem," I tell her, wishing for anything other than our current situation.

It's not that I feel anything romantic toward Sophie, but I feel for her...I feel admiration and respect. I'm so thankful for this small person she brought into this world—*we* brought into this world. I'm grateful for her taking such good care of Sammy for all the years I didn't know her. I just wish things were different. I wish it so bad that I can't swallow down the enormous lump in my throat.

"Not too hot and not too cold," Sammy instructs, stepping up on a stool to grab a fluffy pink towel from the shelf above the toilet.

"Right," I tell her, remembering this routine from the last time. "I'll lay you some pajamas out on your bed, okay?"

"Pink ones," she says.

"Sure you don't need any help?" I ask, always feeling weird leaving her to it. I know Cami said she's fine and I trust her, but I just don't want anything bad to happen to her.

"I'm big." That annoyed expression and tone she used with me and Cami at the farm is back.

"Okay." I hold up my hands in surrender.

"Tucker?" she asks, right before I close the door.

"Yes?"

"You can sit outside the bathroom."

I nod, trying to keep a straight face until the door is closed, leaving it cracked an inch, just in case. She's way too smart for her britches. If she knows I'm sitting outside of the bathroom keeping an eye on her at four, what is she going to figure out at sixteen?

Oh, God.

What will she be like at sixteen?

She's never dating.

Ever.

Maybe we'll become Amish.

What are their policies on dating?

I'm at least in favor of their dress code.

When Sammy is tucked into bed and Sophie is exhausted from reading practically her entire shelf of books, we sit down in the living room. The house is quiet, too quiet really. It's void of Sammy's adorable chatter, so I feel the need to fill it.

"What will happen to the house?" It's a random question, but one I'm sure Sophie's thought about. She's thought of everything.

"We rent it. Now that Mamie's things are gone, there will just be mine and Sammy's stuff and we really don't have much. I've donated things and given things away. The biggest items that'll need moving is the furniture, but I told the landlord he can have it all or give it to the next people who rent the place."

I nod, clearing my throat. "What about your stuff?"

"Well, like I said, I've donated a lot. All I have is in a few boxes in the bedroom, one of them with Sammy's name on it. It's stuff I want her to have later down the road. I contacted a hospice facility earlier today. My doctor suggested it, knowing that I don't have anyone around and well..." she pauses, taking a deep breath. "He said he can't tell me how much time I have, could be a few weeks to a few months. Days even. It's not something he can predict. It's mostly just time and whether or not I catch some crazy illness. Usually, what kills people isn't the cancer, it's the body's inability to fight off sickness."

Everything she's saying I already know. I've been doing research. But again, it makes me feel good that she's opening up to me. I want her to feel like she can talk to me about anything. She needs someone and I want to be there for her.

"What would the hospice facility be like?" I ask, trying to get a grip on what she's telling me.

"It's a place, like a hospital for terminally ill patients. My

Medicaid will pay for it. All I needed was for my doctor to make the recommendation, which he did, months ago."

"You don't have to do that." The words come out of my mouth before I think them over or consider the consequences. "You can stay with me. I'll take care of you and Sammy. I've been working on setting up my house. There's plenty of room—"

"No." Her reply is swift and firm, matching the hard expression on her face. "That's not what I want. It's..." She swallows. "It's a really kind gesture, but I can't. I don't want Sammy around when things get bad. She'll be scared and worried...all the things I've been trying to avoid."

I sit and consider her words, knowing that's one of the reasons she sought me out in the first place. But this part is so hard, much harder than I ever expected. How can I just allow her to go into a hospice facility and die alone? It goes against everything inside me.

"So, you're ready?" I ask, needing her to tell me face-to-face that she's ready for me to take Sammy—ready for this to be over, ready for this final step.

"Can we ever be ready to die?" Her dark curly hair is framing her face, making her look so young. Way too young to be dealing with death. Way too young to plan the end of her life.

"No," I tell her sincerely. "We can't. I remember when my mama died, it took us all by surprise. She was sick and then she was gone. One night, I overheard some of the ladies from church talking about how at least she didn't suffer. It pissed me off. I wanted to yell at them and I didn't even know why, but I just knew there was nothing good about my mama dying. Not that I would've wanted her to suffer, but I wanted more time with her. I wanted time to prepare. But, now that I'm older, I realize there's no such thing."

"You're gonna be good for her," Sophie says, picking at a thread on the blanket that's across her lap. "You know what it's like. She's lucky to have you."

"I don't know about that," I admit, shaking my head. "Every day since you showed up in the barn, all I've thought about is that I'm gonna mess this up."

"Every parent worries about that. I think, if you don't worry about messing your kids up, you're not doing it right." Sophie laughs lightly and then coughs, but it's good to see a smile on her face. I love that she still finds light in the darkness. She can still laugh when everything in her life is so sad. I hope Sammy has that kind of fight and optimism. "You're not gonna mess her up or break her. I thought that for the first year of her life, but it was Mamie that talked some sense into me. She said kids are much more resilient than we realize. They're gonna fall and get bumps and bruises, but that's all part of life. Every trial and tribulation they go through is what molds them into the adults they become. So, don't be afraid of failure."

"How did someone so young get so wise?" I ask, dumbfounded by her strength. "I don't know how you're still so strong."

"It's Sammy," Sophie says. "She's been my lifeline. If it wasn't for her, I would've been dead years ago. She saved me, gave me purpose. I just wish…" her voice breaks, and I see the tears in her eyes, tears I'm not prepared for, but feel deep in my soul.

"She's gonna remember it…all of it," I tell her, my own voice breaking. "I'm gonna make sure of it."

She swallows down her emotions, wiping at her eyes with the blanket. "I'll never be able to say thank you enough or repay you, but just know you have my eternal gratitude."

I lay my hand on top of hers and give a squeeze as I stand up and head to the kitchen. It's getting late and I want to make sure everything is cleaned up before I leave. I wash the few remaining dishes in the sink and place them on a clean towel so they can air-dry overnight.

When I turn off the faucet is when I hear the crash.

I run back into the living room and find Sophie on the floor between the couch and the coffee table.

"Fuck," I spit out, rushing to her side. I check for her pulse and am relieved when I find it, but it's weak and she doesn't react when I say her name or touch her face. Grabbing my phone out of my back pocket, I dial 9–1–1 and glance down the hallway, checking to see if Sammy has heard any of this. Thankfully, she hasn't but I know I'll need to wake her after the ambulance gets here.

She's going to be so scared.

Who am I kidding? I'm fucking scared, too.

Within twenty minutes, the ambulance has arrived and Sophie has been placed on a stretcher to be taken to the emergency room. She still hasn't regained consciousness and I fear this may be the end for her.

What if our conversation was the last thing she'll ever say?

My stomach is twisted in knots and I'm shaking all over but I continue to give the paramedics all the information I can. Once they're ready to leave, the paramedic I'd been talking to pats me on the back and tries to assure me they'll do their best with Sophie. I nod my head in understanding and thank them before running into the house to wake Sammy.

Later, at the hospital, I'm sitting in the waiting room with Sammy asleep in my lap. She wasn't budging when I tried to wake her up at her house, so I just wrapped her in a blanket and carried her to my truck. I buckled her in the best I could since I didn't have a car seat for her and my right hand never left her little body, as I drove quickly but safely to the hospital. We've now been here about thirty minutes. Sammy stirred for a minute but I reassured her that I had her and she fell back asleep.

I'm struggling to stay awake myself when a doctor finally comes to give me an update.

"Are you Sophie's husband or boyfriend?" he asks.

"No, but I'm her friend. I'm the only person she has, really, besides our daughter here." I glance down at Sammy in my arms.

The doctor takes a deep breath and releases it before continuing. "Sophie is conscious now but, as I'm sure you realize, she's not doing well."

"Yeah, I know."

"Are you two living together? Does she have a home health worker checking on her?"

"No, like I said, I'm all she has and I just happened to be at her house tonight."

I watch the doctor scratch the stubble on his chin as he thinks of what to say next. Maybe he's thinking of *how* to say it instead. His job can't be an easy one.

"Sophie won't be able to go home. She's too sick, and at this point, she's going to need around the clock care. I hate to be so direct, but there's no time to beat around the bush. Her time is short. I'm recommending she be placed into a hospice facility as soon as she's stable enough to transport. I've looked over her chart and there's not anything left we can do for her, besides keep her as comfortable as possible."

"She was just telling me tonight that her doctor had already set her up with one," I inform him.

I hate that she was right, that the doctor was right.

This is happening too fast.

"I'll contact her primary doctor and get the transfer paperwork started."

"Can I see her? Can *we* see her?"

He lets out a deep sigh. "I don't think that's a good idea right now. She's conscious, but her vitals are weak. The nurses are cleaning her up right now. My advice would be to go home and get some rest. When she's set up at the new facility, someone will call you."

The doctor offers his hand for me to shake, so I take it but I don't look at him. My eyes are glued to the little girl snuggled up against my chest, knowing she's now my full responsibility.

"Where's Mommy?" A sleepy Sammy asks about five miles out of town. It's now three o'clock in the morning and we're almost to French Settlement.

I was going to go back to Sophie's house for the rest of the night, but it just didn't feel right. So, I drove over there long enough to grab her car seat and the boxes Sophie packed up for her and we left.

"Mommy's in the hospital." I think about softening the truth, but there's no benefit to that. I don't want Sammy to be blindsided by Sophie's death. It's inevitable at this point, so she needs to know.

"Where are we going?" Her voice is a little unsure, but I expected that. It's a lot for *me* to take in, so I can only imagine what's going through her mind.

"We're going home, to my house...our house." I correct myself and reach over to smooth her hair back. "Is that okay?"

"Okay," she says, looking over at me. In the darkness, I can barely make out her petite features, but what I see is a little girl who's scared.

"It's gonna be alright," I tell her, wishing I could give her a hug, but we're almost to the house, so I keep driving.

Before we turn off the main road, I glance over to see that Sammy's dozed back off. When we pull up in the drive, I'm glad I left a light on in the living room because even though this was Cami and Deacon's house, it's still new to me.

Walking around the truck, I decide to get Sammy out first. I'm also glad that Micah and Deacon helped me get her bed put together. At least, she'll have a place to sleep—somewhere to call her own.

"Mommy?" Sammy mumbles sleepily.

"Shhh. I got you," I assure her.

"Daddy," she says so quietly as she nestles her head on my shoulder, wrapping her arms around my neck.

I freeze in the middle of the driveway, my heart pounding in my chest.

That's the first time she's called me anything besides Tucker. It makes me squeeze her a little tighter. I want to ask her to say it again, but she's sound asleep. I wonder if she'll remember in the morning.

Unlocking the door, I take a second to look around the place. There are still a couple of boxes left to unpack and not much on the walls, but the things that are in here are mine. Tomorrow, I'll add Sammy's.

I've always known that it's not the things you have that make a home, it's the people inside.

Hopefully, Sammy will feel like this is her home.

CHAPTER EIGHTEEN

"These pancakes aren't as good as Kay's," Sammy says as she crams another bite in her mouth.

I laugh, shaking my head. "Give me a break, kid. That's my first attempt."

"You'll get better." Her words are mumbled as she talks around a mouth full of food.

If I've learned nothing else about my spunky little girl, I've learned she's honest, sometimes to a fault, but it's okay. I love that about her. I love always knowing what's on her mind. It makes me hopeful that we'll make it through these next few weeks.

After our visit to the hospice facility yesterday, I'm afraid that Sophie only has a few more days, maybe less. She was only awake for a brief time while we were there, but it was enough time for her to acknowledge Sammy, giving her the connection she needed with her mom.

Since Sophie passed out in the middle of the night and Sammy slept through most of it, she didn't understand that her mom was super sick. She needed to see her. She needed that concrete proof, something tangible to help her process.

"After you're finished with my mediocre pancakes, how about we go out to Annie and Sam's to play with Carter?"

"Yes," Sammy replies excitedly, stuffing the last bite into her mouth. "I'm ready. Is Aunt Cami gonna be there?"

"No, Aunt Cami is at the art studio, but we can visit her, if you want. I'm sure she'd love to see you."

It's been my goal this week to keep Sammy busy. I've noticed when it's just the two of us at the house, her questions about her mom are more intense. She thinks about everything and it's too much for a four-year-old. I know she needs to think about it some, but I don't want it becoming all she thinks about, so we play with Carter as much as possible and visit everyone. She's even been to Grinders for lunch, and yesterday, we stopped by the old Pockets site to see the new walls being built.

She thought that was awesome.

Tomorrow, I'll take her back to see her mom, but for today, I want her to be four.

"Go get your shoes from your room while I clean up this mess," I tell her, smiling as she skips down the hallway.

We're still adjusting and things aren't smooth sailing, but we're getting there.

Sammy's had a few meltdowns. The first time she fell apart over me choosing the wrong bow to match her dress, I stood in her doorway like a deer in headlights. I had no clue what to do, so I just let her cry it out. When she was ready to talk, we talked. And I called my sister who assured me that it won't be the last time and to expect her to be irrational about things. For one, she's four. For another, she's going through changes most adults can't handle.

So, we're taking it slow—day by day.

I still make mistakes—like choosing the wrong bow or not knowing what pants go with what shirt.

Sammy still has meltdowns from time to time.

But I'm learning and so is Sammy. She's teaching me what acceptance looks like and what true love is. I'm teaching her that it's okay to feel however you want to feel and that I'll be here for her, no matter what.

As I'm drying the pan I used for pancakes, my phone rings from the living room. Running in to grab it, I see No Caller ID on the screen and my heart stops, and then starts back up, double time.

By the time I realize I need to answer it if I want to talk to her, it's too late. The ringing stops and it goes to voicemail. I wait, hoping for a message to pop up, but it never does.

"Ready!" Sammy exclaims from the hallway. "I got my shoes!"

"Uh, just a second," I tell her, holding up a finger. "I need to make a phone call."

"Okay," she sighs, plopping down on the couch.

When I go to hit redial, nerves flood my body. I don't know why. She called me. All I'm doing is calling her back. So, why the sweaty palms?

The phone rings and rings. Just as I'm getting ready to hit end, Piper answers, "Hello?"

"Hey," I say.

"Hey." She sounds perplexed or caught off guard.

"You called me?" It comes off more as a question than a statement, but I'll be damned if it isn't good to hear her voice. Just the two words she's said are enough to relieve the ache in my chest. I've missed her, more than I'd like to admit.

"I did?" she asks and I don't know if she's playing dumb or if she's serious.

"Yeah, I just missed your call, like a minute ago."

"Oh." She laughs, somewhat nervous sounding herself. "I'm sorry. I must've butt-dialed you." There's a rustling sound and then a thud.

"Piper?"

"Sorry," she yells. "I dropped the phone. Hold on."

A few seconds later, the rustling is back, along with a winded Piper.

"I can tell this is a bad time," I tell her. "I just thought you—"

"No, I'm just running stupid errands and have my hands full. I'm really sorry I called you on accident...well, not sorry I called you, just—"

"It's fine. Really."

"You doing okay?" she asks and it makes my heart pound harder.

"Yeah, we're makin' it."

"We're?"

"Me and Sammy," I clarify.

"So, she's living with you now?"

"Yeah, just the last few days."

"Oh, well, I hope everything's going well."

"It's goin'," I tell her, not wanting to say too much in front of Sammy.

"Sounds like you probably can't talk right now either," Piper says. "Tell you what, how about I call you back later? Maybe after bedtime?"

I laugh, smiling as if she can see me. "Sounds good. Like, nine-ish?"

"Nine-ish."

"Hope you have a good day," I tell her, knowing she needs to go, but not wanting to let her.

"Thanks, you too."

"Later."

The phone goes dead and I stand there for a second, holding it to my chest.

"Who was that?" Sammy asks with a funny expression on her face. Her little nose is scrunched up and she's tilting her head looking at me, as I scramble to think of the right answer.

"That was Piper—my, uh, friend."

"Is it a girl or a boy?"

"She's a girl."

"Does she have blonde hair like us?"

I laugh, shaking my head. "No, it's dark brown, like this," I say, holding up one of my favorite guitars. It's made from mahogany, and ever since I met Piper, I've thought of her every time I pick it up. Which is probably why I've been using it to write a song these past few days.

All my woodworking stuff is still out at the barn, so after Sammy goes to bed, I've been left with nothing but my guitar and time to think. It never fails that my thoughts turn to Piper. Every lyric that's come to me lately has been about her.

"That's pretty," Sammy says. "I wanna hear you play it, like last night. I heard you play a song."

"Oh, really?" I ask. "Weren't you supposed to be asleep?" I walk toward her, hands out in a tickle motion.

"Yes," she giggles, crawling away from me. "But it was pretty."

I reach in for a tickle and then hug her to me. "I'll play for you later, after we go play with Carter."

"Okay," she agrees, hugging me back.

On the short drive out to Sam and Annie's, I glance over to Sammy. The windows are rolled down and she has her eyes closed, letting the breeze blow her hair.

"Do you like it here?" I ask, needing to know if she's happy.

"Uh huh," she replies, opening her eyes, but keeping them on the passing trees. "Mommy likes it here too."

"She does?" I know she needs to talk about her mom, so I let her.

"She said it's a happy place."

"I've always thought so."

"I wish she could live here too."

I know she means that, but I know she also knows that her mom is dying. Sophie told me that she's talked to her about it, not wanting her to be scared, but wanting her to be aware. So, I know when she says things like that it's more of a wish than anything. However, seeing that she's big into fairytales, I don't want her to get her hopes up, just to have them crushed.

"Me too." It's all I can say, anything else feels like it would either feed the fantasy or crush the dream, and I can't bring myself to do either.

When we get to the big house, Annie is waiting for us on the front porch.

"There she is," Annie gushes, holding her arms out for Sammy.

The two of them have become fast friends.

Annie and Kay came over the first day Sammy was here and surprised her with princess bedding for her princess bed. But I don't think it's the gift that got Sammy hooked on Annie. It's deeper than that. There's a connection between them that goes beyond materialistic things. I think for Annie, it's a connection to my mom, plus Sammy is the first little girl she's had to mother since Cami was little. For Sammy, I think she's senses what we all know already—Annie is a mom in every sense of the word. She's a soft place to land. Sammy needs as much of that as she can get right now.

While Carter and Sammy run around back and begin to play, Annie and I find a comfortable spot on the porch to watch them.

"How're things goin'?" Annie asks, keeping her eyes on the kids as they used some old wood and begin building what looks like a castle.

"Good, I guess." I shrug. "I mean, I still feel like it's the blind leading the blind, but I think we're figuring it all out slowly, but surely."

"Has she talked about Sophie much?"

"Some, I try to let her talk when she brings her up, but I worry about her. I worry about her worrying." I laugh, but it's not out of humor. It's because this is all so fucked up and even though on the outside it looks like I'm dealing, on the inside, I'm a mess. "What happens when she's gone?"

Annie sits there quietly for a second, collecting her thoughts.

"She's gonna be fine. It might not be immediate, but eventually she will be. There will always be a hole there. She'll always miss her mama. Look at you and Cami...and Clay...and me. We all miss Jessie, even after all these years, but life goes on. And just like Jessie, Sophie wants that, especially for Sammy."

"I know. She's told me."

"Sammy's lucky to have you," Annie says, reaching over to pat my hand. "When I see the two of you together and think about the circumstances, it's evident that God always has a plan, even when we can't see it."

"I've thought about that, too," I admit.

"You should tell her about Jessie," Annie encourages. "It'll help her, when the time is right."

"She would've loved her," I say, looking out at Sammy running around a tree with Carter hot on her heels.

"Oh, Tucker, I see so much of Jessie in your girl. Cami, too. They have the same childlike wonder and fantastic imaginations. I believe they got it from your mama. But, don't worry. There's plenty of you in that precious child. She's wild and brave and full of life. And, if I'm not mistaken, she's already a daddy's girl."

"I don't know about that, but I'd say she has me firmly wrapped around her little finger. I just don't want to let her down."

"You won't, sweetheart. Parents make mistakes, but it's how you learn and grow from them that matter. Just continue to love that baby girl with all your heart. The two of you are gonna be just fine."

She pats my hand again, and I can tell by the mischievous look in her eyes, she's not done with me.

"I also don't want you to put a wall up when it comes to finding love. I see what you're doing, putting everything on hold for Sammy, and that's very admirable of you. But, Tucker, honey, there's plenty of love to go around. Trust me, your heart is so big; it needs to be shared, and not just with Sammy. Don't be selfish with it, you understand?"

I swallow, wondering how she knows exactly what I need to hear without even knowing what's going on in my life.

I give her a smile and nod, which she returns with a knowing look in her eye.

"I see things," she says. "And I know things. I know that little girl is gonna need someone and be a second mama to her. Sure, she has me and Kay and Cami and Dani, and that's all fine and dandy. We're all more than happy to step in, but she'll need someone to call her own."

"You were that for me," I admit, wondering if I've ever told her thank you for all the times she stepped in and filled the huge gap my mama left behind.

"I was happy to do it."

"Thanks, Mama A."

CHAPTER NINETEEN

"You ready to go see your mama?"

"Yes, yes, yes!" Sammy jumps up and down while waiting for me to open her door to the truck. Once she's buckled in her car seat, I take my place behind the wheel and start the truck.

"Want to listen to some tunes?" I ask.

"Yes, please. Play the tunes we listened to yesterday!" she exclaims, clapping her hands.

"Classic rock, it is, m'lady." I give her a wink, then plug my phone into the outlet before starting up the playlist she requested.

"Thank you, m'daddy." She tries really hard to wink back at me and I swear, it's the cutest thing I've ever seen.

My heart still squeezes every time Sammy calls me "daddy". Sometimes she'll call me by my name but "daddy" seems to be winning out. I freaking love it. I had no idea what it'd feel like to be someone's dad, but it's the greatest feeling in the world, second only to when I was with Piper.

We're well into our trip to Houma when our classic rock jam session is interrupted by a phone call.

Glancing at my phone, I see *No Caller ID* on the screen.

Speak of the devil.

"Hey, Sammy, you wanna answer my phone for me? Just slide your finger across the screen, then say hello."

"Okay. I can do it." I watch out of the corner of my eye as she grabs my phone from the console. She's concentrating so much, her little tongue is sticking out but I make sure to stifle my amusement. I worry the call is going to go to voicemail before she answers but she manages to swipe the screen just in time. Quickly, I reach over and put the call on speakerphone.

"Hello? This is Sammy, who is this?"

Piper waits a few beats before answering. "Well, hello, Sammy. I'm Piper. Is Tucker busy?"

"Piper? You're Daddy's friend, huh? The one with brown hair," she states matter of factly.

"That's me. It's nice to meet you. Are you having a good day?"

"Yes. Me and Daddy are drivin' to see my mama at the hospital. That's why I answered the phone. Daddy's not supposed to talk on the phone while drivin'. It's dangerous."

"You're right, it is. I'm glad you're there to take care of your daddy."

I hear the slight emphasis Piper puts on daddy and it makes me smile.

"Me too. He needs all the help he can get," Sammy continues in a dramatic tone.

"Hey, now," I interject. "Who told you that?"

"Uncle Deke," she answers. "He even said to bless your heart."

Piper's laughter is loud and beautiful through the phone's speaker, and I really wish I was hearing it in person. She's never been one to show her playful, fun side to just anyone, or maybe she was more selective with me for some reason. Whatever the case, I quickly learned how rare and precious her laughs and giggles are and treasured each and every one she shared with me.

"Well, I won't keep you," Piper says, clearing her throat. "I can call back another time."

"No, it's fine. We've got a good ten miles left to drive. What's up?" I ask.

"Just calling."

It's then that I hear something in her voice I don't like—tired, weary. I'm sure, but I'm sure she won't tell me what's wrong knowing Sammy's listening in.

"How's your day goin'?" I ask, smiling over at Sammy who's just enjoying the ride.

"Oh, you know, work," Piper says with a sigh. "Don't grow up, Sammy. You have to get a job and sometimes your boss is stinky."

Sammy laughs, like it's the funniest thing she's heard all day. "He needs to take a shower!"

I wish Piper could see the way Sammy's holding her nose, so she can get a full picture of the four-year-old humor.

"He does, Sammy. He definitely needs a shower." Piper laughs again and I'm hoping that whatever's going on, maybe this phone call will help.

I mean, Sammy is living sunshine.

"I'm glad I got to talk to you, Sammy," Piper says. "Maybe we can hang out one of these days."

"You should come to Nanny Annie's. We're having a tea party with Grandma Kay, Aunt Cami, and Aunt Dani," Sammy says, listing off the people on her fingers. "Nanny Annie says we're having fancy sandwiches and Aunt Dani's making cookies!"

She gets more excited with each passing word.

"That sounds amazing. I wish I could come." Piper sighs.

"You can!" Sammy speaks animatedly to the phone, like Piper can see her. Maybe we should FaceTime next time.

"Did you know Dani is my best friend?" Piper asks.

"I didn't know that," Sammy says, looking over at me. "Daddy didn't tell me."

"Well, she is. I'm glad she gets to hang out with you."

"You should hang out too."

"One of these days, Sammy." The melancholy is back in Piper's voice. "Well, it was great talking to you, but I've gotta go. My stinky boss needs me to run errands."

"Tell him to take a shower!" Sammy yells out.

Piper laughs. "I'm gonna do that, Sammy. I hope you have a good visit with your mom."

"I'll talk to you later," I say, before she gets a chance to hang up, hoping she'll call back later when we can talk more.

"Yeah, we'll talk later."

The phone goes silent and I glance over to make sure the call ended.

"She's nice," Sammy says. "I like her. Maybe she wants to be my best friend, too."

This time, it's me who laughs.

"I bet she'd like that. You can ask her next time she calls."

A vision of Piper and Sammy together hits me like a brick wall, nearly stealing my breath. What I wouldn't give for that vision to be a reality, but I don't know how. Would Piper even want something like that? Would she want what I have to offer?

I don't know.

Everything has changed so much since Piper and I first started out—she's changed, I've changed, my entire life has changed. But even before Sammy, I knew that my feelings for Piper were growing. Looking back, I was falling before I ever realized it. Maybe Piper was too. Maybe that's where the struggle was coming from—both of us feeling the pull, but pushing it away because that's not what we'd intended to happen.

There're so many *what ifs* that float through my mind on a daily basis, but all I have time for are the *right nows*.

A few minutes later, we pull into the hospice facility and I say a silent prayer that Sophie is having a good day. Sammy needs it. After the talk I had with the nurse on the phone yesterday, I know that Sophie's organs are shutting down and her vitals have been low. She encouraged me to come visit and bring Sammy.

I'm not stupid. I know what that means.

Taking a deep breath, I jump out of the truck and walk around to help Sammy out.

"Got your card for Mommy?" I ask.

"Yep." Sammy holds up the pink card she made. It's a little worse for wear, but Sophie will love it, regardless. "I hope she's not sleeping today."

"Me too, sunshine."

Please Lord, let her have one more good day.

"Hello, Sammy. Tucker." The nurse who's always sitting outside of Sophie's room greets us with a smile and I take that as a good sign.

"Hello," Sammy says cheerfully. "I brought my mommy a card."

"Oh, she's gonna love that. Let's see if she's awake." She gives me a small smile as Sammy goes into Sophie's room.

"It's a good day," she whispers. "I'm glad you brought her."

Sophie doesn't look better. She's lost weight, too much weight, and her eyes are practically sunk into her once-round face. But she's still beautiful, especially when she smiles at Sammy.

"Mommy." Sammy's entire face lights up when she sees Sophie awake. Her bed is inclined enough that she's almost sitting.

"Hey, baby girl."

"I made this for you," Sammy says, walking to the side of the bed.

"Get up here and tell me about it." Sophie pats the bed beside her.

I walk over and help Sammy up, giving Sophie a smile.

Thank you, she mouths.

I shake my head, because I have no words and because I need no thanks.

Stepping back, I watch as Sammy and Sophie fall into perfect cadence. Sophie mostly listens as Sammy tells her about the card, and then she goes into a story about being at Sam and Annie's last week when a huge butterfly landed on her arm. That's where she got the inspiration for the card.

"I was gonna draw you a castle," Sammy says. "But I thought you'd like a butterfly better. I'll make you a castle next time."

"I love it," Sophie says.

I watch her work hard to school her emotions, trying to just be in this moment with Sammy.

There's not much to her voice. It's barely above a whisper. But talking to Sammy is a labor of love. She wants this. She wants these last moments.

"I'm gonna walk down and get some coffee," I tell them, wanting to give them some space. "Can I get you anything?"

Sophie shakes her head as she reaches up and slowly runs a hand through Sammy's curls.

She didn't want a ponytail today. She needed a yellow headband to match her dress.

"Need anything, sunshine?"

"No, Daddy," Sammy says and I see the look on Sophie's face—something between shock and awe, but happy.

Leaving them to their talk, I walk out of the room and find a chair down the hall.

CHAPTER TWENTY
Piper

W\ALKING OUT OF THE ELEVATOR FOR THE UMPTEENTH TIME TODAY, I hear Drake calling my name down the hall.

"Grey!"

I don't respond. I'm moving as fast as I can with three cups of coffee and his pants from the dry cleaner, along with the proofs from a photo shoot and my big ass bag.

"Grey!" he bellows again, just as I get to his door.

Again, I don't respond.

I'm here.

I have his fucking coffee and his fucking pants, and I'm so fucking done.

These past two months have been my own living hell. I know, in the grand scheme of things, it's not the worst. I mean, Tucker's dealing with a dying mom and becoming a dad for fuck's sake.

I should be able to deal with a dick for a boss.

I should be able to be a professional and separate myself from the menial tasks he asks of me and go about my fucking life.

But I can't.

I don't want to.

I'm miserable.

And I miss Tucker.

And that pisses me off.

Everything pisses me off.

"I need you to take this to the Williams Building," he says, handing me a manila envelope, but never making eye contact. "The address is on the front. It needs to be there in the next fifteen minutes, but before you go, I sent an email for the restaurant my meeting is at tomorrow. You need to call and confirm my reservation."

"No." I drop the proofs on his desk.

"What?"

"No." I say it a little louder and a little firmer this time.

That finally gets his attention and he glares up at me.

"I don't think I heard you correctly. What did you say?" His tone is lethal, matching the angle of his jaw, daring me to defy his requests.

"I'm not doing it, none of it. I'm an editor. That's my job. If you want me to do *that*, I'm more than happy to, but I'm not being your errand girl. I'm not your scapegoat. I'm not someone you can talk down to. I refuse to jump through your fucking hoops anymore."

"You do remember who you're talking to, right? Is it hot outside? Did the heat go to your head? Make you stupid? I think you remember our conversation and what our agreement was."

"Not anymore. There's no agreement. If you want to fire me over a fucking video, then go ahead, because I'm so done." I draw the last few words out as my shoulders begin to sag under the relief of getting them off my chest.

"You're right." He shoves his hands in his pockets, walking around the desk like the cocky bastard he is. "You're done," he says in a low growl. "And I will ruin you. Don't think for one second you'll ever work in the publishing industry again."

Fire blazes in my veins as I square my shoulders, mustering up every ounce of courage I have left. "I'll be filing a complaint on my way out, accompanied with all of the texts messages and emails you've sent me over the past two months, the ridiculous demands you've made. I'm not a lawyer, but I believe that's coercion."

I don't know if anything I just said is true, but I don't care. Slinging my purse over my shoulder, I storm out of his office and make my way to the elevator, not even stopping at my office to collect my things. I'll get them later or never. There's nothing in there worth having to face him again.

As the elevator doors close, I see him watching me from the hallway, his face red with anger.

Before he's out of sight, I flip him off, making my feelings clear.

Fuck him.

Fuck the video.

Let him show that fucking video. I don't even care anymore. I let out a pained growl as I feel the emotions creeping up my throat—every second of suppressed frustration, every moment of restrained anger, every bit of buried hurt—it's begging to be released.

Somehow, I manage to keep it together until I'm outside of the building, walking swiftly down the sidewalk, until I bump into someone not paying attention to where they're going. It's then that I take a second to think and promptly fall apart.

Bending over, I rest my hands on my knees as I try to control my breathing and fend off a panic attack as the tears sting my eyes.

Holy shit.

I just quit my job.

Or got fired.

What the fuck?

And then again, good fucking riddance.

My heart is at war with my head when I hear a familiar voice call my name.

It's not Drake the Dick.

Quite the opposite.

More like Greg the Gentleman.

"Piper?" he asks with a hint of concern. "Hey, are you okay?"

I don't even try to pretend I'm not falling apart. Shaking my head,

I bite down on my lip to try to keep the tears from falling. This isn't me. I'm not this girl. But for once in my life, I can't put on a good face.

"I, uh, just got fired...or quit," I say with an edge of distaste as the words leave my mouth. "I haven't decided. But I'm definitely unemployed." My voice cracks and I blow out a harsh breath, smoothing my hair back.

"Do you want to get a drink?" he asks, examining me with his dark eyes.

This isn't the first time he's asked me out. About a week after I met him at the airport, he called and asked me out for dinner. A week later, he emailed me about meeting for lunch. I turned him down both times.

It's too soon.

But I need a drink. And he's offering. And I don't want to drink alone.

"Okay."

The smile that splits his face is alarming, because I can see him getting his hopes up, but I hate to tell him they're futile. Nothing's changed. I'm still crazy about Tucker...my heart belongs to him. Even though I'm pissed that he's shutting me out and I'm hurt that he thinks all I want is a convenient relationship, I can't let go. I feel like he sees our potential, but it scares him. Plus, he has a lot to deal with right now, so I'm letting him have his time—time with Sammy, time to deal with everything.

I'm letting him figure his shit out.

If the tables were turned, I know he'd do the same for me. And after all he's been through, he deserves that.

And I deserve a drink.

"I know this great place, just a block from here," he offers. "I was just there last week for a meeting. They have great martinis."

I nod my head in agreement, still trying to prevent the water works and get a grip on myself.

As we walk toward the bar, Greg places his hand at the small of my back, guiding me through the groups of people. It's nice and almost welcomed, because I'm having trouble putting thoughts together, let alone one foot in front of the other. When a group of people pass, he stretches an arm out in front of me, blocking them from running me over. It's chivalrous and polite.

When we get to the bar, he holds the door open for me and asks the waiter if I can get a glass of water before we order.

"Tell me all about it," he says on an exhale, taking his messenger bag from his shoulder and setting it in the open chair beside us.

"You really don't want to hear it," I groan, hiding my face in my hands.

The waiter shows up with a glass of water and a drink menu.

"Thank you," I tell him, taking the glass and chugging nearly half.

"We'll have two Grey Goose martinis," Greg says, smiling over at me and then the waiter.

The fact that he doesn't ask me what I want, just orders for me is so reminiscent of my father that it nearly makes me want to bolt. I physically force myself to stay in the chair, eyeing Greg across the table. Same pristine appearance from before. Same air of confidence. Same polite gestures.

"Go on," he encourages. "You'll feel better once it's off your chest."

So, I do. I tell him all the sordid details, because I figure there's nothing to lose.

Greg is patient and understanding, commiserating with me over every detail from the video to Drake the Dick. He volunteers a business card from an attorney friend of his, if I'm serious about filing a suit against Drake Montgomery.

It's what I need, but yet, not.

I appreciate the drinks. I appreciate him taking the time out of his busy day to make sure I'm okay. I appreciate that he's easy on the eyes and makes me laugh a time or two. But it's not the soothing balm I crave.

He's not Tucker.

"Can I walk you home?" Greg asks, after we argue over who's paying the check. He won, of course.

"No, you've done enough," I say with a laugh. "I can't believe I just had a melt-down and told you my whole life story. Believe me, that was a one-time performance."

"Well, I'm glad I could be here for it. Not that I want to see you upset, but I'm glad I was in the right place at the right time." He smiles and I'm forced to smile back.

"Most sane people would probably say wrong place, wrong time."

"I'd say a few drinks with you is better than any day at the office, even under these circumstances." He walks closer to me, handing me my bag, his hand lingering at my shoulder.

My senses are lagging a bit from the drinks, but when they kick in, I realize he's looking at me like he wants to kiss me.

"Well, I really should go," I say, clearing my throat. "I've taken up enough of your time today." I laugh again, but this time it's a bit nervous. Even though I haven't been in a *public* relationship, I've been in a committed one. Tucker and I agreed a long time ago that if we were hooking up with each other, we wouldn't hook up with anyone else. And I know he told me it's over, but I'm not ready.

"Nonsense," he says in a low voice, moving even closer.

"Remember that guy I told you about from the video?" I ask, deciding being direct is my best policy.

"Yeah," he says, nodding his head.

"Well, we just recently got out of a relationship, of sorts, and I'm not over him. So, I don't want to lead you on. That's not me. And you're a great guy. You don't deserve what I have to offer right now, because it's not much."

Slowly, Greg takes a step back, nodding his head in understanding.

"You're a catch, Piper Grey." He gives me a boyish smile, scratching at the back of his neck. "If you ever change your mind, you have my number."

"I do. Thank you."

"Thank you for letting me finally buy you a drink." Stepping back, he gestures toward the door and I follow his lead.

"At least text me when you get home?" he asks, holding the door open for me. "And let me know what happens with Drake the Dick."

"Okay," I agree with a smile and a nod.

Turning around, I start walking in the direction of my apartment, feeling the weight from the day start to sit heavy on my shoulders. Drinks with Greg was a distraction, but they didn't really help me process.

It's crazy. I'm sure on paper, he seems like the perfect guy—successful, attractive, intelligent, well-mannered, kind, occasionally funny, yet serious.

He's not adventurous, free-spirited, living life on the edge. He's not rough-around-the-edges, soft on the inside. He's not funny as hell and so fucking creative. He doesn't ignite a blaze inside me so fierce I'm afraid it's going to consume me. He doesn't calm every frayed edge by just giving me a look across a crowded room.

That's Tucker.

When I get to my apartment, I shoot Greg a short text, letting him know I'm home, then I toss my bag by the door, kick off my shoes, and call the only person I truly need to talk to right now.

"Hello?" Dani's voice immediately makes me feel homesick, which is crazy, but she's been my home for so long. I can't help it. And she's closer to Tucker. Part of me wants to hang up the phone and drive to French Settlement, but I know that's ridiculous, I can't do that.

"Hey." I don't know why, but the second I hear her voice and go to speak, all of my emotions are back and have to fight back the tears. I thought telling Greg about everything would release some of the pressure that's been building inside, but apparently not.

"Piper? What's wrong?"

"I'm a fucking mess," I sob, finally feeling free to let it all out. "I've messed up big time."

"I doubt that," Dani says in a soothing, yet firm tone. "You're Piper Grey, you never mess up. You've always got your shit together. It's one of your greatest qualities." Even as she's complimenting me I can hear the worry in her voice. For as long as we've been friends, she's never witnessed this side of me.

"Dani, I threatened my boss and quit my job." Even as the words leave my mouth, I still can't believe them.

"Whoa," she says, pausing briefly. "Uh, that's crazy, but I'm sure you had a good reason. Tell me what happened."

"Okay." I let out a deep, cleansing breath and try to collect myself. It's now or never...just like ripping off a bandage. Dani is my best friend and I know she won't judge me for what I'm about to confess, but I don't want to disappoint her. I'm disappointed enough for both of us.

"So, I have to back up a bit and start at the beginning. Please, just listen until I'm done, okay? This is hard enough to admit, so I don't want any interruptions."

"Just spill it, Piper."

"Tucker and I were fuck buddies." I spit it out and brace myself for her reaction but there's nothing. I'm actually surprised Dani is keeping quiet. I'd give anything to see her face right now, but I continue.

"We started hooking up right before Cami and Deacon's wedding. It's been pretty hot and heavy ever since...well, until you and Micah got engaged. That was one of the last times we were together and on that night after everyone went their separate ways, we went to The Cat's Meow. We were completely hammered and—" This part is the hardest for me to say because, even though it was the catalyst for the shit storm I'm in now, I don't regret it. In fact, I wish I could go back in time and do it over but, this time, I'd be happy Tucker proposed.

"And, what, Piper? You can't leave me hangin' like that," Dani blurts out.

"Tucker asked me to marry him. I said yes." I realize that I'm scrunching my face up, like I'm expecting Dani to start screaming or something. She doesn't scream, but I do hear a loud thud.

"Dani, are you okay?"

"Yep, I'm here! Just dropped the phone, nothing to worry about. Please, continue."

I can't help the small smile that begins to break out on my face. I'm impressed at how composed she's being, or at least pretending to be.

"It was actually the first time we spent the night together. When I woke up the next morning, everything went to shit. A friend of Tucker's, one of the guys from the band, was there at Cat's Meow, and he witnessed the whole proposal, took a video and put it on fucking Twitter." I groan, tossing my head back on my couch. "Tucker got a text message with the video attached just as I was storming out the door. Then the shit really hit the fan. He said it went viral. I can't believe none of you saw it. I swear, every time you called for that first month, I was holding my breath, waiting for you to bust me." I laugh at the thought. It really wouldn't have been the worst thing. "My boss did, though, and he's been holding it over my head ever since, making me do anything he asks just so he'll keep quiet."

Dani's also quiet, so I keep going.

"I reached my limit today. I just couldn't take another second of it, so I basically told him to fuck off and he fired me."

Wow. I feel so much lighter, freer getting that out.

"You still there?" I ask, pulling back my phone to see that the call is still going. "Did you pass out or something?"

"Can I talk now?"

"Yes," I say, the word coming out somewhere between a laugh and a cry as I wipe the dampness from my cheeks. "Go ahead."

"Okay. Holy shit. First things first. I can't believe you kept all this from me! You and Tucker? What the fuck?" she yells. "Sorry, but I'm just completely blindsided, yet, somehow not surprised. And no one knows?" Dani takes in a deep breath then continues. "Don't even get me started on your boss. What an asshole! You don't need that job anyway, you can work anywhere." She dismisses the whole unemployed thing like it's no big deal. "But, back to what's important, what the hell is going on with you and Tucker? Why did y'all stop seeing each other?"

"Holy shit, Dani, you were just bursting at the seams, weren't you?" I ask, snickering at my friend.

"You said I couldn't interrupt. It was killing me!"

"To answer your question, we kinda hooked up one other time

after your wedding, but it just didn't work out after that. Tucker's been going through a lot. He didn't even tell me about Sammy. You did. I was really pissed about that, but after we talked, I understood. He's got a lot to deal with. And I've been miserable, putting up with the boss from hell."

"Do you want to see him again or are you just going to be friends? Not that you were really friends before. I mean, how did that work anyway? I thought you two hated each other."

"We did," I say with a laugh. "We pretty much just hate-fucked the entire time. Somewhere along the way, though, our feelings changed." My voice is softer now, especially compared to the loud gasp that Dani just made.

"It's probably best that it didn't work out," Dani says, letting out a deep breath. "I mean, I know he's sweet and sexy and I swear if you ever tell Micah I said that, I'll kill you. But he's also Tucker the Fucker, and he didn't get that name because it rhymes."

"I know exactly how he got his name," I tell her, feeling a prick of possessiveness come over me. I've never felt it before, so it catches me off guard, but I actually *want* to defend Tucker. It's foreign, but I can't fight it. "But he's different. I know everyone thinks he's a player, someone who sleeps around and never commits, but he's not like that. Not anymore, at least."

"You're my best friend and I love you." Dani pauses, but I can tell she's not finished, so I wait. "I'm just looking out for you, like you've always done for me."

"Thank you," I tell her sincerely. "But some risks are worth it."

"So, you really like him...like, *like him-like him*? Like, for real?" I can hear the disbelief still in her tone, and I can't say I blame her. I mean, I did just unload a shit ton of information on her. She has a right to her reservations.

"I pretty much love the asshole," I confess. If I'm being honest, I might as well go all the way. "But he doesn't know that. That's actually the first time I've admitted it out loud." I close my eyes and try to wrap my brain around the day—my life.

"Oh, Piper—" Dani starts but I interrupt.

"It's fine, Dani, I swear. I kinda think Tucker might feel the same, but it's just not our time. He's focused on Sammy and he should be. It makes me love him even more. It just sucks that it didn't work out, you know?"

CHAPTER TWENTY-ONE

My phone ringing wakes me from a dead sleep. I roll over and reach for it, knocking it to the floor. As I grab it, I swipe across the screen answering it before I see who's calling.

"Hello?" My greeting is gravelly and low, so I clear my throat and try again. "Hello?"

"Mr. Benoit?" a female voice on the other end asks.

"Yes." Her tone and unfamiliar voice puts me on edge, so I sit up in bed and try to clear away the grogginess. "This is Tucker."

"Tucker," she repeats. "This is Beth. I'm a nurse at Memorial Hospice."

"Sophie?" I ask, my heart stopping. "Is Sophie okay?"

"I'm sorry. She passed away just a few minutes ago. Dr. Lydel asked me to call. He was called in at two this morning, due to a shallow breath and low pulse. Sophie never woke up. She was pronounced dead at two-twenty-eight. Again, I'm so sorry for your loss. A hospice worker will be in touch with you in the morning to go over the final arrangements for Ms. Martin."

Sophie.

"Okay," I reply numbly.

"Is there anything I can do for you right now?" she asks.

"Uh, no." I shake my head even though she can't see me. "No."

"Call us at any time, if you need someone to talk to or have any questions."

"Okay." It's the only response I can manage.

After the phone goes dead, I sit there, holding it to my ear.

Sophie's gone.

My throat begins to squeeze, pain radiating from there to my chest.

Sophie's...gone.

Swallowing, I feel the sting in my eyes.

Sammy.

I close my eyes and sink back down on my bed, letting the phone fall to the floor. How am I going to tell her? I've thought about this moment quite a bit over the last couple of months, but each time, when I get to the point where I tell her, I hit a block.

How do you tell a little girl her mom is gone?

Reaching way back in my memories, I find the one where my dad told me and Cami. I still remember his words: mama was sick and her body was tired. He told us that she went to heaven and she's always going to be watching over us.

Cami was crying one night and I remember walking down to her room, but my dad was already in there, comforting her. I slid down the wall beside her door and listened. He told her, when she looks up in the sky, that mama would be there...*she's in every star, every cloud. She's not gone, because she lives on inside us. As long as we keep remembering her, she'll always be here.*

I wipe at my eyes, the tears from my memories, mixed with the tears for Sophie...and Sammy. Just as quickly as I wipe them away, they're replaced with new ones.

Memories of Sophie flash through my mind like snapshots. Somewhere, from the back of my mind, a flash of the girl I met out on tour hits me out of the blue—bright, fearless eyes. Who knew? Who knew that a random night would lead to this.

She changed my life.

Blowing out a hard breath, I pull myself out of bed and walk the short distance down the hall to Sammy's room. The door is cracked, just like I left it when I tucked her in bed.

Tonight, her three things she's thankful for were talking to her mom on the phone, playing with Carter, and me reading her a bedtime story.

As I stand there, watching her sleep in the faint light of the moon shining through her window, I wonder if she had any idea that was the last time she'd talk to her mom. I didn't ask what she and Sophie talked about, but I hope Sophie was able to leave her with a lasting impression of just how much she loves her.

I think about waking her up, but I can't bring myself to do it. So, I sit down on the floor and lean against the wall, silently praying it's all going to be okay...that she'll be okay.

My thoughts turn to Sophie as I sit there, watching our daughter sleep. What were her last thoughts? Like, the last one before she drifted off to sleep, never to wake again. I wish I could've been there. I know she wasn't alone, but I wish someone who knew her—loved her—was there for her last breath.

When I first met Sammy, I was jealous of the time Sophie had her...all the time I missed out on, but I know in the end, it was Sophie who was jealous. She wanted to be here. She wanted to watch Sammy grow. She wanted to take her to her first day of school. She wanted to be there for her first kiss, first date...first heartbreak.

And now, that's all on me.

What did I do to deserve the privilege of raising Sammy?

I don't know the answer to that. It's still hard for me to wrap my mind around it. But I know I'm going to do my best to make Sophie proud and to keep her memory alive for Sammy.

It's the least I can do.

I wish I could tell her one last thing. I wish I would've told her thank you. She didn't have to find me. She didn't have to keep Sammy in the first place. She was a young girl, no family, a history of illness. The fact that she was brave enough to take on a baby by herself speaks volumes about her character. I'll be sure Sammy knows that, one of these days, when she can appreciate the sacrifices her mother made for her.

As the sun begins to rise, Sammy stirs in her bed and I drag myself off the floor, muscles aching from sitting there so long. Walking over to her, I sink down beside her, brushing the curls from her sweet face.

"Daddy?" she mumbles in her sleepy voice and it makes my heart clench.

I swallow hard, praying to God I can get through this without falling apart.

"Good morning, sunshine."

"It's too early," she groans, pulling Bubba closer to her. "What's today?"

What's today?

It kills me that today will be a day she'll always remember, even if she doesn't remember the day or the date, she won't forget this moment.

"It's Thursday," I tell her, making her scoot over, so I can climb in beside her. "I have something I need to tell you," I begin, but still feeling so lost on the right words to say.

"What is it?" she asks, opening her little eyes and looking up at me with such blind trust. There's no fear there, no hesitation or uncertainty.

Swallowing again, I close my eyes. "Remember what your mommy told you about where she was going?"

"Heaven," Sammy says in her matter-of-fact way.

"Right." I lean down and kiss her forehead. "Remember what else she told you?" I ask, silently thanking Sophie for giving me this— laying the foundation for this inevitable talk.

"She's always going to be with me," Sammy says, pulling Bubba back and pointing to her chest. "Right here."

"Right. Always, she's always gonna be right there, and in here," I say, brushing back her hair. "We'll always have our memories."

"And pictures," she adds, reaching over and grabbing the one off her night stand of her and Sophie.

"And pictures," I repeat, struggling to hold back my emotions.

We lay there for a moment, in silence, as Sammy looks at the picture of her and her mom. When she looks up at me and sees the tears I no longer can contain, she frowns, reaching up to cup my cheek.

"Mommy's gone to heaven, Sammy." I feel the first fracture in my heart when Sammy's frown turns to sadness and her little face falls. "She's gone to heaven, but she'll never leave you."

Sitting up in her bed, I pull her onto my lap and hold her while she cries.

It's real and raw and part of me is happy she's letting it out, because I was afraid she wouldn't understand. But that was crazy, because Sammy is an old soul. She's intuitive and empathetic. She's smart and caring. She's so much her mother.

I hold her for what seems like hours, but I doubt it's been even an hour. For a while, I think she's fallen back to sleep, but then she speaks in a small, sad voice.

"I didn't get to say goodbye."

Lifting her off my shoulder, I look her in the eyes—those blue eyes that make me feel like I'm looking into my own soul.

"Your mommy didn't want to say goodbye because it's not goodbye. She knows she'll see you again. One day, when you're old and grey, you'll go to heaven too, and you'll see her again. So, you don't have to say goodbye."

Sammy seems to be taking in my words. Her little forehead relaxes from its tensed state of duress and she takes a deep breath, blowing it out and blowing a curl away in the process.

"I'm still gonna miss her."

"Oh, me too, sunshine."

Pulling her to my chest, I hug her to me for a while longer.

"What do you want to do?" I finally ask, knowing we can't stay in bed all day. I mean, we could, but I know she needs to eat and she'd feel better after a shower and getting dressed.

"I want pancakes."

"Pancakes, it is."

We'll take this one thing at a time—one minute, one hour, one day. For now, it's pancakes, and then we'll play it by ear.

THE LAST FORTY-EIGHT HOURS HAVE BEEN A WHIRLWIND. I'VE BARELY slept, worried about Sammy, even though she's been sleeping in my bed or I've been in hers. During the day, I find myself unable to take my eyes off her, worried that she's going to break and I'm not going to be there to pick up the pieces.

Today, we're burying Sophie's ashes and planting a tree in her honor.

After talking it over with Dad and Kay, we decided a place out by the barn would be good. One of Sophie's last requests was to put her ashes somewhere peaceful and give Sammy a place she can visit, if she wants.

I think she'd approve.

She mentioned several times that she loved this place. I know she thought it would be a good place for Sammy to grow up, so I think she'll be happy here as well.

Micah and Deacon went into Baton Rouge and bought a magnolia tree. Annie said a magnolia is a symbol of beauty and perseverance. That was Sophie. So, here we stand, on the south side of the barn, in full view of the late afternoon sun.

"God our Father,
Your power brings us to birth,
Your providence guides our lives,
and by Your command we return to dust.
Lord, those who die still live in Your presence,
their lives change but do not end.
I pray in *hope* for Sammy,
And for all those who knew and loved Sophie."

Sammy squeezes my hand a little tighter as Sam offers a prayer over the small hole where Sophie's ashes are now buried.

"In company with Christ,
Who died and now lives,

may they rejoice in Your kingdom,
where all our tears are wiped away.
Unite us together again in one family,
to sing Your praise forever and ever.
Amen."

I kneel in front of Sammy, getting eye level with her. "Is there anything you want to say?"

She looks at me and then around the circle at Sam, Annie, Dad, Kay, Cami, Deacon, Micah, and Dani. Then she raises her little chin and looks up at the tree that's planted and then over to where we placed the small box in the ground.

"My mommy likes it here." She trails off a little and looks down at the ground. I'm afraid this is all too much and that she's going to fall apart on me, but she doesn't. She keeps going. "She likes pretty trees. And she likes heaven. And now she's with Daddy's mom. Isn't that right, Daddy?"

I nearly crumble to the ground at her feet.

"That's right, sunshine." I force out the words and nod my head.

For that brief moment, it's just me and her. I don't feel the wind or the sun. I just feel the connection between me and Sammy.

One day, I'll take her to the cemetery down the road where my mama is buried. I'll tell her how I made it through. Hopefully, it'll help her heal, knowing she's not alone and that we have this connection. But for today, I'm going to hold her a little tighter, love her a little harder, and be her soft place to land.

We all gather at Dad and Kay's for dinner, but the mood is somber. Everyone is tired from the last couple of days. Kay and Annie have been staying over until late into the night, just in case we need anything. And Cami and Dani have been hanging around during the day, with everyone else popping in sporadically.

"I'm gonna take Sammy home," I tell Cami as we wash up a couple of dishes. "I think she needs to rest, maybe just have some down time."

"I think that's a good idea." She dries her hands and turns around to lean against the cabinet. "I can bring Carter over tomorrow after school, if she's up for someone to play with."

"I'm sure she will be. Those two are thick as thieves these days."

"Yeah, it's good for her. For him too, especially with this one on the way."

"Kinda crazy that we're repopulating the family," I laugh. "I can't imagine what it'll be like in a few years."

Cami smiles, resting her hands on her round belly. "I doubt Micah and Dani wait too long, and Deacon and I have already talked about another, a little closer together this time."

"Geez, keep it up and we'll have enough for a baseball team," I tease.

"Well, you make beautiful babies," she says wistfully, watching Sammy and Carter playing in the living room.

"Okay," I say, tossing the dish towel on the counter. "I'm leavin' on that note."

Cami laughs. "I'm just sayin'."

"Well, just keep your sayin' to yourself. I've got my hands full with Sammy." Even as the words leave my mouth, I know they're not completely true. I do have my hands full, but since calling things off with Piper, I've missed her more than I care to admit. Our timing is shit, but it doesn't mean I still don't want her—want everything about her, everything with her. She's been on my mind a lot the last few of days. But I've been so busy, I haven't had a chance to call her.

After Sammy and I say our goodbyes, and Kay sends us home with enough food to feed an army, we head out.

Sammy is quiet as we drive down the road. I hear her yawn just as we get to the main road, and by the time we turn down our road, she's asleep.

When I pull up to the house, I hardly look twice at the car in the drive. I've been so used to everyone being in and out, it doesn't even dawn on me it's there, until I see someone sitting on the front porch.

"Piper?"

CHAPTER TWENTY-TWO
Piper

"Hey." Standing up from my spot on the porch, I walk toward him, completely caught off-guard by his slacks and dress shirt. I've never seen Tucker in anything besides jeans and t-shirts. And naked, but now is not the time for thoughts like that.

"Hey," he replies, his face full of confusion.

"Dani called me. I was going to come to the farm today, but I thought it was better for it to just be family."

"You're family." He tilts his head as he looks at me, his eyes look tired. Actually, his entire body looks tired. But his words make my heart do funny things.

"Where's Sammy?" I ask, looking around him toward the truck.

"She's asleep right now." He looks back over his shoulder and then back at me. "How long are you gonna be here?"

"Well, I don't have any plans, if that's what you're asking."

I watch as he unlocks and opens the front door, propping it open with a work boot that's close-by. "I'm gonna carry her in and put her to bed," he says, pointing over his shoulder. Then, he jogs back to the truck and gently lifts Sammy from her seat and carries her inside.

Yet, again, I'm stunned into silence at the sight of Tucker while he has his daughter in his arms. I was not prepared for the onslaught of emotions that are hitting me right now. Seeing him again is one thing, but seeing him with Sammy is just...damn. Can a woman die from an ovary explosion?

"Piper? You still outside?" Tucker sticks his head out the front door, looking for me.

"Yeah, I'm here." I wave at him from where I'm sitting on the porch steps.

He smiles as he walks over and sits down beside me, unbuttoning the sleeves on his shirt and rolling them to his elbows.

Focus, Piper.

"I'm really sorry about Sophie." I've wanted to ask about her—about them, but I know now isn't the time. "How's Sammy doing?"

"She's doin' okay, I guess. I mean, she has her moments where she's sad, of course, but she bounces back pretty quickly. I'm amazed at how she handles herself, though. Sometimes I feel like I'm the child and she's the parent. She's just incredible."

I smile, watching him gush over Sammy. "She's lucky to have you."

"I'm the lucky one, believe me." He sighs, looking uncomfortable from my compliment. "Enough about me. What's been goin' on with you?"

I want to ask how he's coping, but I can tell he doesn't want to talk about that right now. So, I tell him the other thing that's weighing on my mind.

"I'm moving."

"What? What do you mean? Where are you goin'?"

I've thought a lot about how I was going to tell Tucker I lost my job, and I've decided to be as vague as possible. He has so much going on in his life, that I don't want to add to his burdens by telling him our proposal video was what started all my problems.

"I'm going home to Connecticut. I, uh, quit my job the other day, and I decided I need a fresh start."

He stares at me for a moment before looking out into the field beside the house. I can't decipher his expression, but from the way his posture goes rigid, it feels like he's already putting a wall up, blocking me out. I wish I knew what he was thinking.

Finally, he speaks. "Why did you quit your job?"

"I just felt like I'd reached my potential at the magazine and had nowhere else to go. My dad set up an interview for me with a division in his company, so, hopefully, I won't be unemployed for too long."

"When are you leavin'?"

"Next week."

Tucker lets out a deep breath and still isn't looking at me. "Wow, that's...soon. Are you not plannin' on comin' back down here?"

"I'm sure I'll be back to visit, but I really don't know what's going to happen in my near future, you know?"

"I do know. I can relate to that very well, in fact."

Finally, he smiles at me. It's small, but it's something.

"For what's it worth, you really seem to have your shit together. I'm impressed."

He barks out a laugh. "I don't know if I can agree with that, but I'm tryin'. It's kinda funny that I'm the one who's settlin' down and you're not. Since when did our lives reverse?" He gives me a wink before nudging me with his elbow. I push back against him and try to ignore the jolt of electricity that surges through my body. Just that small contact was enough to set my body and heart on fire, but I can't give into it.

"How are you?" I ask, needing to know he's okay—that he's going to be okay.

"I don't know. It still feels surreal." He hangs his head, resting his elbows on his knees. "Some part of me thought she'd get better or something, even though the logical part of me knew she wouldn't. But deep down, I felt it comin'. So, I guess I was as ready as I could be, given the circumstance."

"It's a lot to handle," I tell him, not knowing what else to say, except I'm sorry and life sucks sometimes. It really, truly sucks.

"This isn't how I saw my life goin'," he confesses, looking over at me. "But I wouldn't trade it for anything. Now, lookin' back, I can't imagine my life without Sammy."

"I knew when you came off the road, you were searching for something. You were restless and unsettled. But you're different now. You seem content. Maybe it was Sammy you were searching for all along."

His eyes linger on me and I think he's getting ready to say something, but doesn't. Instead, his cheeks fill with air and then he blows it out with a long sigh. Until he finally asks, "Are you hungry?"

"Oh, no. I just wanted to stop by to check on you and Sammy and to tell you about Connecticut."

"Are you plannin' on goin' to Dani and Micah's?"

"Uh, I'm not sure. Like I said earlier, I really have no plans. Dani doesn't even know I'm in town. I haven't talked to her since yesterday."

"Well, you should come inside. It's gettin' dark. And if you're hungry, you should eat, because Kay sent us home with enough food for a month," he says, cracking another smile. This time is less sad and more Tucker—sly and full of mischief.

"Okay," I agree, not needing much convincing.

After a minute or so, he stands, offering me his hand. I gladly accept it and smile as he pulls me up. Our bodies are so close now, we're sharing breaths. Just a couple more inches and our lips would meet. I want to so badly. Just a kiss. I could handle that much. At least, I think I could. Would it be so bad to try?

Why does this have to be so hard? I could reach up and kiss Tucker right now and say 'fuck it all', letting the cards fall where they may. It would feel so good and I'm sure I'd be happy, that *we'd* be happy. But there's this little voice inside my head that whispers negativity, poisoning my happy thoughts. *What if Tucker's settling for you? What if you're settling for him? What if this is just more rebellion?*

And then I think of Sammy. She just buried her mother and isn't looking for a replacement. What kind of replacement could I be anyway? Here lately, I can barely take care of myself.

No. I can't do it. It's just not the right time for any of us and I don't want to push us into something that could eventually destroy us, no matter how good our intentions are. I have to be strong. If it's meant to be, it'll be meant to be later.

"Against my better judgement, I wish I knew what was goin' on inside that head of yours, Piper Grey." Tucker's words are barely a whisper but they make me smile. I'm thankful for the interruption of my thoughts, though, and I squeeze his hands before letting go.

"I really don't think you do, Tucker Benoit." I walk into the house, leaving him on the porch and knowing he's watching my every step.

A moment passes before he finds me in the kitchen, pouring myself a glass of water. He's carrying a large insulated cooler that he sets on a countertop close to me.

"I forgot the food was still in my truck," he says with a laugh. "Good thing the cooler kept everything warm."

"I'm sure it'll be fine. A little food poisoning never hurt anyone, right?" I joke.

Tucker laughs and starts unloading the cooler, pulling out covered dishes and food wrapped in foil, as well as, what looks to be many different types of cookies in plastic baggies.

"Damn, you weren't kidding. That's a lot of food."

"We, southerners, do any kind of life event big like this. Don't you know, food heals all?" Tucker winks at me and I swear, it takes everything I have not to jump him.

"Believe me, I do. My jeans are already too tight from all the self-medicating I've been doing with food lately." I say this as a joke but the look Tucker gives me knocks the humor out of me. It's a mixture of concern and, maybe, desire. No, definitely desire.

He turns to me, his eyes boring into mine. "First, you're perfect the way you are. Don't ever forget that. Second, you can always come to me if something is bothering you. You know that, right?"

Words aren't forming in my brain, so I simply nod my head.

When he's satisfied enough with my response, he breaks eye contact and turns back to the food. Stupidly, I blurt out, "Is there a third?" Why in the hell did I just do that?

I watch as he chews on his bottom lip, thinking. His decision on how to answer will determine how the rest of the night will go. Finally, he smiles. "Yeah, there is. Third," he motions to the food spread out on the counters, "pick your poison. Ladies first."

Relief and, if I'm being completely honest, disappointment rushes through me. Of course, he could've used that opportunity to knock all this food to the floor and take me right here and now, but he chose the safe option. The smart one.

We finish our meal, which was a delicious hodge-podge of southern and Cajun foods, and are sitting in the living room when the sound of tiny feet shuffling down the hall reaches us.

"Hey, there, sunshine. Everything okay?" Tucker asks.

Sammy only acknowledges his question by nodding her head yes because her eyes are fixed on me. I'm not sure what I'm supposed to do, so I smile at her and give her a little wave.

"I heard you talking to someone and I thought it might be Mommy." Her voice is calm and matter-of-fact, but her words absolutely break my heart.

Tucker gives her an understanding smile. "Sammy, this is my friend, Piper. You talked to her on the phone, remember?"

Surprisingly, this makes Sammy smile and she quickly walks up to me. "I remember you. You're even prettier than the picture Daddy has of you."

This catches me off guard for more than one reason and I give Tucker a questioning look. "You have a picture of me?"

He has the nerve to blush, but I know he's not really embarrassed. Nothing embarrasses Tucker Benoit.

"I may have snapped a few pictures on my phone when you weren't looking," he says, shrugging his shoulders.

All I can do is laugh because admitting how flattered I am to Tucker would be a wrong move. Instead, I turn my attention back to Sammy.

"Thank you, Sammy. I'm happy to finally meet you in person. I'm also very sorry to hear about your mommy." It's hard to know what to say, but I want her to know that I mean it.

"Me, too," she says. "But she's still with me. Right, Daddy?" She looks at Tucker and I'm blown away at how much she resembles him.

"That's right, love. Hey, are you hungry? Want me to fix you a snack?"

She nods and Tucker goes into the kitchen to get her something to eat. He's such a great daddy, I can tell by just watching this short interaction. I already knew it, or had a feeling, but now it's in my face and real, and it's making our *just* friends status harder to maintain.

Because Tucker as a dad is one of the sexiest things I've ever witnessed.

While she waits for her food, Sammy climbs onto the couch and then into my lap, making herself at home and snuggling into me. I don't want her to sense how shocked I am, so I wrap my arm around her and run my fingers through her hair. There's something so calming in this moment, so special, but I don't read anything into it. I just enjoy it.

Tucker enters the room and his steps falter a bit when he sees us. I give him a look that says 'I have no idea what's happening' and his smile just grows.

"I've got mac and cheese," he says, holding up a bowl with a spoon.

"That's my second favorite." Sammy looks at me with these amazing, deep blue eyes. "Wanna know what my favorite is?"

"What?" I ask, feeling a little sad when she pulls away, but also grateful for the moment. I barely know what to do with myself—my feelings, instincts. It's all too much.

"Grilled cheese." Sammy smiles and waggles her eyebrows. She's so much like Tucker it's scary. "Do you like grilled cheeses?"

"I love them," I admit. "Have you ever put bacon on your grilled cheese?"

Sammy's eyes light up and then her brows furrow as she turns on her dad. "Why have we never put bacon on them?"

Tucker laughs. "I don't know. I didn't know you liked it."

"I didn't either." She shrugs and hops down, walking over to the table where Tucker sets her bowl down.

I get up and walk over, pulling out the chair across from her. Tucker, pulls out the other, and we both sit and watch Sammy. I wonder how he gets anything done. I'd probably do this twenty-four-seven if she was mine.

After a few bites, Sammy's spoon stops mid-air and her eyes shift from me to Tucker and then back to me. "What?"

Tucker and I both laugh.

"Nothing," he says, shaking his head. "How's the mac?"

"Delicious." Her words come out around a large bite of cheesy noodles. "Did Grandma Kay or Nanny Annie make this?"

"Nanny Annie," Tucker says with a grin.

"That's what I thought." She nods as she continues eating.

"Nanny Annie, huh?" I ask with smirk.

"She pretty much has everyone wrapped around her finger."

"What does that mean?" Sammy asks.

"It means you're cute and we're weak against your powers," he says in a deep, animated voice, causing Sammy to laugh. "Now, finish your mac and cheese."

After she's finished eating, Tucker puts her bowl in the sink and looks over at the clock.

"Super late, sunshine. How 'bout a shower and then back to bed."

Her bottom lip comes out and she rests her chin on the table.

"Sammy," Tucker says, trying to get her attention, but she's staring straight at me.

I look from her over to Tucker. He's leaning against the counter, watching her with a slight smirk on his face. "Sammy," he says again, and she slowly turns her head to look at him. "Shower and get ready for bed, then I'll read you a book."

She turns her head back toward me. "I want Piper to read the book."

Tucker sighs. "Well, Piper might not be able to. I don't know if she wants to stay that long."

Sammy sticks her lip out a little further and then bats her lashes at me, showcasing those big blue eyes.

Of course I'll stay. "Sure," I say, realizing she's still waiting on my answer. "I'll stay."

"Yay!" She claps her hands and hops down from the table, running toward the bathroom.

"Damn," I say after she's out of earshot. "She's good."

"Tell me about it." Tucker starts down the hall. "And she's four."

"Going on twenty," I add.

"Don't say that. I'm not even ready for five, and that happens next month."

While Tucker is helping Sammy, I help myself around the living room. I've been in this house before, but it's different now. It's all Tucker, and as I peruse the contents, I realize I've never been in Tucker's space before. We've always met up on neutral turf.

I love it. It's comfortable and so him. I feel like, even if I didn't know he lives here, I'd still know.

There's a wall of guitars, one that looks like it's used more than others resting against the end of the sofa. Next to those is a side table with Tucker's name all over it, not literally, but I can tell it's something he made. It's a dark wood with smooth edges, and the craftsmanship is superb.

On the table are stacks of papers. I assume they're your typical mail and junk, but on closer evaluation, I realize they're sheets of music and songs. Some have words written on them. Others have chords and notes...things I know nothing about.

When a door shuts down the hall, I jump, causing one of the pages to fall to the ground. Picking it up, I can't help reading a few of the words.

You're trouble of the best kind.
You stole my heart and robbed me blind.
One look from you and I hit the floor.
One call from you and I'm out the door.

Gathering the papers up, I try to stack them like they were, hoping Tucker won't notice that I've been nosing through his personal stuff.

Another sheet slips out and I bend down to pick it up, nearly jumping out of my skin when I hear Tucker clear his throat.

Turning around, I feel heat flush my cheeks. "Sorry." I smile apologetically.

"Find what you were lookin' for?" he asks.

"Are these all songs you wrote?"

"Uh, yeah." Now, Tucker is the one whose cheeks are tinged with pink. He barks out a laugh, taking the stack and sticking them in the drawer of the table. "They're not all great."

"What do you plan on doing with them?" I can't imagine him going back on tour with his band. The road is no place to raise a child.

"Well, I *was* thinkin' about sendin' a couple of them to a guy I know in Nashville," he admits, chewing on the side of his lip. "I'm not sure if they're good enough, but I think it's worth a shot. I haven't really decided what I'm gonna do."

"I think that's a great idea. I mean, all they can say is no, right?"

"Kinda what I was thinkin'." He gives me a small smile. "Now that I'm tryin' to be a responsible adult, I figured it'd be a good idea to have some financial stability. I can't really expect Sammy to live out of a van and eat meals comped from bars."

He laughs, but I know he's serious and that he's been giving this some thought. I also know Tucker and I know he won't be truly happy unless he's doing something creative. He's not the kind of person who works a nine-to-five job.

"What about your furniture?" I ask, looking around the living room that's full of it. "I think you could do really well selling it."

Sighing, he smoothes back his hair. "I don't know. Annie mentioned somethin' about it too, but I don't know anything about runnin' a business like that."

"Wouldn't take much," I tell him. "A little marketing, advertising..."

"You're speakin' a foreign language," he says with a laugh.

"Daddy!" Sammy yells from down the hall.

"Be right back."

Tucker jogs off, leaving me standing there. I'm tempted to go for the drawer where he stuck the papers, but I don't. The few words I read are giving me enough to think about.

Was that song about me?

I'm still standing in the middle of the living room, letting Tucker's words run through my mind when he pokes his head around the corner.

"You're up."

Smiling, I follow him back down the hall and into Sammy's room where she's snuggled into a gorgeous canopy bed with pink chiffon on top and a fluffy pink comforter that has butterflies all over it.

"Wow," I say, checking out the bed and then the rest of her room. "It looks like a princess lives here."

"I love princesses," Sammy says dreamily. "Have you been to Sam and Annie's castle?"

I look at Tucker and he just smiles, shaking his head, so I play along.

"Yes," I tell her, walking over to her shelf where there is a small collection of books. "It's beautiful, especially the gardens, those are my favorite."

"Nanny Annie grows beautiful roses," Sammy adds. "She's secretly a queen." It comes out in a conspiratorial whisper, with her hand up to her mouth.

"Really?" I ask, feigning shock.

"Yes." Her eyes are wide, but sure, like she knows something no one else knows. "Pops told me."

"And by Pops, you mean?"

"Sam. Our names are the same." She yawns and folds her arms behind her head, again looking so much like Tucker. But when I catch a glimpse of the framed picture on her night stand, I see someone else she looks alike. A young woman with dark skin and dark curly hair is smiling back at me, holding a smaller Sammy.

I know it's Sophie without asking. She's beautiful, and even in her picture, I see the kindness and gentleness that Sammy possesses.

Genetics are amazing.

"What book are we reading?" I ask.

"Daddy's been reading this," Sammy offers, handing me a book.

"*Tuesdays at the Castle,*" I read from the front of the book.

"It's about a castle that changes every Tuesday." Sammy's voice is filled with awe. "Princess Celie doesn't know what it's gonna do." Her arms go out wide in exclamation.

"Well, let's find out what's happening," I tell her, looking around for a chair, but Tucker's occupying the only one in the room. I'm getting ready to kneel beside the bed when Sammy pats the mattress.

"You have to lay down here."

"Okay." Kicking my shoes off beside the bed, I climb in beside her.

"Here," she says, giving me a big pink pillow from the other side of the bed. "Use this."

"Thank you."

"You're welcome." When she smiles at me, like she is now, it melts my insides. "You're pretty. I like your hair. So does Daddy. He says it's the same color as his guitar."

I glance over to see Tucker hiding his face in his hand. If it weren't for the slight shake of his shoulders, not doubt from stifled laughter, I'd think he's asleep.

"Well, you're pretty too. Prettiest girl I've ever met." On instinct, I lean over and kiss the top of her head. "Now, let's read."

Opening the book, I see there's a pink ponytail holder between two pages and I assume that's where I'm supposed to start.

I'm only a few pages into the story when I feel Sammy's head lean against me. Looking down, I see that's she's already fallen asleep. I admit, I love looking at her while she sleeps, so sweet and angelic, but I'm a little disappointed she crashed so soon. I was really enjoying being with her. She's had a long, rough day, though, so she's earned her rest.

Tucker takes the book from me and places the ponytail holder inside, marking where I stopped, then gently moves Sammy off me and onto her pillow. When he offers to help me down from the bed, I don't decline. I also don't let go of his hand until we're walking into the hallway.

"You're so good with her. I'm impressed," he says, once we're back in the living room.

"Thanks." I don't want to read more into his words than I should, so I smile up at him. "You're a natural. Pretty good yourself," I say with a wink, trying to keep the moment light. But I mean it—he so is.

Feeling the atmosphere shift, I grab my purse from the coffee table and walk to the door. "I should be leaving."

"I wish you didn't have to."

It's a simple statement but I know what he's saying. He doesn't want me to leave...tonight.

But, maybe, he also doesn't want me to go to Connecticut. I want to ask him—force him to tell me how he feels—but I can't make those kinds of demands. Not now. Not after everything he's been through.

Placing my hand on his chest, over his heart, I look up at him. "I wish that, too."

The words are barely out of my mouth before Tucker's lips are on mine. It's not a needy kiss, like he wants to ravage my body the way he used to; it's a kiss full of meaning, sweet and passionate—saying every word we can't.

I kiss him back, fantasizing about staying with him forever, but stop when it gets to be too much—when my heart feels like it's about to explode. There's one small kiss left to give him, and when I do, it says the word I can't bear to speak.

Goodbye.

CHAPTER TWENTY-THREE

"I'm so happy everyone's here," Annie says, reaching out for Deacon's hand and then Sam's, while the rest of us follow suit. "There's so much goin' on, what with gettin' ready for the baby and Micah and Deacon startin' work on Pockets. Seems like we've all been so busy lately." She sighs, looking down one side of the table and then the other. "Today's message in the sermon reminded me to be grateful for the time, because it slips away too fast."

We all sit there for a minute, no one saying a word. If we've learned nothing else over the years, we've learned that when Annie speaks, we listen. I look down at Sammy who's smiling across the table at Annie, happy as can be.

"Sam, say the blessin'," Annie instructs.

Sam gives Annie a smile, followed by a kiss to the back of her hand, then we all bow our heads.

"Lord, bless the food before us, the family beside us, and the time we share. Amen."

Everyone does the sign of the cross. I watch Sammy from the corner of my eye. She doesn't miss a beat. If you didn't know any better, you'd think she's been coming to these Sunday dinners at the Landry's her whole life.

"Dani, how's Piper?" Annie asks as food starts getting passed around the table. "I miss her."

"Well, she's back in Connecticut." Dani sighs and I watch for any subtle reaction that would give me a clue as to how Piper's doing, because the two times we've talked since she left, she's been vague at best.

Maybe I shouldn't have kissed her before she left, but damn it, I would've regretted it if I hadn't. I regret so many things already, mostly not telling her how I feel. I couldn't add another thing to the list.

Dani cuts her eyes over at me, like she can sense that I'm watching her.

"Is she gettin' settled?" Annie asks, drawing both of our attention back to her.

"She went for a job interview. That's about all I know."

"Well, I just hate that things didn't work out in Birmingham. I was gettin' way too used to havin' her around." Annie continues passing food. She and Kay are always making sure everyone has everything they need before they ever take a bite of food.

"I hate it too. I miss her." Micah pulls Dani over to him, kissing the top of her head. "Hopefully, she'll come for a visit at least."

"Is she seein' anybody?" Annie asks, causing me to choke on my bite of mashed potatoes.

It's a normal question. Annie is always interested in people's love lives, but when it's concerning Piper, it feels off limits.

Dani looks back across the table at me before answering. "Well, she did mention someone by the name of Greg."

Everyone else is so engrossed in their meals and side conversations that this is now mostly a conversation between Dani and Annie...and me, because I can't peel myself away.

Who the fuck is Greg?

"Greg," Annie repeats, smiling at Dani. "That's a nice name."

Dani laughs, shaking her head. "That's what I told her. Doesn't it just sound like a name of a nice, normal guy?"

"That's what everyone says about Sam," Sam chimes in, winking at me across the table.

"What about Deacon?" Deke asks, taking offense, of course. "I'm the nicest guy you'll ever meet."

Pretty soon, everyone is laughing and Annie is rolling her eyes. "Y'all have very nice names. I should know. I picked them out."

"Hey, now," Sam says. "I get a little cred."

"All the credit for Tucker and Cami go to Jessie," my dad says. "I told her she carried them for nine months, so she earned the right to pick their names." He smiles, looking across the table at my sister. "She had Camille picked out from the time we started dating. Always knew she wanted a Camille."

"Mommy named me Samanie because she wanted me to remember where I came from," Sammy pipes up and we all turn to look at her. She just smiles, not fazed by all the attention in the slightest.

"It's a great name," Kay assures her. "Beautiful. Your mommy knew what she was doing, because it fits you perfectly."

Sammy grins up at me, so proud. Leaning over, I kiss her head and squeeze her to me.

As everyone else goes about their conversations, I can't help thinking about what Dani said. Who's Greg? Is he someone Piper met in Connecticut? Is that why she's seemed distant lately?

All the unanswered questions are killing me.

After dinner, Sammy and Carter are playing on the jungle gym Sam and Annie had installed a week or so ago. It looks like something you'd find in a city park; the kids love it. Even the big kids. Micah and Deacon were out here the other day, seeing who could cross the monkey bars the fastest.

"Hey," Deacon says, coming up beside me and nudging me with his elbow.

"What's up?" I ask, keeping my eye on Sammy and Carter. The monkey bars are really high and Sammy insists on figuring them out, but she refuses help. It makes me nervous.

"Everything alright with you?"

"Sure, man. Everything alright with you?" Deacon has been acting weird around me all day. Weirder than usual, I mean. He obviously has something on his mind. I wish he'd just spit it out but, at the same time, I'm gonna play dumb until he does.

"Come on, Tucker, you can talk to me, man." He sighs, folding his arms across his chest. "I know this has been difficult for you, but we're all here to help. Sammy is our family, too."

Deacon is a great friend, the best, but he's really making me feel like shit right now. Since Sophie died, things have been okay with me and Sammy. Better than okay, actually. We have our difficult moments, but we're acclimating to this new normal, or at least we're doing the best we can. I know everyone is concerned and wants to help.

But how do I admit the reason I've been such a moody bastard lately isn't because of my situation with Sophie and Sammy, but because of Piper? She's on my mind more than I care to admit, and I can't do anything about it. I should be trying to move forward with my life like she seems to be doing, but I can't.

"I know, Deke, and I appreciate it, I do. I have a lot of crap goin' on in my life right now that I'm tryin' to get sorted. It's more than just Sammy, although she's the most important."

"Well, maybe I can help with one of the other things troublin' you." I take a good look at my friend's face and see nothing but genuine concern. "I hate seein' you sad and mopey all the time. It ain't right. How about we hit the bar tonight? The kids can have a sleepover here at the big house and you, me, and Micah can have a guy's night out, like we used to do. Lord knows I could use a high-priced beer right about now."

"A beer with you two sounds pretty good, but I don't want to go out." I lived the bar scene for ten years and the thought of going back anytime doesn't appeal.

"When was the last time you got your dick wet, man?" Deacon asks in a low, conspiratorial whisper.

"Dude!" I look over at where the kids are playing and hope to the high heavens they didn't hear what Deacon just asked.

"They didn't hear me. Don't get your panties twisted. That's it, isn't it? You haven't been with someone in so long, you've forgotten how to do it. I swear, I never thought I'd see the day when Tucker the Fucker lost his mojo." The bastard has the nerve to shake his head at me like he pities me.

"Shut up, Deke. You don't know everything about me. I know you think you do, but you don't." I know I'm probably being a little too harsh, but damn. The last thing I need is Deacon all up in my business.

"I bet I know more than you realize."

"Oh, yeah? Try me," I challenge, because he doesn't know shit. No one really knows anything. They don't know about Piper.

He stares at me, clenching his jaws so hard, I see the muscles in his face tense. I know this look. For some crazy reason, he really thinks he has something on me and he's debating whether or not to admit it.

"Just fuckin' spit it out, man. You're obviously dyin' to call me out on my shit, so just do it."

After a moment, Deacon moves closer to me and looks me dead in the eye. "I know about you and Piper."

Well, fuck me running.

"There is no 'me and Piper'. I don't know what the hell you're talkin' about." Deny, deny, deny. There's no way he knows about us. We were way too careful.

"Oh, really? So, that wasn't you and Piper fuckin' each other's brains out in the bathroom last year at my parents' anniversary party?"

Okay, so, maybe, we weren't always careful.

Desperate times, desperate measures. And all that bullshit.

Deacon crosses his arms over his chest while quirking an eyebrow at me, waiting for my response. I think about denying it again, making up some kind of lie, but, really, what's the point? Piper and I are over and, surprisingly, I just don't give a shit that Deacon knows.

"Shit," I mutter under my breath, breaking eye contact with him.

That's all he needs. "I knew it!" he yells and punches his fist in the air.

"Yay, you figured it out. Big freakin' deal. What do you want me to say?"

"For starters, I'd like a 'thank you, Deacon'."

"Thank you? For what?"

"For keepin' your secret! Ya'll shit on me all the time, sayin' I can't keep a secret and I've been keepin' the biggest one for months!"

He's so ridiculous to be so butt-hurt about this, but he's right. On both accounts.

"Fine. Thank you for not tellin' anyone about me and Piper. We didn't want anyone to know and there's no reason for anyone else to know, got it?"

"Why not? Why are you hidin'? And why are you two not together anymore?"

"We never planned on bein' anything other than fuck buddies, with more emphasis on the fuck and less on the buddies. I guess it all fell to shit when I proposed to her."

Deacon starts coughing but manages to squeak out, "You did what?"

"Yeah, the night Micah proposed to Dani. We were drunk and didn't even remember it happenin' until Dave posted it on Twitter or some shit." Thinking back on that night—what I remember, that is— and the following morning brings a smile to my face. I haven't allowed myself to think about it much over the last couple of months. Even though it all went downhill after that, I don't regret a single thing.

"Damn, that's crazy. I can't believe you didn't tell anyone."

"It was right after that that I found out about Sammy. So, to say my priorities changed would be the understatement of the century."

"I get it. I'm guessing Piper didn't want to play house with you and Sammy?"

My gut reaction is to be pissed at Deacon for assuming that about Piper, but he doesn't know her like I do. If he did, he wouldn't have asked. He's just jumping to conclusions.

"I didn't give her a chance." I kick at an imaginary rock on the ground. More and more, I'm realizing this is my fault. I'm the one who pushed Piper away, and now I'm the one suffering for it. I deserve to feel miserable.

"Hmmm," is his only response, keeping his thoughts to himself.

"I fucked this up so bad, man. But shit, this is uncharted territory for me. I didn't know what the hell I was doin' or what was comin' next. All I could think about was Sammy. Piper knows that."

"So, you think it's best for Sammy if you're completely miserable?"

"What? No—"

Suddenly, Deacon thrusts his hand out to me, like he's expecting a handshake.

"What on earth are you doin'?" I ask.

"Hi, I'm Deacon Landry and I'm callin' you out on your shit." He's lost his mind. It's official. This will break Annie's heart. "You do know that I pursued Cami, your sister, when she was a single mom, right?"

"It's not the same thing," I argue.

"The hell it's not. I was in love with her and she'd just had another man's baby. Was it complicated? Sometimes," he says, shrugging. "Was it worth it? Absofuckinglutely. Don't make assumptions about Piper, or Sammy. You're forcin' them to respond to a situation without givin' them a chance to decide for themselves, and in the meantime, you're sellin' them both short. You're doin' the same to yourself. Life is much better when you open your heart to all its possibilities, rather than blockin' everyone out. You and that precious girl of yours have some of the biggest hearts I know. It'd be a shame not to share them."

Deacon walks over to the kids, leaving me completely dumbfounded and with a lot to think about.

CHAPTER TWENTY-FOUR

THINGS HAVE SETTLED INTO A NICE ROUTINE FOR ME AND SAMMY these last few weeks and, for that, I'm grateful. During the day, Sammy stays with Kay or Annie, and plays with Carter when he gets out of school, while I help my dad in the fields. In the evenings, we hang out at home. Sometimes, we have company over, but, for the most part, it's just the two of us getting to know each other and making our own memories. Sammy loves it when I play the guitar for her, especially when I sing. Sometimes, she sings along. She also likes to help me sand furniture. Anywhere I am, there she is also, and I wouldn't have it any other way.

Time seems to move slowly, yet fast at the same time. As a kid, I never knew what my dad was talking about when he would talk about how fast time flies. Now, I get it.

I feel like Sammy changes and grows every day.

I guess I'm doing a little changing too. I'm getting better at fixing Sammy's hair and I've learned to cook something other than grilled cheese and frozen pizza. Of course, Annie and Kay both love bringing us food but they understand I'm trying to do as much as I can by myself. They don't necessarily like it, but they understand.

One thing that hasn't changed is how much I miss Piper, or maybe it has, because with each day that passes, I feel like I miss her a little more.

I feel restless.

Sammy went to bed over two hours ago, but I'm still up. I tried working on some new songs, but I couldn't concentrate. So now, I'm wandering around the house looking for something to do.

Walking down the hall, I peek my head into Sammy's room for the umpteenth time, but she's still fast asleep, arms wrapped tight around Bubba. After watching her for a minute, I end up in my room, staring into my closet. There are a couple of boxes that are still unpacked. Now seems like as good a time as any, so I begin opening them up.

One is full of keepsakes from my time on the road. Band merch, pictures, gifts from fans. They're all reminders of a chapter in my life that's closed. Those ten years I spent on and off the road were some of the best times of my life, but I can honestly say I'm fine with leaving all of that in the past. I know with Sammy in my life I have even better adventures ahead.

I grab a pen from a nearby shelf and write the word "storage" on the outside before taping it back closed and pushing it to the side of the closet.

When I open the second box, I feel like the air has been knocked out of me. There, on top of more band shirts, is a small, black velvet box. Of course, I know what's inside, but I have to open it. Looking down at the ring I proposed to Piper with floods me with emotions I wasn't prepared for. It's an odd mixture of happiness and regret.

And something else that's been brewing inside me since my talk with Deacon—determination. I made this mess. I did this. I pushed Piper away and never gave her a choice. So, I'm determined to find a way to fix it.

Without another thought, I grab my phone from my pocket and dial Micah's number. It's just past closing time at Lagniappe, so I know he's up.

"Hey, man," he answers. "Everything okay?"

"Yeah, sorry for callin' so late, but I was hopin' you and Dani would come over for dinner tomorrow night."

"You cookin'?"

"We can order out if you want."

"Then we'll be there," he says with a laugh.

Fucker.

"Great, see ya then."

The line goes dead and I sit there for a minute, turning over in my mind the plan that's been building. Also, knowing I made the right decision calling Micah. If that would've been Deacon, he'd have asked a million questions and wanted to know everything.

Micah's not like that. Sometimes, he's a man of few words, which works perfectly with my plan, because tomorrow night, I'll be picking Dani's brain.

Looking around my closet, there are no more boxes to unpack or go through. So, after I take the ring box out and tape the second box up, I turn the light off and walk over to my bed, free falling onto it with a thud.

As I hold the ring box up, opening it to display the diamond, I think about calling Piper, but it's an hour ahead in Connecticut. I don't know what her schedule is like or if she's asleep. I feel like I don't know anything that's going on in her life right now and it kills me.

The fear that's been tickling the back of my brain the last few weeks comes to haunt me.

What if I'm too late?

What if she's moved on?

I just wish she would fucking talk to me. Ever since she left for Connecticut, she's been distant, like she's putting up a wall between us. When I ask her about her job, she gives me shit answers. She knows they're shit. I know they're shit. And she knows I know they're shit.

But it doesn't keep her from giving them and dodging the truth.

Everything else I ask her is answered with vagueness. The only time I feel like she's being real with me these days is when we're talking about Sammy, which is often.

She and Sammy even FaceTimed last week. I just sat back and listened, feeling content for the first time since she left.

Eventually, I must fall asleep, because the next thing I know, a small person is climbing into bed with me.

Maybe I shouldn't let her. Maybe it's a bad habit to start, but I can't find it in myself to care. Reaching over, I flip the switch on my lamp and we both go back to sleep.

"Hey, Tucker." Annie's voice sounds chipper. She's always a good person to talk to on the phone, because you instantly feel better.

"Hey, Mama A. Did I catch you at a bad time?"

"It's never a bad time," she croons. "You know that. What's up? Need me to watch Sammy?"

I smile, because that's another thing Annie is always good at. She jumps on any chance to keep Sammy for me. I don't know what I'd do without all the women in my life.

"No, Dad doesn't need me until later and Kay said I could just bring her with me when I come," I tell her, hoping I'm not hurting her feelings.

"Oh, well, that's fine. I was plannin' on coffee with Kay later. So, I'll just see her then."

"Well, I do need something...a favor, actually," I tell her, needing to get to the point of my call before Sammy walks back into the room.

"Of course, what is it?" she asks, already agreeing to something she doesn't even know about.

"Sammy's birthday is coming up," I start. "It's actually the twenty-fifth, same as Mama's." I pause, realizing I hadn't had a chance to tell Annie that yet. I shared it with Dad and Cami, but not Annie. There just hasn't been an opportunity with everything else going on.

"Annie?" I ask, when she doesn't say anything.

"Sorry," she says and I swear I hear a crack in her voice. "I'm just, well, it's amazing how things work out."

"It is," I agree. "Dad says he thinks Mama had a hand in all this."

"I tend to agree with your dad." Annie's words are soft and

thoughtful. "Anyway, what was the favor?"

"Well, you know Sammy thinks your house is a castle."

Annie laughs. "Bless that child. God, I love her."

I smile, feeling the same. "Yeah, well, I was wonderin' if you'd be okay with us havin' her party out at your place? I found a princess bounce house and Mrs. Martin is makin' her a castle cake. I thought it might be fun to have the party at her real-life castle."

"Oh, I'd love it," she exclaims, and I can already hear the wheels turning.

"Now, no goin' overboard. She's just five. This isn't gonna be a Landry shindig. We ain't invitin' the whole town," I warn, knowing how she tends to go overboard on things like this.

"You hush, Tucker Benoit. A girl only turns five once. Besides, we have four years of birthdays to make up for."

"Alright," I finally say, because what else is there to say?

You don't argue with Annie Landry.

"Good," she says. "You leave the food and decoratin' up to me."

"Fine."

"Oh, this is gonna be so fun! Do you know how long it's been since I've planned a birthday party for a little girl? Years!"

And, the beast has been set loose.

"Yeah." I can see there's no turning back now, so I better just let her go. "Well, Sammy's comin', so I've gotta run."

"Okay, we'll talk soon."

Hanging up, I slide my phone in my pocket and let out a deep breath.

"Daddy, are you sad?" Sammy's question startles me, for more than one reason. I didn't hear her come in the room, and I don't want her worrying about me.

"No, sunshine. Why do you think that?" I ask, kneeling to her level, motioning her over to me. She walks over with a thoughtful look on her face, coming right into my arms.

"You just sighed," she says, mimicking me. "You do that when you're sad."

"I do?" I look at her—really look at her, sitting down in the middle of the kitchen floor and pulling her onto my lap. "Well, I'm not sad. I have you. How can I be sad? You're my sunshine."

"Do you miss Piper?" she asks and I swear the air leaves my lungs, but I try to recover quickly.

"Why? Do you miss Piper?" Turning the question back around to her gives me a few more seconds to get my shit together.

"Yes," she admits, so easily. "Why'd she have to go to Connect-icut?"

The way she butchers the state makes me laugh. Very seldom does Sammy miss a beat. Her language skills are better than kids two and three years older than her. But when she does, it's freaking adorable.

Her frown tells me she's not happy that I'm laughing. This is a serious talk. "Ahem, sorry."

"She liked it here. She told me," Sammy continues when I don't answer her question.

"Oh, really?"

"Yeah, when we FaceTimed, I asked her if she moved because she didn't like it here anymore, but she said she liked it here. If you like a place, you stay there. My friend Charles moved because his mommy didn't like their house."

Sammy's four-year-old reasoning makes me smile. And I agree, if you like a place, you should stay there.

"Do you think you could ask her to come back?" Sammy asks and I swallow, trying to school my features, because she's sitting in my lap, facing me, as she plays with the cross I wear around my neck. But she has no idea what kind of loaded question she's asking or how many times I've wondered the same thing.

"It's not that easy, Sammy. Piper is an adult, and adults have responsibilities. They can't just up and move places. She has a new job and a new place to live—"

"No, she doesn't," Sammy informs, interrupting my shitty excuse. "She lives with her parents."

Her little eyebrows arch up and she gives me the cutest expression, like *can you believe that?*

It's then I realize Sammy might know more about Piper than I do, and I'm not sure whether to be offended or happy about it.

"Well, I can't just ask her to move back." Even as the words leave my mouth, I'm not sure I believe them. Can I ask her to move back? If I did, would she?

"Where'd you get this?" Sammy asks, holding up the cross at the end of the chain around my neck.

"Uh," I pause, wondering where all these hard questions are coming from. "My mama gave it to me. A long time ago."

"When she was sick?" She asks the question so nonchalantly, like it's normal conversation. To her, it is. To most kids her age, they don't have the first clue about someone being sick, at least not the kind of sick she's talking about. They don't know about death and loss. They don't know about grieving.

Sammy knows about all of that.

At first, I hated it. I hated that she had to experience the death of her mother. I hated that she had to see her deteriorate, but now, I can't hate it, because I see what's it's making her into. She's becoming one of the most empathetic people I know. And she's four...almost five, going on twenty-five.

"Yeah, when she was sick. She gave it to me as a reminder that she'd always be watching over me. Just like your mama's always watching over you."

Sammy continues to run her thumb over the silver cross. "It's pretty. What was your mama's name?"

"Jessie," I tell her. "Remember you share a birthday with her?"

"Yep." Sammy's smile breaks across her face.

"She's watching over you too, sunshine." I pull Sammy closer, kissing the top of her head and saying a silent prayer, thanking my mama for watching over me all these years, and for bringing me my own personal ray of sunshine.

"Come on, kiddo." I help Sammy off my lap and then climb to my feet. "We gotta get ready for Uncle Micah and Aunt Dani. They'll be here for dinner soon."

"Yay!" Sammy takes off running down the hall toward her bedroom. I've already learned that her prepping for company and my prepping for company are two different things.

She's probably setting up her table for tea.

I look around the kitchen and wonder what I'm making for dinner. I know I told Micah that I'd order something and pick it up, but I don't feel like getting out and I'm running out of time. So, I walk to the fridge and take inventory.

An hour later, dinner is on the table, and there's a knock at the door.

"I'll get it," Sammy yells, running around the corner.

"Ask who it is first," I remind her. Not that we live in some big city, where strangers knock on your door, but I don't want her to get too comfortable answering the door.

"Who is it?" I hear her yell.

"The Avon Lady and Cookie Monster," Micah yells back.

"The Avon Lady and Cookie Monster," Sammy repeats.

"Tell them to go away. We don't need any," I instruct with a laugh, waiting to hear Sammy repeat what I said, but she doesn't. The next thing I know, an annoyed Sammy is standing in the kitchen with her hands on her hips.

"Daddy," she says with way too much sass. "It's Uncle Micah."

"Oh, well, in that case, I guess you can let him in."

She turns and stomps off back toward the door.

"Munchkin," Micah exclaims, doing something to make Sammy squeal.

When they come into the kitchen, he has her turned upside down on his shoulder.

"Hey, where do you want this sack of potatoes?" he asks with a big ass grin.

"Eh, just put them down over there." I gesture toward the table and he sits Sammy down in her chair.

"I swear, Sammy," Dani says, taking the seat beside her. "We're the adults."

"Yeah, not those two." Sammy's winded as she pushes her hair out of her face and gives me and Micah a wide smile.

"Chicken nuggets and mac and cheese?" Micah asks, looking over my shoulder and stealing a nugget. "Really? Are we, like, four?" He kisses my cheek and I elbow him in the gut.

"Hey!" Sammy says, taking offense to Micah's remark.

"Kiddin'." He holds his hands up in surrender and takes the seat across from Sammy. "I love nuggets. You're a pretty cute nugget. Maybe I'll eat you."

"No!" Sammy laughs. "I'm not food!"

I put the nuggets, mac and cheese, corn, and a big salad on the table.

"This looks great," Dani says. "Thanks for the invite. I didn't feel like cooking tonight."

"Well, thanks for comin' over."

After we've all finished eating, Sammy puts her napkin on her plate and looks over at me.

"Can we have tea now?" she asks.

I should've known that was coming.

"Did someone say tea?" Micah asks, wiping his mouth and tossing his napkin on the table. "I could sure go for a cup of tea." He takes on a terrible British accent for that last part.

Sammy giggles, covering her mouth.

"Shall we?" he asks, offering her his hand.

She takes it and skips away.

"God," Dani mutters. "Those two are so cute."

"You should get you one."

She sighs, leaning back in her chair. "Nah, I think we'll just borrow y'all's for now. Besides, Micah's competing for that Best Uncle title, and he's pretty serious about it."

"Yeah, he's kinda puttin' me to shame these days."

"You're not too shabby. These kids are definitely lucky."

I nod, swallowing as I try to think of how to come out with what

I want to say—the real reason I invited them over for dinner tonight.

"Well, let me help clean up dinner," Dani offers, standing up and gathering a few bowls.

"You don't have to do that. Really," I tell her, taking the bowls from her and setting them beside the sink. "After Sammy goes to bed, I wander the house lookin' for somethin' to do."

"This is different for you," Dani says, leaning against the counter, her eyes on the floor. "When I first met you, I thought you were nothing but trouble." She laughs, shaking her head as she looks back up at me.

"I was. Probably still am." I smirk, smoothing my hair back.

"I know about you and Piper," she says, wincing at the words. "I know I shouldn't say this. Pretty sure I'm violating some best friend code, but I just want you to know that I know."

Her words shock me.

But then again, they don't.

I mean, how long could we go without anyone knowing. Deacon obviously caught on a long time ago, and somehow, kept his mouth shut, which is a miracle in itself.

I nod my head, trying to think of what to say now.

Letting out a deep breath, I start. "Well, that's actually why I invited y'all over tonight. I wanted to talk to you."

"About what?" she asks. Her expression is a mixture of leery and hopeful.

"Piper. I just..." I blow out another breath. "I messed up. I should've asked her to stay, or at least told her how I feel—gave her a choice. I need to fix it. But she's not talkin' to me. I can't get her to tell me anything these days. She'll hardly even talk to me about her new job."

"She hates it," Dani says, pushing off the counter. "She's miserable."

"Why won't she tell me?"

"She doesn't want you to worry about her. She says you have enough to worry about without her adding to it." She gives me a tight smile. "You probably don't know about Birmingham either or her leaving *Southern Style?*"

"All she would tell me is that she left because she felt like she had no room to grow."

"That's bullshit," Dani says, a hint of anger coming to her tone. "She was basically coerced into quitting. Her boss found out about the proposal video—"

"Shit."

Mother fucker.

"I can't believe she didn't tell me."

"He held it over her head for a couple of months, making her jump through all his hoops until she couldn't take it anymore. She told him to fuck off. He told her she was finished." Dani sighs, crossing her arms. "She didn't know what else to do. Without you and without her job, she didn't feel like she had a place here anymore. She's miserable in Connecticut—living with her parents, working a job her dad got for her. If you know anything about Piper, you know that's a bad place for her."

My heart squeezes.

Fuck.

I rub my hand over my chest, trying to get the tightness to ease up. "I've gotta get her back," I tell her.

"Do you have a plan?"

"Not exactly, but I'm working on it. Can I count on you for help?"

Dani looks at me intently for a moment before answering. "I wasn't sure you two were right for each other when Piper first told me, but you're more alike than I realized. Bottom line, my best friend is miserable and I want her to be happy. You deserve to be happy, too, Tucker, and I think Piper is the one to make that happen, so, yes, I'll help."

CHAPTER TWENTY-FIVE

I'VE BEEN STEWING OVER MY CONVERSATION WITH DANI FOR THE last two days. The longer I stew, the more pissed off I get. Piper hasn't answered my calls or replied to my text messages. I'm trying not to venture into stalker territory, but I'm close to putting myself on a damn plane and hunting her ass down.

All day today, while I've been running the tractor, I've also been running over in my mind what I'd like to say to her. My pretend conversation varies from "why the fuck didn't you tell me" to "please, come home". I'm not sure what it'll actually be like when she finally decides to return my calls.

As I'm walking through the barn, I look over at an unfinished piece of furniture and think about working on it for a while to help clear my head. But then, my phone rings.

"Hello?"

"Hey," Piper says, her voice sounding small and withdrawn.

"Why haven't you answered my calls?" That's where I decide to start, because the last time I checked we're at least still friends, and friends don't ignore phone calls.

"I'm sorry. Things have been kind of crazy around here...new job and everything." She drifts off, just like she always does, fully prepared to skirt the truth. But I'm not going to let her.

"I know why you left." I figure that's a good place to start.

Piper lets out a deep sigh. "What are you talking about?"

"I know about your boss finding out about the video, and I know he was holdin' it over your head. Did that really happen?" I know it did, but I want to hear it from her.

She's so quiet I worry that she's hung up on me but, finally, she responds. "Yes." Her voice is small and it breaks my heart. It also fills me with rage.

"Why didn't you tell me?" I spit out, taking my anger out on her.

"You had your own shit to deal with; you didn't need mine, too."

"I was in that video. It's because of me that you were in it, Piper. This isn't your fault; it's mine. You should've told me."

"It takes two to tango, Tucker. You know that better than anyone. Besides, it doesn't matter anymore. It's over."

Her words cause me to pause because I don't know if she's referring to the drama with her old boss or her relationship with me.

"I could've helped you. I could've done something."

"What were you going to do?" Her voice rises an octave, with a harsh laugh.

"Something," I tell her, not really knowing what I would've done. Pummeling her boss's face doesn't sound too bad right about now. "Anything. You know I would've helped in any way you needed me to."

"Like I said, it's over." She sounds so resigned, so unhappy, just like Dani said.

We both sit in silence, before I finally say what's really bothering me.

"I'm pissed you didn't tell me. You have to talk to me. How can I know what to do, if you don't talk to me?"

"Like when you didn't tell me about Sammy?" she retorts. "I think we're both pretty good at not talking about important things."

That stings, because it's true, but I'm trying to change that. She's just not letting me. Even from hundreds of miles away, I feel the walls she's built around herself.

"If you don't have anything else to say, I've gotta go."

I have so much to say—so many things I haven't told her, but I can't make my mouth work fast enough.

When she hangs up the phone, I toss mine across the barn, yelling in frustration. Staring at the roof, I will it to tell me what the fuck to do. Somebody, tell me what the fuck to do, because I'm at my wits end. I know what I want, but I have no clue how to get it.

Piper is so frustrating. She's the most stubborn person I know. It pisses me off, but it's also one of the things I love the most about her. She's tenacious and driven. But I'm willing to be just as stubborn. We've always matched each other blow for blow, giving it as good as we get.

I'm not giving up now.

Somehow, some way, I'll tell her how I feel.

I'll tell her that I love her.

I'll tell her that I don't want to live without her.

I'll let her know she has a place here, with me.

Walking over and picking up my phone, I dust it off and check it for cracks. Fortunately, it's all in one piece and the time on the screen reads a little after four. Maybe if I leave now, I can catch Micah or Deacon at Grinders. I could really use someone to talk to right about now. Kay's always a good listening ear, but I don't want to discuss this in front of Sammy.

When I get to the house, I peek my head in and tell Kay I need to run to Red Stick for a few things, asking if she minds watching Sammy, who's preoccupied with a puzzle at the kitchen table.

"Bye, Daddy," she calls out as I begin to shut the door.

"Bye, sunshine. Be good for Grandma Kay. I'll be back in a while."

She smiles up at me and waves, but goes straight back to her puzzle. It makes me feel good that she's become so comfortable with everyone so quickly, accepting everyone as members of this new, extended family. One of my biggest fears after Sophie's death was that Sammy would feel abandoned. I think it's safe to say she's thriving.

Driving down the dirt road in my old truck, with the windows rolled down and the warm May breeze blowing in, I start to feel my head clear a little.

When I pull into the parking lot behind Grinders, I see Deacon's Jeep and Micah's truck.

Good, I need to get all this shit out in the open, so I'm glad they're both here.

Walking into the back door, a few of the kitchen staff say hello or throw me a wave.

"They're in the office," Joe says. "Haven't see you around here in a while."

"Yeah, I've been a little busy."

"I heard." Joe flips a burger on the grill. "You hungry?"

"Nah, I'm good, thanks."

I pat him on his shoulder as I walk out of the kitchen and make my way down the hall to the office. Joe and I go way back. He used to be the cook at Pockets, and back in the day, I played there every Friday night. Even when we went on tour, I still played Pockets when I was in town. Sometimes with a full band, sometimes just me and my guitar. Joe would always make sure I ate well.

Before I even get to the door, I hear Micah and Deacon arguing about something. It's pretty par for the course. They've always had friendly disagreements. Now, that shit that was going on between them during the Alex Debacle, that wasn't normal. I've never seen them so at odds with each other, but I'm glad they're past that.

"Hey, bitches," I say, walking into the office.

"Well, if it isn't Tucker the Fucker," Deacon booms. "What brings you to town? Did you bring Sammy for dinner like I told you to?"

"No, she's with Kay."

Micah looks up from a stack of papers, his pen in midair. "What do we owe the honor of your presence?"

"Cut the shit," I tell them, pulling up a chair from the corner to sit by Deacon. "Can I not just pop in for a visit anymore?"

"Well, you don't." Deacon's tone sounds offended and I cringe a little. I've been really distracted lately. My priorities have shifted and it's gonna take time to figure out how to balance it all.

"Sorry, man. I'm just—"

"Nah, dude. It's cool. We know you have Sammy now and she's more important."

I nod, trying to remember the plan I came up with in my truck on the way here.

"So, what's up?" Micah asks, setting his work to the side.

"I have somethin' I need to show you." Pulling my phone out of my back pocket, I open my text messages, skimming past some recent messages between me and Dave until I get to what I'm looking for.

Pushing the arrow in the middle of the screen, the ruckus that is The Cat's Meow begins to fill the room.

I don't watch the video, because I've seen it plenty. Instead, I watch Deacon and Micah.

Deacon already knows about the video, but he hasn't seen it. Micah on the other hand, he's being blindsided right now, and I feel a little bad about it. But, I figure if I'm coming clean, I might as well start from the beginning.

"What the fuck?" Micah asks, leaning back in his chair with a wide-eyed expression. "When did that happen?"

"The night you proposed to Dani," I tell him, slipping the phone back in my pocket.

"Yeah, but I thought you and Piper hate each other. That did not look like two people who can't stand to be in the same room for longer than ten seconds." Micah's tone turns accusatory and I'm a little surprised, because I was banking on him knowing some of this. I thought Dani would've told him.

"We've been, uh—"

"They've been fucking," Deacon says, finishing my sentence. Normally, it pisses me off when he does that, but I'm actually grateful, because this is harder than I thought it was going to be and I can use all the help I can get.

"Basically." I nod my head and let out a deep breath. "At least, it started off that way. It was an arrangement of necessity and convenience."

"Yeah, you both needed to fuck each other's brains out," Deacon adds, snorting and rolling his eyes. "I can't believe you held out on us for so long. You have no idea how many times I wanted to bust you on it, but it just never seemed like the right time."

"Wait a damn second." Micah stands up quickly, bracing his hands on the desk as he looks at both of us. "He knew?" he asks, pointing at Deke.

"I didn't tell him."

"I overheard their little show in the bathroom at Mom and Dad's anniversary party." The grin on Deacon's face is oozing with self-satisfaction. He couldn't be prouder of himself for this little piece of information.

"And you didn't say anything?" Micah's voice gets louder with each question. "You fucking tell everything else you know, but keep this shit to yourself?"

"I can keep a secret when I want to," Deacon retorts. "I was waitin'."

"For what?" Micah asks, and I just sit back and let them go, because I'd rather the heat be on Deacon at the moment. It gives me a reprieve.

"The right time to use it against this fucker." Deacon points over at me. "I figured I'd save it for a rainy day. Besides, I didn't think it was still going on. I kinda assumed it was a one-time deal."

"But it's not...or wasn't?" Micah turns his glare back to me.

"No, it was...more," I admit. "I'm not even sure when it happened, but I think I fucking love her."

Micah falls back into his chair with a thoughtful look on his face. "I had my suspicions about the two of you, but I didn't expect you to say that."

Smoothing my hair back, I exhale. "Pretty sure that's the first time I've even admitted it to myself."

"So, what are you gonna do about it?" Micah asks.

"That's what I was hopin' you two could help me figure out. You got the girls. Tell me how to get mine."

"It ain't easy, man," Deke says with a sigh.

"No, but it's worth it," Micah adds.

"I feel like I've fucked this all up so bad."

"First things first, you need to tell her how you feel," Deacon says.

"Yeah, but not just that. Personally, I'm a fan of grand gestures." Micah leans forward, resting his elbows on the table. "When Dani was dealin' with all that shit with her ex, I flew my ass to New York. Sometimes, you gotta show them you're serious, make some effort. Dad says actions speak louder than words. So, you're gonna have to do something."

"Think I should fly to Connecticut?" I ask. "What about Sammy? I don't feel like I can leave her right now."

We're all in thinking mode when my phone rings.

I mindlessly take it out of my pocket and answer it.

"Hello?"

"Yeah, is this Tucker Benoit?"

"Speaking."

"This is Coy Smith. You sent me a demo last week of a song you wrote."

Shit. My heart drops.

"Mr. Smith...yes, sir, that was me."

"Well, I love it. I've let my partner listen to it and he's sold on it too. We'd like to see what else you might have for us, maybe hear a live performance?"

The recording I sent was crap. I used some old recording equipment Dave let me borrow. I'm surprised they made it through the first verse, let alone liked it enough to call me. My heart speeds up, as I let his request sink in.

"Uh, yeah, sure...I could probably set somethin' up," I tell him.

"Great," he replies. "Could we maybe arrange something for next week? We have a new recording artist who's in desperate need of some songs and your style is just what we've been looking for."

An artist.

Singing my songs.

Holy shit.

"Mr. Smith, could you hold for a second?" I ask.

"Sure."

Pressing my thumb over the receiver, I look up at Micah who's watching me with a confused expression.

"I'm gonna need to play at Lagniappe next week. Cool?"

"Sure."

"Mr. Smith?"

"Yes."

"I'll call you with the information tomorrow."

"Sounds great. We'll talk then."

He hangs up and I stare at my phone in disbelief for a second, before looking back up at Micah.

"I think I have a plan."

CHAPTER TWENTY-SIX

Tonight's the night.

Finally.

I should be nervous but I'm not. I have a lot going on tonight, a bunch of irons in the fire, if you will, and I'm hopeful everything turns out well. It has to. My future is on the line here, in more ways than one.

Because of the extra adrenaline running through my veins, I have my equipment set up in the corner of Lagniappe's dining area early, leaving me with nothing to do but wait. Sitting at the bar while Micah's staff gets ready for the evening shift, I allow myself one shot of whisky. It's just enough to relax my vocal cords, while tamping down my excitement.

I need to keep my cool.

"Hey, Tucker. Getting some liquid courage before your set? Dani smiles as she sits on the bar stool next to me.

"Nah, I'm cool as a cucumber. This is helping me stay mellow."

"I see," she says with a chuckle. The bartender places her drink in front of her and she takes a sip, letting out a low whistle when she's done. "Whew. I guess Lagniappe also means you get an extra shot in your drink."

"Or the staff knows they'd better keep the boss's wife happy or else," I joke.

"Hmm, maybe so. If I have another one of these drinks, though, I'll be more than happy. I'll be falling down drunk, I'm afraid."

"So, um, I'm tryin' not to ask but you know I have to..."

"Yes, I told Piper about you performing tonight and I did my best to convince her to come down here but she never gave me a straight answer. She did sound very interested and excited about you performing for this music bigwig from Nashville, so I have a feeling she'll show up."

That's not exactly what I was hoping to hear but at least she knows what's going on tonight. All I can do is hope Piper shows up to see me perform. If she doesn't, I guess I'll have to resort to Plan B, whatever that is.

"Oh, look, there's your fan club. Annie! Sam! We're over here!" Dani waves, catching Annie's attention. She waves back and heads our way, followed by Sam, my dad, Kay, and Sammy.

"Daddy!" Sammy squeals when she sees me, running straight into my arms. I squeeze her tightly and kiss her head. "Hey, sunshine. I'm so glad you're here."

"I can't wait to watch you on the stage. You're my favorite singer." She smiles at me and looks so happy, it takes my breath away.

"Well, you're my favorite sunshine. Whatcha think about that?"

"I'm your only sunshine, just like the song says," she says, referring to the Louisiana state song. I sing it to her every morning when she wakes up.

"That's right and don't you forget it." I tickle her side, making her giggle, before setting her feet on the floor. "How about we go to our table? You hungry?"

"I'm starving. I'm gonna ask Uncle Micah to fix me some mac and cheese." I watch as she skips to our reserved table, finding a chair right in the middle and sitting down.

"Son, you ready for tonight?" My dad claps me on the shoulder, which is basically his way of hugging me.

"I am. I feel good," I answer honestly.

"I mean, about Piper, you know. You got this music-thing in the bag but will it be enough to get Piper back?"

By now, all my family and friends know about me and Piper. They may not know all the sordid details but they know I fucked up and am trying to get her back. Even I have to admit how nice it is that everyone is here to support me in both of my endeavors tonight. I just hope I don't let them down.

Shit, I need to get on the stage so I can get out of my head.

Shrugging, I answer honestly. "I don't know, Dad, but I sure hope so."

After a few minutes, Micah motions for me to go to him. The dinner crowd is steadily filling, which means it's close to show time. I stand up, kiss Sammy on the head, and wave to everyone else at our table.

"See y'all after the show."

Various cheers and words of encouragement are sent my way as I join Micah by the hostess stand.

"Tucker, this here is Coy Smith. He's here to watch your show." Micah points to a man who looks like a perfect example of Nashville hipster. A goatee, glasses, and fedora greet me first, followed by a classic rock T shirt and ripped jeans. The cowboy boots on Coy's feet wrap up his ensemble perfectly and I quickly assess him as being a cool dude.

"Hey, man." I stick my hand out for him to shake. "Good to meet you. Thanks for comin'."

"The pleasure's all mine. I'm excited to watch you perform."

"Let me show you to your table, while Tucker gets ready. He'll be performin' shortly." Micah leads Coy away but manages to turn toward me, giving me a quick thumbs up.

I honestly don't know what I'd do without my support system.

While Micah gets Coy settled, I take the opportunity to look around the room for Piper. I know if she were here, she'd be at the table with my family but I also wouldn't be surprised if she was hiding in a corner somewhere. I don't see her but I keep the disappointment at bay. There's plenty of time for her to get here and I have a good amount of songs to perform before I do the one I want her to hear the most.

I roll my shoulders and stretch my neck, loosening up my muscles and forcing the tension away, before I head for the stage. Micah beats me there and introduces me, before walking back to the bar to watch.

"Hey, y'all," I speak into the microphone. "My name is Tucker Benoit and I'm gonna play a few songs for y'all, if that's alright."

The crowd instantly claps and cheers, sending me the positive vibes I need to make me feel at home. Being on stage is second nature for me, but it's a hundred times better when the audience is excited and receptive, like this one is.

I grab my guitar and place the strap around my shoulder before strumming a couple of times. After making another quick glance across the room and coming up empty, I close my eyes and begin to play.

Throughout my set, I try to force myself to not think about Piper but it's hard. She's in everything I do, especially when I sing the songs I wrote for her. In the end, though, the fact she's not here works to my favor because I'm able to pour the emotions coursing through me—anger, disappointment, sadness, loneliness—and give one of the best performances of my career. The crowd is right there with me, too. They're feeling what I'm feeling and supporting me in ways they'll probably never understand.

"Well, it's time for my last song." The crowd boos a little, making me smile. "I want to thank y'all for bein' so great tonight. I really appreciate it. Here's a song I wrote called 'The Best Kind of Trouble.'"

I begin strumming my guitar, playing an up-tempo rhythm, and soon, the audience is clapping along. Originally, I was going to play my song to Piper at this point but, since she's not here, I've decided to save it. It's always better to end a set with a song that leaves the crowd pumped up, rather than melancholy, in my opinion.

"You're trouble of the best kind.
You stole my heart and robbed me blind.
One look from you and I hit the floor.
One call from you and I'm out the door.
You told me I was convenient.
I told you I didn't care.

But the truth is I love you,
And I'm too scared to share.
Somewhere between the kissin' and fightin',
I fell hard.
Somewhere between now and then,
I lost my heart.
It's yours.
You own it.
You're the best kind of trouble."

By the end of the song, the crowd is clapping and singing along, giving me the high I used to live for. It still feels great, don't get me wrong, but it's a quick high that I know will leave me feeling empty once I'm done.

Something catches my eye and I look to the side of the stage and see Sammy dancing. Her wild curls are bouncing all over the place and she's singing and giggling, having the time of her life. It's then that I realize the empty feeling I was expecting isn't there. As much as I miss Piper and want her here with me, I know I'll be okay because of that little girl. Some people may think I saved her but, really, it's the other way around.

When the song ends, I wave my thanks to the audience and set my guitar on its stand before scooping Sammy up in my arms, giving her a kiss on her cheek before setting her back down. My parents and the Landrys join me, showering me with praise. I feel good about the set, and I hope Coy likes my songs enough to buy them.

Occasionally, throughout the set, I'd give him a glance while I played. Each time, he seemed to be enjoying himself, but I won't know until I speak with him.

Micah steps up to me and hands me a bottle of water. "Great job, man."

"Thanks," I tell him, before taking a big gulp of water. "Thanks for all of this."

"Any time. You know that. And, for what's it worth, I'm sorry she didn't come. Dani really thought she'd be here."

I wave him off. "It's all good. I guess it just wasn't meant to be." I hand him back the bottle and go into the bathroom to splash some cold water on my face. I don't want to be a sweaty mess when I talk to Coy.

When I step out of the bathroom, Coy is waiting for me.

"Hey, Coy. Thanks, again, for comin' all the way to New Orleans to hear me play."

"No, man, thank you. I love your music and think it'll be a great fit with the artist I'm workin' with. I have to ask, though, why aren't you tryin' to get a music deal? You know how to put on a show and I think we could help you make a big name for yourself."

I take a moment to think about what he's offering. A year ago, I'd be on this opportunity like white on rice and I can't deny the appeal. It's what I worked so hard for when I was on the road. But, then I look over at Sammy and know that life isn't for me anymore and I have no regrets.

"I appreciate what you're sayin', I really do. The road life just isn't for me anymore but, if my songs can help other artists make a livin' and reach their dreams, then I'm more than willin' to keep writin'."

He gives me a long look before nodding his head in understanding. "If you ever change your mind, you know where to find me. I'll definitely be in touch after I play these songs for my people, so don't go anywhere."

"I'll be here," I promise.

He shakes my hand and gives me his business card before leaving the restaurant. As I watch him walk out the door, I feel a tiny body slam into the back of my legs.

"Daddy, you sang so good," Sammy gushes.

I turn and pick up my daughter, giving her a peck on her nose. "Thanks, sunshine. I'm glad you had fun tonight."

"She sure did," Kay agrees. "I think it's time for the little party animal to go home, though."

Sammy makes a pouting face, but I know she's tired. It's way past her bedtime and I'm sure she's worn out from all the dancing she did.

"Grandma Kay is right, Sammy. It's time for you to go home with her and Grandpa. I'll see you tomorrow, okay?"

Her shoulders sag, but she accepts her fate, reaching out for my dad to carry her.

"You did great, son," he tells me, hugging Sammy close to him. "I'm proud of you."

I give him a small smile and wave as my family, plus Annie and Sam, make their way out the door.

"Tucker, I'm so sorry." I turn and see Dani looking at the ground.

"Don't apologize. I'll be fine. It doesn't mean I can't try again. There's gotta be a Plan B, right?"

"I hope so," she admits. "I really do."

"So, what's a guy gotta do to get a burger around here? I'm starvin'!"

Dani laughs and nudges me back toward our table. "Sit here. Micah's already cookin' you something special."

"That's what I'm talkin' about."

After I eat, I kill time talking to some of the guests that stop by and congratulate me on my show. It makes me feel good to hear they had fun because, ultimately, that's what it's all about for me...doing something that makes others feel something, anything with my music.

"You still here?" Micah asks, sitting down next to me.

"Yeah, I figured I'd hang out, help with the clean-up or whatever else you might need."

"Tucker—" he starts but I cut him off.

"I'm not ready to give up yet, okay?"

He nods his head in understanding and stands up. "In that case, get your ass to work, wipin' down these table, would ya?"

"You got it, boss man." I grab a rag from one of the busboys and start doing as Micah asked.

I take my time, allowing the leftover adrenaline from my set to settle down. By the time I'm done, I look around and see I'm the only one in the dining room. I hear a few voices in the kitchen, but other than that, I'm completely alone.

I guess there's no reason for me to stay any longer, so it's time I face the inevitable. I walk to the stage and grab my equipment. First, tearing down the mic and stand, placing them in their carrying bag. Then, I pick up my guitar, unplugging it from the amp. When I go to place the guitar in its case, I hear a knocking sound. Looking around the room, I try to figure out where the sound is coming from. It's not until I see Piper at one of the front windows with her fist in the air, that I realize what's happening.

Holy shit, she's here.

She's late as fuck but she's here.

After setting my guitar back down, I make my way to the door and open it. She walks up to me, staring, waiting for me to let her inside. I'm still in such shock that she's actually here, it takes me a minute to realize I'm blocking the door. But, still, I don't move.

"I didn't think you were coming," I admit.

"I didn't think I was either. I mean, I wanted to but it seemed like everything was against me getting here on time. I'm sorry."

I look at her, really look at her. She looks tired and frustrated and worried and she's still the most beautiful woman I've ever seen.

Finally, I move out of her way and allow her to come inside the restaurant. "Come in. I was just packin' up."

"Tucker, I really am sorry I missed your show. I know it was important to you. I didn't even expect you to be here this late, but I had to try."

"I was waitin' for you. I've been doin' everything I could think of to put off leavin', but I'd just given up when you knocked on the window."

"Given up?" I can see the tears forming in her eyes and it kills me.

"Can I play you a song?" I ask, rather than answer her question.

"Of course." She wipes under her eyes and takes a seat at a table in front of the stage. I take my guitar out of the case and, instead of getting on the stage, I sit in a chair across from her.

"I was saving this song for you," I tell her as I begin to play.

"You're everything I was looking for, but never knew I needed.
You're the answer to my prayers and every song I'm singin'.
I should've told you sooner. I should've changed my plans.

I should've listened to my heart and taken the chance.
Now, I'm sitting here with a hole only you can fill.
And I'm wonderin' if you think of me still.
A sad goodbye on a warm Louisiana day.
A broken heart in the middle of May.
That's not how our song ends.
The right place at the wrong time.
The change of heart on a dime.
That's not how our song ends.
I don't want to live without you.
I don't even want to try.
So this is me loving, changing the story.
Standing in front of you saying, "I'm sorry!"
Darlin', let's do some daring, fight under the covers.
Let's take this story from enemies to lovers.
We can show the world how true love looks.
We'll give them something for the books.
A sad goodbye on a warm Louisiana day.
A broken heart in the middle of May.
That's not how our song ends."

When the song is over, I stand up and walk over to the stage, placing the guitar back in its case. As I turn to sit back down, Piper is standing right in front of me, tears streaming down her face. Cupping her jaw, I use my thumb to wipe her tears.

"Why are you cryin'?"

"Because I don't want our song to end." Her voices breaks and I feel the familiar squeeze in my chest.

"What do you want?"

No more games, no more avoiding our feelings. Now's the time to be honest and whatever she's about to say, I'll have to honor.

"I want you, Tucker Benoit."

I quirk my eyebrow at her, because I can't help myself. "Is that so?"

"Yes, dammit. I want you and everything that comes with you... Sammy, country living, dirt roads, and loud music. I want it all."

"So, no more job in Connecticut?" I ask, searching her gorgeous face for any hint of reservation.

"Nope. I'm officially free and unemployed."

"No more Greg?"

"Greg? No, Greg was never an option, just a distraction." She gives me a small smile and shakes her head. "It's always been you, Tucker, no matter how hard I've tried to fight it."

"But, you have to admit, some fightin' is fun." I grab her hips a little tighter, pulling her to me.

Her face lights up as she tries to fight her smile. Then she goes serious, an intensity in her eyes that I've always loved, even when it used to scare the shit out of me.

"Stop being an asshole and kiss me already," she demands.

Sliding my fingers through the hair at the nape of her neck, I pull her close to me, breathing her in for a second. "Your wish is my command."

I touch my lips to hers, trying to be soft and take it slow, but Piper is having none of that. She deepens the kiss and wraps her arms around my neck, not afraid to show her true feelings anymore. I don't hold back either, expressing myself with every kiss, every swirl of my tongue, and nip of my teeth.

"I missed you so much," Piper groans out in between kisses.

"Just me?"

"No, I missed your demon dick, too. I might've missed him more than you, now that I think about it."

I can't help but break our kiss and laugh loudly. This is us. This is how we are and what I've missed, and I fucking love it.

Grabbing her by the waist, I pull her body flush with mine, so she can feel my reaction to her. "I can't wait for me and my demon dick to show you how much we've missed you, too."

"For the love of all things holy and righteous! Would you two get the hell out of my restaurant?" Micah yells from the kitchen door.

Still laughing, I grab my guitar case and the rest of my equipment. When I look back at Piper, her lips are swollen and her eyes are bright.

I know we still have some things to work out, but we have all the time in the world for that. For tonight, though, it's all about getting back to us.

"Come on," I tell her. "Let's go home."

"Home, huh?"

"You have a better idea?"

She pretends to think for a minute before smiling at me. "Nope. Home sounds perfect."

CHAPTER TWENTY-SEVEN

Unfortunately, or probably fortunately, piper rented a car at the airport, so she's currently in front of me, driving a few miles over the speed limit.

I'm still trying to process that she's here and she wants me—everything about me, including Sammy. I'd hoped. I'd prayed. But there was still a nagging doubt in the back of my mind that Piper would ever settle for small town life. She's always seemed bigger than that in my mind, more than what a place like French Settlement has to offer. But if she's willing to make the sacrifice to be here with me, and Sammy, then I'm willing to do everything in my power to make her happy.

Finally, we turn off the main road and onto the street that leads home.

When I pull in the drive, I barely remember to turn my truck off before I'm out the door and jogging up to Piper's car.

"In a hurry?" she asks with a soft smile and a quirk of her eyebrow.

"Just to get you in my bed, then I'm planning on takin' my time."

No quickies tonight. No leaving. Nowhere else to be, except exactly where we're meant to be.

She steps out of the car and up to me, grabbing me by my shirt. Leaning up on her tip-toes, she's almost eye-level with me. "This isn't a quick fuck. I don't know about you, but I'm ready for slow."

"You read my mind."

"What else is going through that brilliant mind of yours?"

"I love you," I breathe out, touching my nose to hers, but refraining my need to kiss her until I get out what I want to say. "I should've told you a long time ago. I was just scared and stupid. So fucking stupid. I should've never let you go. I should've asked you to stay. I should've given you a choice when it came to Sammy. Not sure why I ever doubted you. I should've known that you'd be amazing with her. But I couldn't see past my insecurities. Forgive me. Tell me you're gonna stay forever."

"I'm here. I'm not going anywhere," she says softly. "And I forgive you. Although, there's nothing to forgive. I can't fault you for being cautious...it's my middle name. I think you and I are a lot more alike than we care to admit. But, hopefully, our incredible differences will keep some balance in the force." She laughs, with a hint of emotion in her voice, and I crush her to me, wanting nothing more than to just hold her and know she's mine.

For real.

"I love you," she whispers into my chest. "I think I've loved you for a long time, but I just recently admitted it to myself or let myself believe it. Being without you was worse than dealing with my parents. I knew I had to find a way back here. Dani calling was what I needed to make the move."

"I made the move," I tell her.

"You told Dani to call me," she counters. "I got on the plane."

"Yeah, but you wouldn't have got on that plane, unless I told Dani to call you."

We both pull back a little, as the usual banter between us fires up.

"Let's just agree that we both made a move," she suggests.

"Compromise, I like it," I tell her with a waggle of my eyebrows.

"You're so infuriating sometimes." She rolls her eyes while trying to hide her smile.

"And you love me for it." I pin her against the car, my arms caging her in.

"I do." Her eyes bore into mine, straight to my soul. "I love every infuriating thing about you. I love that you're rough around the edges. I love the way you can piss me off faster than anyone else I know. I love that you call me on my bullshit, and that I can all you on yours."

"I love pissing you off," I admit. "But not because you're mad. I love the way your face lights up, like you're ready for the challenge. It fucking turns me on. So, I hope you're okay with me pissing you off for the next sixty years."

"Only sixty?" she asks.

"Well, I figure when we're ninety, I'll trade you in on a new model."

A slight punch to my gut makes me laugh, and then Piper's arms are wrapped around my neck and her legs are around my waist. There's nothing left for me to do but carry her in the house—straight to bed.

WAKING UP THE NEXT MORNING, I ROLL OVER AND AM MET WITH the greatest sight known to man—free-range titties.

And they're mine.

Well, not technically. But unlike in the past, I know exactly who they belong to, and *she's* mine.

Again, not technically, or in the eyes of the law, but I'm hoping to change that one of these days, along with her last name.

Pulling myself away from the view, I roll over and grab the black box from the drawer of my nightstand. I roll it over in my hand, thinking about it and the night that eventually led us here.

Life, man, what a fucking roller coaster. If you'd have asked me a year ago where I'd be, I wouldn't have said this. I didn't even know what *this* was. All I knew was life on the road, with my band, living one day to the next. I didn't even know I wanted this—settled down, being a dad to Sammy, lying here next to Piper.

This is happiness.

"I expected you to be ogling my boobs," Piper says in a sleepy voice.

"I was," I admit, rolling back over to face her, getting a look at all the goods—from her perfect tits to her beautiful face. "But then I remembered something I want you to have."

A sly smile forms on her lips. "Round two?"

"Yes, but first, this." I take her left hand and slip the ring on her finger. Last time this happened, I don't even remember it. Vague snippets of that night have come back to me over the months, but for the life of me, I couldn't remember actually putting this ring on Piper's finger. And now, I'm glad, because it's one of the best feelings in the world.

"You want me to wear this?" She looks up at me with a soft look on her face, and then she looks down at the ring, splaying her fingers out to get a good look.

"I do," I tell her, nodding my head. "*Technically*, I asked you. And *technically*, you said yes. So..."

"I did." She smiles up at me. "I thought maybe you sold it or something. Why did you keep it?"

"For now."

"You're lying if you said you knew we'd be here, right now, under these circumstances," she challenges.

"Okay, so I didn't know, but I hoped."

"And if you hadn't pulled your head out of your ass...or I hadn't come back? Then what?"

"So, I'm the only one who needed to pull their head out of their ass?" I question with a pointed look, earning a guilty smile. "I guess I would've had an expensive souvenir from our time together."

"I think it would've worked out, regardless," she says, with a thoughtful expression. "I think when two people are meant to be together, the universe makes it happen."

"That might be the most romantic thing I've ever heard you say." I pull her to me, loving the feel of her bare skin against mine.

"I can be romantic."

"If you really want to be romantic, tell me you're gonna wear this." I pick up her hand and kiss where the ring resides. "And that you're gonna marry me one day."

"Okay," she breathes.

"Okay, what?" I ask, needing to hear her say it.

"I'm gonna wear this ring...and I'm gonna marry you one day."

Rolling her over quickly, I climb on top of her. She laughs, tossing her head back and giving me access to her neck, which I could feast on for hours alone, but the rest of her body is calling to me, as well. I still feel like a starving man who can only be satiated by this woman beneath me.

As I make my way from her neck, down to her sexy shoulders and over to the Promised Land, Piper moans her appreciation.

"I'm still holding you to my condition," she says, already a bit breathless as she moves her body under mine, searching for what she wants.

"What's that, darlin'?"

"The one where you promised me a mind-blowing orgasm every day, for the rest of my life."

EPILOGUE

"Yes, tucker. Oh, fuck, right there."

Piper moaning in my ear spurs me to take things up a notch, hitting my stride, but also trying to keep the bed from banging against the wall. Having sex with a kid in the house is no joke. Our sessions have been relegated to late at night or super early in the morning, which is the case right now.

I have to admit, there's nothing like waking up to Piper in my bed, especially when she's naked.

"Oh, God, Tucker!" I muffle her scream with my mouth, kissing her until she hits her climax.

With a few more thrusts, I follow her, my arms giving out as I collapse in a heap. Wrapping my arms around Piper's shoulders, I roll us over until she's resting on my chest.

"I swear, I thought there was never going to be anything better than the awesome hate-sex we used to have, but I was so wrong," she whispers, kissing my neck. "This is better, so fucking better. I wish I could go back and slap that girl silly. She should've got her shit together a long time ago. We could've been having these amazing orgasms this whole time."

"I don't know. I remember you getting your fair share of *mind-blowing* orgasms back then. Lots of screamin' and makin' a scene." I laugh, kissing the top of her head.

"How about round two?" she asks, getting on her knees and climbing on top of me. I love the way her hair falls in a curtain around us. It used to be shorter, but she's let it grow out some and it's gorgeous, just like the rest of her—from her stunning eyes to her kind heart. I love her, every inch of her.

A small knock on the door makes Piper jump, her eyes growing wide with a knowing smile.

"Daddy!" Sammy yells from the other side. "Why's the door locked? It's my birthday party today!"

"How about a rain check?" I whisper, kissing Piper's nose and then her lips...just one more to tide me over until later.

Piper scurries off the bed and throws on a flowy dress, tossing her hair up in a messy ponytail. I finally pull myself from our oasis and put on some shorts. As I open the door, I pull a T-shirt over my head and smile down at my little girl standing in the doorway with her hands on her hips.

"Who's birthday is it?" I ask, playing dumb to get a rise out of her.

"Daddy!"

"Oh, right. It's your birthday." I slap my forehead and lean down closer to her. "Like I'd ever forget your birthday, sunshine. One of the most important days of the year." Kissing her nose, I finally get a smile out of her.

"How about some pancakes?" Piper asks, coming up behind me. She's no chef, definitely no Nanny Annie or Grandma Kay when it comes to skills in the kitchen, but she's learned to make a mean pancake.

"Yay! Pancakes!" Sammy's hands fly in the air and she runs down the hall toward the kitchen.

She still misses her mama. She still cries sometimes. She still wakes up in the middle of the night and needs someone to sleep with. But she's doing good, better than good. She loves Piper being here. They have their own special bond. Just in the couple of weeks since her return, they've fallen into a routine—breakfast in the mornings, lunch with Aunt Cami or Aunt Dani, afternoons at the big house or the farm.

Eventually, Piper will have to find work, but for now, she's just enjoying some much-needed regrouping time. We'll figure the rest out as it comes.

After pancakes and showers, Piper fixes Sammy's hair and puts her in her special princess dress that Kay bought her for the party. I can't wait to see her face when she sees everything we've planned for the day. There won't be many kids, just her and Carter, but it should still be a fun day.

"Who's ready for a party?" Piper asks, causing Sammy to whoop and holler.

When we pull up at the big house, Sammy's already unbuckling herself out of her seat. The three of us barely fit in my old truck, proving that we're going to need a new vehicle soon. Piper's still renting a car. She sold her old one before she left for Connecticut, but again, we'll figure all of that out as we go.

"Happy birthday, Sammy," everyone yells as we walk into the house. Annie has the entire place decked out. There's not an inch of foyer space that doesn't have crepe paper or balloons attached to it. As we walk into the kitchen, it's the same. The whole family is there, including my very pregnant sister. She's been sticking close to home for the past month, practically on bed rest due to early contractions, but she's finally in her thirty-eighth week and her doctor thinks she can go any time.

My dad and Kay take turns scooping Sammy up and showering her with kisses before we finally make it into the dining room where the cake is on display.

The large castle cake sitting in the middle of the table catches Sammy's eye and she runs over to it. "A castle cake! Daddy! A castle cake!"

Walking over, I kneel beside her as she takes it all in. "I know, sunshine. A princess has to have a castle cake for her birthday."

She turns and throws her arms around me, hugging my neck

fiercely.

"Thank you, Daddy. I love it."

"Tell Annie thank you, too. She's the one who put all the pink stuff up."

Turning around, she runs to Annie and hugs her too. "I love it all."

"Oh, I love you, baby girl. Happy birthday." Annie's eyes are a little misty as she hugs Sammy to her. We share a glance that lets me know she's thinking of my mama. Me too. I always think of her on this day, but today, a little more than usual. It's a happier thought, though—one of gratitude and appreciation.

"This place looks amazing," Piper says, walking around and checking out all the balloons, bouquets, and streamers. "Magazine worthy."

Annie smiles over at her. "I can't tell you how good it is to have you home."

"I can't tell you how good it is to be here," Piper replies, and it's still music to my ears to hear her call this home. "Pretty sure this is where I was always meant to be, just took me a while to realize it."

"I want in on this love fest," Dani chimes in, walking over and hugging her best friend to her.

"Let's eat so we can have cake," Annie suggests, sending everyone into the kitchen for plates.

"I don't think I can fit anything else into this belly," my sister says with a moan, rubbing her protruding stomach. "I seriously feel like I'm gonna pop."

"I wasn't gonna say anything, but," I tease, earning a slap to my chest. And then another upside my head. That one came from Deacon.

"My wife is perfect and gorgeous," Deke says, giving me a look of warning. I'm going to guess this has been a subject of conversation at their house recently.

"Of course she is," I agree.

"Sammy, have you seen your giant blow-up castle in the backyard?" Deacon asks, like the big kid he is.

"Deacon!" Annie, Micah, and Dani all say in unison. Cami normally would be right there to return the slap he gave to my head, but she's barely standing on her own two feet right now, so she's not quite up to par.

"What?" he asks, looking puzzled. "There *is* a big blow up castle in the backyard."

"It's a surprise, dip shit," Micah says, rolling his eyes.

"That's a bad word," Carter chides, snagging a tiny sandwich, taking a bite, and then going back for more.

"I wanna see the castle, Daddy! Please!" Sammy begs, pulling on my arm. "How big is it? Is it pink?"

I glare at Deacon, but I don't say anything, because I feel like I still owe him for keeping mine and Piper's secret all those months.

"Sure, Sammy. We'll go see the castle." I mean, you only turn five once. So, I sit my plate down and follow her to the back door, with Carter hot on my heels.

Once the kids see the castle, it's all over. It's huge, like Olympic size, and has a bounce house with a tall slide on one end. There's even a tower they can climb up inside.

Sammy's face is pure joy as she claps her hands together and gives a silent squeal. Her hair bounces with her, the excitement oozing from her pores.

"Go, on. It's your birthday," I encourage.

And they do. They take off running, straight for the door to the bounce house.

"Take your shoes off," my sister yells from somewhere behind me.

"Hey," I say, as she walks up beside me, or waddles, rather. "Aren't you supposed to be resting?"

"Yeah, but I'm sick and tired of resting...and hurting...and being pregnant." She sighs, but it comes out almost as a whine, which is not my sister.

"Anything I can do?" I ask, as we watch the kids play.

"I wish. Not unless you have some magic juju to make the baby come out."

"Fresh out," I laugh.

"I have been noticing a ring on an important finger of Piper's left hand." She says it so nonchalantly, like she's commenting on the weather, never taking her eyes off the bounce house.

We'd thought about making some kind of announcement, but we just haven't gotten around to it. We've been enjoying just being together, without any pressure about the future or plans.

"Yeah," I acknowledge, but don't offer up any information.

"That's good." Cami nods her head. "I'm happy for you."

"Thank you."

She sighs again, stopping mid-breath. Her hand comes out and grasps my arm.

"Cami?" I ask, turning my attention on her.

"Uh, I think my water just broke," she says, looking down at the ground between her feet where there is a significant wet spot.

"Deacon!" I yell. "Deke, get your ass out here!"

The back door flies open with my brother-in-law blowing through it like the house is on fire.

"Cam?" he asks, coming around so he can see her face. "Are you okay?"

"My water broke," she repeats, while I stand there like an idiot with no clue what to do.

"You got Carter?" Deacon asks me.

"Of course." I nod, looking up to see everyone else running out of the house.

"Micah, get my car and pull it around the side of the house."

Micah runs back into the house and is back in an instant with a set of keys, jogging around the side of the house.

"We're going to the hospital," Deacon yells to everyone. "Can you walk or do you want me to carry you?" he asks Cami.

"I can walk." She's panting now, holding tightly to her stomach.

Annie and Kay come out with their purses and a bag. "We'll follow y'all. Sam and Clay can put the food up and lock the house."

"Me and Piper will keep the kids. Y'all call us when it's close and we'll come up."

I catch Piper's eye across the yard, and she smiles back at me, completely unfazed by everything. "We're having a baby," she mouths excitedly.

It makes me laugh, easing a little of the tension I'm feeling.

Maybe one of these days, it'll be us having the baby.

I think I like that idea.

Looking back over to the bounce house, I see Sammy and Carter still playing happily without a care in the world.

This is life. It goes on, with or without us. I feel like Sophie's looking down on us. I don't know why that thought comes to my mind in this moment, but it does. And I think she's happy—happy that Sammy is a part of this big, crazy family.

I am too. I don't know where I'd be without my family, and I'm happy that now includes Sammy and Piper. They make me feel complete, like everything is right in my world. I'm the same person I always was, just a tamed, less troubled version, and it's all thanks to them.

Everyone sets into motion, working like a fine oiled machine, like we do this every day.

And, in a way, we do. It's chaos, but it's perfect chaos. That's what it's all about, right? It's life and death and change; love and acceptance and growing. It's good times and bad and everything in between.

I'd be crazy to think my mama didn't have a hand in all this. I bet she's sitting up there, organizing the whole, chaotic thing.

"I see you, Mama."

THE END.

ABOUT THE AUTHORS

JIFFY KATE IS THE JOINT PEN NAME FOR JIFF SIMPSON AND JENNY Kate Altman. They're co-writing besties who share a brain and a love of cute boys, good coffee, and a fun time.

Together, they've written over twenty stories. Their first published book, Finding Focus, was released in November 2015. Since then, they've continued to write what they know—southern settings full of swoony heroes and strong heroines.

You can find them on most social media outlets at @jiffykate, @jiffykatewrites, or @jiffsimpson and @jennykate77.

Made in United States
North Haven, CT
03 March 2023

33425701R00161